Guardians of Earth
III
Book Three: The Emissary

P. R. Garcia

1

I dedicate this book to my daughter, whose consistent willpower and perseverance inspire me to improve and keep going no matter the odds.

And to my granddaughter for always making me laugh.

Treat the Earth well.

It was not given to you by your parents,

It was loaned to you by your children.

We do not inherit the Earth from our ancestors,

We borrow it from our children.

Native American Proverb

Contents

Chapter 1: THE SIGNAL

Tim jolted upright in bed, his chest heaving. Cold beads of sweat clung to his skin, tracing chilling paths down his body. He could feel each droplet gathering at his brow before sliding, slowly, off the tip of his nose, plummeting into the darkness below. The silence around him was thick, tense - he didn't dare move, didn't dare breathe, as if the faintest sound might summon the shadows from his nightmares into reality.

"What the hell is happening to me?" he whispered to his reflection in the mirror, as if it could offer answers.

The dreams began two nights ago, right after he received the communique from Xavier, the android Head Commander aboard the space station. Since then, searing images clawed their way into his mind. Sleep had been a battleground, an unforgiving landscape where shadows of memories and nightmares collided. He couldn't shake the feeling that these dreams were more than just fragments of his subconscious - they were a prelude.

Tim's legs finally felt strong enough to carry him without shaking, so he made his way to the kitchen. The remnants of his last meal sat forgotten on the counter, but what caught his attention was the half-full cup of coffee. Or at least what passed for coffee on Rigel Six. He reheated it, the bitter aroma doing little to soothe his nerves. Taking a seat at the small kitchen table, he sipped the brew. The room was silent. The only sound was the faint hum of the ship's systems, but Tim's mind was anything but quiet.

With a sense of dread, he picked up Xavier's communique, reading it for the tenth time, each word cutting deeper than the last:

Tim: I need you for a secret mission to Earth. The ISC received a signal from the blue planet and wants a team to investigate. Meet me on Thursday at twenty-one hundred hours in my office. Come prepared to leave. Xavier.

Thirty-eight years. It had been thirty-eight years since Tim had left Earth, turning his back on the blue planet as he embarked on a life among the stars. In all that time, he had never once considered returning. Earth was a ghost, a distant memory shrouded in the fog of time and overshadowed by the life he had built out here, far from its gravity. But now, it seemed the past had caught up with him. Xavier's message wasn't a request - it was a summons.

Tim frowned, sipping the lukewarm coffee. Why now? His life was finally stable, almost perfect. He was on the brink of completing the design for a new intergalactic ship that would revolutionize space travel, cutting a ten-day journey down to six. His social life was a series of thrilling adventures, each port city offering a different flavor of companionship. And he had just earned a promotion to Captain, solidifying his place among the stars. Everything was falling into place.

Did Earth, once indifferent to the Interstellar Space Coalition, now need the ISC's aid? What catastrophe had driven them to send a signal across the vastness of space to seek help from those they had once shunned?

Tim set the communique down, his gaze lingering on it as if it might offer the answers he sought. The mission to Earth loomed over him like a storm on the horizon, dark and unavoidable. And deep in the recesses of his mind, where logic and fear battled for control, Tim knew one thing: whatever awaited him on Earth was something he couldn't escape from. Not this time.

The countdown had begun, and there was no turning back.

Standing atop a stack of crates for a better vantage point, Jeremy peered down at the disembarking passengers. They were a motley crew-- spacefarers of every stripe, their clothes a vibrant tapestry of cultures. He scanned the travelers, and his attention snagged on two figures who stood out. Identical uniforms, stark and severe, encasing their forms, shrouding them in an air of mystery.

Catching sight of his brother, Jeremy raised his arm and waved. Tim waved back, then pointed to Jeremy, saying something to the soldier with him.

Time seemed to rewind as the brothers pushed through the crowd and collided in a fierce hug. Despite being the elder, Jeremy found himself enveloped in the warmth of Tim's embrace. Their roles had reversed - Tim, once the skinny kid he had to protect, now towered over him, his strength evident as he lifted Jeremy off the ground.

"You grow taller every time I see you," Jeremy said with amazement and brotherly pride. Tim stood Jeremy back on his feet, the room still spinning from the exuberant embrace.

"Naw," Tim laughed. "You're shrinking with old age." Tim moved his gaze toward the soldier beside him. "I'd like you to meet Lieutenant Comstock."

Jeremy softly clasped the hand of the uniformed individual. "It's a pleasure to meet you, Lieutenant." He glanced over the being's body shape and features. "Human, Lieutenant?"

"Yes, Sir. Please call me Opal."

"I don't remember you being on the space station," Jeremy said. "And you appear too old to have been born on New Earth. May I ask about your origins?"

Tim chuckled. Opal smiled. "You and your brother think alike. That was Tim's first question for me. I was born on the station during the third year of our journey. I would have been too young for either of you to pay attention to either on the station or here on New Earth. You might remember my parents or oldest sister. My parents were Daniel and Lorraine Comstock. My dad was a member of the aviation team. Maggie Comstock was my oldest sister. She would have been several grades below you."

"Wing Wizard Comstock?" Jeremy's jaw dropped. "Your dad was THE Wing Wizard Comstock? I grew up on his wing designs! I worked alongside him for years. The man was a genius and came up with ideas that even Xavier scratched his head over. Irreplaceable, that's what he was. It's a pleasure to meet you." Jeremy shook her hand up and down.

"Perhaps you can show her your pleasure by not breaking her hand," Tim teased, his eyes twinkling.

"Oh, sorry." Jeremy released her hand. "I was sorry to learn that your father passed away three years ago on Delta Prime. How's your mom and siblings doing?"

"Mom's great. Maggie, Albert, and Heather are doing well also."

Jeremy wrapped his arm around Tim's shoulder. "So, Little Brother, what brings you to New Earth? And why so secretive? Mom won't be happy when she learns you stopped here and didn't give her a visit."

"With any luck, she won't find out. And I hope to have time to visit before my journey continues. But secrecy was necessary. Xavier sent for me."

"Xavier?" Jeremy asked. "What does he want?"

"I'm unable to discuss specifics. All I can say is he needs someone for an important mission, and he thinks I'm it."

"Really?" Jeremy turned to Opal. "Are you also the perfect person?"

Opal smiled. "Head Commander Xavier gave no reason for choosing me other than he needed a second human. I was available, so here I am."

"What could Xavier possibly need two humans for?" Jeremy asked, rubbing his chin thoughtfully. "Can you at least tell me where you're going or when you'll be back? Mom and Dad are going to ask."

"We're meeting Xavier at twenty-one hundred hours aboard the station," Tim replied. "Once I have the details, I'll know what I can share with you - and Dad and Mom. I'm sure Xavier won't send me off without letting me say goodbye."

"Dad still has top security clearance," Jeremy noted, recalling the years their father served as Commander under their grandfather. "News of a secret mission shouldn't be withheld from Dad."

"I wouldn't think so, but Dad has been out of commission for some years."

Jeremy noticed Tim's jaw clench and his shoulders tighten. He stopped and pulled his younger brother around to look him in the face. "Tim, is everything okay? You appear to be worried or scared. What kind of mission is this?"

Tim pulled free from his brother's graph and walked three steps away before turning. "I'm not worried about the mission. It's dangerous, but nothing the team can't handle."

"Who's going?"

"Xavier didn't say. He will fill in those details when we meet."

"So, what's the problem?"

"I'm afraid he will ask me to take the lead."

"Did he say you were going to be in charge?"

"No, but he didn't say a senior officer would be over me, either."

"If you're not ready, tell him."

Tim's eyes widened. "I can't do that. If Xavier puts me in charge, it's because he thinks I'm ready. Crap, Jeremy, I can't disappoint him. Not Xavier. I just don't know what to do?"

"It would be easier to advise you if I had some idea what the mission entails. Can't you tell me anything? Remember, I still have my top-secret clearance, too."

Tim fidgeted, then glanced across the platform. Most of the passengers had departed. No one was close to them. Tim grabbed

Jeremy's arm and pulled him behind a pillar. "Not a word to ANYONE, not even Dad. The ISC received a signal from Earth. We're going to investigate."

Jeremy's eyes widened to the size of silver dollars. "Earth? Are you kidding me?" he whispered. "It's been, what, over thirty years?"

"Closer to forty."

"Did Xavier say what the signal said?"

"No."

"That's why Xavier wants you and Opal. He needs humans. After the way we left, Earthlings might not be too happy to witness metal androids again."

"That's my guess. So, what do you think I should do?"

"Meet with Xavier and find out the details and who Xavier plans to put in charge - you or someone else. Once you know the specifics, you can decide. If it's not a good fit, tell him. He'll understand. Besides, Xavier would rather have you be honest than take on an operation you're not ready for." Jeremy paused, reminiscing of what life had been like on Earth. "Boy, I'd give anything to be going along."

"I'm sure Xavier would let you go in my place," Tim said with a smile.

"Maybe he would, but Martha would have my hide. I don't think the wife of my children would appreciate her husband being gone for three to five years."

"You're probably right.

"Reporting as requested," Tim said as he entered Xavier's office, bringing his right hand to his forehead.

"Welcome aboard," Xavier greeted, extending his right hand. "Remember, this is not a military ship. No saluting is necessary."

"In that case, I'd say a hug is necessary." Tim walked over and placed both arms around the android. Even though Tim had grown, Xavier still towered over him.

Xavier wrapped his arms around the human, although hugging still did not bring him joy. "I am glad to see you, Tim. You resemble your grandfather more every day."

"That's what Mom says," Tim said, releasing his embrace and taking a seat.

Xavier extended his hand to the female human. "You must be Tim's partner."

"Yes, Sir. My name is Lieutenant. . . I mean, Opal Comstock. It's a pleasure to meet you, Head Commander. Tim's told me so much about you."

Xavier lowered his eyelids as he stared at the male human. "A word of advice, Opal. Don't believe everything Tim tells you. He exaggerates."

"I do not!" Tim said.

"Might I remind you about the flying squirrel incident?"

"Well, maybe that one time." Tim and Xavier laughed. Opal's head snapped back, her eyebrows flying upwards in a question mark.

"Are you surprised, Opal? Have you never heard an android laugh?" Xavier asked.

"Yes, a few times," Opal said. "Those were soft chuckles. You did a full-blown belly laugh. I didn't realize humor was a concept androids could understand."

"I did tell you that Xavier was different from other AIs," Jeremy said.

"That I am. I am the only one of my kind. There was another, but she passed some years ago."

"Tim's grandmother, Jenny," Opal said.

"Correct. Tim really has informed you of his past."

"I wasn't sure what you needed us for, so I thought it best to apprise her of mine and your past," Tim said.

"A reasonable conclusion."

"So, what about this mission to Earth?"

"As my communique mentioned, at fifteen hundred hours three days ago, the ISC received a signal from Earth," Xavier said. "The signal lasted for three minutes, then ended. Two hours later, it repeated for another three minutes, then stopped. The signal continued at this exact interval for forty-eight hours, then ceased. We've received no further transmissions since fifteen hundred hours yesterday. After thirty-eight years of silence, you can imagine the ISC's surprise."

"It contained no message?" Opal asked.

"No, just the signal. ISC believes there are two possible reasons why no message was attached. First, things on Earth have gone terribly wrong, and they cannot send a message. Or two, although unlikely, the transmitters we left behind have malfunctioned."

"Didn't the ISC leave numerous transmitters behind?" Tim asked.

"Thirty-six, scattered across the planet," Xavier stated.

"I can't believe they would all malfunction in such a short time," Opal said. "The transmitters were designed to last for three hundred years."

"The ISC also believes they didn't malfunction, which leaves the first scenario as reality," Xavier said.

"I fear something major has occurred," Tim stated.

"As do I. The ISC wants a small squad of humans, backed by security androids, to head to Earth and discover what's happened. Our last run-in with the inhabitants of Earth was a disaster, so we hope they will react favorably with others of their species. We don't want a repeat of what happened."

"I agree," Tim said, recalling when he and his family were held against their will. He also remembered the people of Earth's reaction when his grandfather and the green alien Glogg appeared at the U.N. Assembly. "Will Opal and I be the only humans?"

"No. A member of ISC Security will be the third human," Xavier answered. "You will pick him up at Zaylara Prime. His name is Robert Hellsworth. He was born on the station forty-six years before we left, lived on Earth by choice for thirty years, and served in the French military. Robert continued his security career with ISC. He is skilled in negotiations and will be the one to bring the ISC's proposal to the humans and analyze Earth's options. Since he is the senior officer, he will be leading this mission."

Tim closed his eyes and sighed. He wouldn't be the leader after all.

"Is there a problem, Tim?"

"No, Sir." Tim wiped all emotion from his face. "Why do you ask?"

"Your face demonstrated you disagreed with the assignment of duties. And you sighed quite loudly."

Tim forgot how well an android's hearing was. "Sorry, I didn't mean for you to hear that."

"Then you do have a problem."

"No."

"Why did you sigh?"

Knowing he had to be truthful with Xavier, Tim scooted his chair closer to the android's desk and looked him in the eye. "The reason I sighed was relief that I was not going to command the mission."

"You don't think you're ready to lead a mission? Did I pick the wrong human to be the Captain? Should something happen to Robert, it will be your responsibility to step into his shoes and lead the mission."

"Yes, Sir, I realize that."

"Can you replace Robert if needed?"

"I believe so."

"There is no believing, Tim. You either can or can't. Which is it?"

"Honestly, Xavier, I'm not sure. I've led other missions, but nothing of this magnitude, duration, or importance."

"Would you be more confident knowing Juaquin will be top android and second in command?" Xavier asked.

"The fact that Juaquin will be at my side does give me more confidence."

Xavier leaned back in his chair. "After hearing your reservations, I am afraid I need to rethink my choice of crew members."

"You don't need to do that. I'm simply a little nervous," Tim protested. "You asked me why I sighed, and I told you the truth. I shouldn't be penalized for being honest."

"The ship doesn't leave for another six hours. Fly down to New Earth and visit with your family. Talk to your father and Jeremy and listen to their advice. In the meantime, I will investigate who else is available to go. Report back here at zero two hundred hours, and I will advise you if you are still on the roster. Be prepared to leave in case you stay assigned."

"But, Xavier…"

"No buts. You're dismissed. The matter is closed. Opal, do you still wish to go even if Tim doesn't?"

"Yes, Sir," Opal shouted, a little too eagerly.

"I need you to remain. Tim, I will see you in five hours."

Tim left the office, closing the door behind him. Clenching his fingers in his right hand, he slammed his fist into the wall.

"You stupid idiot," Tim murmured. "Why did you question your assignment?"

"Trouble in paradise?" came a familiar voice. Tim turned to see Juaquin walking down the hallway.

"I think I persuaded Xavier NOT to send me on the mission to Earth." Tim walked over and hugged the android. "It's been a few years, Juaquin. How are you doing?"

"I am operating in accordance with my parameters," Juaquin answered.

"Same old Juaquin," Tim laughed.

"Why do you think you're off the team?" Juaquin asked.

"I told Xavier I wasn't ready to command the mission."

"Did he ask you to?"

"No. But I gave him doubt about if I could step up if something happened to the mission's leader, Robert Hellsworth. He's looking at other personnel to go in my place."

"I'll talk to him." Juaquin grabbed the office door handle.

"How many security androids are going?"

"Six besides myself. All top-of-the-line security droids whose main purpose is to protect Mr. Hellsworth, Opal, and you, or whoever else goes in your place. Go and say goodbye to your family. Be ready to leave in case Xavier keeps you on the team. Be sure to pack everything you can't live without. We'll be gone for around four years, and you won't receive cargo shipments."

Maybe I should remain at the station.

"No. I understand your doubts but let me assure you that you're exactly the right person for this mission. Even if you can't see it, I have full confidence in your abilities. The challenges ahead might seem daunting, but I believe in your strength and your capacity to overcome them. Trust in yourself, as I trust in you. You've got this."

"Thanks, Juaquin."

———————

Tim ate little at the family dinner. He couldn't shake the impression that he ruined his chance to return to Earth.

"What do you think Xavier will do?" Jeremy asked.

"I have no idea," Tim said. "Juaquin said he'd talk to Xavier and get me back on the team."

"Tim, you've headed several away missions and had no problems being in command," Tim's dad, Steven, said. "Why are you doubting yourself now?"

"I'm not sure," Tim replied. "I've been having bad dreams ever since I received Xavier's communication."

"Nightmares?" Steven asked.

"I think so. I wake up in a cold sweat. My heart's pounding, and my body shakes. Something terrible happens in those dreams, but what I can't remember."

"So you don't want to go because you're having bad dreams?" Jeremy asked.

"It's more than bad dreams," Tim said. "It's like the universe is trying to tell me something, warn me of imminent danger." Tim stood and took his plate to the sink. "Or maybe I'm afraid because it's Earth. I've been gone for so long. And this mission is so important. It could be the last chance for Earth to be saved. If I screw this up, I would be responsible for destroying our home planet. How would I ever live with that?"

"Tim, you're too hard on yourself," Steven said. "I wish your grandfather was here to speak with you. Or even Grogg. Both felt like they failed when they left Earth."

"Glogg and Grandpa thought they failed?" Tim asked. "Why did they think that? They saved Earth. Without their confrontation with the Kett, Earth would have been stripped of her resources and left as a lifeless rock."

"True, but they didn't convince the people of Earth to join the ISC and regain their protection."

"Do you think you're right for the mission?" Sarina, Tim's mom, asked.

"Hearing that Glogg and Grandpa had doubts helps me feel more confident about going. But I still can't say a hundred percent I'm the right person."

"That, in itself, is a good thing," Jeremy said. "Xavier would rather have someone on the team with doubts instead of some cocky and overly confident asshole."

The beeping sound of Tim's transmitter interrupted the conversation. Tim peeked at the caller ID. "It's Xavier. He wants to see me right away. Guess he's made a decision."

"Give us a hug and kiss in case Xavier still wants you to go," Sarina said.

"Good luck, son."

"Send us some pictures of Earth," Jeremy said.

Sarina dashed over to the counter and placed a number of the cookies she baked earlier into a bag. "Take these for Opal and yourself. And no matter what Xavier decides, make sure you give him one, too."

"Mom, androids don't eat chocolate chip cookies."

"No, they don't, but Xavier does. I can't tell you how many times I caught him sneaking one when I used to bake them for your grandfather. Trust me. He'll be hurt if you don't offer him one."

Tim stood outside Xavier's office, gathering his courage. No matter what Xavier's decision was, he would be happy about it. He knocked and entered. Juaquin was seated inside.

"Don't bother sitting," Xavier said. "Your ship leaves in fifty-two minutes."

"Thank you." A huge smile spread across Tim's face. "You won't be sorry. I will make you proud."

"Be sure you do."

Tim turned to leave, then stopped and turned back around. He reached inside his bag and removed a chocolate chip cookie wrapped in a napkin. Tim placed it on Xavier's desk and slid it towards the android. When the young human turned and left with Juaquin, he was sure Xavier smiled, and his eyes twinkled.

Chapter 2: DEVASTATION

Walking beside Juaquin, Tim and Opal walked down the hallway toward hanger number eight, their duffle bag of clothing and toiletries slung over their shoulders. Turning the corner, Tim's eyes grew to the size of half-dollars.

"Is that what I think it is?" Tim asked, staring at the gray airship docked on the walkway.

"It's the latest model of the V-647 inter-stellular airship you, Xavier, and I designed," Juaquin said. "The engineers made a few modifications to help with our mission, which I think you'll like."

"Have you tested her yet?" Tim asked, barely able to speak from the excitement. The prototype had taken the two androids and Tim five years to design and build.

"Took her out for a spin yesterday. She handles like a dream, just as you said she would. She's another reason Xavier thought you were the perfect choice for this mission. He said since you helped design her, you should be the one to go on her maiden voyage."

"I wish he were coming with us," Tim said, grinning.

"I'm sure he tried to think of some reason why he should have come along," Juaquin stated. "But his duties as Head Commander keep him tied to the space station."

"She looks tiny," Opal said. "Are you sure it can accommodate all ten of us, our food, supplies, and communication equipment?"

"How can you say that?" Tim asked. "She's the perfect size. We designed her for maximum capacity. You'll not find an inch of wasted space inside."

"Plus, since androids do not need to eat, our supplies are minimal," Juaquin said. "We require little rest, so we don't need bunks to sleep in. The V-647 can accommodate thirty androids inside without a problem. Twenty-three with humans aboard." Juaquin observed the skepticism that remained on Opal's face. "I assure you, Miss Comstock, the ship is of sufficient size and comfort."

"Opal," the female said. "Call me Opal."

"Shall we go aboard, Opal? You can see for yourself."

Opal stepped to the door and heard the familiar "swoosh" as it opened. "Xavier said she can take us to Earth in a year and a half. Is that correct?"

"I would estimate more like fourteen months," Juaquin said. "I'll show you to your quarters and then take you to the bridge to meet your crew."

"Sir, Earth should be within viewing range in another thirty minutes," Jules stated.

"Which one is she?" Opal asked, her body filled with hundreds of needles pricking her skin.

"That large body to the left," Juaquin said. "Jules, raise the magnification to 100 plus."

Robert, the third human, stepped closer to the screen. "I can't wait to see her. I always hoped I would return one day. She's such a beautiful planet."

All three stared up at the overhead screen as the image grew in size and clarity, their insides filled with butterflies, feeling like kids in a candy shop. Opal gave a light giggle at the joy of seeing, at last, the blue planet her parents once called home.

An image of a desolate, dying planet filled the screen. The surface was a lifeless, dull brown, stretching endlessly under a hazy, toxic atmosphere. A sickly, grayish-green sludge filled the ocean basins. Above the equator, any trace of greenery had long vanished, leaving behind only a landscape of blackened, charred earth, as if scorched by endless fires. The northern tip displayed no ice cap. The entire planet exuded an aura of decay, as if it had long since given up the struggle to sustain life.

"Jules, I think your instruments are malfunctioning," Tim said. "That can't be Earth. Where's the blue seas and white clouds?"

Jules checked his readings. "My instruments confirm that this is indeed Earth, Sir."

"That doesn't resemble the Earth we learned about in school," Opal said.

"Or the Earth I lived on," Robert said. "Jules, can you increase the magnification? Maybe space interference is causing our instruments to alter Earth's colors."

"Raising magnification another two hundred," Jules stated.

The screen flickered, and a new image materialized - more horrifying than the last. The northern landscapes were scarred by massive blast craters, each the size of a football field, marring the terrain with jagged wounds. Lakes had been reduced to sunbaked basins of cracked mud, their waters evaporated. Once-thriving forests had been shattered into splinters, leaving nothing but desolate expanses of broken trees. The mighty mountain ranges were all but erased, their stone foundations obliterated as if they had never existed. Iconic cities lay in ruins, their former grandeur now reduced to skeletal steel frames, glinting weakly under a dim and sickly sun.

"What in the hell happened here?" Tim asked. "Did the Kett come back and start harvesting the planet?"

"I don't think so," Juaquin said. "If the Kett had returned, we would see evidence of mining, and huge sections of earth would be missing. And they would not have left the metal beams visible in the cities. Earth's metals bring a hefty price on the interstellar black market. This was not an act of harvesting but of something more sinister, I fear."

"Sir, I'm picking up high amounts of radiation in the northern hemisphere," Jules reported.

"Continue our course, but stay twelve *killigs* above the planet," Robert ordered. "Tell me if the radiation levels rise. Keep the deflectors to a maximum. Run a scan and check for signs of animal or plant life."

"Yes, Sir."

Tim remained silent as they drew closer to the brown planet. His heart pumped faster, and his mouth grew dry, making it hard to swallow. *"Please make this a computer malfunction."*

After fifteen minutes, Jules broke the silence. "Sir, I detect no life forms, either plant or animal, above the equator."

"None?"

"No, Sir. Not even a blade of grass."

"What about below the equator?"

"I cannot scan the southern hemisphere from this trajectory. I'll need to change our heading to scan the southern half of Earth."

"Make it so."

All eyes were fixed on the screens as the ship altered its course. Much like the northern hemisphere, the southern half appeared as a muted canvas of brown and gray. Devastation, drought, and destitution was evident on every continent.

After another ten minutes, Robert shouted, "Well, what do you find? Is there life?

"I am detecting signs of both animal and plant life below the equator, although on a reduced scale from what our records show."

"Are any of them human?" Tim asked.

"Yes, although sporadic. Around the 20th parallel south, I detect a limited number of humans. Below the Tropic of Capricorn across Africa and South America is a larger accumulation, with the largest concentrated at the south pole. I estimate the combined total to be under two hundred thousand."

"Two hundred thousand?" Robert whispered.

Hearing the news, Tim collapsed in a nearby chair. "That can't be. When we left Earth, over eight billion humans lived there. How can there be so few left? What happened here?"

Juaquin pulled off a report from the computer. He read the words and then handed the report to Robert. All eyes turned to Robert, waiting for him to speak.

Unable to read aloud the report, Robert asked, "Juaquin, please tell the others what the report said."

"The computer analyzed the data and offered the following possibility. Based on the amount of damage, amount of radiation, and pollution in the air, the computer hypothesized that five years ago, someone in the north launched a nuclear attack. In defense, the other northern countries followed suit, resulting in the obliteration of all life north of the equator. A nuclear winter followed and destroyed most of the southern hemisphere, including the vast majority of the animal life on land and in the oceans. The computer estimates that between one and five percent of life still exists."

"Could the computer be wrong?" Tim whispered.

"Never," Juaquin said.

Robert swallowed hard, forcing back his tears. "Jules, continue to circle the southern hemisphere. Have the computer determine what life remains."

"Jules, maintain a height of 15 *conks* over the Earth," Juaquin interjected. "Keep a close eye on the radiation index."

"Yes, Sir," Jules replied.

"I'd like to drop a little lower." Robert turned to Juaquin. "I want a better view of the oceans and land masses."

Jules turned to Juaquin for confirmation. "What is the current radiation reading?" Juaquin asked.

"The needle is holding at six *giffs*," Jules said. "That is well within the limits humans can withstand."

"What were the readings in the Northern Hemisphere?" Tim asked.

"The highest we recorded was twenty-three *giffs*. The lowest was fifteen. Exposure to either would cause human death within hours to days."

"Remain at this altitude," Juaquin ordered. "What is our current location?"

"Coming across a large body of water known as the Atlantic Ocean," Phillip said. "Our first land mass will be Africa, a region called Namibia."

Opal and Tim rushed to the observation window. "I can't see much from up here. The atmosphere is too hazy."

"I want to start with our first pass from up here," Juaquin said, his voice steady but laced with caution. "From this altitude, we can assess the situation without exposing ourselves to unnecessary risks. If the sensors don't pick up any signs of danger, we'll make a second sweep at a lower level, where we can get a clearer, more detailed view of what we're dealing with."

"I'm detecting signs of plant and animal life forms on most land masses," Jules stated. "As previously reported, sporadic settlements of humans. The major cities show no human life forms." After five minutes, the android continued. "We're now passing over the Indian Ocean. In addition to marine life forms, I'm detecting high water pollution and acidity levels. We will pass over Australia in six minutes."

The pass over Australia showed the same results - no life in the larger cities and small congregations of human life. They continued their journey, crossing the vast expanse of the Pacific Ocean, and approached the South American continent. Suddenly, a red light began to blink on the screen, drawing their attention and signaling something unexpected.

"Sir, I'm picking up a signal in South America," Phillip reported. "It's the same configuration as the signal the ISC received."

"Location?"

"It appears to be originating from an area in Patagonia, Argentina," Phillip said. "On the southern corner of Lago Argentino, fifty miles outside of the city of El Calafate."

Juaquin looked out the side window. "Jules, what's the radiation level?"

"I'm picking up a higher level than we anticipated," Juaquin said. "But it's still within the range that a human can tolerate."

"Drop us down to ten *conks*. Stay hidden in the clouds. There's no sense in revealing our presence to Earth's inhabitants until we're sure what's happening down there. Don't you agree, Robert?"

"Yes, I concur. The humans will be anxious, and I don't want our ship to frighten them."

"Won't staying hidden in the clouds make it hard to determine what's happening below?" Tim asked as the ship dropped lower into the atmosphere.

"You probably weren't on the space station long enough to remember we have the technology to penetrate clouds," Juaquin said. "Keep watching the viewer."

Tim gazed up at the overhead screen. Earth remained hidden behind a thick veil of clouds. As he watched, the fog gradually cleared, revealing a sharp, detailed image of the planet.

"Why wasn't I aware of this?" Tim asked, his eyes wide in wonder. "Why didn't we use this technology when flying through the nebula clouds in space? It would make traveling through those thick clouds a lot simpler."

"Because the clouds in space are made of star particles - dust and gases like helium, hydrogen, and other ionized gases. Earth's clouds consist of water particles, which are much easier to penetrate."

"The signal is getting stronger," Phillip announced.

The landscape unfolded in stark contrast. A few scraggly trees gave way to a sprawling expanse of brownish-green grassland that stretched endlessly. At the northern edge of the field, a patch of scorched earth marred the scenery, its blackened soil stark against the muted tones of the grass. The remnants of a small settlement came into view, crumbled huts barely recognizable through the rising columns of dark smoke that twisted into the sky like ominous signals. Even from afar, the still forms scattered across the ground were unmistakable, their lifelessness casting a heavy pall over the desolate scene.

"Looks like we're too late to the party," Tim said. "Can you tell what happened? Was this deliberate or an accident?"

"Based on the evidence of the bodies and the still smoking debris, someone attacked the settlement less than two hours ago," Phillip said. "From this height, I cannot hypothesize who attacked who and if these were the people who sent the signal."

"Is the signal still being transmitted?" Robert asked.

"Yes. It's originating from those caves east of the settlement," Phillip said.

"What caves?"

Jules reconfigured the cameras to scan left. A series of caves carved into a nearby mountain range came into view. "Second cave from the right."

"Look, there are people in those caves," Opal said as they watched two humans emerge from behind three enormous boulders in front of the cave entrance, each holding automatic rifles.

"Are they survivors or the attackers?" Opal asked.

"Unable to determine," Juaquin said. "The only way to find out what happened or who is sending the signal is to go down there."

"I agree," Robert stated. "Tim, you and I will go down with fliers. Juaquin, you and three other androids will accompany us." Robert's expression turned serious. "There is a good chance the humans we encounter will react with hostility. I need you, Juaquin, and the other androids to bypass your programming and not react with deadly force."

"Sir, we are programmed to defend you. I cannot change mine or the other androids' algorithms."

"No, you cannot. You can, however, choose to delay deadly force until you determine if a threat cannot be neutralized by other means, such as negotiation," Robert said. "That's all I am asking. Evaluate the situation before using deadly force."

"That we can do."

Robert turned his attention to the female human. "Juaquin, Phillip, Andrew, and B-25 will accompany us. Jason and Jules will remain aboard the ship with Opal and provide support from above if needed. Jules, send a message to the ISC and advise them of the destruction of Earth's northern hemisphere. Ask them to dispatch a relief ship with supplies, medicine, and security androids."

"Shouldn't we wait until we know what's going on down there first?" Tim asked.

"The relief ship will be much larger than the one we arrived on," Robert said. "Its journey will take up to three years to arrive. It needs to leave now. Besides, even if the humans are hostile, we need to provide support to this planet. It is doubtful that humanity will survive without our intervention."

"I will prepare the fliers for launch," Juaquin said. "We leave in forty-five minutes."

"Is there any way to inform them you're coming?" Opal asked. "No matter if they're friend or foe, the sight of three alien ships landing might be unsettling and provoke a defense response."

"How will they know we are alien?" Phillip asked.

Opal giggled at the android's innocence. "I think the craft's design and ability to land without a sound might give us away."

"Is there a way to contact them through their transmitter?" Tim asked.

"There might be," Juaquin said. "We can send a transmission to their radio, which should make it beep. We can't send a message, but the beeping might be enough to make them aware of our presence."

"Make it so," Robert said.

––––––––––

Due to the limited storage space, the fliers were secured upright, their sleek wings folded neatly against their sides like resting birds of prey. This vertical arrangement limited maneuverability. To access the cockpits, the crew had to scale the ships themselves, climbing carefully along built-in footholds and handholds integrated into the craft's frame. The ascent required skill and balance, a ritual that underscored the intimate connection between pilot and machine.

Tim crawled into the first flier's cockpit, slid into the seat, and strapped himself in. Andrew crawled into the co-pilot's seat. Robert and B-25 slipped into the second, and Juaquin and Phillip took the third ship.

Tim flicked the controls, listening closely for the faint hum of the engines. Satisfied that everything was running smoothly, he said, "Okay, Jason, lower her down." The ship began to tilt, shifting into a horizontal position. Tim could feel the subtle movement as the rollers locked onto the flier's wheels, guiding it toward the bay door. Through the windows, the view shifted from the ceiling to the walls as the ship descended and then to the bay door as it opened to the vast expanse of space.

"Releasing the clamps," Came Jason's voice over the intercom. "You're free to move ahead."

"Roger." Tim acknowledged, feeling the slight jolt as the rollers propelled the plane into the emptiness of space. He let the aircraft drift away from the ship, the silence of the void enveloping him. Once he reached the sixty-yard mark, Tim started the engine and pushed the throttle forward, smoothly turning the plane ninety degrees. He waited, eyes fixed on the bay door, as the other two planes emerged one by one, joining him in the vast, star-filled expanse.

"Everyone ready?" Juaquin asked.

"Echo Two ready," Tim said.

"Echo Three ready," B-25 added.

"We'll fly in and hover over the field in front of the caves to announce ourselves," Juaquin said. "If the humans demonstrate no aggression, we'll land the craft. Andrew, B-25, and I will exit first. Tim, Robert, and Phillip, stay on your ships with the engines running. Keep the force field active until I give the okay to lower it. If the humans accept our arrival, Tim and Robert will join us. Phillip will stay with the planes and monitor the situation. At the first indication of aggression, Tim, Robert, and Phillip are to take off."

"I'm not leaving you alone down there," Tim said.

"Remember, Captain Spalling, that I am in charge of security, and you will do as I say," Juaquin said, his voice crisp. "We will retreat to the east side of the settlement where you can land and retrieve us. Is that understood?" Silence. "Tim?"

"Yes."

"You are so like your grandfather," Juaquin said. "He, too, had trouble following his security droid's orders. Especially Xavier's. How about you, Robert? Do you understand?"

"Unlike my young friend, I respect your authority."

"Hey, I don't disrespect his authority," Tim blurted. "I consider Juaquin, B-25, and Andrew too valuable to abandon."

"I assure you, Tim, that unless there is a major military army down there with nuclear weapons, we have nothing to worry about," B-25 said. "Even their nuclear weapons wouldn't be a problem, now that I think of it."

<hr />

Jessica carried the radio transmitter to the injured man lying on the cave floor. "Robert, your transmitter is beeping."

"Give it to me," Robert said, holding his breath as he reached out his hand. Jessica placed the transmitter in his palm. Robert's face lit up when he witnessed the lights flash three times and then stop. The signal repeated every ten seconds.

"Does that mean they got our signal?" Jessica asked. "Are they coming?"

"For the signal to reach the receiver, they have to be within a few miles of us. I'd say they not only got my signal, but they're here," Roger shouted, wincing as a pain shot through his side. "Tell those on watch to expect several fliers to appear within the next ten minutes." When Jessica went to leave, Roger grabbed her arm. "Remember, Jessica, if there are humans, they will have security androids with them. The androids will not hesitate to fire upon you if they feel threatened. DO NOT show any aggression towards them."

Jessica smiled. "I remember your stories."

———————

The three fliers emerged from the clouds overhead and hovered twenty yards before the cave opening. A woman and three men poked their heads out from behind two boulders, each carrying a weapon.

"Remember, no deadly force," Robert cautioned.

"Set your ships down," Juaquin announced. "They appear to be friendly."

The android waited three minutes before issuing the command to dismount. In unison, the three hatches opened with a soft hiss. Juaquin, Andrew, and B-25 stepped out, their eyes locked on the humans. They moved to the edge of the force field and halted.

"Hello," Juaquin shouted. "My name is Juaquin. I am a Rz-GAG security android. My fellow AIs are AV-152 droids. We are here with three humans. The ISC received your signal. We have come to investigate Earth's situation."

"Welcome," Jessica said. "We have been waiting for you."

"You have? If that is true, why do you have your weapons trained on us? Please lower them. Once you do, the humans accompanying us will exit the planes and formally greet you," Juaquin said.

"We can't do that," Jessica said, her eyes scanning the landscape. "Our attackers could be hiding on the rim of the settlement, waiting for a chance to take us down."

Robert stepped beside Juaquin, Tim following to his right. "You may keep your arms."

"That is not allowed," Juaquin countermanded. "Robert, you and Tim were to remain in the plane until I gave the all-clear."

"We'll never discover anything if we remain hidden in the plane," Robert said. "They have the right to protect themselves. They may keep their weapons."

"We would have picked up any intruders on the radar," Juaquin commented.

"Perhaps we should recheck," Tim stated, looking around at the many places attackers could hide.

Juaquin looked at Tim with squinted eyes. Keeping his comments to himself, he said, "Phillip, how does the radar look?"

"A herd of animals is being stalked by a predator to the south. In the trees to our west, a group of what I believe humans call monkeys are scampering across the branches. A flock of birds is flying this way and should pass overhead in five minutes. No signs of humans other than those inside the cave and the four outside."

Juaquin tilted his head. "Are we happy now?"

"Yes," Tim laughed. "I agree with Robert. Let them keep their weapons and feel safe."

"Very well," Juaquin sighed. Even after all these years together, humans still questioned their androids' decisions. "Keep your weapons if you must," Juaquin shouted. "Just keep them pointed to the ground with their safety locks on. Any elevation of the nozzles will be considered an act of aggression, and we will shoot. Do you understand?"

The female said something to the three men. Each flicked on their gun's lock and lowered the nozzle towards the ground. Two of the men kept their index finger close to their gun's trigger. "Yes, we understand."

"Phillip, turn off the force field," Juaquin ordered. "Robert and Tim, you two stay between Andrew and B-25. I will take the lead. Are you ready?"

"Yes," Robert said.

"Yes," Tim confirmed. "Let's go meet the humans."

As the group advanced, the security droids kept vigil on the humans' trigger fingers. Each android was prepared to execute the men before they could fire their weapons.

Robert extended his hand once they reached the boulders. "Hello, I am Robert Hellsworth, ISC Emissary."

"My name is Jessica Steinberg." The female looked into Robert's eyes and giggled.

Robert turned to the others in his company. "Did I miss something? Why is she laughing at me?"

Jessica laughed louder. "I assure you, you do not. I wasn't prepared for you to look so much like Roger. He said you two were hard to tell apart."

"Roger? You're familiar with my brother?" Robert asked.

"He's inside waiting," Jessica said. "Juaquin, was that your name? Would it be okay if I place my weapon over my shoulder and ask the men with me to do the same?"

"Yes," Juaquin said. "Do it slowly."

"Okay, you guys. It's time to put your weapons away," Jessica instructed. "Gentlemen, please follow me."

Jessica led the group into the cave entrance. The interior was dim and narrow. The air was stale and carried the stagnant scent of people living in close quarters. As they ventured further into the depths, armed adults emerged from the shadows and down narrow corridors, their presence a silent but unmistakable warning. Juaquin and the other androids raised their weapons, prepared to react at the first sign of aggression.

"Juaquin, remain calm," Tim whispered. "They're only guarding their habitat, not attacking."

"Please lower your weapons," Jessica shouted. "These men and androids are the ones we sent for. They are here to help us." She paused. "This way."

The group followed Jessica down three more corridors until they reached the back of the cave. But instead of growing darker, it was getting brighter. They rounded a corner, and a circle of light appeared ahead. Through it, they observed vegetation, trees, and sunlight. Laying under a shade tree was an elderly man resembling Robert, his arm bandaged and resting inside a sling, a medical wrap around his abdomen.

"I'm sorry to tell you that your brother was injured during an attack that happened two days ago," Jessica said. "We don't have much in the way of medical supplies. All we were able to do was set his arms."

Juaquin knelt beside Roger. "Hi, Juaquin."

"Hello, Roger," Juaquin said. "It's nice to meet again after so many years. How are you doing?"

"Been better," Roger said in a whisper. He tried to laugh but grimaced in pain instead.

"Hold on. We'll get you feeling better soon." Juaquin ran a medical instrument over Roger's body, watching the readout. "B-25, get the medical kit from the flier. Tell Phillip to return to the ship and bring down the Havoc unit and two more medical kits."

"Yes, Sir."

"I had the foresight to bring a Quantum Medical Kit with us. It's in locker BIB. Tell Phillip to bring that as well.." Juaquin motioned for Robert to come forward. "That's all I can do until B-25 brings me the med kit. He's in pretty bad shape. He's lost a lot of blood, has three broken ribs and a broken arm, and he's bleeding inside where his liver was nicked by a bullet, which is still inside. I can get him stabilized, but I can't remove the bullet or repair his liver until Phillip returns with the Quantum Medical Kit."

"I understand." Robert sat down beside his brother. "I thought you might be the one who sent the transmission."

"I was hoping you'd get it and come," Roger said.

"There will be time to talk later," Juaquin said. "Right now, he needs to rest." When B-25 returned, Juaquin removed several syringes from the med bag and injected Robert. "I've given him a sedative, some antibiotics, and something to help with the bleeding. He'll be out for the next day or two."

"Shouldn't we transport him up to the ship?" Tim asked, reading the medical scanner.

"That is not advisable," Juaquin said. "I fear if we try to move him, the bleeding will become worse. I don't need the medical facilities aboard the ship to save him. The Quantum Medical Kit will do that."

Chapter 3: A HELPING HAND

"B-25, stay with my brother. Inform me the moment he gets worse," Robert said. "Jessica, is there somewhere we can talk? Can you explain what has happened to this planet and who attacked you?"

"Before that, might you have any food with you?" asked a tall man with long blond hair and a straggly beard. His shirt was dirty and stained with blood. "The marauders took what food we had in the gardens and in our storage units. We haven't eaten much in the last two days."

"You are?" Robert asked.

"This is my co-leader, Gerald," Jessica said.

"How many survivors?" Tim asked.

"We have twenty adults and eleven children," Gerald replied.

Tim pulled out his communicator. "Echo One to Echo Command Ship."

"Echo Command Ship here."

"Jules, is Opal around?"

"I'm right here," came Opal's voice. "Is everything okay?"

"Phillip is on his way to you to get some medical supplies. We have injuries that need special attention. There are thirty-one survivors in need of food. Advise Phillip to bring back five cases of food."

"What about water?"

Tim looked at Jessica. "No, we have fresh water here in the cave. Food and medical supplies will be sufficient."

"Negative on the water," Tim said into his transmitter.

"And your situation? Is all well?" Opal asked.

"We are fine," Tim said. "We made contact with the inhabitants with no altercation. I will send you a detailed report within the hour."

"Advice Opal to send another security android," Robert ordered.

"Opal, we're going to need another security droid down here to help with the locals."

"Affirmative. I'll send Jason down. Echo Command Ship signing off."

"Gerald, are you injured?" Tim asked. "You have a lot of blood on your shirt."

"No, I'm fine. Most of the blood is from one of the injured children I carried inside."

"Do you have more wounded?" Robert asked.

"Gerald, take the android to our injured," Jessica said.

"Negative," Gerald said, his jaw growing firm. "I don't want any hunk of metal touching my children."

"Gerald, I said take him to our injured," Jessica repeated. "They are here to help. We discussed this, remember?"

Gerald walked away, his feet stomping across the cave floor. Andrew followed.

"You'll have to excuse Gerald," Jessica said. "He doesn't like robots. He's had some unpleasant encounters with mechanical beings like you."

"We are not robots," Juaquin said. "We are AI androids who have been sentient since before humans walked upright. You said Gerald encountered others like us? We left no androids behind when we left. How is this possible?"

"When you abandoned Earth, many of the advanced nations poured billions of dollars into building robots, I mean androids," Jessica said. "Many were used to wage war on other countries. Or keep the poor from advancing."

"Do these androids exist here?" Tim asked.

"We haven't seen any for about a year," Jessica said. "Rumor has it that some big organization took them to a superhuman colony in the Antarctic," Jessica said.

"Our surveillance of the Antarctic showed a substantial accumulation of humans," Robert said. "I don't remember any androids."

"We did not scan for nonhuman life," Juaquin said.

"Jessica, who attacked your village?" Robert asked.

"A group of marauders that settled in our area about six months ago," Jessica said. "The leader is a former member of the Argentina drug cartel, a Miguel Costa. We were trading with them, but they soon demanded more than we could give. When we refused to give them the majority of our harvest, they attacked and stole what they wanted."

"Do you think they would be willing to negotiate?" Robert asked.

"Negotiate? Why would you want to negotiate with them?" Jessica's voice grew louder.

"The only way for the remaining humans to survive is to unite all the human fractions," Robert said. "To save this planet, we need a majority rule, not a minority."

42

"You're kidding, right?" Jessica raised her right eye.

"Why would you think I'm kidding?"

"Although less of us, we are more fractured than ever. We will never agree on anything."

"Oh, ye of little faith," Robert chuckled. "I have negotiated treaties that were believed impossible. I assure you, it can be done. But I am getting ahead of myself. Before I continue, I need to know what happened in the north. Who destroyed half the planet?"

Jessica sighed. "Let's sit on those boulders under the two beech trees over there." The three travelers followed her to the trees and sat down. Tim looked up. Through an opening above, a hazy grayish sky showed.

"Is the sky always that color?" Tim asked. "Our surveillance of the planet showed a cloud of dust covering the Earth."

Jessica looked up. "Ever since the destruction, we haven't seen a blue sky. For the first two years, the sunlight seldom got through. Most of the forests and plants died, causing a big shortage in edible food. Acid rain took its toll, too. With food sources low, animal and livestock numbers plummeted. Thankfully, the lakes were not as polluted and fish survived, although on a reduced level. Many species died out."

"So, what happened?" Robert asked, shifting his position on the boulder.

"We don't know for sure," Jessica said. "Most of what I'm about to tell you is based on rumors and speculation. It began five years ago. I was on vacation in Santa Rosa. I am, I mean, I was a schoolteacher in Bedford, Michigan. Three friends and I went on vacation together during the summer, a decision that saved my life. It happened on our third or fourth day here in Argentina. We went sightseeing ten miles outside of Santa Rosa. At 1:18, the ground trembled. We thought it was an earthquake. I remember the exact time because I had just checked my watch to see if it was lunchtime. I had no idea that exact time would be the end of my world as I knew it. A dozen or more aftershocks occurred, then silence."

"We returned to our hotel around six that evening to find the city abuzz with alarming news. Every city in the Northern Hemisphere had gone dark. Reports flooded in, describing thick, black smoke clouds visible north of the equator. Investigation planes were sent to assess the situation, but none came back. The next morning, we awoke to a world without cell service, electricity, or any means of communication. Authorities canceled all flights to and from the country. People exited the city in droves. Fearing we'd have trouble getting back home, we made our way to the airport and waited for six days. It was a nightmare - there was little food, and what was available was being exploited for five times its worth. Water was scarce. The bathroom facilities were deplorable. Rebecca, one of my friends, became very ill. Medical help was more or less nonexistent, and after another two days, she died. People gathered into gangs, preying on the weaker, taking whatever they wanted. After Rebecca's death, Sara, my other friend, and I decided we needed to get somewhere safer and left with a small band of fifteen people. We walked for days until we arrived here. It was a small farming village. They offered us food and shelter. Since they didn't have many living comforts, the lack of electricity or cell phones did not hinder them. They had what was important - fresh water and food."

"The skies grew menacing, heavy with an unnatural darkness that swallowed the land whole. Day after day, the sun hid behind a suffocating wall of thick, acrid smoke, plunging the world into an endless twilight. Crops, starved of sunlight, shriveled into brittle husks; streams turned lifeless as fish succumbed to poisoned waters, and once-pure wells ran foul with contamination."

"Desperation gnawed at us as the men hunted relentlessly, their efforts barely enough to fend off starvation. As the vegetation crumbled to dust, the animals we relied on for sustenance fell one by one, their carcasses a grim reminder of the mounting toll."

Jessica wiped a tear from her cheek. "For six harrowing months, the sun remained obscured. Rain was a rare mercy, and when it came, it carried with it drops of blackened ash that stained the earth and burned the skin. The very air reeked of decay, a pervasive stench that clung to every breath, every surface - a constant, oppressive reminder of our approaching death slowly creeping across the land."

"How did you survive?" Tim asked.

"The villagers knew this land like the back of their hand. They knew where to find uncontaminated water and thick undergrowth where some fruit, reptiles, roots, and insects could be found. Not the most appetizing food, but it kept us alive. One such place was this cave, where food and fresh water never stop. Then, one day, the sun emerged as the smoke dissipated. But with the lighter days came survivors. They poured out of what was left of the forests, many sick and dying, covered in sores and blisters. Amongst the new arrivals were several doctors who told us the people were suffering from radiation sickness. They surmised a nuclear war had been launched in the north."

"We didn't have enough food to feed ourselves, let alone all these newcomers. When the rain returned and washed the streams clean, allowing the fish to return, our food supply was replenished. Hoping the rains had cleansed other lands, many new arrivals continued the journey to find better living areas. Only two have ever returned and they reported living conditions were even worse to the south and west. The drug cartels used the lack of law enforcement as a way to raise their status in the world and rule over many areas."

"Did you ever hear who started the war?" Juaquin asked.

"No. We weren't even sure a war happened, but we had no other explanation."

"When did my brother show up?" Robert said.

"About two years later. New stragglers arrived every couple of months in groups of three or four. Robert walked into the village one day, accompanied by six forest people. Robert remained, but the forest people returned to their forest hideouts."

"By your account, Roger arrived three years ago," Robert said. "Why did it take him three years to send us a message?"

Jessica chuckled. "It seems fate was not done punishing us for our destruction of nature. Roger and his group had to fight against

45

many factions on their way here. In one of those encounters, his communicator for the ISC was damaged."

"That's impossible," Juaquin said. "They're built from the same material I am and are therefore indestructible."

"That's what Roger said, but it was damaged. He tried explaining it to me, but I didn't understand."

"How did he get it working?" Tim inquired.

"He knew the problem was a broken wire, but he had no way to fix it. He tried everything, but nothing worked. One day, a survivor passed through, and she had a robot's hand attached to her belt. After hours of negotiating, Roger finally persuaded her to trade him a finger - only the little finger, not the entire hand. It cost him an enormous bag of prickly pears. He wove together several wires from the robot's hand and repaired his communicator. He never knew if the wiring worked, but since you're here, I guess you got his message."

Tim checked his timepiece and stood. "I need to contact Opal with my report. Please excuse me."

"Ask her if Phillip has left to return yet." Robert stood as well. "I need to check on my brother."

"Robert, can you tell me if it was a nuclear war and how many survived the onslaught?" Jessica asked, her face ashen white.

"As you feared, our computer's analysis stated the probable cause was a nuclear war. I'm sorry to say that our scans of the northern hemisphere showed no signs of life - animal nor plant. It is now a barren land of ash, dust, and radioactivity."

A heavy silence filled the room. Finally, a reply came, quiet yet cutting, like a blade tempered by sorrow. "So, humanity's greed was finally unshackled, and the devastation unleashed." A pause, then a soft, resigned sigh. "Thank you for your honesty." Jessica rose, her face stoic, as if chiseled from stone. Grabbing her weapon, she proceeded to the cave's entrance to take her turn standing guard.

Robert walked to where the injured were housed. Five adults and four children lay on piles of old clothing and leaves. Two of the children and two adults were badly burned.

"Most of their injuries are superficial," Andrew reported. "Abrasions and several broken bones. I've cleaned and stitched several wounds. For the burned victims, I gave them pain medication and removed the charred skin. Once Phillip returns with the Quantum Medical Kit, I can regenerate new skin. They should be fine in several days. The only one that concerns me is the young woman to the left. She took a bullet to the abdomen. The scanner shows her spleen and liver are damaged. I'm not sure there's anything in the Quantum Medical Kit that can repair her organs."

"Could she survive a trip to our ship? We could use the regeneration chamber."

"Like Roger, I don't believe she would survive the trip. I might be able to use the Havoc to build some chamber to repair the injured organs, but it's no guarantee it will work."

"Do what you can," Roger said, his face solemn and strained. "What is her name?"

"I heard one of the women call her Lucy."

Robert walked over to the young woman lying on the floor. "Hello, Lucy. My name is Robert Hellsworth."

"You're Roger's brother. You two really do look identical."

Robert smiled. "So I've been told all my life. How's your pain?"

"The robot gave me a shot of something. I'm much better now," Lucy whispered.

"An android. He's not a robot, but an android." He leaned in very close and whispered. "They don't like being called robots."

"I'll remember that. Robert?"

"Yes?"

"Am I going to die?"

"I won't lie to you, Lucy. Your injuries are severe, but we're going to try something to repair your internal injuries once another android returns with more medical supplies. Until he does, you rest and keep fighting."

––––––––––––––

Tim stood with Jessica and the two human guards at the cave entrance. The flier returned and landed inches before the boulders they hid behind.

Jessica and the two men gasped. "I've never felt that before."

"The energy produced by the flier tends to send a tingle through your body and make the hairs on your arms stand up. After a few times, you won't even notice it."

"I doubt that," said the man with a red beard.

Phillip popped open the cockpit shield. He and Jason jumped out and removed the medical equipment from the storage area.

"Cutting it a little close, aren't we?" Tim asked as Phillip walked by.

"Radar picked up a group of humans hiding in that undergrowth five hundred feet to the south," Phillip said. "I would assume they are getting ready to attack again. Their weapons can't hurt us or the flier, but I didn't want to chance them hitting the Havoc Quantum Medical Kit. Keeping both within the force field until they were out of danger was the only solution."

"I agree." Three bullets ricochetted off the force field and fell to the ground. "Our unwanted guests seem interested in what we brought. How many humans appeared on the radar?"

"Eight, each holding an impressive weapon."

"Anything I need to worry about?"

"Not unless you intend to go for a stroll outside the force field. The survivors will be safe as long as they remain hidden inside the cave or behind these boulders."

"Can what's inside those bags help our wounded?" Jessica asked.

"Yes," Phillip said. "Tim, if you take the equipment to Roger and the wounded, Jason and I will unload the food supplies. We also brought a small replicator to help with needed items."

"Jessica, can you show my men a good place for the food?" Tim asked. "They will ration it to your people and take some to your wounded. Phillip, keep a guard posted with the food at all times."

"That's not necessary," Jessica blurted.

"I understand your people are starving, and hungry people don't always make the best decisions. To ensure the food lasts and everyone gets a share, my men will distribute and maintain the food. That's the way it must be for now."

Jessica gave Tim an annoyed look. "You can store the food down the right tunnel with our other supplies. Follow me, and I'll show you where. Once you're ready, I'll tell everyone they can get something to eat."

"Jason, once you have the food stored, return here and monitor our hidden visitors. Inform me if they decide to try something," Tim said.

"Will do. Might I make a suggestion?"

"Of course."

"Since the attackers' main purpose is food and supplies, why don't we eliminate that need by dropping some food over them?"

"An interesting idea. Let's ask Robert what he thinks."

Chapter 4: SURPRISED COMPOUND

"I still say this is a bad idea," Jessica yelled as she ran after Juaquin, Tim, and Robert. "Forget about the fact they destroyed our settlement. They've been shooting at us for the past three days."

"The ISC sent me here to not only find out why a signal was received but also to unite the various factions of humanity." Robert lifted a case of food into the flier. "I can't do that sitting here."

"But they've been shooting at us for days. There's no talking with them."

Robert signed. "And why do you think they are shooting?"

Jessica scowled. "I don't know. Maybe because they're a bunch of bloodthirsty murderers who want to take everything we have?"

"Or could it be because they're a bunch of hungry people with little options?" Seeing the expression on Jessica's face made Robert chuckle inside. No wonder they blew themselves up; no one wanted to trust anyone. But he did. "To persuade them to our side, I need to find a common ground. That's rule number one in all negotiations. Food is that common ground."

"It's not going to work."

"Then I'll keep trying until I find something that does." Murmuring something under her breath, Jessica stomped off into the cave. Sighing, Robert turned to Jason. "Why can't she see that to stop the attacks, we must eliminate the reason for them?"

"I don't believe she's had much reason to have hope these past few years."

"True. Is that deer you shot aboard the plane?"

"Yes, Sir. But it doesn't seem right to give them a dead animal. Besides the humans here in this colony, I've never known men to consume animal flesh."

"That's because you're only familiar with New Earth's and the space station's humans. We don't eat meat, but here on Earth, it is part of their daily food consumption."

"Except for my brother and Ronald," Tim laughed as he walked towards them. "Remember that fiasco with the chicken, Juaquin?"

"That is a chapter in my life I would rather forget and have nothing to say on the matter." Ignoring the topic, the android climbed into the pilot's seat.

Tim laughed. "I guess you would." He extended his hand to Robert. "Good luck."

"Don't tell Jessica, but we'll need it," Robert whispered. "You're in charge, Tim, until we return. It should take us forty-five minutes to reach their main camp. Say, another fifteen to twenty for negotiations. If you don't hear from us by twelve hundred hours, send two of the androids after us. Do not come yourself. If the worst happens, return to the ship and ask the ISC for further instructions."

"I am confident it won't come to that." Tim forced a smile onto his face.

"*I wish I were,*" Robert said silently as he climbed into the passenger seat. "Let's head out, Juaquin."

The plane lifted off the ground, banking southward toward the camp of Miguel Costa, the former drug lord. As they flew low over the terrain, the devastation below was starkly visible. As at the campsite, the ground was scorched, with vast stretches stripped bare

51

of vegetation. Yet, against all odds, they saw signs of resilience scattered across the desolate landscape. Bands of guanaco grazed atop the parched hilltops, their silhouettes stark against the barren horizon. In shallow lagoons, herds of capybaras waded and fed, their movements bringing a rare flicker of vitality to the bleak surroundings. Mule deer darted through clusters of skeletal trees, their lean frames a testament to the harsh conditions they had endured. In the distance, a solitary patch of vibrant green trees stood in stark contrast to the barren expanse around it, a poignant reminder of what this landscape had once been. The cluster of foliage seemed almost out of place, a fragile yet enduring fragment of a world now lost.

"Robert, I'm detecting a thriving forest to our left."

"A forest?" Robert scanned the horizon. "I don't see anything Where is it?"

"It seems to be cloaked from the naked eye. Let me bring it up on your screen."

Juaquin turned a few nobs and a thriving forest appeared on Robert's view screen. "Hello beautiful! What are you doing out here all alone? Juaquin, fly towards those trees. I want to check them out. Keep this altitude and fly over the sector. It might contain what we need."

"And what is that?"

"Lots of indigenous food. And let Tim know of our detour. Tell him to add an extra thirty minutes to our time frame."

As they neared the designated region, it remained undetectable to Roger's human eyes. Juaquin was able to switch to another view and see it with no problem.

"Why did you stop?" Robert asked when the airship halted.

"I'm detecting a force field."

"Is it detrimental to our ship?"

"Not that I can detect."

"Then proceed."

"Yes, Sir."

Juaquin inched the flier through the shield. Waves of hidden energy flowed through Robert's body, making the hair on his body stand on end. Once inside, Robert saw a lush, green forest flowing for hundreds of miles. The vegetation was bright green with no signs of dead or dying leaves. Radar showed an impressive congregation of wildlife, including the larger herbivores. Numerous streams of clean, fresh water snaked through the land. Trees were laden with various fruits. Vines of grapes and squash entwined around the tree trunks.

"How is this possible? How can the rest of the land be half-dead while this land appears to be untouched? Why wasn't this area affected by the nuclear winter?" Roger asked.

"The locality is located inside a valley. Perhaps the surrounding mountains sheltered it from the worst of the fallout?"

"No. The lack of sun would still have prevented the vegetation from conducting photosynthesis. Somehow, these plants found a way to get the needed light from another source. But what?"

"Perhaps those towers." Juaquin pointed to fifteen massive green towers scattered amongst the vegetation.

"What are they?"

"I do not know. But my readout said they are artificial. And, Robert, they're made out of *iggium*."

"*Iggium?* Are you sure?"

"I've run the scan three times. It's *iggium*. They're connected to that extensive building fifty feet to the left."

"What building? All I see is a grassy knoll."

"That's not a knoll. It's a bio-dome. I am reading an enormous output of energy."

"I can't wait to check that out. Are you getting any readings of human life?"

"Unsure. I'm picking up some form of life inside, but I'm unable to tell what kind. The bio-dome has a dampening field preventing my instruments from getting accurate readings."

"Humanity shouldn't have been able to create a dampening field that would affect our instruments. I wonder if it could be alien?"

"Or perhaps a project conducted by some of the space station's inhabitants."

"But the ISC would have listed it."

"Perhaps not. Whoever built this place might have wanted it to remain secret."

"Contact Opal and advise her of our discovery. Tell her to use the ship's radar to penetrate the dome. The mystery of this place will have to remain a secret until another day. We need to return to our mission of contacting Señor Costa's camp. Advise Tim also and tell him we're on the way to our rendezvous. And scan the terrain. We'll analyze the data when we get back to camp."

Forty-two minutes later, Juaquin sat the flier down in a clearing a half mile from the camp. Within fifteen seconds, twenty men and women came running towards them with assault weapons.

"Ready for this?" Juaquin asked.

"As ready as I can be. Pop the lid."

As the two climbed out of the cockpit, the distinct sounds of bullets ricocheted off the force field. Soon, dead bullets littered the ground along the rim of the field.

"We mean you no harm," Robert said, walking to the edge of the force field. "My name is Robert Hellsworth. I was one of the humans aboard the space station hidden in your moon. The Interstellar Space Coalition sent me to investigate what has happened to Earth since our departure. I wish to talk with Señor Miguel Costa. Can you please tell him I am here?"

Above the sound of more bullets hitting the shield was the humming of Juaquin's firearm charging. "Stand down, Juaquin,"

Robert said. "We won't use any force today. They can't hurt me inside the force field." The humming stopped.

"Is Señor Costa available? We need to speak." Once more, only silence greeted them.

"I don't think he's coming," Juaquin stated after twenty minutes.

"I agree. Let's unpack the supplies and leave." Addressing the crowd of angry mercenaries, Robert shouted, "To show you can trust me and am a man of my word, I have brought you food. We will leave it here for you to retrieve after we depart. Please tell Señor Costa I will return at twelve hundred hours in two days to meet with him."

Juaquin and Robert unpacked the boxes of food rations and placed them on the ground just inside the force field. On top of the crates, they placed the gutted deer and several live guinea fowl. After climbing inside the cockpit, Juaquin lifted the plane off the ground and headed north. The moment the plane disappeared from view, the mercenaries dashed to the boxes, ripping them open to reveal the military rations.

"Why would they leave us food?" one man asked. "Surely, they knew we were the ones who attacked their village."

"That's for Miguel to figure out. Pedro, run back to camp and get some mules to take this food to our hungry families."

———————————

"How's he doing?" Robert asked Andrew.

"About the same. As I told you, I was not able to repair the spleen. The spleen was too damaged for the Quantum Medical Unit to repair it. I am not a surgeon, and even if I had the training, I don't have the necessary equipment here. He needs a hospital with a surgical team."

"And those are in short supply here," Robert sighed. "How long would you say he has?"

"At best, a week. All I can do is make him comfortable."

"That is enough. Were you able to use the Quantum Medical Unit to help Lucy?"

"I'm sorry to report that she died from her injuries while you were gone."

Robert walked to his brother and sat down beside him. A soft breeze blew in from the opening above, carrying the scent of flowers to his nostrils. "Roger, are you awake? I need to talk with you."

Roger opened his eyes and smiled. "What do you need? And before you even ask, I am doing well and am in no pain."

"That's excellent news."

"You look like you just lost your best friend," Roger said.

"I just learned that Lucy, the young lady who had been shot during the attack, has died. I told her I wouldn't let that happen. I failed her."

"Don't say that, Robert. You're not the one who shot her. Your team gave her a few extra days of life without pain. You did all you could. Tell me how your trip went?"

"As expected, Miguel did not show. But on the way, we discovered something. About ten miles west of Miguel's camp, we found a section of forest alive and growing. It shows no ill effects from the nuclear winter. Animal life is abundant, and the streams are uncontaminated and filled with life."

"How is that possible?"

"There are towers made of *iggium* throughout the forest."

"*Iggium?* That's impossible."

"That's what I said. And it gets stranger. The towers somehow supply the native vegetation with what it needs for photosynthesis."

"But that would take a hell of a lot of power for such an operation. And electricity is non-existence at the moment. How are they getting power?"

"There's a huge bio-dome giving them all the power they need. And Juaquin couldn't penetrate the dome with the plane's sensors. I had Opal try our ship's radar, and she got the same results."

"Impossible. Nothing can deflect our radar."

"But this structure can. You worked with the scientists aboard the space station. Do you remember any of them setting up an experiment on Earth? Or hear of anyone attempting to correct Earth's pollution?"

"There were so many experiments being done aboard the station and on Earth by humans and aliens. I remember the Caladrine were always trying something new to strengthen Earth's ecosystem. They would be the logical guess, but I can't imagine any of them would have traveled down to visit Earth. Those long trunk-like noses and blue skin would have instantly given away the fact they were alien. They couldn't go unnoticed for long, even hidden in the deep forest."

"But if they could have remained hidden, do you think some Caladrine would have remained on Earth when we left? Would they have sacrificed their future?"

Roger smiled. "All of them would have remained if they thought they could discover new ways to garden and produce food. Remember, they were natural-born farmers and dedicated their lives to that industry. But I can't imagine they chose to live on Earth with the allergies they had. That would be a double-whammy sacrifice. But I can think of one particular Caladrine that would have stayed if given the opportunity - -a fourth-year-belted female named Hiinew. But that doesn't make sense. The ISC would never have given her permission for such an assignment. Utter secrecy was always their top priority."

"Maybe she didn't ask for permission."

"That's the only way she could have gotten down here. But someone on the space station must have helped her, and possibly others, sneak off the station."

"You think there's more than her?"

"If those towers are as sophisticated as you say, she would have needed help. Plus, *iggium* metal is heavy. Caladrine don't have the strength to lift it. She'd need a few androids for that part of the project."

"So, there's the possibility that there's a Caladrine settlement with alien androids existing not far from here?"

"Appears so. When are you going to check the facility out?"

"Making friends with Miguel is my number one priority. The possible Caladrine will need to wait for a while."

"I think I have a solution for that. Let Tim take me to make contact with the Caladrine."

Robert crossed his arms and leaned back. "Are you crazy? You're in no shape for such a trip. Absolutely not!"

"Robert, we both know I'm dying. I've got what, a week or two at most left? Andrew can inject me with enough medication so I can make the trip. It's not that far."

"No."

"Let my life down here count for something. Let me contact another life form one last time. Please."

"No."

"They might be able to help me medically. They wouldn't have set up a lifelong project without a chance of leaving the planet without doctors and advanced medical equipment. Andrew told you I needed a hospital, something we didn't think existed. But now I think it does."

"It's too dangerous."

"I'm going to die for sure if I don't go. At least, this is a chance. And if it turns out they don't have a hospital, I will die content."

Robert stared at this brother, unable to think of a worthy argument. If the settlement contained Caladrine, they could save Roger. "Tim and Andrew would have to go with you."

"Yes, yes, of course. I wouldn't want it any other way."

58

"I'm still against this, Roger, but I can't deny you the possibility of recovering."

Tim set his flier down beside the grassy knoll. The radar showed no entrances, so he took an educated guess of where one might exist. Using the frequency from the space station, Tim sent a message stating who they were and advising them of their arrival. The ship's cockpit had not fully opened when a side panel in the hillside opened a few feet from the flier. From within came the sound of a loud sneeze.

A huge smile filled Roger's face. "I remember that sound. That's a Caladrine sneeze."

Tim jumped down onto the ground. From the opening emerged three Caladrine and two security androids.

"Tim, you've grown into a fine-looking human male," the first Caladrine stated as she extended her hand. "The last time I saw you, you were around nine. What are you doing here? You're supposed to be on New Earth."

"I might ask you the same thing?" Tim stated, shaking the alien's hand. "Why are you on Earth? And how did you get down here?"

"I asked first."

"Hey, don't forget me," came Roger's voice from inside the flier.

"Is that Roger Hellsworth?"

"Yes, it's me. Are you O'jin Hiinew?"

"Yes, get down here so I can give you a human hug."

"I'm sorry to inform you that Roger sustained severe injuries in an attack at the camp where he lived. He is dying but insisted on coming. Our equipment was not sufficient to correct his injury. We were hoping you might have the medical capability to save him."

"Of course," Hiinew said, waving to the two accompanying androids. "Remove Roger from the cockpit and take him to the medical center. He needs our doctor's expertise."

The androids lifted Roger down with Andrew's assistance and placed him on a carrier.

"Hello, Roger," Hiinew said. "It is wonderful to see you again."

"As it is to see you." Roger beamed. "I can't wait to learn about what you've done here. I'm already impressed by the little I've seen."

"Let's get you healed first." Hiinew lowered her head and placed it on Roger's. "We have some excellent surgeons here. I am sure they can fix your injured body."

"I don't think there's a doctor in the entire universe that can do that," Roger chuckled.

"While our medical staff attends to Roger, you and I will have a long talk." Hiinew slipped her arm into Tim's and escorted him inside.

"Tim, if you have no objections, I will go with Roger," Andrew stated.

"Of course."

Tim's jaw dropped as he entered the dome. Crisp white walls lined an array of tunnels snaking through the structure. Multi-colored flowers lined the walkways, their fragrance filling the air. Despite being underground, warm sunlight filled the building.

"How is this possible? It reminds me of the greenhouses on the station," Tim whispered, afraid if he said the words out loud, the dream would disappear.

"It's exactly like the greenhouses on the station," Hiinew said. "If my memory serves me well, humans like coffee. Would you like a cup?"

"I do like coffee, but might you have any Quivia juice? I haven't tasted that treat in over twenty years."

"You like our Caladrine drink? I can assure you, we have lots of it. Come, we'll sit on the patio. There's always a fresh pitcher of Quivia juice waiting there."

Tim and Hiinew continued walking arm in arm down a small hallway to a beautiful veranda overlooking the pristine forest. Tim observed a family of coati munching guava in a nearby fruit tree. Below, hungry deer ate the fruit pieces the coati dropped to the ground.

"This is magnificent. How did you manage to build this without anyone knowing?"

"Remember, I asked first." Hiinew handed him a glass of juice. "Your message stated you were here on assignment from the ISC."

"Yes." Tim took a drink, letting the thick, sweet drink slide down his throat. "The ISC received a signal from Earth about two years ago. It was only a signal, so to determine why, I was sent here with Roger's brother, Robert, and another human named Opal and several droids."

"Robert's here too? I can't wait to see him. Why didn't he come?"

"He's trying to make contact with the people that injured Roger. That's how he found your bio-dome and forest. He was on his way to their camp when Juaquin spotted your trees."

"Juaquin is here, too?" Hiinew giggled. "This day just keeps getting better. Juaquin and I had some wild adventures in my day."

"Really?" Tim asked. "You must tell me about them."

Ignoring Tim's statement, Hiinew continued. "You said Roger's trying to make contact with the marauders?"

"Yes, He hoped by bringing them food, he could entice the mercenaries to lie down their arms and join our group. The original order from the ISC still stands. Humanity must stop fighting amongst themselves and ask for help before the ISC intervenes. And their help is needed now more than ever."

"So, you saw what they did to themselves up north?" A tear slid down from Hiinew's golden eye. "So much death and destruction."

"Do you know what happened?"

"Only that someone launched a nuclear bomb. Who it was, we never learned. We believe that in retaliation and defense, the other countries launched theirs. Within minutes, nothing remained. So many warheads erupted that the atmosphere itself caught fire. The shockwaves and intense heat obliterated anyone or anything that survived the initial blasts. Mother Nature herself revolted as the earth opened and magma poured out. The inferno lasted for two years and spread as far as below the midpoint of the Earth. I think you call it the equator. The sun was blocked out by so much smoke and ash, causing plants to die across the southern part of the planet. When we realized what happened, we were able to adjust our towers to compensate for the lack of sunlight and save this forest and several more we have across the world."

"You have more of these bio-domes?"

"We had six. Now, we only have three: this one, one in Costa Rica, and one in the Congo Basin in Africa. The bombings destroyed the one in Siberia and the Artic. We had another one on a small island in the Pacific Ocean, but with the high temperatures in the north, the snow completely melted in the Arctic, and sea levels rose. The island was submerged. Not enough ice has reformed in the Arctic to bring the water levels back down so we can restore that location."

"You snuck down enough personnel to man six stations like this?"

"How I wish." Hiinew refilled Tim's glass. "Had we tried that, we would have been discovered for sure. No, this is the only fully manned facility. The one in Costa Rica has two Caladrine and two androids. Before they were destroyed, we monitored the ones in the north and on Palmyra Atoll by computers."

"So, how did you manage to sneak androids and Caladrine down here without getting caught?" Tim asked.

Hiinew giggled, then sneezed through her long nose. "Even with all our advanced technologies, Earth's weather and fauna still wage war on our allergies."

"I remember your allergy problems. I can't tell you how many times I got sneezed on by Caladrine." Tim took another drink. "So, how did you pull it off?"

"With much planning and a lot of luck and help from some wonderful friends on Earth and on the space station. If I told you more, I'm afraid I would have to silence you." She smiled and sneezed again.

"How many inhabitants occupy this station?"

"Besides myself, there are fifteen Caladrine and ten androids."

"You realize I will have to advise Robert of what I've found, and he, in turn, will need to report your existence to the ISC."

"Yes. But ask Robert to delay telling the ISC until he and I speak." Tim gave her a perplexed stare. "We are needed here. Earth cannot survive without our work. Humans already know aliens are real. Glogg saw to that when he addressed the United Nations, so there's no reason to keep our existence a secret."

"You're wrong," Tim said. "Now, more than ever, the fact you exist puts you in danger. Humans are desperate. They would not hesitate to kidnap you and exploit you for your knowledge."

"The androids will protect us. They always have."

"While true, I fear that may have changed. You don't realize what desperate men are capable of."

———————

While Tim visited with Hiinew, Robert and Juaquin made another attempt to talk with Señor Costa. They landed in the same clearing and exited the plane, remaining behind the force field. As before, a mix of men and women walked toward the aircraft, but this time, they didn't shoot.

Juaquin snickered. "It appears they have learned our technology can't be breached."

"I believe you have acquired Xavier's sense of humor," Robert said.

"He is my idol."

"After what he did to you?"

"Water under the bridge."

"If you say so."

Robert walked to the end of the force field. "I ask to speak with Miguel Costa. Has he come here today?"

"He says you're to talk with me," a bearded, red-haired male said.

"No, I will only speak with Señor Costa."

"He wants to know why you gave us the food?"

"I will explain that to Señor Costa."

"Do you have more? We have many mouths to feed."

"Can I speak with Señor Costa?"

"Did you bring more food?"

"Yes. Is he going to speak with me?"

"No."

"Juaquin, let's unload the food." Robert and Juaquin unloaded the crates of food and piled them to the side of the flier. This time, they brought boxes of figs, tomatoes, corn, plus boxes of rations. Instead of a deer, they brought two male boars and four ducks.

"Tell Señor Costa that I will be back in three days. Tell him I expect to talk with him, or I will bring no more food. The choice is his. Do you understand?"

"Yes. I will give him your message."

"We will meet again in three days."

64

"Might you have medicine?" shouted a scruffy woman. "We have sick people."

"There are medical supplies in the small crate. I will bring more medicine when I return. But, as with the food, it will not be left unless Señor Costa speaks with me."

"I understand. Thank you."

Juaquin and Robert climbed back into the aircraft and left. The moment it was safe to retrieve the supplies, the humans rushed in.

———————

Robert hurried to the plane when Tim landed. His heart dropped when he realized his brother was not inside.

"Is he, is he . . ." Robert couldn't say the word.

"No, he's fine," Tim said. "The facility contained Caladrine, and a few of them were doctors. They repaired Roger's injured spleen. He's in good hands, and the recovery process is going smoothly. If all continues as expected, he'll be back at the camp within the week, good as new."

"Thank goodness. So, it was Caladrine, as Roger suspected. What did you find?"

"You won't believe it. It's amazing. They've not only found a way to give the vegetation the sunlight it needs, but they've also engineered plants that produce more fruit and edible leaves with less sunlight. This may be our way to solve the food problem for the rest of humanity."

"How many inhabitants?"

"Sixteen Caladrine and ten androids."

"Androids? The Caladrine have ten androids? ISC androids?"

"Yep!" Tim was glad he wasn't the only one astonished by that fact.

"How in the hell did they pull that off?" Roger paused, bringing his hand to his head, thinking. "The androids are highly monitored to ensure none go missing, so how can someone confiscate ten androids without ISC knowing? I'll need to notify the ISC immediately."

"The Caladrine in charge, Hiinew, asked that you not inform the ISC until she talks with you. She said you two were friends a long time ago and hoped that friendship would allow her some leniency."

"We weren't that close. But I'll wait until I talk to her, just so I have the whole story."

Chapter 5: MIGUEL

"I stayed on Earth to help humanity have a better future," Roger argued. "That objective is more important now than ever. What better place to continue my work than here with the Caladrine?"

"But you need to recover," Robert said. "Plus, I can't assure your safety here."

"Robert, I can recover here as well as I can laying inside that damn cave opening. Plus, here, I can accomplish something. I promise to take it easy and rest each day. And the doctors here are better equipped to care for me than Andrew. Plus, this place is actually more secure than the camp. There are ten security androids here. You only have four back at the cave."

"I'll concede that the security here may be better. But the two of us have just gotten back together and, well ..."

"You'll miss me." Roger beamed. "Just admit you love me and tell me to stay here."

"I love you, and I will miss you. But if I agree to this, you must report in every day. I'll expect a detailed report from you and your doctor."

"It's a deal. Have you granted Hiinew's request and delayed informing the ISC about her being here?"

"I have decided to postpone that part of my report. But not because she asked me to. I am still gathering information and want to send an accurate report when I do notify the ISC of her presence."

"Do you think they'll make Hiinew and the others leave?"

"I don't know. She's a talented speaker, so she might persuade them to allow her and the others to stay. If the ISC decides to help, they might even give her more staff and open up a few more facilities." Robert scanned the beautiful landscape with its towering trees. A flock of macaws flew past the windows. "This is an amazing place, and it is hard not to call it a major success. Now, if my meeting with Señor Costa were half as successful,"

"When do you plan on meeting him?"

"Tomorrow morning. I said this was his last chance. If Miguel continues his refusal to speak with me, there will be no more food, and my negotiations will end."

"What are you going to do if he doesn't show?"

"I have no idea. Any suggestions?"

"No. Besides food and medicine, I can't think of anything you can offer him. You can't give him our technology, and you certainly can't give him any weaponry. How about blankets and clothes?"

"I don't have a supply of those items."

"I'm sure the Caladrine would help. With all the natural fiber growing around here, I am confident they could whip up some blankets and clothing with no problem. Those items will come in handy when winter arrives. I'll ask Hiinew for you."

"Let me know what she says. Remember, send me a report every evening starting tonight. I'll stop back in a few days."

The next day, Robert and Juaquin returned to the enemy's village. As they arrived at the designated rendezvous point, they noticed a line of ten men and women already waiting. At the front of the group stood a dark-haired, tan-skinned man in his late thirties. Robert and Juaquin exited the plane and walked to the end of the force field.

"Buenas dias, Señor Hellsworth. I understand you've been asking to speak with me."

"If you are the man who goes by the name of Miguel Costa, I have."

"I am the only person here by that name."

"You are younger than I imagined. From your reputation, I expected a much older man."

"A reputation comes from experience, not age. I am here, as you asked. What do you want?"

"I do not know if you know this, but when the space station left your moon…"

"If I might interrupt for a moment, Señor Hellsworth." Miguel took a step forward. "Whatever you're about to say, you will want me to accept as truth. It's hard to trust a man who hides behind a force field. Let us talk as men, one on one, with no shield dividing us."

"I remain behind this force field because your men have repeatedly tried to kill me, both at my camp and here on this field. But if you give me your word they will not fire upon us, I will lower the shield."

"You would believe my spoken word?"

"Yes, I would. I believe you are an honorable man."

Miguel turned to his small army. "Amigos, guarden sus armas. Nadie debe disparar contra estos dos." He turned back to Robert. "I have told them they are not to fire on either of you."

"Thank you. But in accordance with ISC rules, I must warn you that if any of your men decide to disregard your directive, my security android will not hesitate to fire and kill them. There may be ten of you, but he is capable of destroying much larger groups in seconds."

69

"Do you tell me this to instill fear in me? I am not easily frightened."

"No, Señor Costa. I want you to understand the android's capabilities and directives. Juaquin, lower the field."

Juaquin did as instructed, then stood beside the human. Together, they walked towards Miguel, stopping halfway across the expanse. Miguel and one other man walked to them.

"It is a pleasure to finally meet," Robert said, extending his hand.

"That remains to be seen," Miguel said, ignoring the hand gesture. "You were saying something about the space station."

"Yes. When we left here, we allowed the people of Earth to put their differences aside and live in peace. If they did that, another station would be sent to protect the Earth from outside alien invasion and ensure Earth prospered. Most of the dignitaries who were to make that decision are now dead, which makes you one of the few people who can now make that decision. I ask you to put your differences aside, lay down your weapons, and join us in a peaceful coalition."

"What's in it for me?"

"A better life. Food, water, medicine, protection from other sanctions."

"I have that now."

"I beg to differ. Your people are starving, and from what one of your people told me last time, you have sick who need treatment. Plus, winter is coming, and we can provide shelter and blankets."

"Again, I have that now. We survived last winter, and we can survive this one."

"True. But we can also provide you with more advanced techniques to grow food even in the winter, sustainably hunt animals, and more.

"You would share your advanced alien technology with us? Can we have one of your fliers? And several of your rifles?"

"No, I cannot do that. The ISC forbids the sharing of advanced alien technology, but we can share some techniques with you."

"Then you have nothing for me," Miguel said. "If you're not prepared to offer us your technology, there's nothing else to discuss. I will wait until the forest claims you like it does all foreigners and take what I want when you are dead."

"Then you will be waiting until you are an old man. I will leave the food, but this will be the last time. I will not return. If you change your mind, you know where I am. And, Miguel, think about changing your mind. I can offer you and your people a better life."

"Answer me one more question, por favor. You said all must agree to lay down their arms. What if we agree and others do not? What happens to us then?"

"We will still give you a better life. An ISC ship is on its way here with supplies and personnel to make this planet habitable again, at least the southern half."

"And the moment they are gone, a stronger coalition will sweep in and destroy us. No, Señor Hellsworth, you offer me nothing. I thank you for the food, but our conversation is over. The next time we meet, my men will not hesitate to shoot." Miguel turned his back and walked towards the tree line.

"If that is true, on that day, your men will die and leave their children without anyone to feed them," Robert shouted. Miguel paused for a minute, then continued to walk away.

"Well, you tried," Juaquin said. "I'll unload the food."

Robert walked back to the ship, silent and disappointed. Was this the way all his negotiations were going to go? Without something of significance to offer these former drug cartels, there was little hope of success. He had to find something that would change their minds.

———————

For the next 5 weeks, Robert and Juaquin contacted various groups living within a hundred miles of the camp, aided by Opal and the spaceship's radar. Opal searched the countryside for people, animals, and edible plants, letting Robert know where she found them. Upon detecting villages, Robert performed a flyover and analyzed their openness to his arrival. If the village showed signs of civilization, Robert visited and tried persuading them to join their organization. If forest people inhabited the village, Roger left them in peace.

Soon, the number of residents in the camp grew to two hundred and seventy-six, straining the camp's food and material supplies. Once the number reached sixty, the cave was no longer feasible as a place to live. The androids and humans began building a permanent village on the flat plain a half mile from the caves. Trees were felled to make barracks and a food hall. A force field was placed around the encampment to defend themselves from marauder attacks. But the availability of trees was scarce.

As the sun dipped behind the west mountain range, Robert, Tim, and the androids huddled together. It was now a daily ritual to meet somewhere away from the other inhabitants and discuss that day's events or strategize new activities.

"I don't see any other way to obtain the needed wood," Tim said. "We need to use Hiinew's forest. Even if we cut down every tree in a fifty-mile region, we couldn't obtain enough lumber."

"The Caladrine settlement must remain a secret," Juaquin said. "No human can know of their or the forest's existence."

"Hiinew's jungle may solve our lumber problem, but what do we do about the labor problem?" B-25 asked. "We have exceptional strength, but three androids cannot cut and deliver the wood."

"Make that four androids," Andrew said. "I can help."

"No, you're needed here to attend to the wounded and ill," Robert said.

"So, we're back to Phillip, Jason, and myself," B-25 stated. "Do you think Hiinew would lend us a couple of her androids to help?"

"I don't see why not," Robert said.

"Is there a possibility we could bring a couple of them back here to help with the lifting and construction?" Tim inquired. "We could always say they were from the ship."

"I wouldn't bring any more than two," Juaquin stated. "Otherwise, the humans will question why they didn't come down before and help."

"Agreed. I'll talk with Hiinew tomorrow."

"When I'm not accompanying Robert, I can help build the camp," Juaquin added. "If the humans dig the post holes, we can use the planes to lift the tree trunks into place and erect the protection barrier." He turned to Jason. "How's the modification on the force field coming?"

"The current force field was designed for a small sector," Jason answered. "I've made some modifications, but it won't be sufficient to encompass the cave, the planes, and the new settlement. Something is going to have to go unprotected."

"Each plane has its own shield," Tim said. "If we line the three planes in front of the cave entrance, their combined radius should keep the cave safe. Besides, once we build the settlement, we won't require the cave anymore."

"Since more and more people are arriving each week, the barrier should be priority number one," Robert said. "Jason, contact Opal and have her double-check the cargo hold for an additional field generator. I can't believe we only brought one. In the meantime, let's bed the humans outside beneath the planes at night. The fliers' force fields can protect them. How is the food supply holding up?"

"The group that arrived yesterday brought bags of nuts and figs with them. And some women came across a wild patch of strawberries this morning."

"Mmm, fresh strawberries." Robert's mouth watered. "Remind them to leave enough for the local life."

"Jessica's crew planted a second field of squash and beans. The seeds Hiinew gave us are growing faster than normal seeds, but like everything, they take time to mature, flower, and produce edible food. It will be another three weeks before we can harvest the crop. We limit meat to two or three times a week, but the additional visitors may require us to hunt more often."

"I don't like the fact that we're killing these animals to feed these people," Tim muttered.

"Right now, I don't see any other choice," Robert said. "They must eat something. And full bellies keep the bickering down. As with the fruit, we will monitor the number of animals we take from each species. We don't want to deplete an already hindered population."

The sound of loud voices broke the peacefulness of the air. The team ran towards the sound to find two men arguing.

"I need more food," a man in a red shirt shouted. "My wife's pregnant, and she needs more to eat."

"You know the rules, everyone gets the same amount," the woman serving the food shouted. "Right now, food is in short supply."

"I need just a ladle more," he shouted.

"You heard her," Gerald yelled. "Move it. I'm hungry."

"Mind your own business."

"I said, move it." The man in the red shirt snarled, shoving Gerald with such force that his plate of food went flying. The meal of meat and potatoes landed in the dirt with a heavy, muffled thud, scattering dust and bits of food across the ground.

"You bastard." Gerald balled his fist and struck the man in the jaw, knocking him backward.

The third man in line reacted, defending his friend, and attacked Gerald. More joined in. Soon, the brawl grew to fifteen. Several men were pushed against the food table, knocking it over. The screams of the servers intermingled with the shouts of the fighting men. As Robert and his team drew near, Tim saw one man pull a pistol he had hidden in his boot.

"Stop, Don't shoot," Tim shouted as the man pulled the trigger, hitting the man wearing the red shirt in the arm.

Without hesitation, B-25 reacted and fired his weapon, hitting the man with the gun. The man was propelled backward onto the ground, a hole over his heart from which his body's blood poured out.

The crowd stood motionless, stunned by the actions of the android.

"You son of a bitch," Gerald screamed. "You killed him." Gerald grabbed a nearby log and ran towards B-25. "I'll smash your face in."

Another shot rang out as Juaquin fired, hitting Gerald in the arm. "The next person who tries to harm any human or us will not be so lucky," Juaquin said. "I will not hesitate again to kill the next one."

"Stop this," Jessica shouted, running forward.

Knowing Juaquin would not hesitate to shoot, Tim grabbed Jessica, locking her into a tight embrace. "No, Jessica. He will kill you." Tim dragged her towards the safety of the cave boulders.

"Let go of me," Jessica screamed, twisting her body to break Tim's hold. "I have to stop them." She sank her teeth into Tim's arm.

"It's over," Tim said, struggling to keep his voice calm and reassuring. "As long as no one else attacks or fires a damn gun, no one will get hurt. Stop biting me."

"Your robots killed one man and injured another."

"My ANDROIDS are programmed to defend. I've explained that to you and everyone out there over and over." Feeling Jessica's body relaxing and her breathing slowing, Tim released his hold "Lordy, Jessica, you're strong. And have a painful bite." Tim watched the blood drip from his arm. "How did that man get a gun into camp? And why did he fire it?"

"You may accept your android's superiority, but the rest of us don't. Artificial live forms should not have the capability of killing humans!"

"I will not debate with you android ethics. These androids were designed and programmed thousands of years before man existed. Their makers wanted a life free of aggression and war, so they gave the androids domain over them in matters of hostility. Be thankful Juaquin can distinguish between deadly hostility and defense. Otherwise, Gerald would be lying out there dead, too."

"Go to hell." Jessica's footsteps echoed across the stone floor as she stamped outside to try and rectify what happened and console the dead man's family.

"Let's get that wound attended to before it gets infected," Juaquin said. "I can't believe she bit you."

"Me either." Tim laughed.

"I'm thankful only one man was killed," Roger said, in an attempt to ease his brother's guilt. "If those other men had had weapons, the count would have been higher."

"Why was the dead man so foolish as to think the androids wouldn't react?" Hiinew asked.

"We've lived with the androids and the fact that they will not hesitate to kill to save us for centuries," Robert said. "These campers have only been aware of the capability for a little over a month, some only days. I guess he forgot how they'd react to an act of aggression."

"Or didn't believe it," Roger said. "How did the humans react?"

"Not well." Robert stood and walked over to a planter of flowers. He took a deep breath, his mind oblivious to their sweet fragrance. "The next morning, about a third left the encampment for somewhere devoid of murderous monsters. Their words, not mine."

"Why are you surprised?" Roger asked. "When has the human species not felt superior to other beings or each other? Or not taken what they wanted by force?"

"After they blew up half this planet and poisoned the rest, I hoped they had learned something."

"Are they even capable of learning? You had to take a space station full of animal specimens hundreds of light years away from here so you could save them from humanity. We are destined to destroy ourselves and all we touch."

"I don't believe that," Robert said, trying to convince himself humanity could change. "New Earth is a testimony to what humanity can accomplish if they try."

"I fear that is true only because those humans were gifted with alien intervention," Hiinew said softly, placing a gentle hand on Robert's arm. "Here on Earth, humans never received the wisdom held by many alien nations. They're driven by their instincts, products of their environment. You can't expect to change them overnight, nor can you undo what's already been done."

"As I see it, Brother, you have two choices. You can continue to try to unite the various fractions so the ISC will bring Earth into the organization. Or you can admit defeat, return home, and leave Earth's humans to their own destruction. They will either learn or destroy themselves. Their future is not yours to save."

"No, it's not," Robert said. "I wish there was an easy way I could get through to them."

"If it was easy, it wouldn't be worth doing," Hiinew said. "Do you still want two of my androids?"

"Yes. I still plan to build the new compound."

"Then you plan on staying?" Roger asked.

"I agreed to give this plan a try for three months. I've still got six weeks left. Let's see how much more can get screwed up." Robert walked to the end table and poured himself a glass of Quivia juice. "Although, for a chance to keep drinking this delicious brew, I might consider staying even longer." He laughed. "So, Hiinew, what about the Quebracho trees? Can I harvest a few?"

"The jungle is stable enough to allow the felling of thirty-three trees scattered throughout the region. But I must tell you, I fear that their transportation may make the discovery of this place a possibility. How do we hide the fact that you are harvesting virgin, healthy trees from the west of the camp? What if humans come to investigate the area? The humans could destroy all we have built." Hiinew paused, letting the gravity of the situation sink in. "We need a plan, something that ensures secrecy, or else the consequences could be disastrous."

"That problem keeps me up at night. It is imperative that we protect the secrecy of this place." The skin on Robert's face grew taut. "But I may have thought of a way. Hiinew, if your people can fell the trees and transport them to a region north of here, we can fly in and pick them up. That way, if anyone sees the fliers with the logs, they will assume we harvested them from the section far north of here."

"That might work," Roger said.

"Quebracho trees are indigenous in the north," Hiinew stated. "Your androids can cut down some. That way the humans will believe they came from the north. And if we leave their branches and vegetation growth on them, they will resemble ordinary fallen trees."

"But won't their bright and healthy leaves give away the fact they're not from that area?" Roger asked. "The trees in the north are barely hanging on."

"If we allow your trees to lie on the ground for a week, their leaves will wither," Hiinew replied. "The new trees will look sickly, just like the northern ones."

"Then we agree. I'll take two of your androids back with me today, and you will start harvesting the trees. Can you have them at the rendezvous in, say, seven days?"

"That sounds like a reasonable time frame," Hiinew replied. "Seven days should be enough time for their leaves to start to wither."

"Remember to instruct your crew not to clean them. We must maintain the deception."

Robert's jaw dropped open as he stared at the scene when he landed. The camp was in shambles, reminding him of a war zone. Three of the newly constructed huts were gone, replaced by a burning pile of smoldering wooden beams, burning cinders, and smoke. The androids were carrying dead bodies to a funeral pyre. The field where corn and beans existed were now bare, its vegetables pulled out by their roots. The door to the small meat house was yanked off its hinges and lying on the ground.

"What happened here?" Robert demanded as Tim advanced towards him.

"About twenty campers that left after the shooting incident decided they wanted more than the food we sent them with."

"Casualties?"

"Four of our people were killed, six are wounded, and ten of the attackers were killed."

"How did they get past the androids?"

"A small number of attackers created a diversion down by the stream, screaming for help for a young boy attacked by pumas. B-25, Jason, and Phillip went with me to help. One of the campers kept Andrew busy and away from the radar while the assailants advanced. We rushed back the moment Andrew advised us about the attack, but by the time we got here, they had already taken the meat and destroyed the crops. The androids opened fire and repelled the attackers."

"Make that five of our own killed," Jessica said as she walked up. Her cheeks were wet with tears. "Gerald has died. He saved my life by stepping in front of me and taking a bullet meant for me."

"I am sorry for your loss," Robert said, his voice soft and sincere. "He was a great asset to this camp. His presence will be missed. But perhaps you can now better understand why our androids were designed to respond to any act of aggression. If they had not reacted according to their programming, everyone might have been killed."

"Yes." Jessica gazed deep into Robert's eyes. "Although I don't completely agree with it, I understand now."

Tim's communicator beeped. "Sir, Andrew reports Opal is calling from the ship."

"It appears you have everything under control. Carry on."

Robert walked into the cave and into the section where a temporary communication center had been erected. "Robert, here."

"Hi, Sir. I have exciting news. A Triilon freighter in this parsec contacted me. The Triilon nation is a member of the ISC and heard of our mission. They are offering food, medicine, some less advanced technological equipment, building materials, and *sybock* rods."

"It couldn't have come at a better time. The settlement was attacked."

"Tim informed me."

"*Sybock* is just what we need. It's similar to *iggium*, but less dense and lighter. It will make excellent material for the huts and outer wall. With the recent attack, I can't spare any androids to retrieve the supplies. Can you contact the Triilon and see if they can deliver it?"

"Yes, Sir," Opal said. "Do you think the humans will tolerate aliens landing on Earth's soil?"

Robert laughed. "Humans now know that aliens have walked on their soil for several thousand years."

"Yes, but knowing something happened and actually witnessing it are sometimes two different things, Sir."

"True, but I think they'll survive seeing a few Triilon and strange-looking spacecraft. Besides, the Triilon are beautiful beings. They resemble Earth's fairies."

"I will contact their commander and get back to you. Echo Command Ship One out."

Robert ended the communication. He saw the odd expression on Andrew's face. "What?"

"You really think the humans will accept aliens landing outside their door?" Andrew asked.

"Due to current events, they have lost half of their food supply. Their desire to survive should overcome their fear of the unknown. At least, that's my hope. And I wasn't kidding when I said the Triilon are beautiful creatures. Humanity's history is filled with stories of fairies. I'm simply going to give them a chance to meet one in person."

That night, the dining zone buzzed with the news that fairies were arriving the next day to deliver supplies and replace the stolen food.

"You told them real fairies were stopping by tomorrow?" Tim asked Robert. "Fairies?"

"Have you ever seen a Triilon?"

"No."

"Trust me. They're identical to the pictures humans have of forest fairies: long pointed ears, flowing blond hair, blue eyes, and a pair of exquisitely colored wings."

"And when have you ever seen pictures of fairies?" Juaquin asked.

"When I was in New York, I visited the library several times a week. I loved reading books in the Fantasy sections and became well-versed in the concept of fairies. I had met the Triilon some sixty years ago and was intrigued by their similarity. It made me wonder if the Triilon hadn't visited Earth over the years and were responsible for the fairy legends."

"Really?" Jessica asked, intrigued at the idea. "You think this alien race has been here before?"

"Jessica, if you knew how many alien races have visited Earth, you'd never have a restful night's sleep again."

"How many species are you talking about?" Everyone could see the concern on Jessica's face.

"More than you can imagine."

"But take comfort in the fact that none of them have been hostile," Tim added.

"At least not yet," Jessica whispered.

The next day, at 0-eleven hundred hours, five massive pink and yellow cargo ships landed in the field beside the camp. The vessels were ten times the size of the ISC fliers, displaying swirls of pink, yellow, lilac, and blue. Ornate filaments decorated the ship, reminding one of a shiny Christmas tree ornament. When the side doors opened, a creature emerged who was so beautiful he made the humans gasp in wonder. They really were fairies. They were unisex, scantly clothed, with gentle facial features and slim bodies. After exiting the ships, each spread their semi-transparent gold wings and flew across the meadow.

"Commander Hellsworth, I am Commander Undii of the Triilon cargo ship Ooodee," said a female voice from the translator. The Commander's actual voice was a series of whistles and clicks.

"It is a pleasure and an honor to meet you, Commander Undii," Robert said, placing his hands together and bowing his head.

A smile spread across Undii's face. "You do not remember when we met before? I visited the ISC's space station when it was hidden inside Earth's moon."

"I recall a troop of Triilon visiting the station many years ago. I did not realize you were a part of that convoy."

"The Triilon have maintained a cargo route through this system for over millennia. That is the reason I can offer you assistance today."

"Assistance I am grateful for. On behalf of the ISC and those here in the camp, I deeply thank you. Can I offer you something to drink?"

"No, I am on a short time frame. If you tell me where to place the supplies, I will ask our androids to unload them."

"You have androids too?" Jessica asked, her face a jumble of confusion.

"All ISC ships have androids," Undii said. "Might I ask your name?"

"Commander Undii, this is the leader of the humans, Jessica Steinberg."

"Miss Steinberg, it is a pleasure to meet you."

Jessica giggled, the feeling of a thousand ants running across her body. Her stomach churned. "I can't believe I'm meeting a real fairy."

"A fairy?" Undii asked, one of her feathery eyebrows rising.

"A little something I told the humans," Robert whispered. "A mythical creature that humans adore. After all that has happened, I didn't want to upset them by saying ships of aliens were coming."

"I understand," Undii whispered back.

"Some of the children and adults were wondering if they could meet you?" Jessica said, her cheeks blushing.

"I would like that."

"I must place restrictions on that meeting," Juaquin intervened, stepping forward. "There may still be conspirators amongst the humans. I have no way to tell who is friendly and who is not."

"At least allow the children to meet us," Undii said.

"I will allow groups of five children to greet Undii once they have been inspected for weapons."

"You think the children are dangerous?" Jessica asked.

"I am not willing to endanger Commander Undii's life. As for the adults, only two at a time may meet her and her staff. Again, we will screen them for weapons. An android will escort each."

As the cargo was unloaded, the children marched forward in groups of five and met Commander Undii and her four lieutenants. The children giggled, softly touching the Triilon's wings, their three blue-tinted fingers, pointed ears, and soft blond ringlet hair. The children asked many questions, which the Triilon answered with smiles. Each group was allotted ten minutes. Once the children had finished, it was the adults' turn. Only sixteen adults wished to meet the aliens. Those not brave enough watched from behind the cave boulders, giggling and pointing.

"Thank you again, Commander Undii, for the supplies," Robert said. "I don't think we could have survived without them."

"Commander, the ISC assignment given to you is almost an impossible task to accomplish. Let me help you even further. The humans have been living with your androids and are used to them being around. You need more help here. Let me leave you an additional fifteen androids to assist with security and help rebuild the settlement." Undii raised her hand in the air. "And before you object, you can signal us when you are ready to return home, and we will stop and pick them back up."

"That is too generous. Are you sure you can spare them?"

"The androids are aboard for security and to do any necessary heavy lifting. They are often bored and are always eager for new assignments. I assure you, they will welcome the change of scenery. And if need be, I can always recruit a few at our next port."

"Then I will be happy to accept your help. Might I ask you for one more favor?"

"Of course."

"Might you have any extra fliers you could lend us? We only have three fliers, and that number is a hindrance to my mission. I need to spread out more and explore other continents to find more humans and recruit them for our cause. But I can only use one flier for that. The other two must remain in camp to help in the construction and to maintain safety."

"I am sorry, we do not have small fliers, only the massive cargo ships. But I can pick up several at Felix Three. We can make the trip and be back in three weeks. Would that be okay?"

"I don't want to cause you undue hardship."

"No hardship. I would consider it an honor to help."

"Thank you. They will help a lot."

"How many fliers do you need?"

"Can your ship accommodate seven fliers?"

"My cargo bay can accommodate thirty if you'd like that many."

"Seven is sufficient. I don't want too many fliers about tempting the humans. There are still those around who would love the chance to get their hands on a flier."

"Seven it is. Farewell for now. I will see you in three weeks. And next time you visit Hiinew, tell her I have a case of Quivia fruit for her."

"Hiinew? You know about Hiinew?"

"Who do you think arranged for her emergence on Earth without the ISC knowing?"

"You are as mysterious as she is."

Offering only a smile as further explanation, Undii shook his hand, turned, and flew back to her ship. Robert watched as the five cargo fliers rose in the sky.

"Robert, what's that in your hand?" Tim asked.

Robert stared at a shiny, golden star-shaped stone in his hand. "I'll be damned. My star."

"Your star?"

"Now I remember Undii. She visited the space station when I was young, around nine or ten. The Triilon mesmerized me, their

85

three-fingered hands, and, of course, their wings. Undii was a sub-adult, and she went by her child's name. That's why I didn't realize who she was until now. We became friends and spent a lot of time together over the three days she was aboard. When the Triilon left, I gave my friend this star as a symbol of our friendship. I bought it from a shaman on board. He told me it would bring her luck and keep her safe on her travels. It appears to have worked."

"Why did she give it back to you?" B-25 asked.

"I guess she thought I needed luck and something extra to keep me safe."

Chapter 6: AUSTRALIA

Juaquin walked from the loading zone to Robert with two new androids in tow. "Sir, I'd like to introduce you to A-16 and S-32. A-16, S-32, this is our leader, Robert Hellsworth."

"Welcome to our camp." Robert shook both android's hands. "Your help is appreciated."

"Our purpose is to serve, Sir."

"Do you prefer to be called by your designations, or would you like to choose a real name like Scott or James?"

"Is that allowed?" A-16 asked. "On Triilon ships, we all go by our designation. Even many of the Triilon have designations instead of names."

"I have an idea. How about, for now, you each keep your designation," Juaquin said. "After a few days, you can decide if you want to switch to another designation."

"How will we know which designation to choose?" A-16 asked.

"There's no right or wrong way to determine a name," Robert said. "Often names are derived from the name of a person you admire or are fond of, an ancestor, or a fond designation. Sometimes, it's a nickname, a loving name someone else gives you, such as shorty or smiley. Names come from many factors. But I believe you will know when you hear one you like."

"Can the other androids choose a name?" S-32 asked.

"Of course," Robert chuckled. "All androids have the same rights. Have either of you ever worked with humans before?" Robert asked.

"No. Is that what these beings are called, humans?" S-32 asked. "Both of us have worked with many alien races, but this is our first time on this planet."

Juaquin laughed. "You will find they are a strange lot, capable of great emotion, caring, and anger. They are not logical but are ruled by their emotions. You cannot ask for a better being to be your friend and always be there for you."

"What is a friend?" A-16 looked at S-32, who shook his head negatively.

"A friend is the person who knows all your quirks and still sticks around, even after witnessing your most embarrassing moments. A friend is your personal cheerleader, therapist, and partner-in-crime, all rolled into one. They're the ones who turn ordinary days into adventures and boring conversations into hilarious inside jokes. In short, a friend is the family you get to choose, the one who makes life a lot more colorful and a lot less serious."

"Will you or Commander Hellsworth give us a friend?"

"No, that is something you need to find for yourself."

"How do we do that?"

"I believe Tim or Jessica can explain that better than me," Robert said. "Or perhaps one of our androids. But I have found it is easier to make a friend when you are yourself and go by a real name."

"Robert, Robert," Jessica yelled as she ran from the cave. "Henry's on the ham radio with a man from Australia." She stopped speaking when she witnessed the two new androids. "I'm sorry. Am I interrupting something?"

"No. These are two of our new androids."

"More androids, Robert?" Jessica asked, her face emotionless.

Robert wondered if she was happy, upset, or indifferent. "Yes, besides the supplies, the Trillion commander left us fifteen new androids to help with the construction and protection duties."

"I see."

"You were saying, Jessica?"

"Remember, I told you that Henry can contact various people worldwide on his hand radio every few months? Sometimes, when the airwaves are just right, he can speak with a man in Australia. He's talking to him now."

Robert's eyes widened, and little pinpricks traveled up and down his body. "Lead the way!"

Jessica and Robert rushed into the cave and down a small tunnel to a section where Henry and his son sat. Henry's ham radio was on top of a small table, and in front of the radio was a microphone into which Henry was speaking.

"I'm sorry to hear that," Henry said. Jessica tapped Henry on the shoulder. "Maattie, the man I was telling you about is here. I'm going to let him talk with you." Henry stood and gestured for Robert to be seated. "Speak into the microphone. You should have no trouble hearing him, but if you do, give me a thumbs up, and I'll increase the volume. I'm speaking with Maattie. He is a member of the Nyungar."

"Hello, Mr. Maattie. My name is Robert Hellsworth. I have come to Earth on behalf of the Interstellar Space Coalition to investigate what has happened since we left Earth thirty-eight years ago."

"It is a pleasure to speak with you, Mr. Hellsworth. But there is no reason to address me as Mister. My name is Maattie."

"And you can call me Robert."

"Why have you returned after so many years, Robert?"

"The ISC received a transmission from Earth. The Coalition thought Earth might be in trouble or, better yet, had finally taken our offer to join the ISC. You can imagine our surprise when we discovered the Northern Hemisphere countries had annihilated themselves and left the rest of Earth in dire peril."

"So, it is true. The northern countries did launch their nuclear weapons?"

"Do you have knowledge of this occurrence?"

"Only from what Henry told me. We had gone on a walkabout and were unaware of anything happening until after we returned."

"A walkabout? I am not familiar with that term," Robert said.

"A walkabout is a journey taken by foot across Australia. The First Nation's people have taken such walks for centuries. It is a way for us to reconnect with our culture, the land, and the spirit world. Ten of us had gone on the walkabout and were gone for five weeks. When we returned to our home outside of Perth, we found many of the town's residents were gone, dead, or dying of an unknown sickness. No one knew what was going on. Several days after we returned, half of our people also became ill from this illness and died."

"My condolence. How did you learn what happened?"

"A man stumbled into our town telling stories of nuclear weapons striking Australia's cities. He said that even though our country possessed no nuclear warheads, some leader somewhere decided that because Australia was a partner of NATO in the Indo-Pacific region, we posed a threat. We learned the mysterious disease killing us was radiation poisoning."

"About the same time, the skies over Australia turned dark," Maattie continued. "The sun was blotted out in thick dust and smoke. The sparse vegetation perished, followed by the animals. Those who had managed to survive the bombings died of starvation, including the First Nation's people. We realized that if we wanted to survive, we needed to depend on our traditions. We left our urban communities for the Outback. That is where we have lived these past several years."

"How many are you?"

"We number only twenty-two. Many are still sick. Food and water are scarce, but we manage to survive."

"What can I do to help you?"

"Unless you can turn back the hands of time, nothing, Robert."

"Nonsense. I have fliers available at my disposal. I'd like to come visit you and bring you food, water, supplies, and medicine."

"I thank you for your offer, but you cannot come here. I fear the radiation levels are still too high and will kill you."

"Part of my organization consists of security androids. I can have an android team scan your region and determine the amount of radiation. From that, I will determine whether a visit is feasible or not. But even if I cannot visit in person, I can still send you what I promised. High levels of radiation will not harm my androids."

"What about your ships? Won't the radiation harm them?"

"No. They are built to withstand the radiation from twin suns."

"Then, Robert, we would welcome a visit and supplies. Run your scan."

"Thank you, Maattie. Are you aware of other survivors?"

"We've encountered no one, but we talk with three other groups by radio."

"Where are they located?"

"Two are in the center of Australia; the third is located in Mount Isa in Queensland."

"Do you know how many survivors are in each group?"

"No. I asked when I first talked with them, but I haven't inquired for over a year. It became too depressing to learn of so many deaths each time we spoke. If you'd like, I can try contacting them and find out."

"Yes, please do. Also, ask if they need supplies."

"Will do." There was a brief pause. "Robert, how bad was the destruction in the north?"

"I'm sorry to tell you that nothing remains. It's been completely destroyed."

"The greed of the northern leaders always ruled their thinking." Maattie went silent. Robert could only imagine the man's sorrow.

"I will talk with you in two days once I learn your radiation levels."

"Robert, that might not be possible," Henry interrupted. "Usually, things line up only every few weeks or even months to allow us to communicate."

"In that case, Maattie, if conditions are favorable, I will visit you within the week. If not, I'll talk to you when conditions allow it."

"Agreed. Can you put Henry back on the line? We still have some chess moves to discuss."

"Chess?" Robert asked, standing up to give Henry back his seat.

"Even in the chaotic world, there's always time for a game of chess." Henry gestured to the side of the table. To the radio's left, a chessboard was set up, partially hidden by the expanse of the radio.

"Who's winning?"

"I am," came Maattie's voice.

"But not for long. I have him on the run this game."

"Only because I let him think that." Maattie's laugh echoed through the cave.

Robert stepped outside into the crisp evening air, his gaze sweeping over the open yard. Shadows stretched long as the last light of day faded. In the distance, he spotted a lone figure near the storage shed, its outline familiar. Quickening his pace, Robert approached, the gravel crunching underfoot as he called out, "Juaquin!"

"Do you need something, Commander?"

"I have an assignment for B-25 and one of the new androids. I need them to fly over Australia along the southwestern coast, the northern coast, and the middle and take radiation level readings. I need to know if it's safe for me to visit there. If not, what would the danger be to the androids and ship if they landed."

"Radiation does not interfere with the flier's capabilities or us androids. Did you forget that?"

"No, but I want to make sure. Neither you nor the fliers have ever been exposed to the radiation caused by nuclear weapons."

"You think the radiation from the north traveled this far to cause possible problems with us?"

"No. Some idiot decided it was a worthwhile idea to bomb Australia with nuclear weapons."

"Why? We detected no launch facilities on that continent."

"I can only guess why such a decision was made. Bombing an innocent people with no counter-strike capabilities is either mentally ill or paranoid."

"I'll send the two tomorrow morning at 0-six hundred hours."

The sound of laughter and music drifted across the small breeze. "What's that?"

"Undii left a little surprise for the humans in the cargo boxes - musical instruments. Some campers decided we needed a little fun for a change and are preparing to play a few songs. Why don't you go join them, Sir?"

Robert smiled. "I think I will."

As he neared a roaring bonfire in the distance, the sound of twanging music drifted into his ears. Upon drawing closer, he saw three people playing odd musical instruments that reminded him of a cross between a banjo, a guitar, and a violin. Another person played the accordion. Circling the fire were people dancing, some as couples, some dancing alone.

"I wonder where in the world Undii found these musical instruments?" Robert said as he stepped beside Tim.

"They sure are strange looking," Tim chuckled. "Jaime already had the accordion. He brought it with him across the Andes. He's a natural."

"That he is," Juaquin said. "There is something so soothing about the sound of music."

"That, I believe, is a truth amongst many civilizations," Tim replied. "Have you always enjoyed music?"

"I'm not sure that 'enjoy' is the right word," Juaquin said, his tone measured. "As androids, we have no evidence or data to suggest that we experience enjoyment from sounds in the way you understand it."

Tim chuckled. "Just like Xavier doesn't enjoy my mom's chocolate chip cookies."

"An acceptable comparison. All I know is that the moment my ears were blessed with a Caladrine blowing a note on a wind instrument, I was a fan."

"Do all androids appreciate music?" Robert asked.

"I think so. I've never met one who didn't, but I'm sure there's at least one or two out there who don't."

Jessica ran over, weaving around the dancers on her way to Tim. She reached out her hand and grabbed his. "Come dance with me."

Tim tried pulling his hand free. "Oh no, I don't dance." A nervous giggle escaped his throat.

Jessica held his hand tighter. "I won't take no for an answer." She leaned back toward the dance floor, pulling Tim forward.

"No, no, I can't."

"Go on, Tim," Juaquin teased. "Nobody out there knows what they're doing. Go and have some fun."

"Come on." Jessica pulled harder, getting Tim to take a step forward. Seeing she had him on the move, she dragged him out into

95

the center of the dirt dance floor. She placed her arms around Tim's neck, lifted her feet, and laughed as her partner did his best to keep up. The two danced intermittently throughout the night with each other and different partners. Each time Tim danced with Jessica, he detected the smell of liquor was more pungent.

Tim grabbed her as Jessica tripped, almost knocking over one of the musicians. "I think you'd best sit a few dances out."

"Oh, the world is spinning." Jessica chuckled. "I think I've partied a little too much." She held onto Tim's arm, steadying her walk. Letting go, she took two steps and then fell forward. Tim quickly grabbed her.

"Perhaps I should help you home," Tim said.

"That is a ... a ... a dupper, I mean a pupper idea." Jessica snorted a laugh. She smiled, holding her hand up to her mouth. "Oops!"

"How much did you have to drink?"

Jessica held up her hand, showing the measurement of an inch using her thumb and her index finger. "Only a widdle."

Tim steered Jessica towards the cave entrance, passing Robert and Juaquin on the way. "I'm going to make sure Jessica gets home safely, and then I am retiring myself. See you two in the morning."

"Good night, Tim."

"Good night."

Walking a curvy line, Tim guided a very drunk Jessica towards the cave and inside. Now having to almost carry Jessica on his hip, Tim used his free hand to guide himself down the dimly lit tunnel. After some swearing and near falls, they arrived at Jessica's room.

"Thanks," Jessica slurred. She leaned forward and kissed her escort. Being intoxicated himself, Tim kissed her back, barely pressing his lips against her. But when he felt her tongue slip inside his mouth, he reacted. His kiss deepened. He encircled her tongue with his, allowing his passion to grow. Without warning, Jessica grabbed his crotch.

96

Tim broke the kiss and took a step back. "Damn, Jessica, you're forward." Jessica smiled and reached again. This time, Tim was prepared and grabbed her hand. "Time for me to leave. You've had too much to drink, and I don't want us to do something we might regret tomorrow."

"I want you to stay with me tonight."

"That's the alcohol talking."

"Don't you like girls?"

"Of course I like girls. But tonight's not the right time."

"That's not what the hardness in your pants says." Jessica leaned forward, closed her eyes, and prepared to give him another kiss.

Tim's cheeks turned red, and he backed up. "Night, Jessica." He turned and left, hearing her swear as she fell into bed.

———————

"You don't appear well this morning," Robert said as he placed his breakfast tray on the table and sat beside Jessica.

"Damn tequila," Jessica said. "I know better than to drink that shit."

Robert glanced around the sparse table. "It appears a number of people should have abstained. Breakfast attendance is a little down this morning."

Jessica belched. She placed her hand over her mouth. "I can't eat this." She rose and ran towards the bathrooms.

"Where's she off to in such a hurry?" B-25 asked.

"Upset stomach."

"Did she eat something that didn't agree with her? Andrew can give her something for an upset stomach."

"I think it has more to do with what she drank, not ate, but I will tell her. Are you and S-32 ready?"

"Yes, Sir. We plan on leaving in ten minutes. I wanted to inform you of our departure and tell you that S-32 has chosen a name."

97

"Good for him. What did he choose?"

"He decided on Quinn."

"Any reason why he chose that particular name?"

"He did not say, Sir."

"Did you get the latest scan report from Opal?"

"Yes. It shows an extreme concentration of radiation over southern Australia. Has Henry heard anything from Maattie this morning?"

"No, the radio waves are still silent. Such interruptions are normal and can occur for days to weeks." Robert read the report on the screen. "Remember, fly over and check the radiation levels. Send me your report, and I'll decide if you should land or not."

"If I might remind you, radiation will not harm the aircraft, Quinn, or myself. We are immune."

"That is an assumption. To date, no one has encountered radiation that is detrimental to you. However, Opal's report stated that this radiation is different, and the computer's analysis advises it to be a threat. Assume that this radiation is harmful to you two and the plane. No compromises. Is that understood?"

"Yes, Sir."

"I will expect your call at seventeen hundred hours."

"Talk to you then." B-25 turned and headed to Juaquin to give him an update. Then, the two walked to where the newly named Quinn waited with the plane.

"Congratulations on your new designation," Juaquin said.

"Thank you, Sir. I could find no other android listed with that name."

"Then it was a good choice. Remember, the moment you encounter any radiation, call it in," Juaquin ordered. "As reported, this radiation is unlike anything you or the plane have encountered before. Take no chances. Keep an eye on that flower in the cockpit. At the first sign of it dying, advise me."

B-25 flew the alien flier at an altitude of 6.6 miles above sea level toward Mattie's last known location. The alarm sounded two miles from the coordinates, signaling high radiation levels.

"Echo-Two reporting to Home Base," B-25 radioed

"Home Base here," came Juaquin's voice.

"We're picking up high levels of radiation."

"What is your location?"

"Two point two miles west of Maattie's last transmission."

"Opal, are you picking up any increase in radiation?" Juaquin asked the ship in space.

"No, I'm not showing any increase on our instruments," Opal replied.

"Do another sweep of the region," Juaquin said to Opal.

"Roger," Opal ran a new scan of the designated area. "Juaquin, I'm getting the same reading. Do you want me to drop the ship down ten clips?"

"Negative. You are at your maximum gravitational pull. Do you have Echo-Two on radar?"

"Yes."

"Echo-Two, Opal can detect no increase in radiation," Juaquin reported to B-25.

"It just jumped another fifteen arcs," B-25 reported. "Some instruments are showing distress.."

"That's impossible," Juaquin said. "Radiation does not affect our planes."

"What's going on?" Robert asked, walking up and overhearing the conversation.

"I don't know," Tim said. "It appears the radiation is causing problems with the plane. I've never heard of this happening before."

"It never has," Juaquin said. "What kind of bomb did they build?"

"Quinn, how's the flower doing?" Tim asked.

Quinn lifted the tiny floor pot with a red flower growing in its soil. "The flower is dead and has patches of white on its petals."

"Something is happening we have no knowledge of," Robert said. "B-25, are you low enough that you can see the ground below? Can you see if there is human life?"

"No. There is too much cloud cover."

"Juaquin, can we have them go lower?" Robert asked.

"B-25, what's your radiation reading?" Juaquin asked.

"The instruments are recording 12 Sv's,"

"What's the rem reading?" Tim inquired.

"The panel shows 300 rem."

Juaquin looked at Tim. "That's well within boundaries for the ship and them," Tim said. "They should be okay to drop down for a few minutes to get more information."

"Agreed. B-25, I want you to drop down another fifty feet but make the descent in small increments," Juaquin said. "At the first sign of trouble, discontinue and raise back up."

"Yes, Sir." B-25 put the plane in a gradual decline as he headed towards Maattie's location. When they reached thirty feet, the plane shook. "Radiation has risen by eighteen *arcs*. The ship is experiencing tremors."

"Juaquin, I am picking up fluctuations from Echo-Two," Opal reported. "However, there is still no radiation increase."

"B-25, abort the mission," Juaquin shouted. "Return to base."

"Yes, Sir. Heading back now. I am ..." Silence.

"You are what?" Juaquin asked. "Echo Two, respond."

Silence.

"Echo Two, I'm not receiving your broadcast. Say again."

Silence.

"What happened?" Tim asked. "Why aren't they answering?"

"We've lost communication with them."

"Did they crash?" Robert asked.

"I don't know," Juaquin said. "Echo Home Base to Echo Command Ship. Opal, do you still have Echo Two on your radar?"

"Echo Command Ship here," came Opal's voice. "Yes, Sir. Echo Two has turned around and is heading towards base camp."

"Try to reach them on their radio," Juaquin ordered.

The radio went silent as Opal attempted to reach the aircraft. "Sorry, Sir, I am unable to reach them."

"What in the hell is going on?" Robert yelled.

"B-25, is anything odd happening up there?" Quinn asked.

"Like what?"

"I don't know. I feel strange."

"Strange how?"

"Just different. I don't know how else to describe it."

"I feel nothing different,"

"Maybe it's my imagination."

B-25 felt a sudden twinge in his hand, a sensation that was both unfamiliar and unsettling. He glanced down to see a soft, pulsing glow emanating from his palm, casting an eerie light throughout the dimly lit cockpit. The glow intensified, spreading warmth through his circuits.

"I don't think it is," he murmured, his eyes fixed on the radiant hand, unsure of what was unfolding within him, his voice tinged with an uncharacteristic note of uncertainty.

"Opal to Home Base." Juaquin heard the tension and worry in her voice.

"Go ahead, Opal," Juaquin said.

"We're picking up something strange on Echo Two. Radar shows Echo Two emitting a trail of radiation advancing at 15 *arcs*. It is also irregular."

"Irregular, how?"

"It's shifting about five miles back and forth in a zig-zag line," Opal replied. "We're also detecting some weird readings in the atmosphere."

"What about the radiation levels?" Tim asked.

"Unchanged."

"Have you been able to re-establish communications with Echo Two?"

"No, Sir."

"Keep monitoring the trail and keep me advised," Juaquin said. "Echo Home Base out."

Chapter 7: ILL ANDROIDS

"It's the damnedest thing I've ever seen." Robert gazed at the flashing red light. His mind raced with possibilities and theories, struggling to make sense of the situation despite being baffled by what appeared on the radar screen "Why is Echo Two showing signs of radiation that keeps increasing as they come closer to Base Camp?"

"Unknown," Juaquin stated for the fourth time. Did Robert not remember he had asked three previous times, or did the occurrence dumbfound him? "The skin of the plane is designed to repel radioactive particles. Radiation contamination shouldn't show on radar at all."

"Juaquin, does the ship pose a threat to us?"

"It is possible," Juaquin answered.

"Echo Two to Echo Base Camp."

"Finally. We were concerned when we lost communication with you," Tim said.

"Sorry, but we're having mechanical problems," B-25 replied. "Quinn worked some magic and got the radio working again."

"How are you two doing?" Juaquin asked.

"Not the best. Echo Two is giving us a few problems. The integrity of the hull is deteriorating. I've established a small force shield around the plane to keep her together. We've only got about another twenty minutes before we arrive. I think I can keep her together until I can land."

"B-25, I want you to cut your airspeed by half," Tim said.

"Won't decreasing my speed make us arriving intact problematic?" B-25 asked.

Juaquin looked at Tim. Tim nodded. "Follow Tim's advice. He's the plane expert."

"Slowing your speed will reduce the drag on your hull and tail section and help the plane stay together," Tim stated. "I'm now able to view you on our radar. From your readout, your craft will break up at your present speed in eleven minutes."

"Reducing my speed by half."

Tim stared at the flier's readings. Before his very eyes, he witnessed the flier's integrity deteriorating even more. Would it hold together?

"How are Quinn and you doing?" Juaquin asked.

"About the same as the plane." Quinn's voice crackled through the comms, carrying a note of concern. "Our skin is glowing with this strange, unusual shade of yellow. Both B-25 and I are feeling this warmth spreading through our systems, almost like a slow, creeping heat. It's as if our circuits are reacting to something. I am also having trouble seeing clearly. Whatever this is, it's affecting us both, and it's intensifying."

"Has B-25's vision been affected?" Juaquin asked.

"Not yet, Sir."

"I want both of you to listen to me," Robert said. "We have no idea why this has happened to you or the plane, or what danger it imposes on the other humans and androids in camp. I want you to land the plane 5.2 miles west of the south hill. Both of you will stay with the aircraft until we can analyze if you're a threat. Do you understand?"

"Yes," both androids said.

"Juaquin, do we have any radiation suits that will fit an android?" Robert asked.

"No. Androids never needed anti-radiation suits. They were designed specifically for humans."

"And they're way too small to fit an android even if we tried to enlarge them," Tim said quietly, mostly thinking out loud. "But I think I remember something that will work just as well. When we encounter problems aboard the space station on our way to New Earth, the Caladrine built an anti-radiation tent."

"I don't remember that," Robert said.

"I do." Juaquin stood. "The wall on the space station breached, and the created vacuum sucked a cargo hold of our food out into space. To decontaminate it, the Caladrine built a containment tent made from *plidillium*. We can do the same thing here with B-25, Quinn, and the plane."

"Do we have a supply of *plidillium* I'm unaware of?" Robert asked.

"No, but I bet the Caladrine do," Juaquin said. "And if not, I'm sure they can make it or another suitable material."

"Before we can neutralize the radiation, we need to understand its nature and how it's interacting with our alien technology," Robert said, his tone firm. "We can't just eliminate it blindly. We have to know what we're dealing with first."

"Agreed. How do you think the humans will react to the Caladrine?" Tim asked.

"And how do we explain their presence? We can't say they live west of here," Juaquin added.

"The humans had no reverse reaction to the Triilon," Robert said. "I imagine their reaction will be no different with the Caladrine."

"There is one major difference," Juaquin stated "The Triilon look like mystical fairies, something that appears in human folklore. Caladrine look like blue aliens with long noses. I don't remember reading anything in human history about such creatures."

"If we tell the humans what to expect, they will be okay. As for the Caladrine presence, we can say they were on our ship, and we decided to bring them down to help."

"That won't work," Tim said. "We've told them too many times the ship only has one human and one android aboard. I believe our best option is to tell them a Caladrine ship was passing by, like with the Triilon."

"I'm not sure that explanation will work either. Like with our ship, we told the humans the Triilon were buzzing past Earth. If we tell them another alien species was doing the same, humans might become a little fearful at learning what exists in their solar system. They remember the space station was not replaced, and their planet has no protection anymore."

"True," Tim stated. "Let me talk with Jessica and learn what she thinks. Maybe she can envision a solution we haven't."

"Agreed. Robert, contact Hiinew and ask her for an answer to the *plidillium* question."

A large beep sounded from the radar screen. "The ship's breaking up," Tim shouted "B-25, abort your mission. Eject, eject."

"No, Sir," came B-25's voice. "I can land her. I see a clearing less than a mile away. I can reach it."

"No. Both of you eject now." Juaquin ordered.

A muffled voice came across the waves. "Quinn has ejected. I can do this. The craft must remain intact if we hope to discover why the radiation infected the plane."

"B-25, eject!!" Juaquin said. "That's an order."

Only silence filled the air.

"B-25, are you with me?"

Again, silence.

The two humans looked at Juaquin, their faces frozen in fear.

"Even if the plane crashes and burns, B-25 is an upgraded Rz-47G android, the same material construction as myself," Juaquin said. "He will survive the crash."

"You don't know that," Tim shouted. "We can't be sure what damage the radiation did to his construction and skin dynamics. He might die."

"Androids don't die."

"Well, he might be damaged beyond repair. Remember, we don't have Master Kim here to fix him."

"If he is unrepairable, we will put him in storage and take him back to the space station at New Earth. Master Kim can restore him."

"Damn you, Juaquin, you have an answer for everything, don't you? This is B-25 we're talking about."

Tim was sure he witnessed Juaquin grimace. The android was known for his stoic demeanor, a mask that rarely slipped even in the most dangerous situations. Yet, something in Tim's words had pierced that armor.

"Like your grandfather, Tim, you are often governed by your emotions." Juaquin placed his hand on Tim's shoulder. "I assure you, all will be fine."

"Stop telling me I'm like my grandfather, Renn," Tim screamed.

"You just proved my point."

Tim's eyes narrowed as he glared at Juaquin. Tim hated it when the android was right. Sometimes, his emotions did get the better of him. Thinking of a hundred things to say, Tim remained silent and concentrated on the blinking red light. It stopped.

"Did she crash?"

"I have no way to tell."

"B-25 here," came a voice over the radio. "She's pretty broken up, but I was able to land her. Quinn is on the ground and walking towards me. Awaiting further orders."

"Sit tight," Juaquin said. "We'll discuss your insubordination later."

"Yes, Sir."

"Tell him you're glad he's okay?" Tim said.

"Why?"

"Just do it."

"But he disobeyed my orders."

"Do it, Juaquin."

"B-25, I'm glad you landed safely."

"Ah, thank you? B-25 signing off."

"Both the androids and plane were contaminated?" Hiinew asked. "And the two androids glowed?"

"That's what B-25 reported," Robert said.

"How is this possible?" Roger shook his head in amazement. "The designers engineered androids to withstand every known type of radiation, ensuring they would be resilient in even the most extreme conditions. The ISC used the same advanced materials in constructing our ships, making both the androids and our vessels impervious to this looming catastrophe."

"Unbelievable as this occurrence is, it does appear humans designed something new and unimaginable – a radiation which can infect anything."

"Did either android report any other effects besides the glowing skin? Any skin deterioration or headaches?"

"Not yet. I have ordered them to report any changes the moment they occur, no matter how minor. Do you think other abnormalities are possible?"

"Yes," Hiinew said. "If the flier was infected, their skin may also suffer from radiation damage. Remember, the android's skin is alive, just like yours and mine. Therefore, if damaged, it should react the same way."

"Did you receive any communication from the humans in Australia?" Roger asked. "The ones B-25 and Quinn went to meet?"

"No. This morning, the cloud covering cleared enough for Opal to view the area from the ship. She found no life at the settlement. She discovered human remains a few miles from their camp, but we have no way to verify if they were Maattie. It appeared dingoes and other animals feasted on the remains. Opal was not able to determine how the person died or if male or female." Robert placed a small black pouch on the table. "I brought a piece of the metal for your analysis." Hiinew's face grew taut upon seeing the bag. "Do not worry. The pouch is heavily shielded. No radiation can escape. And the piece is tiny. I can bring a larger piece if you need it."

"That won't be necessary. My scientists only need a small piece to check the molecular composition and structure. And I don't want to take the chance of a larger piece leaking radiation into my complex. Once they complete their examination, we can determine if the ship and androids can be decontaminated and how to treat them."

"What do you mean if?" Robert's throat tightened.

A loud sigh escaped her throat as Hiinew dropped into a nearby chair. "As we have been discussing, androids CANNOT be affected by radiation, yet B-25 and Quinn were. This may mean that the contamination is on a molecular level which cannot be reversed."

"And what happens to them if it can't be?"

"Decommission and disassembly." The color drained from Hiinew's face, leaving it pale and stark. Her forehead creased in a frown.

"I can't believe it would come to that!" Robert said. "No android has ever been disassembled. How do you even decommission an AI?"

"I wouldn't know the first step to accomplish such a thing," Hiinew admitted. Rising to her feet, she paced towards the vast glass window overlooking the vibrant forest, a stark contrast to the turmoil brewing within her. "The only option seems brutal - shutting them down, severing their connection to this world, and returning them home. But even then, their creators might be powerless." Hiinew turned to face her visitors. "The creators built these machines to defy deactivation and designed them for an unending purpose. We might have no choice but to condemn them to an eternal slumber as we lock them away in a sterile prison and forever cut off from all they were."

"Do the creators even still exist?" Roger asked. "Has anyone encountered them in the past five thousand years?"

"Not to my knowledge," Hiinew said. "And I think the time is closer to fifty thousand years or longer. But just because no one has had contact with them does not mean they don't still live. Remember, their planet is at the end of the known universe."

Robert interjected, "We're becoming too morbid here. We have no idea how bad their contamination is. They might be okay."

"Let's work on that assumption," Roger stated.

"Hiinew, the Caladrine aboard the space station used a tent constructed of *plidillium* to decontaminate some food sucked into space. Can you do something similar here?"

A twinkle appeared in Hiinew's eyes as a ray of hope emerged. "Yes, we can. We always keep a supply of *plidillium* handy for unexpected happenings like this. We even have a *plidillium* tent, believe it or not. I'll have some of my people make it ready."

"Should we wait for the test on the piece of the flier first?"

"No. The sooner we start the decontamination process on Quinn and B-25, the better. But constructing the tent will take five or six Caladrine. How do we explain their presence to the humans?"

"Tim's working on a solution as we speak."

"Has anyone seen Jessica?" Tim walked toward a group of people planting corn seeds.

"I think she went down to the stream to freshen up," shouted one of the ladies. "She's been having trouble with her stomach the past few days."

"Still?" The tequila she had several days before shouldn't still be upsetting her stomach"

"Tequila affects everyone differently," the woman chuckled.

"That it does. You said she went down to the stream?"

"Yes, the one to the north by the three Quebracho trees."

Tim wandered down to the stream. Since the incident, Jessica and he had barely exchanged words, much less spent time alone together. At first, he thought she might have forgotten what happened, but her deliberate avoidance made it clear she hadn't. Tim licked his lips, biting down on his lower one. He could still taste her lips' sweetness and feel her tongue's warmth against his. The memory stirred something deep within him. He halted, reminding himself he was a soldier with a mission to complete. There was no room for emotions or romantic distractions.

A song drifted across the wind as he neared the hill behind the stream. Jessica was singing. *What a beautiful voice.* He wondered if she sang to advise creatures of her presence, she was happy, or she simply enjoyed singing. Maybe her song was a combination of all three.

Tim crested the hill, his heart hammering a frantic rhythm against his ribs. His eyes, desperate and searching, scanned the glassy surface of the lake for Jessica. A gasp escaped his lips, a strangled sound torn free from a throat gone dry.

In the dappled sunlight filtering through the leaves stood Jessica. Bathed in the cool embrace of the hidden stream, she was a vision of pure beauty. Tim tried to call out her name, but the sound died on his tongue, lost in the sudden symphony of emotions thundering through him. A potent mix of surprise, awe, and a delicious pang of desire left him frozen in place. He'd always realized Jessica was beautiful, but seeing her like this, bathed in the golden light and the cool spray, stole the air from his lungs and sent a jolt straight to his heart.

His cheeks blushing, Tim quickly turned his back to the beautiful sight. He cleared the lump in his throat and called out. His voice was silent. He coughed slightly, then yelled, "Hey, Jessica, are you around here somewhere?"

"Give me a minute. I'm taking a bath." Jessica hastily exited the cool water and dressed, almost falling over when she tried to put on her pants. "Okay, you can come down."

Tim turned and walked down the hill.

Jessica's voice was a frigid spear that pierced the warmth of the moment. "What are you doing here?" Her icy blue stare held him captive, a world away from the playful sparkle Tim was used to.

"One of the ladies told me you were down here."

"And?"

"And what?"

"Tim, what do you want?"

"Roger asked me to discuss something with you?"

"He did, did he? Did he tell you to spy on me while I was naked?"

"I wasn't spying on you?" Tim's voice rose an octave. How dare she think he'd do something like watch her.

"Yeah, right." Jessica walked past him, purposely bumping into his shoulder.

"Hey, look, I don't know what your problem is, but I'm here doing my job."

"Were you doing your job the other night when you walked me home and kissed me?"

"You kissed ME, Lady."

"Well, excuse me for having feelings." She walked away.

Tim reached out, his hand closing around Jessica's arm with a firm yet gentle grip. He spun her around to face him, his eyes locking onto hers with a mixture of urgency and regret. "Jessica, listen to me," he began, his voice low but intense. "I'm sorry. I really am. I didn't mean for things to go the way they did. Our kiss… it just happened. You caught me off guard that night. I wasn't expecting it, and to be honest, I had a few drinks too, which didn't help."

His gaze softened as he searched her face for any sign of understanding, his thumb unconsciously brushing her skin where he held her arm. "I never wanted to make you uncomfortable, and if I did, I'm truly sorry. I just… I wasn't thinking clearly."

Tim felt the tension in Jessica's muscles beneath his grip. Her eyes flashed with a mix of anger and something else he couldn't quite place. "Let go of me," she demanded, her voice sharp and edged with frustration.

Tim hesitated, his grip loosening slightly but not releasing her completely. "Jessica, we need to put this behind us," he urged, his tone pleading now. "We have to work together. What happened between us… it was a mistake. I know that. But we can't let it affect the mission. We're a team, and we can't afford to let personal stuff get in the way."

Jessica's eyes narrowed, her voice firm as she repeated, "I said let go of me."

Tim's jaw tightened, his grip remaining steady despite the growing storm in her eyes. "Not until we settle this," he replied, his voice unwavering. "We need to talk this through, Jessica. We can't keep avoiding each other."

She tugged her arm, trying to break free, but Tim held on, not out of force, but out of a desperate need to make things right. "Please, Jessica," he whispered, his voice barely audible over the pounding of his heart. "We have a problem I need your help with. We need to fix this thing between us."

Jessica raised her free hand and slapped Tim's face. The force of her strike knocked him back a step. He reached out and grabbed her wrist in a tight grip before she could strike him again. Jessica tried to break free, and in the commotion, both fell to the ground. Tim held his grip, knowing Jessica would attack him if her hands were free.

"Get off me, you son-of-a-bitch."

"Jessica, calm down. I'm not trying to hurt you."

"Don't tell me what to do."

Tim gazed into her eyes, finding no trace of fear, only raw, unfiltered emotion. Acting on impulse, he leaned in and kissed her. Jessica resisted, shaking her head in an attempt to pull away, but Tim held the kiss, his lips firm against hers. Her body softened, and she kissed him back with fervor, her tongue slipping into his mouth and intertwining with his. Tim responded in kind, releasing her hands. Jessica tugged off his shirt, her fingers exploring the contours of his muscular chest. He mirrored her actions, removing her shirt and bra, cupping her breasts before letting his hands trail down her sides to her hips. Jessica unbuttoned his pants, reaching for the growing desire within. Without breaking their kiss, they each struggled to push down their pants, hindered only by the boots they wore. On the green grass beneath the midday sun, the two surrendered to the intensity of their passion, their bodies united.

Afterward, Jessica lay smiling in Tim's arms, relishing the feeling of his naked skin against hers. "So, is this what Robert wanted you to discuss with me?"

Tim laughed. He kissed her on the forehead. "We have a bit of a situation."

"I'd say." Jessica entwined her fingers around the hair on Tim's chest.

He slapped her hand lightly. "Stop, I'm being serious."

"So am I." Jessica sat up and leaned over, kissing him once more. Tim gave her a quick peck. But she kissed back harder, with renewed passion. Unable to resist her powers, Tim reciprocated.

Within minutes, they were in the throes of passion and once again consummated their affection for each other.

The cry of a hawk flying overhead brought Tim back to reality. "Girl, you're insatiable. You're going to kill me," Tim sighed.

"It's been years since I've been with someone. I have a lot of passion pent up inside me." Jessica raised up on one elbow and kissed Tim's chest. "So, what's the situation?"

"Remember when I said our androids are indestructible?" Jessica nodded yes. "When B-25 and Quinn flew over Australia, both androids and the plane were somehow infected with radiation. In fact, the flier suffered so much damage it came apart and crashed."

"Are B-25 and Quinn okay?"

"No."

"So, what do Robert and Juaquin plan to do? Could B-25 and Quinn make the people in camp sick?"

"I don't have an answer for you. As a precautionary measure, we have them quarantined south of the camp so there's no chance of contaminating the campers. As for what we're going to do, that's where the situation comes in. I must tell you something, but I don't want you to freak out."

"When do I ever freak out?"

Tim tilted his head, giving her a smirk. "When don't you?" He brushed a piece of hair away from her face. "We recently learned another group of aliens are here on Earth."

"Besides the ones who looked like fairies?"

"Yes. But these are very different. They have blue, slimy skin and long noses."

"Like an elephant?"

"Yes."

"Do they have big ears too?" Jessica giggled, a look of amusement and fascination on her face.

"No. Will you please be serious here and let me finish?" Jessica pretended to lock her lips and throw away the key. "We had an incident aboard the space station while en route to New Earth. The Caladrine, that's what these aliens are called, used their scientific expertise to decontaminate some food supplies. Robert wants them to try to decontaminate B-25, Quinn, and the ship. To do that, the Caladrine must bring a tent to the crash site. Robert feared the campers would see them and he's worried about their reaction to another alien species and their appearance. He hoped you might have some suggestions for us."

"What happens if the aliens can't help B-25 and Quinn?"

"I don't have an answer. If the Caladrine can't help, I fear what might happen to B-25 and Quinn. The Caladrine are our only hope. Nothing like this has ever happened before, not since they were made millennia ago. The androids were built to withstand all forms of radiation."

"Why didn't they this time?"

"No clue. The only thing we can think of is an unknown human from the north created a super strand of radiation capable of killing anything."

"Why would someone create such a thing?"

"You tell me. These are your people, not mine. I can't even fathom how they think most of the time."

Jessica sat up, her face cold and hard. "I can think of only one reason - to make sure they rose to number one. That's why they did it. They wanted to be superior to everyone else. And if the others wouldn't comply with their rules, they'd wipe them out until only they and those loyal to them remained."

"You really think someone would do this on purpose?"

Jessica's shoulders slumped. "Yes."

"Why?"

"Didn't you hear what I just said?"

117

"I heard you, but that can't be the explanation. No one is that inhuman or greedy."

"Tim, I hate to say it, but whoever launched those weapons did it simply because they could. Since the dawn of humanity, there have always been those driven solely by their own desires, blinded by their thirst for power and self-importance. They aspire to play god, and history is littered with their examples. It seems yet another one has emerged."

"I fear you are correct." He softly kissed her cheek "So, do you think the camp's inhabitants will accept another group of aliens? Or will they freak out knowing another alien race visits Earth?"

"After Glogg's speech to the U.N., most of humanity accepted the fact aliens exist," Jessica said. "I imagine our campers are no different. They've been around your AI androids for months. When the group of aliens landed in spaceships, they accepted them without fear. I think that as long as we tell them what is going to happen and what they look like, there will be no problems. In fact, I'd be more worried about keeping them away from the aliens. Everyone, including me, will want to have a look at them." She raised up on her elbows. "And I'm warning you right now, you better make sure I meet them."

"Oh, so you think that because you slept with one of the space Earthlings, you can receive special treatment?"

A huge smile crossed Jessica's face. "Yes, I do!"

Tim laughed a deep, heartfelt laugh. Jessica was going to keep him on his toes. "I suppose we should dress and return to camp before someone comes looking for us and finds us lying here naked."

Jessica put on a pouty face. "Do we have to go? This was so nice." Her face turned into a mischievous smile. "And I was hoping we might go again in a few hours after you had time to rest."

Tim's eyes opened wide. "Girl, you really are going to kill me if you keep this pace up. I'm not eighteen anymore."

"How old are you?"

"Old enough to know better."

———————————

"I was getting ready to send the cavalry to look for you," Robert said as Tim and Jessica walked into camp. Jessica bid farewell and headed towards the cave entrance.

"It took me a while to find Jessica." Tim redirected his eyes from Robert and Juaquin. He wasn't ready to explain the happenings of the day. Plus, fraternizing with an Earthling was forbidden. "We were down by the creek discussing the Caladrine's arrival and how the humans might react. Time got away from us."

"Did she have any ideas?"

"Quite a few."

Juaquin stepped forward and whispered in Tim's ear. "You might want to erase that stupid smile off your face." Juaquin winked.

"Am I smiling?"

"If your smile were any bigger, you wouldn't have a face. Jessica had the exact silly grin. I wonder what you two were really doing for four hours."

"I have no idea what you're talking about. But I'd appreciate it if this was our little secret." He took a step forward, then stopped. "And, Juaquin, tell me if I start smiling again."

"Will do."

"Hey, Robert, mind if I go grab something to eat before I tell you Jessica's idea?" Tim shouted, skipping away. "I'm starving. After I tell you what Jessica said, you can tell me about the Caladrine's upcoming visit."

Robert, Juaquin, and two of the visiting droids observed as Tim practically bounced his way to the feeding area, his carefree whistle filling the air with a cheerful melody.

"What in the hell's gotten into him?" Robert asked. "I've never seen him this happy." Robert thought he witnessed a smile flash across Juaquin's face "You know something, don't you? What is it?"

"I assure you I do not, Sir." Juaquin turned his back to his commander, knowing he wouldn't be able to hide his smile. Sometimes an android just couldn't hide those damn smiles that snuck up on you, especially when your friend found something special one summer day down by the stream.

Chapter 8: A SPEEDING TRUCK

"Robert, wake up," Juaquin whispered, shaking Robert's shoulder. "We've got a situation."

"Hmm? What?" Robert yawned and sat upright. "Another situation? What's happening this time?"

"Radar's showing a motorized vehicle heading this way."

"What kind of vehicle?"

"Unknown, but it's big. Radar indicates three human and two Artificial Intelligence life forms."

"AIs? Are you sure?" Juaquin frowned. "Of course, you're sure. I'm sorry. Force of habit to ask such questions. From what direction are they coming?"

"From the southeast. They should be here within two hours."

"South-east. That's drug cartel territory. It might be our friend Miguel coming for a visit. Might not be. Let's prepare for the worst."

"Already in progress."

"Why would he bring AIs?" Robert pulled on his trousers. "Wake Tim. Tell him to meet me at the Android Station right away. Best to wake Jessica, too. Maybe she'll have some information that might help."

Juaquin left Robert's area and traveled through the cave entrance to the inner garden. Tim had problems sleeping with Robert's snoring and moved to a secluded area, making his bed on lush green grass. Juaquin was a little surprised to find Jessica asleep in his arms.

"Tim, you're needed." The young human remained sleeping. "Tim, I need you to wake up," Juaquin spoke louder and with more authority. "Robert wants to meet."

Tim's eyes fluttered open. He attempted to move his right arm but found it unresponsive. As the fog of sleep lifted, he suddenly remembered Jessica was beside him. "Juaquin." Tim's gaze darted from the still-sleeping Jessica to the android. "I can explain."

"We'll talk about this later. Right now, you're to meet Robert at the Android Station. We have a motorized vehicle headed this way from the southeast."

With his free arm, Tim shook Jessica. She whimpered and turned to her other side. "Jessica, you need to wake up. I have to go."

"Hmm?" Jessica opened her eyes. Upon seeing Juaquin standing three feet away, she bolted into a sitting position. "Juaquin? What's going on?"

"We have a situation. Robert would like you to join him, Ms. Steinberg. An unknown motorized vehicle is headed this way with AIs."

"No humans?" Tim asked as he dressed.

"Yes, three."

"How many AIs?"

"Two."

"Robots or androids?"

"Probably robots."

"How can you tell they are robots?" Jessica asked.

122

"Because our radar shows five beings, but only three have life signs. This means the other two are a form of robotics - either functioning robots or intelligent androids." As Tim turned to leave, Jessica followed. Juaquin raised his arm, halting her advance. "I recommend you return to your quarters and leave in five minutes."

"Why, I'm not ashamed of being with Tim?"

"I didn't think you would be, but fraternizing with the populous is against ISC protocols and subject to disciplinary action. If Robert discovers your little romance, he will place a reprimand in Tim's file and might remove him from the second-in-command position."

"He can do that?"

"Yes, and more."

"Like what?"

"He can send me back to the ship for the rest of this mission and bring Opal down," Tim said, his face stressed and somber. "Worst case scenario, he can send me back home on the next alien transport to face Xavier, and he'll throw me in the brig."

"That's not fair," Jessica said, her voice becoming louder. "We're consenting adults. We're not doing anything wrong."

"You're not, but I am," Tim whispered. He leaned over and, in front of Juaquin, gently kissed Jessica's lips. "I don't have time to explain it to you right now. It's important we act like nothing has changed between us. Juaquin will help me figure out our options."

Jessica hurried from the room. *"Why didn't I realize fraternizing with Tim could damage his career? I'm so dumb."*

Once Jessica was out of hearing range, Juaquin turned to Tim. "You crazy kid. What were you thinking, lying here with Jessica? Anyone walking by might have seen you two."

"She surprised me in the middle of the night. I didn't think we'd sleep till sunrise. You won't tell Robert?"

"No."

"Are you going to tell me I have to stop seeing her?"

Juaquin looked at the young human. "Again, no. I won't prevent you two from seeing each other, even if your actions are against ISC rules. I can tell from the way you two look at each other that you are fond of her and she of you. Tim, I know you have struggled with romance since your unfortunate breakup with Arianna. You deserve to find happiness."

"Thanks, Juaquin. And do me a favor? Don't mention Arianna when Jessica's around."

"Will do. But I have some major concerns. What will happen when our mission ends and it's time to go home? Are you prepared to leave her here? Or did you plan on taking her with us? We have no room on the ship for another human."

"I guess I didn't think about the future," Tim confessed. "I got caught up in the moment and ..." Tim smiled, remembering the moment he saw her standing naked in the stream. "She was so damn beautiful yesterday, and she pushed all my buttons. I got so angry when she wouldn't listen. I grabbed her arm to keep her from walking away. She hit me, hard." Tim rubbed his cheek, still feeling the sting of her strike. "We wrestled and fell to the ground. The next thing I knew, I kissed her. I never considered the damn rules. I just reacted. I never intended to have sex with her. What do I do now?"

This time, Juaquin laughed out loud.

"What?" Tim's voice begged for a reason for the laugh.

"I remember you hate when I say this, but once again, you are acting like your grandfather, letting emotions govern your actions. You two never do anything the easy way, do you?"

"You keep saying that, but I only remember Grandfather let his emotions get the better part of him a few times, usually for justified reasons. He was always this staunch being, someone always in-control, a bigger-than-life human. He never let his desire or emotions get the best of him."

Juaquin laughed again. "Renn lost control of his emotions more times than I can count. He would even get so mad at Xavier that he tried to kill him?"

"Grandfather tried to end Xavier?"

"He almost succeeded – TWICE!"

"Why? I thought they were best friends."

"They were, but their friendship didn't stop Renn from reacting. But that's a story for another time. For now, you need to meet with Robert and help him figure out who the humans and robots are. I will walk past Jessica's domicile, so it looks like I went and told her about the meeting. Later, you and I will have a serious discussion, after which you will have a heart-to-heart talk with Jessica. She needs to realize her options before this affair goes any further."

"Okay."

Five minutes later, when Juaquin arrived, he found Robert and Tim discussing the scene on the radar with Phillip, C-85, and two of the new androids, C-49 and Samuel.

"Is Jessica coming?" Robert asked as he looked up.

"I woke her from a sound sleep," Juaquin said "It might take her a few minutes to get dressed. Any additional information on our visitors?"

"I have confirmed it is a gas-powered vehicle," C-85 said. "I estimate it to be ten feet long, six feet wide, and eight feet high. It's traveling pretty fast for the terrain, averaging fifty miles per hour."

"Someone's in a hurry. Anything more on the robots?"

"No, Sir. They appear to be riding in the back. The three humans are in the front; two adults and one smaller human, possibly a child."

"A child?" Jessica asked as she walked into the conversation. "We don't see many of them around. Can you tell how old?"

"Not at this distance, but the child appears small."

"Jessica, when we first arrived, you told us that the northern governments spend billions of dollars developing and manufacturing artificial life forms," Juaquin said. "You said they were taken to the Antarctic. Is there the possibility some still exist here?"

"Yes. The drug cartels used them to fight other cartels. But once the majority of the robots were taken to Antarctica, the few left behind were used only for defense."

"Did they ever attack your village?"

"No. We were always too insignificant for the robots to bother with."

"Why waste your big gun on small adversaries?" Juaquin said.

"Can you tell us anything about their capabilities?" Robert asked.

"I know they were built for war. They are covered in thick armor, possess heavy artillery, have night vision, and can defeat their enemy."

"I don't like the sound of that," Robert said.

"Do you think that's why they're coming here, to attack us?" Jessica's face showed her fear.

"Not if they're bringing a child with them," Juaquin said. "Something else is going on."

"Will their appearance interfere with the Caladrine's visit to the crash site?" Robert asked.

"No, Sir. B-23 and Quinn are southwest of here. This vehicle is approaching from the south-east. Unless they have binoculars and are examining the sky, the Caladrine should land undetected."

"Have Quinn and B-23 reported in this morning?" Juaquin asked.

"Yes, Sir. Quinn reports both are developing patches of dying or dead skin on their body. Both also report a decrease in energy."

Robert looked at Phillip. "I have no explanation, Sir, for why this is happening to them. I checked our data banks, and no android has ever shown the slightest signs of radiation poisoning."

"Can you give me an educated guess?"

"No, Sir. Without samples of their skin to examine, there is a sixty percent chance my guess would be wrong."

"Let's hope Hiinew has some answers later today," Tim said. "What is the ETA of the Caladrine?"

"Hiinew stated their droid ship would pass over the area at 0-eight hundred hours. If the radiation level was within acceptable limits, they would land and erect the decontamination tent."

"And if the radiation levels were not acceptable?" Tim asked.

"The Caladrine will drop the tent and needed supplies for B-25 and Quinn to erect."

"Sir, might I make a request?" Andrew asked. "If the Caladrine land, I'd like to request Hiinew's team to obtain a sample of the androids' dying skin. I need it analyzed to determine why it's dying."

"Juaquin, make it so."

"Right away, Sir."

Robert turned to Jessica. "The people must be warned the crash site is off-limits. And any attempt to steal a peek at the new aliens will result in a gruesome death by radiation."

"I'll make sure everyone is informed. But I'm not sure the threat of death will keep everyone away. People are curious. Hell, even I want to see a slimy blue elephant. Can you ask one or two to come to camp like the other aliens did so we can meet them?"

"They're not elephants." Robert sighed. "But I'll make you a deal. If everyone stays away from the crash site, I will ask the Caladrine leader if two of her people can stop by the camp for everyone to meet. Do you think that would satisfy everyone's curiosity?

"Oh, yes!"

Robert glanced at his timepiece. "We have seventy-eight minutes before our mysterious visitors arrive. I suggest Tim, Jessica, and I grab some breakfast while we can. Meet back here in one hour."

Robert sat down with Tim and a bowl of hot oatmeal. Jessica went to another table to sit with friends, wanting to keep up an indifference to Tim. As Robert slipped his last bite of oatmeal into his mouth, he noticed C-49 walking towards him. He took a sip of coffee, swished it inside his mouth, and swallowed. Robert raised his arm and looked at his timepiece.

"You're a bit early. I still have fifteen minutes."

"The vehicle picked up speed when it hit the dried riverbed. They will arrive in eight minutes."

Swallowing the remainder of his coffee, Robert set the metal mug on the table. "Guess it's game time. Are you ready, Tim?"

"Yes, Sir. Should I advise Jessica our timeline has changed?"

"Yes. She may be needed."

Tim whistled loudly. "Hey, Jessica," he screamed. "Time to dance."

Robert raised his eyebrows and stared at the young male. "Tim, a word of fatherly advice. Women NEVER like being whistled for or screamed at. Be prepared for the wrath of femininity."

Tim witnessed the smile on Jessica's face disappear, replaced by two slits for eyes and clenched teeth. He may have played the indifference card too high. Tim rushed past Robert, leaving him behind to deal with the disgruntled female.

"What's the ETA?" Tim asked upon arriving at the Android Station. When Jessica arrived, he skirted around the area, avoiding her reach. When Phillip wandered into Tim's escape route, cutting off his retreat, Jessica caught up and grabbed his ear, pulling it hard and yanking his head towards her.

"Listen here, Mr. Smarty Pants, just because I danced with you the other night doesn't give you the right to whistle for me. If you EVER do that again, I'll cut your frigging balls off." She stomped over to the wood pile and sat down, her anger still raging.

"Sorry." Tim winced, rubbing his ear, which throbbed with pain. Was their relationship always going to be this painful?

128

Tim felt Robert's stare. "I did warn you"

The now audible roar of a motor pulled Tim's focus away from his pain and Robert's expression. Jessica stood up, her anger giving way to a mix of curiosity and caution. Without hesitation, she stepped closer to Juaquin, seeking protection.

"Sir, Paul reports the air drone shows it's a large pickup truck covered in armor. He counts two Gatling guns; one is mounted above the cab, and the other one is pointed out the back. Two more artillery guns are on each side in the back. He still reports only two AIs. The driver is a human male with dark hair. The drone cannot get a visual on the other two humans, but one is slender in build, and the other appears to be a child, as we suspected. No weaponry is detected inside the truck cab. A white cloth is tied to the driver's door handle."

"A white cloth?" Tim asked.

"That's the universal signal stating they come in peace," Jessica said, walking towards the front of the group as the engine sound increased.

"Paul reports a red substance on the windshield which appears to be blood. The drone also detects a large amount of blood inside."

"Andrew, I believe you'll need your medical kit."

As the android sped off to retrieve his case, a monstrous truck roared into view. It hurtled closer, its trajectory unwavering, and panic clawed at the human onlookers. With a silent, metallic resolve, three androids surged forward. They formed a defensive line before the cowering humans and the approaching truck, their weapons trained on the barreling menace.

"Hold your fire," Robert shouted "No one is to shoot. Let's discover who they are."

Tense and alert, the androids braced themselves, ready to dodge at a moment's notice. The rest of the group retreated. With a screech of brakes and a sickening lurch, the truck driver slammed on the brakes, sending the vehicle into a desperate spin. A cloud of dust and debris erupted around them, punctuated by the metallic clang of rocks and pebbles ricocheting off the androids' armor. The truck screeched to a halt, a mere three yards shy of the Android Station. Dazed and bloodied, the driver stumbled out of the wreckage.

"Help her." It was Miguel. He limped across the front of the hood, holding onto the grill to avoid collapsing. He pulled the passenger door open, leaned inside, and emerged with a woman also covered in blood. Andrew and C-85 ran forward.

"Give her to me," C-85 said, taking the unconscious woman in his arms.

"What happened?" Andrew asked, rushing forward with his bag.

"A Puma attacked us yesterday," Miguel said. "She's hurt bad. We don't have any medical personnel capable of fixing her, so I brought her here." Miguel looked up into Robert's eyes. "I'll give you anything you want. Just save my wife."

"Can we move her inside?" Robert asked.

"I don't advise it," Andrew said. "She appears to have lost a lot of blood. Her breathing is shallow and labored. I need to treat her right here."

"Andrew, what do you need?" Robert asked, his voice tight with urgency.

"Get a blanket on the ground," Andrew answered. "Someone construct something for shade. I don't need the sun's heat reducing her chances of survival."

Tim moved swiftly, grabbing a blanket and spreading it across the hard surface. While two androids constructed a lean-to for shade, C-85 gently lowered the motionless body onto the blanket with precise care. Andrew knelt beside her, his movements methodical and focused. He opened his medical bag, carefully laying out an array of instruments in a neat line beside the body. His hands worked quickly, yet with practiced precision, as he activated his medical scanner, passing it slowly over her body, his eyes narrowing in concentration.

130

Satisfied with the scan, Andrew selected a syringe filled with a shimmering pink liquid. He tapped the glass vial lightly, watching the bubbles rise to the top, then plunged the needle into her arm with a steady hand. The solution disappeared into her veins.

"I need fresh water, rags, and a couple of bottles of *mavine* NOW," Andrew said.

"Where's the *mavine*?" Robert asked.

"On the ship. *Mavine* has to be kept cool, so we can't keep any here. Someone will have to travel to the ship and retrieve it."

"Is there time for that?"

"Probably not."

"What about Hiinew?" Tim asked. "They treated Robert. There's a good chance she has some or something equivalent."

"Contact her, Tim," Robert said. "Tell her we need it right away. Tell her not to worry about how the humans will react; land in the field."

"Daddy, can I come out?" came a tiny voice from inside the cab. Miguel did not answer; due to his amount of blood loss, Miguel now lay unconscious in C-85's arms.

Jessica walked to the open passenger door. Sitting on the floor was a small girl about three years of age. Her clothes, like the adults, were covered in blood. "Hi, Sweetie. My name is Jessica. You don't have to be afraid. These tall creatures are our friends and will not hurt you."

"Stand away from the child," came a loud, masculine voice. Jessica gasped as she turned and witnessed a husky black robot standing over her. A red beam emanated from his eyes, projecting a red circle on her forehead. In silence, Jessica stepped back from the door.

"B-1, I want to come out," came the small voice.

The beam disappeared. The giant robot reached inside and withdrew the child. Juaquin hurried over and stood between Jessica and the metal being. Juaquin's eyes widened, a reaction Tim and Robert had never seen the android do before. Juaquin looked up at the unknown AI, who stood twelve inches taller than he did and had shoulders four inches wider.

"It's okay, Big Guy. No one is going to hurt the child. Do you remember Miguel's orders?"

"Yes. Bring Sandy and Esperanza to your camp. He said you would help them."

"Did you say Sandy?" A shiver slid down Jessica's spine. Fearing to turn her back from the black robot, she walked backward for five yards, then turned and ran to the blanket. She plopped down on her knees and stared at the blood-covered face. Could this be her friend Sandy? Using a wet rag Andrew had sitting beside him, she carefully washed away some of the blood. Tears rolled down her face.

"Do you know her?" Andrew asked.

"She is one of my friends I came on vacation with. She left with a group of people about four years ago. I never knew what happened to her until now."

"Jessica, I need your help," Andrew said as he worked to stop Sandy's bleeding. "I can't tell the extent of her injuries with all this blood. Use the knife on the blanket and cut her clothing off. Just leave her underwear on. Then wash her body so I can see where all this blood is coming from. Can you do that?" Silence. "Jessica, did you hear me?"

"Yes." Jessica sniffled and wiped her nose on her shirt.

"I'll help her," Rosa said, kneeling down.

"Me too," Sally said. The three women proceeded to do as Andrew asked, revealing multiple puma scratches.

Juaquin never removed his eyes from the giant robot. "Do you have a designation, a name they call you?"

"B-1."

"B-1, you and the others are safe here. My designation is Juaquin. I am an advanced Rz-47 G android." Juaquin glanced at the child in his arms and noted the blood drenching the child's clothing. "Is the child hurt?"

"No, the blood is from her parents."

Tim advised Andrew that the Caladrine were on their way with the *mavine*, then hurried to Juaquin to meet B-1. Between the color of B-1's black armor and his size, he was quite intimidating.

"Hello, B-1. My name is Tim. I am second-in-command. As Juaquin told you, you are all safe with us, and we are doing everything possible to save Miguel and Sandy. May I take the child?" Tim held out his arms.

The small child tucked her head beneath B-1's chin. "No, she stays with me."

"That's not a problem," Tim said, lowering his arms. "Can you tell us the child's name?"

"Her name is Esperanza."

"B-1, Esperanza needs to be washed up and dressed in clean clothes. Would you be willing to take her over by the flier next to the tree? I'll ask some women to bring water to wash her and a change of clothing. You can hold her the entire time."

B-1 remained silent.

"B-1, I think you would agree the child has already endured much. She shouldn't have to witness her parents being operated on. Won't you please take her to the plane so she can be cleaned? I'll have someone bring her some food and water, too. Can you do that?"

"Yes, I can do that." B-1 looked down at the child. "Esperanza, can you walk, or do you want me to carry you?"

"Carry me," Esperanza whimpered.

"Good job, Juaquin," Tim said as he watched the large robot carry the child towards the plane. "He's a big one, isn't he? Maybe you can work your magic again and convince the one in the back to come down from the truck bed."

"I can do that."

Ten minutes later, the sound of whirling blades filled the air. From over the hill appeared a blue alien flier - the Caladrine.

"How'd they get here so fast?" Robert asked.

"Thankfully, they had brought the equivalent of Andrew's needed *mavine* with them in case they needed it for B-25 and Quinn," B-25 said. "They were only minutes away. I heard Hiinew say it's the same liquid they used on Roger."

"Damn," Robert said. "That radiation is still viable and causing problems. Andrew will be disappointed the Caladrine couldn't get the needed skin sample he wanted."

A crowd gathered at the edge of the field, watching as three Caladrine emerged from the flier and ran on their chunky blue legs toward the truck. Fingers pointed, and giggles floated on the breeze as the humans witnessed their second new alien species.

"It appears the humans are accepting the Caladrine," Robert said. "Andrew, how is the female doing? Will she make it?"

"Too soon to tell. The puma inflicted some major damage, but I've stopped the bleeding." He handed the Caladrine, who was holding a bag of *mavine*, the IV line. "Here, connect this to the medication and hold the bag up a little higher." Andrew injected the IV needle into Sandy's arm.

"The Caladrine's medicine should replenish her liquids and start generating new flesh. She's going to have some good scars, though. She also has a broken arm, hand, and leg." In the Caladrine's language, Andrew instructed the alien to start an IV of the solution on Miguel. "Samuel, ask some of the humans to help you build a recovery room inside the cave. I need two bedframes raised off the floor with blankets and sheep skins for softness. Grab two coverlets from the flier and place them on top of the bedding. These wounds will continue bleeding for a while, and I want an easy way to dispose of the bloodied bedding. Advise me when the room is ready. We'll put both on stretchers and carry them inside."

Robert walked over to where Miguel lay. "C-85, how is the male doing?"

C-85 asked the Caladrine the question, then translated his words for Robert. "He says the male has lost a lot of blood. His injuries appear to be not as bad as the females, but his scanner shows a broken hand and two breaks in the left lower arm bone."

Robert turned when he heard Esperanza laugh. The third Caladrine had walked over to examine her once the ladies had washed and redressed her. To win the small child's favor, the alien was making funny noises with his long blue nose. Esperanza was impressed with the demonstration, and she and the mighty B-1 were adding their own nose sounds.

Robert surveyed the area. "Where's the other robot?"

"He's talking with Juaquin and Tim," C-85 reported. "They're trying to find out what happened."

Chapter 9: A NIGHT TOGETHER

Robert watched as Juaquin and Tim approached the Android Station with the second android. The tall robot continued past and walked to where B-1 waited with the child.

"Pretty impressive robots," Robert said.

"I believe either of them could almost beat me in an encounter," Juaquin stated.

"Really, Juaquin? I didn't think anything could intimidate you."

Juaquin looked at Robert. "I said almost."

"Glad you haven't lost your humility," Robert chuckled. "What did you learn?"

"As Miguel explained, they were attacked by a puma. He, his wife Sandy, their child, and another woman had gone out for a picnic, taking advantage of the day's clear skies and tranquil surroundings. The day had been uneventful, even pleasant, until their walk back to the village. That's when things took a terrifying turn."

"They were cutting through a patch of forest when they encountered a mother puma and her three cubs. According to B-2, that's the second robot's designation, the mother puma perceived them as a threat. She attacked, targeting Sandy first. She clenched her teeth around Sandy's throat while ripping her claws through Sandy's clothing and flesh. Before B-2 could react, Miguel rushed to his wife's defense, throwing himself at the puma. Despite her teeth and claws, Miguel somehow managed to rip the puma away from Sandy and toss it aside. But the puma wasn't finished. The cat turned her attention to the other woman who was fleeing. The puma charged, locking her teeth onto the woman's throat and severing her windpipe with brutal efficiency. While B-1 protected the child, B-2 neutralized the threat, killing the animal by strangulation."

"Apparently, Miguel did not tell us the truth that day he said they had medical facilities. They have nothing, only the medical supplies we brought. Miguel ordered both robots to bring his wife and child to our camp."

"You said the second robot's name is B-2?" Robert asked. "And the one with his child is B-1?"

"Correct," Tim said. "Apparently, Miguel's not into formal names."

"So, it seems."

"Robert, when I talked with Hiinew, she reported that the Caladrine couldn't land with their tent. They had to drop it about a mile from the crash site. The radiation levels were too high to go any closer."

"Damn, that shit's still lethal, "Robert said, the vein in his temple pulsating. "Andrew's not going to be too happy they couldn't get a sample of the androids' dying skin."

"Andrew's right. We need a sample to learn why B-25 and Quinn's skin is dying," Juaquin said. "We need to devise a plan to safely obtain a sample."

"Agreed," Robert stated. "But how can we get it? What can we use that won't become contaminated with the radiation?"

There must be a way to safely obtain a sample. I'll discuss our options with Andrew."

"Make it so."

Miguel's eyes fluttered. "Sandy?" came a faint voice.

"Your wife is alive and recovering," Andrew said, resting his hand on Miguel's arm. "You made it to our camp in time. You've been here for three days. We've treated both of your injuries. Your wife is sleeping on the bed to your left. I need you to rest for now."

"Esperanza?"

"She's fine. She had a good night's sleep and a good breakfast. She's currently outside playing with some children from camp. Jessica is taking care of her."

Miguel closed his eyes and drifted off, oblivious to the pain or what was happening outside.

———————

"Good afternoon, Hiinew," Tim said into the mic. "I understand you have a report on B-25 and Quinn. How did you ever get a skin sample?"

"Never underestimate the creativity of a Caladrine," Hiinew giggled. "We can always find a way, especially when androids like Juaquin and Andrew are involved." She paused, composing herself. "I'm afraid the news isn't good. We examined the skin from both androids. The results were the same - their skin is dying."

"But androids were built to be indestructible."

"That is the question we keep asking: how is this possible? The android creators constructed their skin from a synthetic substance manufactured only on their alien world. No one has ever been able to duplicate it, or their internal systems and positronic brain. Although incomprehensible, a flaw appears in the android's construction."

"A flaw? What flaw?"

"Although artificially made, an android's skin is alive like yours and mine. The skin cells are constantly replenished by the flow of android blood through the circulatory system. It was designed to be impervious to every known substance in the universe - until now. Somehow, the humans, either by design or accident, have developed a form of radiation which can stop cells in our android's skin from processing the nutrients needed to maintain their health."

Tim looked at Juaquin. The look on the head android's face sent shivers down Tim's spine.

"Hiinew, the implications of what you're saying are incomprehensible," Juaquin said.

"Believe me, I know. For centuries, species who have opposed the ISC have searched for a way to terminate our security droids."

"If news of this ever got out, every android across the galaxies would be in danger," Tim said softly, afraid voicing the words would make it happen.

"I have already notified the ISC," Hiinew stated. "They have dispatched a convoy to Earth to deal with this problem. But it will take a minimum of two years to arrive."

"We can't wait two years, Hiinew," Juaquin said, his face taut, his eyes glazed.

"No, we can't. That's why Earth is now a quarantined planet. To keep this information secret, effective immediately, no one is allowed off the planet. A fleet from Station Proxima Eight will arrive in four days to establish a net around Earth to ensure no unknown alien visitors leave."

"What about our ship in space?"

"When is Robert due back?" Hiinew asked.

"Not for three weeks. The fliers the Triilon brought go faster and further, so he extended his stay to contact eight more settlements in Africa."

"Since it is imperative that this information remains top secret, Robert, too, must not be told of the findings," Juaquin said. "One never knows who is listening to our conversations. As second-in-command, you will have to make the decisions, Tim. You must say if our ship stays or goes home."

"No, no, no, I am not qualified to make that decision. Besides, Robert is aware that B-25 and Quinn are sick. He will demand the latest updates. And when he learns what's happening, he'll make the decision."

"We will tell him there are no new findings," Juaquin said. "Hiinew, I am sure Robert will contact you. You must tell him you have nothing new to report."

"He's going to ask why our findings are taking so long."

"Tell him that sensitive material can only be discussed in person due to the ISC's rules and regulations."

"There's no such ruling," Hiinew said.

"I know. And so will Robert," Juaquin stated. "He's seasoned enough to realize something major is happening and will not press the issue."

"There are a few other things you must know. In addition to the fleet, a delegation is being sent from Delta One to oversee the barrier's construction and ..." Hiinew paused.

"And what?" Tim asked. "Don't go silent on us now."

"And to begin investigating how it's possible for this radiation to affect the androids and flier. Both Quinn and B-25 will be transported in specially designed tubes to their space station for analysis."

"No!" Juaquin roared, his voice echoing with raw fury, causing everyone around him to flinch. "We are not guinea pigs, not experiments for them to toy with! We have rights, and I will not stand by and let those bastards strip them away!"

"Yes, you do," Hiinew replied, her voice steady yet edged with concern. "And believe me, I share your anger. But if we fail to stop this, your entire population is in grave danger."

"No!" Juaquin thundered, his resolve unyielding. "I won't allow it! Not now, not ever!"

Tim stepped forward and lightly touched Juaquin's arm. "Although you have rights and are sentient, you are under the rule of the ISC. You belong to them."

"We belong to no one," Juaquin snapped, his eyes blazing with defiance.

"Juaquin, you know that's not true," Tim said, his tone firm but gentle. "Your makers manufactured and sold you to the ISC many millennia ago to maintain peace across this galaxy. No one ever talks about it, but it is a fact. To my knowledge, no papers have ever been signed stating you are not property. Do you know of any?"

Juaquin's silence was heavy, his shoulders stiff with the weight of reality. "No," he admitted, his voice subdued. "Such papers do not exist."

"So, our options are kind of limited. In fairness to B-25 and Quinn, let's ask them what they'd like to happen."

Juaquin looked into Tim's eyes. A tear filled the corner of Juaquin's right eye - -one of those android secrets his grandfather told him about. Androids feel emotions. They could cry.

"You and I both know what they'll say. To keep this from infecting other androids, they will submit to whatever experiments are needed."

"Juaquin, to ensure B-25 and Quinn are handled with empathy and respect, I'm assigning two Caladrine to accompany them," Hiinew said. "I'll have them report to you daily on their progress."

"Thank you, Hiinew."

"No thanks are necessary. My goals are twofold: not only must we ensure their safety, but we also need to keep this situation under wraps. The Caladrine involved cannot be reintegrated into my collective. Caladrine are notoriously poor at keeping secrets, and I fear they will spread this information about this radiation to the others. From there, it could spread across the galaxy. No, they must be kept away until this problem is resolved."

"When will the Delta One delegation arrive?" Tim asked.

"In three days," Hiinew answered. "From my crew reports, the meeting with the humans went well,"

"Yes," Tim said. "That at least went better than we hoped."

"Have any of your campers become sick from the radiation?"

"No. The security androids have been able to keep anyone curious away from the crash site. Your crew coming to camp was a big help. Why go to a place that might kill you when you can see the same spectacle in camp? Right?"

"Humans are unique."

"That they are."

"If anything else develops, I'll be in touch. Caladrine One signing off."

"You know, Juaquin, Robert is not going to like being kept in the dark. And I don't like the idea of lying to him."

"You're not lying. You're choosing not to reveal certain information."

"He's going to be pissed."

"Maybe a little. But he'll understand once he thinks it through. Plus, his negotiations will keep him busy. And Tim?"

"Yes?"

"There's no way around it. You're going to have to make the decision about our ship."

———————————

"Hey, Phillip, can you watch Esperanza for a while?" Jessica asked, a smile spreading across her face. "I have an errand to run."

"I told Juanita I would visit her hut and examine the new litter of puppies. Would it be okay if I took Esperanza with me?"

"Would you like that, Esperanza?"

The child looked over at B-1 standing in the corner. "Can I?"

"Of course, if that's what you want to do."

143

"Great. You, B-1, and Phillip will go see the puppies." Jessica turned to Phillip. "Thanks. I should be back in about two hours."

"Are you going outside the compound? If so, you will require an escort?"

"No, I'm staying inside."

"Have a fun time."

"Oh, I will."

Jessica slipped out of the back cave entrance. She followed the worn trail to a small building hidden amongst tall grass. Looking around to make sure no one was watching, she opened the door and slipped inside.

"I thought you weren't coming," Tim said, grabbing Jessica and kissing her. "Did anyone see you?"

"No, I made sure I wasn't seen." Jessica kissed Tim back, then pushed him away. "I was surprised to get your message. I thought we weren't going to meet like this anymore, that you could get into a lot of trouble if Robert finds out."

"I can be in deep trouble, but since Robert's in Africa at the moment I thought we could meet again. Besides, I've missed the taste of your lips and body too much. I couldn't wait any longer to be with you." Tim grabbed her again, pulling her close to his body, allowing his feelings to flow through his lips. This time, Jessica didn't push him away but passionately kissed him back. Tim reached over and unbuttoned her blouse, sliding the garment down her arms and allowing it to drop to the floor. He ran his thumbs down her back, up and down.

"I'm short on time, so we can't do a lot of foreplay," Tim whispered in her ear.

"Okay." Jessica reached down to unbutton her belt.

Tim grabbed her hand. "No, let me undress you." Tim removed her hand from the belt buckle and unhooked the latch. He undid the pant button, then unzipped the zipper. He slipped his hand inside her pants' waistband. Slowly, he slid her pants down to her ankles.

144

"Lift your leg." Holding onto Tim for support, Jessica did as asked. Tim reached down and pulled off her boot, then her pant leg. "Now, the other leg." Jessica switched legs.

"My turn," Jessica said, standing there in nothing but her socks. She lifted Tim's shirt up over his head and tossed it onto a nearby box. She undid his pants, sliding them down to his knees. Tim opted to try and stand on one foot while Jessica attempted to remove his footwear, but he soon tumbled over. They both laughed. Jessica dropped to her knees and pulled the boots and pants off.

"Come here, Beautiful," Tim said, bringing her body to his. For the next thirty minutes, the two lovers expressed their love for each other, each ignoring the danger, each unwilling to think what the future held for them.

Jessica lay nestled in Tim's arms, the warmth of his embrace a temporary refuge from the chaos surrounding them. Tim gently brushed a strand of hair from her face, his voice soft but edged with the weight of unsaid words. "Jessica, with everything that's been happening, we haven't had a chance to talk about us, about what the future might hold. The day will come when this mission ends, and I'll need to return home."

Jessica stiffened, her body tensing against his. In one swift motion, she sprang upright, turning her back to him. "I don't want to talk about that," she muttered, her voice laced with an emotion she struggled to suppress.

Tim sat up slowly, reaching out to take her hand, his touch gentle but insistent. "Jessica, we need to discuss this. We can't keep avoiding it."

She yanked her hand away as if his touch burned, standing abruptly. "No!" Her voice was sharp, cutting through the stillness. She grabbed her shirt from the floor, slipping it over her arms with a sense of finality as if each movement was a wall being erected between them.

"Jessica, please," Tim pleaded, his voice dropping to a whisper, desperation creeping in. He watched her, his mind racing. *How do I make her listen?*

"I said NO," she snapped, her tone final, leaving no room for argument.

Tim shot to his feet, frustration bubbling to the surface as he reached out, gripping her shoulders and spinning her around to face him. "Okay, fine," he said, his voice rougher than intended. "We'll postpone it for another day. But we can't run from this forever. We have to face it sooner or later."

Jessica's eyes locked onto his, her gaze stern and filled with irritation. For a moment, the tension hung heavy in the air, the unspoken words weighing down on them both. But as she looked into his eyes, something softened. She let out a small sigh, the fight leaving her, and she leaned in, accepting his kiss.

Tim's arms wrapped around her again, pulling her close. As they sank back to the floor, he held her tightly, as if he could hold back time itself, if only for a little longer.

"How are B-25 and Quinn?" Jessica asked, pushing the subject of his departure into the recesses of her mind.

"Holding their own. The Caladrine are working on a cure and having some results. I expect they'll be back in camp in no time." Tim hated lying to her, but he had no choice. "How is Esperanza doing?"

"She's a great kid. Phillip took her to go see some new pups."

"I need to ask Phillip if he detected any radiation abnormalities in the pups." Tim said. "I never asked you how your friend ended up with Miguel?"

"A few months after we arrived here at the camp, a new group of wanderers arrived. Sandy started hanging around with them. She hated the life here and believed there had to be someplace better. The new arrivals told her they had heard of a camp further south where living conditions were much better. When they left, she went with them. I tried talking her out of it, explaining why there was no

146

guarantee the place existed. We had a huge argument. She left, and I've not seen her since that day. I had no knowledge she was married to Miguel or had a child."

"Do you think you two can patch up your friendship?" Tim asked.

"I don't know. We both said some pretty nasty things to each other."

A beeping interrupted their conversation. Tim reached inside his pants pocket and pulled out his timepiece, shutting off the alarm. "Time to get dressed," he said.

"Do we have to?"

"Yes. Otherwise, someone will come looking for me." He kissed her on top of the forehead. "If you'd like, I can ask Juaquin to stand guard tomorrow night so we can spend the night together."

Jessica jumped up. "Really? Do you think he'd do that? I thought he objected to us being together?"

"He does. But he might be okay if I tell him we talked about our future and you were okay with the possibilities. Although a staunch android, he has a heart of gold. Juaquin has been like an older brother to me since the day we met."

Jessica picked up Tim's clothes and pushed them in his arms. "Get dressed." Jessica slipped on her boots, pants, and shirt as fast as her hands could move. She leaned in and kissed Tim on the cheek. "See you tomorrow night."

"Don't you want to know what time?" Tim called after her as she rushed from the building.

"Ten o'clock. As soon as it gets dark."

Tim stood there holding his clothes, a big smile spreading across his face. He was going to spend another wonderful night with Jessica. Now, if he could only convince Juaquin it was a good idea.

After dressing, he strolled from the hideaway along the winding, overgrown trail around a hill and behind the cornfield. As he walked, he allowed himself the joy of whistling. He wasn't sure if he was this happy because of being with Jessica or if it was because he'd be spending the next night with her. "Please say yes, Juaquin."

Getting a dish of black beans and two tiny round loaves of bread, he sat down at the table. He flagged down Rosa and asked her to bring him a glass of water. He broke off a piece of bread and soaked it in the beans. He was starving, probably because of his latest "activity". He chuckled to himself. Looking up, he was shocked to see Juaquin sitting across from him.

"You're smiling too much again," Juaquin warned. "I take it you had an enjoyable afternoon?"

"Yes." Tried as he might, Tim couldn't remove his smile. "I was surprised you weren't waiting for me outside the shack."

"I stood guard until I heard you stirring inside this morning. I received notification that Hiinew was on the line.".

"What was her latest report on B-25 and Quinn? Any change?"

"She reported their skin decay has slowed but is still present."

Tim's face went from happy to sullen. "Hell, Juaquin, how am I going to make the decision about those two? Robert isn't going to be back before the delegation arrives. It's going to fall upon my shoulders to make the hard calls."

"I believe you will make the right decision."

"I wish I did."

"Tim, you are second-in-command. When Xavier gave you this assignment, he did so knowing something could happen to Robert, and you would become the primary leader. At least that's what I told him."

"So, Xavier still had doubts about me?"

"Maybe some, but he wouldn't have placed you as second-in-command if he didn't think you could handle the responsibility. He believes in you, as I do."

"Thanks. Your confidence in me means a lot."

"I'm always here if you need advice or help."

"I'm glad you said that." Tim looked around, making sure no one was close enough to hear what he was about to say. "Once the delegation arrives, there won't be much time for everyday life. I want to spend tomorrow night and the following one with Jessica in the shack. Would you be willing to keep watch so we're not disturbed?"

"Or discovered?"

"Yeah." An embarrassed laugh escaped Tim's throat.

"Tim, you know my feelings on this relationship with Jessica. Have you talked about what will happen when the mission is over, and it's time for you to go home?"

"We talked today. She knows I will leave when this mission is done, but she wants us to continue." Well, that was almost the real truth.

Juaquin stared at the young male across the table, scrutinizing his subtle muscle movements and expressions. "Why do I think there's more you're not telling me?"

"Because you're always convinced everyone is hiding something." Tim forced a smile onto his face. He had to remain calm and convincing. The slightest muscle twitch or side glance would convince Juaquin he was lying. He couldn't give Juaquin any reason to doubt his words.

"They usually are." Juaquin looked down, analyzing his choices. "All right. As long as she accepts the fact that you ARE returning home, I'll help."

"Thanks, Juaquin. When I leave here, I'm going to check on Miguel and Sandy. Afterward, I have a meeting with a group of farmers. They are asking to have more land cleared for another field. And I'm supposed to meet with Phillip. He was going to check on some newborn puppies. I want to ask him if they showed any signs of contamination."

"I'll meet with Phillip. You take care of the other two matters. After you finish your dinner, I'll contact Hiinew to see if she has an update on the plane fragment. What time do you need my help tomorrow evening?"

"Jessica said when it was dark: ten o'clock." Tim ate the last of the beans and bread.

"I hope you both know what you're doing."

"We do." Tim smiled broadly, then scampered away, unconsciously humming as he left.

"That's what they all say," Juaquin whispered to himself.

Tim entered the cave and followed the tunnel on the right to the hospital wing Andrew had set up. His eyes opened wider when he saw Miguel and Sandy sitting in bed.

"Well, it looks like you two are doing well. How are you feeling?" Tim said.

"Much better," Miguel said.

Sandy raised her hand and turned it over from side to side. Tim looked at Andrew for clarification.

"When the puma attacked, he did what most predators do: he grabbed her by the throat. Her vocal cords are still bruised, so she can't talk. If you want to ask her questions, keep to ones she can answer yes or no to."

"Or ask me," Miguel said.

Tim sat down in a chair beside Miguel. "Sounds like a plan."

"I wish to thank you for saving my wife's life. I don't know what I would have done if I had lost her. Is Esperanza okay?"

"Yes. Your wife's friend, Jessica, is taking care of her. Esperanza is thriving and happy."

Jessica knocked on her bed and pointed to herself.

"She wants to know if Esperanza can come and visit her?"

"Of course. I'll ask Jessica to bring her here. It might be awhile because she's visiting a new litter of puppies with one of our androids."

150

"Is B-1 with her?" A brief flash of fear crossed Miguel's face.

Tim gave Miguel a warm smile. "He never leaves her side."

"B-1 is not like your androids," Miguel said. "He does not possess their alien brain or their ability to reason. But he does have their strength and conviction. He will protect my daughter and wife against all odds."

"Then he and our androids are not so different."

"When will Robert return? I promised him payment if he saved my wife. He did, and now I am in his debt."

"Robert should return in eleven days. But you have incurred no debt. He did not save your lives for what he could retract from you. He did it because this is our way."

"Then you are fools."

"Perhaps."

Chapter 10: AN INJURY

"Oh, we shouldn't have tried that movement," Tim said, curled up in a fetal position as excruciating pain coursed through his groin.

"It was fantastic while it lasted," Jessica said, trying to give encouragement, a sorrowful look on her face. "I didn't expect you to move the way you did."

"I didn't either. Ouch."

"How bad is it?"

"On a scale of one to ten, about a fifteen."

"Do you want me to get Juaquin? He's outside by the tree."

"NO," Tim shouted, grabbing Jessica's arm so she didn't leave. "He'll never let me live this down. I think if I just lay here, the pain will subside."

"Okay, but if you become worse, I'm getting Juaquin."

"Can you curl up next to me and cover us up? I can't extend my legs, so I won't be able to hold you."

Without another word, Jessica grabbed the blanket and flipped it into the air. Opening up, it floated down gently over Tim. Jessica lifted the side and slid underneath, lying beside her lover. Tim extended his arm, resting it on her shoulder. Even this simple act was painful.

Both tossed and turned through the night. Every time Tim moved, he groaned in pain, waking both himself and Jessica. After a long night of darkness, dawn finally arrived.

A knock on the door woke both humans up. After waiting thirty seconds, Juaquin poked his head through the door. "Okay, lovebirds, time to rise and shine."

"We did that last night," Tim chuckled, only to wince in pain.

"Tim, are you okay?" Juaquin asked.

Damn android. He never misses anything. "I'm fine. Just not used to so much activity." *Put a smile on your face, Tim. Be convincing.*

"Do you need help?"

"Nope. I'll be ready to leave in a moment."

Juaquin looked from Tim to Jessica, then back to Tim, debating his next move. "Make it sooner rather than later. Hiinew has already called this morning." Juaquin closed the door. "Crazy kid."

"Jessica, can you help me sit up?" Tim asked.

"You're still in a lot of pain, aren't you?"

"Yeah. But I didn't want to inform Juaquin. If I can rise to my feet, I'll be okay."

"Let me put my pants and shirt on, then I'll help you up."

Amidst a symphony of muttered curses and pained yelps from Tim and sheer brute force and questionable technique from Jessica, Jessica managed to maneuver Tim into a standing position. She helped him over to a nearby crate to sit.

"Damn, that was not good," Tim said, sweat beading on his forehead, his face pale.

"You sit there, and I'll dress you." Tim did not argue. Jessica lifted his foot to put on his sock, and Tim cried out in pain. "Tim, this isn't going to work. You need medical attention. I'm getting Juaquin."

Tim didn't argue "Throw me the blanket so I can at least cover my crotch." Tim reached out to grab the tossed blanket and cried out again in pain. The blanket crumbled to the floor.

"Sorry," Jessica said. She picked up the blanket and laid it across Tim's lap. Kissing him on the cheek, she opened the shack's door.

"Juaquin, I, uh, I was wondering if you can come inside?" Jessica asked bashfully, her voice barely above a whisper. "We kinda have a situation in here."

Without hesitation, Juaquin walked inside. He noticed Tim's painful look and reddened cheeks.

"Not a damn snickering remark," Tim said through clenched teeth.

"What have you done?" Tim remained silent.

"We got a little carried away," Jessica said "I think he pulled a muscle in his groin area. He's in a lot of pain. He can't even dress himself."

"So, I witnessed." Juaquin removed his communicator. "Andrew, I need you to bring your medical bag to the shack at the north cave entrance hidden behind the hill."

"Great! More visitors," Tim grumbled.

"Andrew, keep this between us," Juaquin added. "Top secret."

"Understood, Sir," came Andrew's voice.

"So, how was your evening?" an embarrassed Tim asked, trying to kill time until Andrew arrived.

"Evidently better than yours." There was that snicker again. "I met a cute opossum and several rats while standing outside. I heard two wolves in the mountains, too. We'll need to monitor them to ensure they don't raid our sheep herd. We'll also need to upgrade the surveillance equipment with their specs to detect if they come too close to camp."

"That sounds like a job for William."

"I'll have him begin work on it right away." Juaquin went silent, sending the new android William a message. "He'll have the drone up in ten minutes."

A knock sounded on the wooden door. Andrew stepped in carrying a small satchel. "Someone here needs medical assistance?"

"Our young human here has injured his penis while engaging in a night of overzealous sex," Juaquin said.

"There it is," Tim said, throwing his arms in the air, then grimacing in pain. "You couldn't resist, could you?"

"Where's the fun in that?" Juaquin asked.

"You are really sick, Juaquin. You realize that, don't you?"

This time, Juaquin allowed the smile to show on his face. "I'm not the one in pain."

Andrew grabbed the blanket and pulled it off. "I'll need to examine your penis. Can you spread your legs for me to examine what you injured?"

"Do you mind?" Tim shouted, his voice two octaves higher than normal. He grabbed the blanket and recovered his private parts. "Not with Jessica here."

"I do not understand, Tim," Andrew said. "I believe you two have engaged in sex numerous times. Therefore, she has already seen your penis and testicles and is familiar with what they look like."

"That's different." Tim's cheeks were a bright red. He averted his eyes to the left, avoiding Jessica's. She turned her head, unable to hide the amusement on her face.

"Perhaps you and I can wait outside," Juaquin said, grabbing Jessica's boots and socks "You can finish getting dressed out there while Andrew does his examination." He gently pushed Jessica towards the door.

"I'll be outside," Jessica called as Juaquin moved her through the entrance.

"Have fun," Juaquin said, giving the injured human a huge smile as he disappeared outside.

"Sick, really sick, Juaquin," Tim shouted. "Ouch, I must stop shouting. It hurts like hell."

"Now that Jessica's gone, can I examine you?" Andrew asked.

"Yes. And please give me something for this pain."

Forty minutes later, Tim arrived at the Android Station to call Hiinew. Thanks to the drugs Andrew had injected him with, his pain had lessened significantly, but he still had a lot of trouble walking. He glanced at Juaquin every few minutes to determine if the android was smirking. But the android was respectful and made no gestures or comments.

"Good morning, Hiinew," Tim said. "Do you have some information for us?"

"Actually, it's early afternoon," Hiinew replied.

"Sorry for the delay. I got tied up with some necessary business." Tim glanced at Juaquin. Still no smirk.

"We've finished our preliminary results of the plane and have found the reason for its crash. While the Beta and gamma particles in radiation normally generate a small amount of heat, this radiation causes super heating. The particles were super energized, resulting in molecular loops being broken and cavities in the metal forming. That's why the force field couldn't hold it together."

"Did this super heating cause the damage to B-25 and Jason?" Juaquin asked.

"Unknown. The coalition will have to determine the answer. They have the equipment to inspect the metal much closer than we can. But I do have some hopeful news about B-25 and Quinn. Caladrine nose mucous contains an antibacterial substance that, in some cases, can heal injuries. It has even been used to repair machinery. We have applied a layer of mucus to the androids' skin."

"Snot?" Tim asked. "You covered them in snot?"

"I am not familiar with the term snot."

"Trust me, it's snot." Tim chuckled. "I never knew Caladrine mucous had therapeutic properties. Is it working?"

"We don't advertise it," Hiinew said. "There's always a species somewhere who is willing to exploit such beneficial properties for profit. While the mucous hasn't repaired the damage, it has stopped its progression."

"Have you been able to determine if B-25 and Quinn suffered any internal damage due to the radiation?" Juaquin asked.

"No. Since we cannot bring them to our facility, we cannot do a proper body scan to determine any damage. But judging by the amount of damage on their outside, there must be internal injuries."

"Can't we drop them down a scanner for them to scan themselves?" Tim asked.

"We tried that. The residual radiation caused the unit to malfunction before the scan was completed."

"So, the radiation still remains active, after all this time." Juaquin didn't like that bit of information. The deadly radiation still posed a threat.

"I am afraid so. It's still strong enough to damage metal and living flesh. But it is showing signs of weakening."

"Any word from the coalition?" Tim inquired.

"No, I don't anticipate any updates until they arrive. They're maintaining a low profile, trying to keep their mission under wraps until the net is fully operational. Have you decided whether to place your ship in or outside the net?"

"I gave Opal until today to make her decision. Since she is the one with the opportunity to return home, it's her call."

"Understood. Caladrine One out."

Juaquin turned to Tim. "How are you holding up? Are you well enough to call Opal and get her response?"

158

"Pain meds are still working. I'm fine as long as I don't have to stand and walk."

"I did warn you."

"You just can't let it drop, can you?"

"I'm only stating a fact."

"I suppose I will have to listen to your jibs for the next five years. I told Jessica I didn't want her to tell you I was injured."

"I'd never used such an injury to tease you for five years. Perhaps two or three, but never five. I am thankful you were man enough to admit your mistake and send for me to save the day again."

"I didn't make a mistake."

"What would you call injuring your pectineus and adductor brevis muscles? How did you manage to injure both muscles at the same time? They aren't even on the same side of your body."

"None of your damn business."

"Echo one here," came Opal's voice over the radio.

"Hey, Opal, how's it going?"

"A little boring. How are you doing?"

Tim held his finger to his lips, signaling to Juaquin to remain silent about his injury. "Not too bad. A little tired from double duty while Robert's gone."

"You're loving it."

"Not really." Tim winced in pain. "So, did you come to a decision? Do you want to stay with us for an undetermined length or go home?"

"I've thought about this long and hard. The service side of my brain tells me I should go under the net and stay here for as long as it takes to rectify this problem as a soldier should. But the emotional, civilian side says to go home and have a life, maybe even a husband and kids someday. If our mission was only going to be extended by

159

another year, I could live with that. But the thought of ten, twenty years, or forever, is more than I can do. I'm sorry, Tim, but I have decided to remain outside of the net. I want to go home."

"Going home is a wonderful choice," Tim said. "You should go home to your family, start one of your own. You've always wanted lots of kids. And maybe I can impose on you to take a message to my parents and siblings?"

"Of course." Opal bit her lip, struggling to find the right words. "Tim…" Her voice wavered, and she took a shaky breath, trying to steady herself. "I wish we had another way. I really do." She paused, swallowing hard before the words spilled out, barely more than a whisper. "I feel like I'm deserting you." The weight of her words hung between them.

"Don't be sorry, Opal. I would have made the same decision. Before they lock us in, we'll need to make a trip to the ship and collect anything we may need. I'll have Juaquin and Jules coordinate the trips and put protocols into place that ensure we don't bring any radiation contamination to you."

"Anything special you want me to have ready for you to take?"

"We're going to need whatever medical supplies you can spare."

"Especially pain meds for Tim's extracurricular sexual activities, Juaquin whispered.

"What did Juaquin say? I didn't understand what he said."

Tim gave Juaquin a stern glance. "Nothing. He was talking to one of the campers."

"Oh. If you think of anything else, send us a message. Jules and I will try to come up with a list of items, too."

"Sounds good. As soon as Juaquin gets a list together, I'll have him contact you with the details. Echo Home Base out."

Tim stared at the android, his eyes narrowing, his chin growing firm. "One of these days, you're going to go too far, Juaquin."

160

"The moment was getting too serious. You needed a distraction. Admit it or not, the fact Opal has decided to go home hit you hard."

"She made the right decision."

"Even if it's the right one, it doesn't make it any easier to hear. Did you mean what you said? If the roles were reversed, would you opt to be outside the barrier? Would you leave her here and go home?"

"I would never leave her behind."

"Why did you tell her you would?"

"So she didn't feel any worse about her decision than she already does."

"You really will make a fine commander one day, Tim."

"Not if I'm stuck on this planet for the rest of my life."

"Well, at least you'll have me to keep you company."

"Is that supposed to make me feel better or worse?"

"Whichever you prefer. Now, I suggest you lie down for a few hours and let those muscle relaxers work. You need to heal as much as possible before Robert returns. We'll also have to develop a story on why you're injured."

"Juaquin, are you saying you'll lie to your commander?" Tim teased.

"Not a lie. Just an extra-long stretch of the truth. Do you need help to get up?"

"No, I can do it." Tim pressed on the table to rise but quickly sat back down as pain shot through his muscles. "I might need a little help."

Juaquin reached under Tim's armpits and lifted him into the air. "Put your legs down."

Tim did as told, amazed at the lack of pain. "Can you hand me the cane?"

Juaquin handed Tim the long tree branch he used for a cane. Keeping his eyes on the ground, Tim asked, "Are you still willing to stand guard tonight?"

"You're kidding? Right?"

"No."

"You can barely walk, and you still want to spend another night with Jessica?"

"We are not going to do anything. I want to spend time with her alone before Robert returns and the coalition arrives."

"You promise me you're not going to try something?"

"Juaquin, I couldn't do anything even if I wanted to. I promise."

"Very well, I take you at your word. I'll escort you to the shack at twenty hundred hours. Jessica can come at twenty-one hundred hours."

Chapter 11: MISSING ANDROIDS

"Commander Buutay here," said the tall insect-like alien on the com screen. "Am I addressing Robert Hellsworth?"

"No, Sir. Commander Hellsworth is on assignment visiting survivors on the large continent to our right. My name is Captain Timothy Spalling. You can call me Tim. You're a Caelifera, are you not?"

"Yes. Not many recognize my kind. I take it you have encountered other of my species."

"Yes. I was on the space station Hope commanded by Head Commander Glogg."

"Ah, yes, I remember reading about his assignment. Glogg is a fine representation of our species, an excellent Head Commander and leader."

"He was also my grandfather's best friend."

"You are Renn Spalling's grandson?"

"Yes, Sir. You are aware of my grandfather?"

"There are few beings in the known universe who are unaware of the great Renn Spalling and his love for the Artificial Live form named Jenny. I have visited their graves three times."

"Are you acquainted with Xavier too?"

"I have only had the pleasure of meeting him once. A very impressive android."

"The android standing beside me is Xavier's second-in-command, and he is as impressive as Xavier. His name is Juaquin."

"If you are as young Tim says, we should accomplish much here."

"Thank you, Sir," Juaquin said. "I look forward to working with you, your crew, and your androids. May I ask what your crew consists of and your android accompaniment?"

"We have a mixture of species: Caelifera, Caladrine, Alphinians, Flicks, and two Kett. Our android count is eighteen."

"Kett? You have Kett aboard your ship?" Juaquin immediately asked. "They cannot be trusted."

"While generally a true statement, Juaquin, some Kett have grown discouraged by their species' occupations and have contracted themselves to the ISC. They have been indispensable in several treaty negotiations. You can put yourself at ease. We keep our two under heavy surveillance. Plus, we believe they may be able to withstand this deadly radiation's effects."

"I wouldn't count on it, Sir. This stuff destroys everything."

"We shall see."

"Commander Buutay, with so many beings aboard, your ship must be a substantial size."

"She's impressive, about a sixth of the size of the space station you were on. She possesses a small complement of military weaponry to defend us from space pirates. We also have a bay holding twenty fliers. She has a complete medical facility stocked with the latest instruments. And a newly created anti-radiation facility where we plan on ending this radiation threat."

"What do you need from us?"

"Your two droids and what's left of their ship. I am sending an unmanned flier to pick up the androids. It will transport both to our secured facility."

"Their names are B-25 and Quinn," Juaquin said.

"Excuse me?" Buutay asked.

"Our two companions' names are B-25 and Quinn. I ask you to show them respect and call them by their names."

"I meant no disrespect to them or yourself, I assure you. I have found it better to remain indifferent in circumstances like this. For our duration, B-25 will be called Android One and Quinn as Android Two. Is that acceptable?"

"No, it is not. And I am uncomfortable with you taking them to your ship to experiment on."

"I assure you, we have no plans on experimenting on your companions, Juaquin."

For the second time in his life, Tim witnessed Juaquin becoming angry. "Commander, is there a way to treat B-25 and Quinn here on Earth?" Tim quickly interjected.

"Only if you want them to die."

"Die?"

"With the amount of damage done to their skin, we suspect each has substantial damage to their inner workings. We need them aboard to open them up and determine the extent of the damage."

Juaquin slammed his fist into the desk, creating a significant impression into the hard, thick wood. Startled, Tim jumped and fell to the ground, screaming in pain. "You have no authority to open them," Juaquin screamed. Juaquin stopped, composing himself. "I wish to inform you, Sir, that the moment I learned of your desire to take B-25 and Quinn, I lodged a formal complaint with the ISC. You may not bring them to your vessel."

"I have every authority." Commander Buutay glared at the android. "As for your complaint, it is the ISC who authorized me to come to this planet and rectify the situation. I have been given an open hand in this matter. The ISC will not intervene."

"We shall see," Juaquin said.

"This conversation is over. Commander Buutay, out." The screen went dead.

"Damn his Caelifera sense of superiority. He has no right." Juaquin walked over to Tim. "I'm sorry, Tim. I hope I didn't re-injure you. Are you okay?"

"I've been better. Can you help me up again?"

"Of course." Juaquin lifted the injured human once more and sat him on the chair. "It appears this Commander Buutay is not as kind-hearted as our Glogg was."

"So, it seems."

"He has no idea who he is dealing with."

Tim smiled. "Go get 'em, Juaquin."

"Stay put. I need to contact B-25 and Quinn." Juaquin turned to C-85, who was manning the radio. "C-85, contact Echo Two."

C-85 dialed the android's frequency. "Echo Home Base calling Echo Two. Come in, B-25." No response. "Echo Home Base to Echo Two. Quinn, do you copy?" Again, silence.

"Where are they?" Juaquin asked. "Jason, try to reach them on your radio."

Jason entered several digits into his communicator. "There's no response, Juaquin."

"Is William done with his wolf surveillance?" Juaquin asked.

"Yes, Sir," C-85 said. "He finished it at dawn."

"Did he return the drone yet?"

"It's sitting on top of the wooden crates."

"Get it in the air and fly it to Echo Two's location. I want to know what's going on down there."

166

Within minutes, C-85 had the drone in the air and zooming over the terrain to where the two missing androids were housed. Tim's eyes remained fixed on the screen as the terrain flew by.

"Hey, wait," Tim shouted. "What's that?"

C-85 stopped the drone and let it hover over the ground. "I don't see anything."

"Back up, about twenty yards. I swear I saw something."

All three kept watch as C-85 flew back over his flight path. As they scanned the video, two human bodies lying on the ground came into view. Both were dead.

"You've got keen eyes, Tim," Juaquin said. "Even I missed them. Can you tell who they are?"

"No. Their faces are unrecognizable," C-85 said.

"Their skin looks like B-25 and Quinn's," Tim commented. "But it shouldn't be. They're still six miles from the crash area."

"Either they walked away after being exposed, or the contamination area has spread. C-85, raise the drone up and let me examine the vegetation in the area. Also, advise Commander Buutay there are two human bodies for their investigation."

The picture expanded in width as the drone rose. "The vegetation is dying, but we cannot determine if it's been that way or if the radiation caused the plants to die. C-85, note the position. Add the vegetation's condition to your report so the coalition can check it out, too. Continue toward the crash site. Keep a close eye on the radiation meter. Let me know the instant it rises."

More dying vegetation filled the screen as the drone continued its journey. As the drone advanced, the trees gradually vanished, replaced with brownish-green grass. When the drone flew over the hill, there was no sign of the broken flier or the two androids. Without being asked, C-85 raised the drone higher into the air, expanding the view of the area. Only grass and dirt were visible.

"Sir, the drone is unable to pick up B-25 or Quinn's signal."

167

"What's the drone's radar range?" Tim asked.

"If they were within ten miles, the drone would locate their trackers. They're not in the vicinity."

"Those bastards!" Juaquin roared, his voice reverberating through the command center. "They took B-25 and Quinn to their ship before they even advised us of their intentions. How dare they! Get them on the com, now!"

C-85 punched in their calling numbers but to no avail. He repeated the sequence several times. "Juaquin, they're not answering."

"Figures. Still send the report. They need to be aware of this new contamination and the dead humans. Keep trying and notify me the moment someone answers the damn link. I need to take Tim to his quarters for some rest."

"That's okay, Juaquin. You've got a lot to do here. I can make it on my own." He stood. Leaning on his makeshift cane, he took two steps, trying to hide his pain.

"Not much I can do here if they don't answer. I might as well be useful and escort you to your bed." Tim walked slowly. His pain meds were wearing off, and his pain was becoming more excruciating with each step.

"Would you like me to carry you?" Juaquin asked.

"Not yet. I'm trying to keep some dignity for myself." His walk slowed even more. "You know, with all that is happening today, you don't have to stand guard tonight. I can cancel with Jessica."

"Nonsense. If they already have B-25 and Quinn, the only thing I can do is scream at them on the comm link. Of course, I could always take a flier and fly up there and confront the Head Commander."

"I wouldn't advise that," Tim said. "And we've already seen what that accomplished - radio silence."

"Those were my thoughts, as well. Besides, as you said, Robert's due back, and this will be the last time you two can spend quality time together for a while. While I do not comprehend the desire to be intimate with someone like you are with Jessica, I do understand that humans do not do well without such encounters. I still remember the dramatic change in your grandfather when Jenny was brought online. He was so lost when the real Jenny died. I thought he would die, too. But when Master Kim brought the android Jenny online and filled her with the real Jenny's memories, your grandfather had a renewed love for life. He was happy and whistled a lot. He always had a smile on his face, just like you do lately."

"I remember him whistling all the time," Tim said. Then, his face saddened. "I also remember when the AI Jenny's life ended and the difference in Grandfather. I was young, and it was the first time I learned androids could stop functioning. I felt so helpless. Grandfather was so lost without his Jenny. That's what he always called her - his Jenny. I vowed never to love someone that much, never to want to die because they did."

"I am saddened to learn your grandfather's reaction influenced you to not find your own true love. What he and Jenny shared was special. Renn was a much better man because of his love for Jenny. It's something I have always wished you would find. And remember, Renn did find love again in Penny," Juaquin helped Tim inside his room. "I had Jaxon raise your bedding up on blocks. I realized you'd never be able to lie down on the ground or stand up again."

"Thanks. I never thought of that."

"Take your next pain medication. Grab some sleep. I'll come by when it's time for dinner, after which I'll escort you to the shack. When I leave here, I will stop and inform Jessica what time to arrive." Juaquin witnessed Tim trying to sit on the bed. "Here, let me help you."

Tim held onto the android's arm as he lowered his body onto the bedding, unable to hide his painful expression. Juaquin walked over, removed a pain capsule from the bottle Andrew had given the human, and placed it in Tim's hand. Once he swallowed it, Juaquin removed Tim's boots. He lifted his legs slowly, swinging them around and onto the bed. He then lowered Tim's upper body into a prone position.

"Should I kiss you goodnight?" Juaquin asked.

"Only if you don't value your life."

"How was your night?" Juaquin asked, finding Tim and Jessica already dressed in the shack.

"It went fine. And I behaved myself as promised," Tim said.

"Any word yet on B-25 and Quinn?"

"Phillip finally got one of the radio operators to answer aboard Delta One. He confirmed both androids were in isolation at their own request."

"Right, like they'd agree to imprisonment."

"Knowing they had no chance on Earth, they might have agreed to go. But not without informing me first. Both are seasoned soldiers and would not leave their post without notifying command."

"Would notifying command possibly mean telling Buutay?" Jessica asked.

"No. No matter where they are, I am still their assigned commander until I tell them differently and file the appropriate papers. Both are still my responsibility."

"Anything else happen overnight?" Tim asked. "Did Opal move the ship?"

"At 0-four hundred hours, Opal moved the ship further into the atmosphere, about a mile past where the net would be. The coalition started their construction at 0-six hundred hours."

"How long will it take to complete construction?" Tim asked.

"Fourteen hours, twenty-two minutes, and eighteen seconds."

"That's specific," Jessica commented.

"Yes, it is," Tim said.

"While I agree with the decision you made, it was not yours to make," Robert yelled. His face was a bright red. His temple vein pulsed rhythmically. "As the leader of this team, you should have advised me of the findings the moment Hiinew gave you the news about the radiation."

"I debated doing that exact thing countless times," Tim said. "Given the sensitivity of my information, I decided to refrain from discussing it openly. And because the work you were conducting in Africa was essential to our mission, I did not wish to call you back. We can't unite the people if they have no idea of what we offer. Plus, Juaquin was at my side to ensure my decisions were correct and within ISD guidelines."

"Although sound, your reasoning is no excuse for keeping me in the dark," Robert screamed. "I am in charge, not you."

"Sir, please, take a moment to calm yourself," Andrew urged gently. "Your blood pressure is dangerously high. If you don't slow down, you could risk a heart attack."

"I agree, Robert," Juaquin said. "You don't look well."

"I am fine. Don't interrupt me. In addition, I've learned a quarantine net now seals us inside this planet. If I had been aware of it, I would have contacted the ISC and stopped it."

"I beg to differ, Sir. No one, not even the Head Commander of the ISC herself, could have stopped the net," Juaquin said. "Nor could you have stopped the coalition from stealing B-25 and Quinn. Why call you back if it wouldn't have mattered? Timothy fulfilled his duties as second-in-command in accordance with ISC rules and your instructions while you were gone. But I can assure you, he is glad you're back."

"Yes, I am," Tim said. "Being in charge isn't all it's cracked up to be."

"And what about Opal and Jules?" Robert looked at Tim. "You allowed her to place my ship, **MY** ship, outside the boundary. She has deserted her post."

171

"She did not abandon her post." Juaquin took two steps towards Robert. "Tim gave her the choice. She chose to go home someday, as is her right when this mission ends. She still sits in space, circling this planet, hoping we will join her on her trip home."

"I say when this mission is over." Robert thundered.

"Not anymore, Sir," Juaquin said, taking another step forward, staring Robert in the eyes. "Due to the danger of this radiation, the ISC is now in charge of this mission. Like it or not, it is what it is. Deal with it. Go lay down before you collapse. When you wake up, eat something. Afterward, you, Tim, and I will sit down and discuss our options rationally."

"You cannot tell me . . ."

"Either do as I say, or I will have my men drag you to your room. I will order Andrew to pump you so full of drugs that you will not wake up for a month. All of this will be sorted out by that time. Do you understand me, Sir?"

"You can't do this."

"According to ISC Rule 54, section 3, subsection 18, item number 6, I can. If you don't believe me, ask Phillip to bring up the rule book. If you still don't believe me, challenge my resolve. Trust me, you will lose."

The vein on Robert's forehead pulsed faster. Roger turned and stormed off to his domicile, knowing Juaquin never lied or gave unsubstantiated information.

"Andrew, go with him. Make sure he drinks something, and you dissolve a sleeping sedative in it. His heart cannot keep up that rapid beating. He must calm down."

Andrew followed Robert to his room, a powder of sedatives in his pocket. He'd make sure their commander slept for eight hours.

"Wow, how long did I sleep?" Robert asked, rising from his bed to a sitting position.

"You've been asleep for twelve hours," Juaquin said, pouring Robert a glass of water. "Here, drink this."

Robert took the glass and stared at its contents. "Is what you slipped in this water going to make me sleep another twelve hours?"

"Sir, I assure you, it is only water."

"I never sleep twelve hours. You slipped me something earlier."

"I assure you, Commander, I slipped nothing into this drink."

Robert looked at Juaquin's stoic face. His chiseled-in-stone expression neither denied nor confirmed Robert's suspicion. He raised the glass to his lips and took a deep drink.

"Rosa has a meal ready for you outside," Juaquin said. "When you're done, we'll contact the coalition and find out what they've done to our androids."

A little unsteady on his feet, Robert stood and meandered to a table sitting in the shadow of the south cave wall. He ate a small portion of the meal displayed on the table, citing a lack of appetite for his sparse consumption.

As they walked to the Android Station, Robert reached out twice for Juaquin's arm to steady himself. Juaquin sent a silent message to Andrew, asking him to run a complete medical review of their leader. Something wasn't right. Did he become exposed to radiation while in Africa?

"Okay, C-85, raise that bastard Commander Buutay on the com."

On the third attempt, the face of an Alphinian from Proxima B filled the screen, and Tim was struck speechless. Though he had heard of these beings, he had never seen one before. The creature was magnificent, its serpentine body balanced on two powerful legs that glowed softly with bioluminescent light. Its head was crowned with multifaceted eyes, each containing numerous lenses that radiated their own gentle illumination. From its chin dangled three glowing antennae, swaying slightly as though sensing their surroundings. Tim couldn't tear his eyes away, wondering if those

173

flashing lights were more than decoration - perhaps a form of communication, an elegant solution for navigating the dark, lightless depths of the Alphinian world. It was a moment that felt both alien and profoundly beautiful.

"I am sub-Commander Sl@%#^&@. How can I be of service?" came a metallic voice across the waves. The flashing lights shifted to hues of yellow and orange, their rhythm quickening into an increasingly rapid pulse.

"I am Commander Robert Hellsworth, commander of the ISC Earth expedition. I wish to talk with Commander Buutay."

"He has been waiting for your call. He is currently talking with the medical team caring for your androids so he can give you the latest information concerning their welfare."

"Can you tell me on whose authority you kidnapped my androids?" Robert asked, his voice stern and authoritative.

"Kidnapped? Oh no, no, no." The Alphinian's lights pulsed faster and shifted to shades of red. His antennae beneath his chin swayed in the air as he shook his head. "We rescued them."

"Like hell you did," Robert shouted. "My android commander specifically told your commander …"

The Alphinian's multifaceted eyes flickered briefly before its bioluminescent lights flared a bright red, casting an ominous glow across its shimmering skin. Then, without warning, the screen went black.

"What happened?"

"It appears the Alphinian ended the transmission," C-85 said.

"Get him or her back."

For the rest of the day and through the night, C-85 tried every ten minutes to re-establish contact, but to no avail. The coalition remained silent. He had Opal send ten hateful correspondences directly to the ISC complaining of Commander Buutay's activities. But even with the recent updates in communicating over long distances, it would take days to receive a reply.

While he waited, Roger corresponded with the settlements he had visited in Africa. Several of them had contacted distant villages, and all but one had agreed to join their cause and ask for ISC help. Now, if he could persuade Miguel to join.

"How's Miguel and his wife doing?" Robert asked Andrew as he stepped into the medical wing.

"I am releasing Miguel today," Andrew said. "He can finish healing faster in the sunlight. As for his wife, Sandy, I will keep her for two to three more days. Her injuries were more severe, and I'm still not happy with her vocal cords. So far, she hasn't been able to speak."

"Is it okay if I talk with them?"

"Yes. Go right in."

Robert walked to where Miguel and Sandy were being housed. Miguel sat in a chair beside his wife's bed, his daughter on his lap.

"That was a close call," Robert said. "I am glad you and your wife are doing well."

Miguel looked at his sleeping wife. "Your second-in-command told me you do not expect payment for what you did for her. Is this true?"

"Yes. I helped you because you needed it, not for what I could extract from you. Like I said the day we met, we mean you no harm. We want nothing from you except to consider joining the ISC and going under their rule."

"To be enslaved and ruled by robots?"

"First of all, they're androids, not robots."

"So everyone keeps reminding me. But to me it makes no difference what you call them. They are still lifeless mental machines that have no feelings."

"You probably don't hear this often, Miguel, but you're wrong. Our androids are sentient and intelligent, and many possess feelings. While it's true, the androids have authority over us in matters of aggression, it involves giving up no freedoms except the choice of making war on others."

"Can we carry our weapons?"

"Yes, as long as you do not use them on other humans or use them to intimidate and dominate others."

"Can we continue to hunt?"

"For a while, but once we can produce enough food to feed Earth's population, hunting will need to stop. The animal species of this planet are depleted, and constantly hunting them is not enabling them to rebound. We will teach you how to live without meat on a plant-based diet." Miguel scowled. "Believe it or not, it's quite delicious."

"Would we have to live here in your camp, or can we remain where we are?"

"The choice is yours and your people's. If you wish to remain where you are, we will assign security androids to protect you in your village. Members of the ISC community will help you become self-sufficient. They will provide you with food, medicine, and necessary supplies."

"So, if I don't agree to join the ISC, you allow us to starve?"

"Of course not. We will help you in any way we can. An ISC supply ship is currently on its way loaded with everything you'll need, but it will take about another two and a half years to arrive. In the meantime, other alien nations will bring whatever supplies they can to tide us over. These supplies will be distributed to all of Earth's people."

"And you expect me to believe you want nothing in return?"

"You are correct. I understand this is hard for you to believe, Miguel, but I am telling you the truth. If you'd like, bring your people here and stay a few weeks or a month. Learn if you like it. If you don't, you will be free to return home. You don't need to decide now."

Phillip ran into the room. "Excuse me, Sir. C-85 finally has Commander Buutay on the screen. They're waiting for you."

"We'll talk more later, Miguel. At the moment, I have a crucial call to attend to. Roger bolted from the room.

Chapter 12: ROBERT'S ILLNESS

When Robert arrived at the Android Station, sweat covered his body. Droplets of sweat dripped off Robert's hair and down his face, and his shirt was drenched in perspiration.

"Robert, you don't look well," Tim said, noting Robert's excelled breathing and pale face.

"I'm fine," Robert grumbled, pulling a chair closer to the screen and plopping in it.

Andrew walked up and ran his scanner over Robert's body.

"Take that thing away from me," Robert ordered, hitting Andrew's hand and the scanner away. "I don't have time for your nonsense."

Andrew looked over at Juaquin. Juaquin nodded, giving Andrew the okay to continue.

"Juaquin, I mean it. Tell him to keep his needle away from me, or I'll demote both of you to latrine duty."

"Sir, as we discussed several times of late, I have authority over you in medical matters." Juaquin paused. He saw Roger was still agitated. "Robert, what is the number one rule of being a great negotiator?"

"To always remain calm." He looked at Juaquin. "Thank you for reminding me of what I know all too well."

"Any time. And to help you calm down, I want Andrew to give you a mild tranquilizer." Robert glared at the android. "Once again, we can do this the hard way or the easy way. Which is it?"

Scrunching his mouth into a deep wrinkle, Robert held out his arm. Andrew jabbed the needle into the commander's vein as the screen flickered. An image of Commander Buutay's face appeared, filling up the entire screen.

"Good day, Commander Hellsworth. I'm glad to meet you finally."

"Where in the hell are my androids?" Robert asked, forcing his voice to be calm despite the rage coursing through his body. "I want them returned immediately."

"Commander, just remain calm and listen."

"You kidnapped by men."

"That is not entirely true."

"Bring them back, now."

"Robert, I wish I could, but we both know I cannot comply with your request. Both androids are contaminated with deadly radiation, and they endanger human and android life.

The tranquilizer was working. Robert's blood pressure was dropping. He could think more clearly. He didn't like it, but Commander Buutay was right. The two androids were too dangerous to remain on Earth. "If you had asked, I would have let you take them to your ship. But you just swooped in and grabbed them."

"You weren't there to ask."

"Captain Spalling was. As my second-in-command, Tim is my authority when I am not here."

"Perhaps I was in error not to ask Captain Spalling."

"I want to speak to B-25 and Quinn."

"I am afraid that is not possible."

Taking a deep breath to calm his rising anger, Robert scooted his chair as close as possible to the screen. Startled by the abrupt action, Commander Buutay took a step back.

"Let me rephrase my sentence. I demand you allow me to speak with B-25 and Quinn within the next two minutes, or I will report you for war crimes to the ISC. Do you understand?"

"Yes, but I assure you I have committed no crimes."

"You took them without their permission."

"I assure you, I did not."

"You took them without their commander's consent and knowledge."

"I am guilty of bringing them to my ship without your knowledge. But such an action is not a crime."

"I want to speak to them."

"It is not possible to speak with either android. Both are currently offline. Our initial examination showed each suffered from internal damage. To evaluate its extent, I authorized the opening of their external access panels, and a complete internal exam is being conducted as we speak."

Upon hearing the news, Juaquin stepped forward. Robert grabbed the android's arm, signaling him to remain silent.

"And what does the report say?"

"I wish I had better news. The radiation penetrated the android's shielding. It caused their A-18, B-2 and C-4 circuits to grow brittle and crack. Android One's radius has splintered. Both positronic brains suffered damage, but we do not know to what extent."

Juaquin collapsed to the ground.

"How... how can this be?" Robert stammered, his voice trembling as the words barely escaped his lips. His heart pounded, each beat echoing the shock that gripped him. He struggled to comprehend the impossible news given him, his mind reeling in disbelief.

"I am sorry to be the bearer of such terrible news," Commander Buutay said. "But not all my news is bad. The nasal mucus the Caladrine used on their outer skin to stop the decay worked. We are hoping it will do the same for their insides. My medical team has designed a specially made solution of the Caladrine's mucous. They are going to wash the android's internal systems in an attempt to eradicate the radiation."

"Will it work?" Robert asked, his face frozen.

"Unknown, Robert. In the ISC's history, we've encountered nothing like this radiation. No android has ever been contaminated with any substance. All we can do is hope."

"And pray," Tim whispered.

"Commander, please understand this. Bringing Android One and Android two up here and opening them was the last thing I wanted to do. I had no other choice."

"Their names are B-25 and Quinn," Tim said.

"Excuse me?"

"Their names are B-25 and Quinn, not Android One and Android Two. Please have enough respect for them and call them by their name."

"I see no reason for such distinctions."

"Do it," Robert sternly said.

"Very well. As I was saying, we cannot allow this radiation to spread beyond Earth. Imagine if it did. It could eliminate half the life forms in the universe, wipe out our androids, and cripple ships everywhere."

"Were you able to determine what caused the flier to break apart?" Tim asked.

"Ah, our second-in-command," Buutay said. "I do apologize for not advising you I was going to take the androids."

"Do you have an answer for him?" Robert asked.

"A partial one. We confirmed the report you sent us regarding a possibility of why the androids and ship were affected. It is a high-intensity alpha radiation capable of displacing atoms within the metal's network by colliding with the metal nuclei. Might I ask how you came upon this discovery? Your equipment is too primitive for such an analysis."

"We have our ways," Robert stated, unwilling to divulge the Caladrine's existence on Earth.

"Isn't this displacement true for all alpha radiation?" Tim asked.

"Yes," Commander Buutay said. "But this normally only occurs in thin metals, like aluminum. This new form of radiation can affect thicker, stronger forms of metal like the *güzerite* our fliers are made of. It creates holes in the matrix, causing the metal to become brittle. And this morning, my engineers found a second problem. The affected metallic nuclei are joining with healthy metallic atoms and creating atoms with one additional neutron. These mutated atoms make the material unstable, and it disintegrates."

"That's how B-25 described what was happening to the flier," Juaquin said, rising to his feet, brushing off the dust on his legs. "He said it was coming apart before his eyes."

"That's why the force field didn't keep it together," Tim stated. "Is there any chance the humans used *tilithium* to create their new weapon?"

"An intriguing thought," Commander Buutay said, his right eyebrow lifting. "A young engineer suggested such a possibility, but it was quickly dismissed due to his inexperience. One suggestion can be overlooked, but the same suggestion from a different source warrants investigation. Why do you think *tilithium* could be involved?"

"*Tilithium* caused the breaches on the space station we took to New Earth. We know in certain circumstances it can destroy the metal matrix."

"I am unfamiliar with this incident," Commander Buutay said. "I will have my personnel investigate the report immediately."

"True, it was *tilithium* that caused the breach, but it didn't affect the androids - except me." Juaquin's mouth twitched, remembering back to when Xavier infected him with *tilithium*. "Why would it affect the androids now?"

"A re-engineered form?" Tim suggested.

"Is *tilithium* available on Earth?" Commander Buutay asked.

"We never scanned for the alloy when we were hidden inside the moon. I know it was available up there." Juaquin answered.

"How do you know it existed on the moon?"

"Because I authorized numerous repairs on the station. *Güzerite* was unavailable, so I searched for an alternative and found large deposits of *tilithium* across the moon landscape. Since the moon is basically made from leftover pieces of Earth, I surmised if it's available on the moon, it's available on Earth."

"I'll have my crew scan for *tilithium* right away," Commander Buutay said. "Wouldn't it be ironic if your old friend *tilithium* is the culprit once again?"

"Yes, it would." Robert sighed, wiping away sweat from his brow. Suddenly, his stomach was upset. He should have eaten more at breakfast. Or declined Andrew's shot.

"Were you able to determine the cause of death on the bodies we located?" Tim asked.

"Preliminary exams indicate they died of a high level of radiation, the same radiation that infected the flier and androids. My staff are still conducting their research."

"The moment you learn more or if anything changes with B-25 or Quinn, let me know. I still want to speak to you about their future, but I am needed elsewhere at the moment. We'll talk later. Echo Command out." Robert held on to the desk and drew his hand across his throat, signaling for C-85 to end the transmission. "What in the hell was in that shot?"

Tim looked at Andrew. "I only gave him a mild dose of valium."

"I need to lie down for a while. Tim, you're in charge until I return."

"Yes, Sir."

Robert clutched the edge of the desk, his knuckles white as he fought to steady his swaying body. The world around him spun violently, every breath a struggle. He took a faltering step forward, then another, his legs trembling beneath him. After six steps, his strength gave way. He crumpled to the ground, his body seizing in uncontrollable convulsions. The impact sent a jolt of pain through him, but he was barely aware of it as his mind slipped into darkness.

"Robert, Robert, what's wrong?" Tim screamed as he rushed to his leader's side. He looked over at Andrew who was already beside his commander. "Is he having a heart attack?"

Andrew ran his scanner over Robert's still body, injecting him with a syringe of medication. "Quick, take him to the medical room. He has a temperature of 103.5."

"Radiation poisoning?" Tim asked.

"No. This is something else."

Phillip picked Robert up off the ground and ran with him to the medical unit. Juaquin, Andrew, and Tim followed; Tim trotting to keep up.

Upon seeing the commotion, Jessica ran over. "What happened?"

"Robert collapsed," Tim said. "He's running a high fever."

Phillip laid the unconscious leader on one of the beds. He removed the human's shirt and tossed it aside.

"Phillip, put an IV in him. Start two *decas* of salt solution, a shot of *Penvine*, and a shot of *Sarron*." Andrew ordered while listening to his heart. "Damn, his heart's beating way too fast." Andrew removed a syringe of heart medication and plunged it into Robert's pounding muscle. He listened again. The heart rate dropped only a few beats. "Hurry up, Phillip, get those drugs in him, or we'll lose him."

Andrew ran the scanner over the body again. "Still 103 temperature. We need ice."

"Where do you think we'll find ice?" Jessica asked.

"Hiinew," Andrew answered. "She has that cold pond."

"Can't we use the stream by the triple tree?" Tim asked. "Hiinew's compound is a long way away."

"The stream won't be cold enough," Andrew said. He looked up at Juaquin. "I need to take him to Hiinew's immediately."

Juaquin sent silent messages to the androids. "William, bring a flier as close to the cave entrance as possible. I need you to fly Robert to the Caladrine base. C-85, contact Hiinew and tell her we have a medical emergency, and William is bringing Robert to her. Tell her he has a temperature of 103, and she needs to immerse him in ice water."

"Come on, Tim. Let's clear the people out of the way so William can land the flier," Juaquin shouted as he rushed from the room.

Juaquin and Tim quickly guided the humans to safety, clearing the area. Within moments, William arrived with the flier, wasting no time. Phillip gently lifted Robert and carried him toward the plane. As they reached it, Andrew climbed into the back seat, carefully taking Robert into his arms.

"Go."

The flier lifted off, the hatch closing as they flew forward. William set a course for the hidden Caladrine location.

"Where are they going?" Jessica asked "The Caladrine live in the mountains. The mountains are behind us."

"Trust me, they're going the right way," Tim said. He turned to Juaquin.

———————

185

A medical team was waiting with an ice-cold water trough when William landed at the Caladrine base. Andrew handed Robert's still body to the Caladrine, who immediately placed him in the liquid. Running as fast as their legs allowed, the group ran through the halls into the medical unit. The water sloshed inside the tub, spilling over the rim and onto the floor.

"We've got to bring his temperature down," Andrew yelled, slipping on the water droplets. "And his heart will explode if we don't reduce his heart rate."

A second medical team began working on the human. Keeping his body in the cold water, they injected him with medication and connected him to machines to keep him alive. Their more sophisticated medical scanner diagnosed Robert was suffering from malaria.

Standing on the sidelines, Andrew intently watched the monitors. 102 degrees. 101.5 degrees. 100 degrees. Robert's temperature was dropping. He was going to make it.

An alarm shattered the silence with a piercing wail, a sound so final it seemed to rip through the air. Robert's breath caught in his chest, his heart stopped.

"No," Andrew shouted, pushing the Caladrine aside and grabbing Robert's body out of the iced water bath. He laid him on the nearby table and started performing CPR on his chest. "I have no breath to give him." Andrew looked at the Caladrine. "I need one of you to blow into his mouth when I tell you."

A Caladrine stepped forward. "How do I blow air into him?"

"Put your damn trunk over his mouth and blow when I tell you to," Andrew shouted.

"It's okay, I've got this," Roger said as he rushed into the room.

Andrew pressed on Robert's chest five times, then stopped. "Now." Roger placed his mouth over Robert's and blew. Andrew watched as the human's chest rose and fell. The android pressed five more times. "Do it again." For five minutes, Andrew and Roger fought to restore life to their leader.

"He's gone," Roger said, stepping back.

"No, we can do this," Andrew screamed.

Roger placed his hands over Andrew's. "He's not coming back."

"I should have been quicker," Andrew said, staring at the still, wet body before him.

"You did all you could, Andrew. Robert always had a bad heart. It wasn't your fault."

Andrew stared at Roger. "But malaria? It's a preventable disease. He takes a pill every day to prevent contracting malaria. How could he die like this?"

"I have no answers for you, Andrew."

"How did Robert contract malaria? We all take quinine pills. And I know Andrew sent a supply with him when he went to Africa."

"He wasn't taking the pills," Jessica said. "I caught him one day putting his quinine pill back into the container. He told me they upset his stomach, so he sometimes didn't take them. Since the wind blowing across the desert usually keeps any mosquitos away from camp, he must have thought he'd be okay."

Tim allowed the tears to flow freely down his face. The moment you witnessed Robert's actions, you should have informed someone. Why didn't you say anything?"

"I, I don't know," Jessica cried. "I was busy with camp business and forgot."

"Had you spoken up, he might still be alive," Tim said, his face turning red.

"This is not Jessica's fault," Juaquin said as he walked over to the two. "And it was not her responsibility to report on Robert."

"Why didn't he take those damn pills?" Tim asked.

187

"Why do humans do what they do?" Juaquin said. "He probably thought not taking the pills was the lesser of two evils. He chose not to have stomach pain."

"Now what do we do?" Tim asked. "With the net preventing us from leaving, how do we end the mission and go home? How are we to proceed without Robert? Can Roger take over as leader?"

Juaquin's eyes fixed on the male. "Tim, you're second-in-command. As such, the job and responsibilities of being the commanding leader fall upon you. Roger is not a negotiator or leader."

Tim's jaw tightened. His eyes panicked and opened wide, showing more white than usual. "Me? No way. I'm not qualified to step into Robert's shoes."

"Tim, you've been wearing his shoes for the past four weeks while he was gone. What do you mean you're not qualified?"

"I'm not," Tim shouted, jumping to his feet, almost collapsing in pain. Placing his hands on his head, he limped around in a circle. "No, no, no. I was able to run things here because Robert was still out there. I had a safety net. With him gone, I am responsible for EVERYTHING." Tim stopped. He turned to look at Juaquin. "You should be our leader. You're better qualified than I am. You should do it."

"Tim, I am an android. Leaders of missions such as this need to be human. I cannot negotiate with the inhabitants of this world. They will not accept an android dictating their lives. It needs to be you."

"Roger then. Yes, we'll secure Roger."

"I already informed you Roger is not acceptable. You are now our leader."

"Stop saying I'm the damn leader," Tim screamed. He turned and hobbled away, blindly heading nowhere and crazed with fear.

"Well, that didn't go well," Phillip said as he approached Juaquin.

"No, it did not."

"Want me to follow him?"

"I believe Jessica is a better candidate for that. Jessica, would you please see what you can do?"

"Since he thinks I'm partially responsible for Robert's death, I'm not too sure he'll want to see me either," Jessica said.

"You may be right," Juaquin replied. "Let's give him some alone time to think things through. B-25, put a surveillance on Tim. Don't let him know you're watching him."

"Will do. Should I send the drone up to keep a visual on him?"

"No, a simple tracking should be sufficient. Notify me if he leaves the camp or does anything stupid."

"Clarify 'stupid'."

"Anything out of the ordinary."

"Sir, we're talking about Tim. Out of the ordinary is his normal."

"True. Just keep me advised on what he's doing. Make sure he doesn't get eaten by one of the locals."

Juaquin turned to Jessica. "Tim is more than capable of fulfilling the duties of a team leader. He just doesn't remember he is. The abruptness of Robert's death has caused him to question his qualifications. Once the initial shock wears off, Tim will realize he is the logical choice."

"I hope you're right."

Juaquin's right eyebrow lifted. "I am always right."

"I came to report Miguel is gone," Phillip said as he ran into the Android Station. "I have searched the camp, and he is nowhere to be found. His truck and B-2 are also missing."

"What about his wife and child?"

"Sandy is still in the hospital. The child is swimming at the stream with Maria and B-1."

189

"Did you ask Sandy where Miguel is or why he left?"

"No, Sir. I thought you might like to question her yourself."

Juaquin looked into the distance, watching Tim's figure getting smaller. "Yes, I do."

Juaquin walked into the medical facility. Sandy was sitting up in bed enjoying a bowl of soup. "Hello, Sandy. How are you doing today?"

Still unable to speak, Sandy lifted her right hand, placed her index finger and thumb into a circle, and signaled she was well. She smiled.

"Sandy, Andrew just informed me your husband is missing. So are his robot B-2 and his truck. Might you know where he is?"

Sandy nodded yes. She held up her hand again, this time making her index and middle fingers move as if walking.

"He left?"

Sandy nodded.

"Do you know where he went?"

Sandy shook her head no.

"Do you know why?"

Again, a negative response.

"But he told you he was leaving, that he left B-1 here to watch over you and Esperanza?"

Sandy nodded.

Juaquin briefly considered whether B-1 might have insight but quickly abandoned the notion. Although highly sophisticated for an Earth AI, B-1 did not possess the capability to comprehend such advanced thinking processes as human departure, temporal concepts, and complex decision-making. His capabilities extended to simple commands, such as guarding Esperanza and Sandy twenty-four hours a day, seven days a week, with the child being priority number one.

With Sandy's inability to speak, Juaquin's questions were limited. He was left with the hope Miguel would return soon. *When Miguel was unconscious, why didn't I put a damn tracker in him? It would make keeping tabs on him so much easier.*

"Andrew said you'll be able to leave the medical unit tomorrow. I planned on placing you and your family in one of the huts by the cornfield. But since Miguel is gone, doing so might not be the best option. How would you like me to ask Jessica if you and Esperanza can move in with her until Miguel returns?"

A smile spread across Sandy's face. Her head nodded vigorously.

"I'll leave you to your meal. If Miguel returns, please ask him to see me."

Sandy nodded again, waving goodbye with her free hand.

Juaquin stepped outside the cave, stopped, and looked around. *"C-85, what's Commanding Officer Tim's current location?"*

"He is sitting inside the shack at the north cave entrance."

"Is he alone?"

"Yes, Sir."

"What's he doing?"

"Just sitting there."

"Send Jason to make sure he doesn't leave. Tell him not to engage. I'm heading there now."

"Aye, Sir."

Juaquin walked briskly towards the hidden shack, searching his data files for examples of pep talks given to humans over the centuries. Thousands of entries flooded in. He limited the selection to the past hundred years, but the number was still too large to search in the allotted time. Juaquin reduced the files further, limiting the content of talks by Xavier and Tim's grandfather. Twenty-three files. He could manage that number. Juaquin quickly listened to the twenty-three recordings and devised a speech for Tim.

191

After dismissing Jason, Juaquin knocked on the door. He entered without waiting for permission and saw Tim sitting on a crate. His face was soaked with tears, but it was a gentle, helpless cry Juaquin heard, not a hysterical one.

Juaquin grabbed an empty crate in the corner and sat it before the sorrowful human. "How are you doing?" Tim shrugged his shoulders. "I can't comprehend what you're experiencing, Tim. My sub-routines weren't designed to give me empathy or experience your devastating emotions. But I can surmise what it is like. It must be scary and overwhelming. You must feel like the world's weight is on your shoulders, that you're trapped. Perhaps you believe the life you envisioned is over. Am I right?"

Tears still flowing, Tim nodded.

"Trust me when I say it's not. If your heart's not in being the mission leader, or you truly believe you can't do this job and want out of it, I'll make it happen."

"Really?"

"Yes. But first, I want you to listen to what I say. Afterward, take the time to think about my words and search your heart thoroughly."

"Being a leader isn't always about having all the answers. It's about having the courage to make decisions, the strength to stand your ground, and the compassion to inspire others. You've got that fire in you, that determination. Your grandfather had it, your dad had it, and you have it. Don't let fear hold you back. Being nervous and afraid is okay; it just shows you care. And frankly, I'd be worried if you weren't afraid. But remember, doubt can cloud your judgment. Trust yourself, trust your training, and trust the people who have your back."

"Remember, great leaders aren't born - they're forged through challenges and determination. Leadership isn't easy. Tim, this is your time to step up and become the leader we need. Look around you, see who's counting on you - your team, the people of Earth, maybe the galaxy. We need your guidance, your strength, and your vision."

"Tim, I believe you can do this. And so did Xavier. He was aware of Robert's heart and the possibility something could happen."

"I wish I could believe what you're saying."

"When have you known me to lie?"

"Two or three times." Tim smiled.

"Never. I may have stretched the truth or omitted parts of it, but I've never lied. Androids are incapable of lying."

"Xavier did."

"Xavier is special. He is capable of things no other android is capable of."

"Like secrets."

"I see Renn has told you things he should not have."

"Actually, it was my brother, Jeremy."

"If Jeremy knew, Renn told him. And yes, androids do have secrets."

"Do you?"

"Yes."

"Do you really believe I am capable of the job of a leader, or are you just saying things your circuits are telling you I want to hear?"

"Both. You have the qualities of a true leader inside you, waiting to be unleashed. I do not doubt for a second you can do this if you want it. The choice is yours and yours alone. Now dry your eyes and wash your face. Jessica is down at the stream with Esperanza and B-1."

"I was pretty rough on her, saying what I said."

"Yes, you were. Your words brought tears to her eyes."

"I really am a jerk, aren't I?" Tim looked up at the android.

"Since I never lie, I will have to answer yes." Tim smiled. "Ask the robot to take Esperanza to her mother. Bring Jessica back here to the shack. I'll make sure no one disturbs you. Spend tonight with

193

the woman who has won your heart. Ask for her forgiveness. Forget the decision you must make. When you wake up tomorrow, a new day will bring brighter things. Juaquin reached out and rested his hand on top of Tim's. "Trust me, Commander."

Tim's eyes grew wide. "Did you just call me Commander?"

"That is now your designation," Juaquin said. "As the new leader of the expedition, you are entitled to the rank of Commander. I have already dispatched a communique to the ISC and Xavier informing them of your rank increase."

"Can you do that?"

"As the mission's head android and Xavier's first-in-command, I have that power. I believe you are the youngest human to ever attain such a rank."

"Really?" Juaquin gave the human a chiding look. "You're right. You can't lie, and I should just accept your word for it."

"Now you're learning."

Chapter 13: MIGUEL'S RETURN

A chill traveled over Jessica's body. She moved closer to Tim for his body's warmth, only to find the space beside her empty. Rising on one elbow, Jessica scanned the dimly lit room. Standing against the wall, peering through a slit in the boards, she spotted Tim.

"Did you injure yourself again?" Jessica asked, wrapping her arms around Tim's shoulder.

"No. I couldn't sleep." Tim shifted his vision to Jessica. "I'm still sorry for what I said."

"I already told you I forgave you."

Tim looked up at the night sky. "Come and take a look at tonight's moon. It's beautiful."

Jessica stood and walked to where Tim stood. Through a knothole in the wood wall, a full moon shone, hanging in the night sky like a giant pearl, its cratered surface bathed in a silvery light. The moon was the size of a porcelain dinner plate, and its color was crisp white.

"It's beautiful. But I don't believe a desire to see such a beautiful moon woke you. What's wrong?" Jessica wrapped her arms around Tim.

"Do you have any idea what Robert's death means for me?"

"You'll be the one in charge now?"

Tim turned around to gaze into her eyes. Her eyes were caring and concerned, but Tim's eyes were dark, fearful, and confused. "Not just in charge of the mission, but in charge of EVERYTHING." He broke her embrace and walked to the other side of the shack. "I will be responsible for every human, every android, every animal, every blade of grass on this dying planet."

"No, you won't," Jessica said. "You are not responsible for us or this planet. Your only responsibility will be to show us a different way to live and allow us to make our own decisions about our future. We created this mess, not you."

"Do you think I can do it?"

"Yes, I do. Tim, the people in the camp have been following you, not Robert. They turn to you for guidance and leadership. Robert being dead makes no difference."

"But when Robert was alive, he made all the hard decisions. Not me. And if I made a wrong decision, he took the blame for it, not me."

"Whose decisions kept us calm when Miguel burst into the camp? You had no idea who was driving or their intentions, yet you remained calm and did what was needed. Who chose to let Opal decide if she wanted to go home? You did. And who confronted Buutay when he took B-25 and Quinn? Once more, it was you. But if you don't want the job because you might make a bad decision, and trust me, you will, then you're not the man I thought you were."

Tim remained silent.

"Did you hear what I said?"

Silence.

Jessica walked over and spun Tim around. "Tim, I asked you if you heard what I said?"

Jessica's heart melted when she witnessed the expression on Tim's face.

"I'm scared, Jessica."

"Of course you are." She pulled the vulnerable man into her arms. "You wouldn't be worth your weight in beans if you weren't." Jessica shivered.

"You're freezing," Tim said, rubbing his hands over Jessica's arms.

"That's because my personal heater left my bed."

"Let's dress and warm you up."

The two quickly dressed. Laying inside Tim's arms, her body soon warmed, driving away the night chill. Within minutes, sleep overtook the exhausted female. But for Tim, sleep did not come so quickly. He couldn't stop thinking of Jessica's words of encouragement. Was she right? When he could finally quiet his thoughts, his dreams were filled with possible future scenarios.

"Hey, you two, time to wake up," came a familiar voice. "Dawn is in an hour. The camp is already stirring."

"We're dressed," Tim shouted. "You can come in."

Juaquin opened the door and stepped in. "How are you doing this morning?"

"As you said, today is a new day. I am better."

"Have you made a decision?"

"Not yet. But thanks to you and Jessica, I stopped feeling sorry for myself. I need to ask Opal to send a message to the ISC and notify them of Robert's death."

"I've already done that. But we have one little problem that needs your attention right away."

"And that is?"

"Miguel is missing."

Roger returned to camp, cradling the urn containing Robert's ashes. Robert had given everything to save the people of Earth, and both

Tim and Roger believed he should become a part of the planet he loved.

As the sun rose on a clear, bright morning, the two men, accompanied by the androids and several camp members, climbed the hill behind the camp. At the summit, Roger opened the urn and, with a deep breath, released the ashes into the wind. The ashes swirled and danced on the gentle breeze, glinting briefly in the sunlight before drifting far and wide, eventually settling into the earth and blending with the soil.

"Now he'll be a part of this world forever," Roger said. "You probably didn't realize this, Tim, but my brother thought highly of you. Robert once told me that he never worried about the mission if something happened to him because you would make a fine leader. He said you would succeed where he failed."

"He thought he failed?"

Roger laughed. "All the time. That's the thing about great leaders - they always doubt themselves. I watched Robert do it. I saw your grandfather do it. And I've seen you do it this past month or so." Roger grasped Tim's shoulder. "Have no doubts, Tim. You are a great leader. Fulfill your destiny."

"Thank you. Hearing that means a lot to me. Will you return to Hiinew's or stay here?"

"Actually, neither. My years, too, are drawing to a close. I've decided to go back and live the remainder of my years with the forest people. When I left their village several years ago to send the message for help, I didn't plan on being gone this long. They must think I am dead. I will be happy to see Chief Anku again. I can't unite Earth's people like Robert and you do, but I can make the forest people's lives better and safer."

"When will you be leaving?"

"Tomorrow morning."

"So soon? I hoped you'd help me through these first couple of weeks of being the new leader."

"You don't need an old man like me, Tim. You have the best mentor possible - Juaquin. Jessica, too, will be a great asset, if you let her. But I do have one piece of advice."

"What's that?"

"We have no way of knowing how long this planet will be under quarantine or if the net will ever be removed. Nor can we determine if those who survive on Earth have learned from their past and will decide on a better future and join the ISC. If you determine the people of Earth are not going to change their ways, do yourself a favor. Grab Jessica, find some small uninhabited spot, and have a slew of kids. Will you do that?"

"I'm not sure I'd make a good family man, Roger."

"Then promise me you'll find some happiness somewhere."

"I promise."

The next morning, Tim and Juaquin watched Roger leave with two androids. They would escort Roger to the edge of the forest people's domain, protecting him from predators of all kinds, both animal and human. Once they delivered Roger, the two would return to camp.

"It's going to be strange having both brothers gone," Tim said.

"That it will."

"What's on my agenda for today?"

"We need to sit down and devise a plan to contact the settlement in Antarctica. They're our last big hurdle. Oh, and C-85 picked up on radar this morning a convoy headed this way from the southwest. It contains three gas-powered vehicles, approximately thirty-three humans, and one huge robot."

"Miguel?"

"That is my assumption, but androids never act on assumptions."

Tim laughed. "So, I've been told. It's been, what, almost two weeks since he disappeared? Why is he returning now?"

"If I were a guessing android, which I am not, I would say he left us to retrieve his people. This may be how he intends to pay his debt to Robert for saving his wife."

"Robert would be pleased."

"That he would be." Juaquin gently slapped Tim on the back. "Let's go find out what news C-85 has for us on their arrival."

"Do you have an estimated time of arrival?" Juaquin asked when they reached the Android Station.

"If they can keep up their present pace, they should arrive on the outskirts of camp in four hours, eighteen minutes, and fourteen seconds."

"Why do you say if?" Tim asked.

"Two of the vehicles are in bad condition," C-85 said. "One is already having trouble. The road before the south hill has a slight incline. I'm not sure it or the second truck can make the climb."

"Phillip, gather ten of the androids together and take them to the south hill. Be prepared to assist Señor Costa and his group if needed. Take the sleds with you. They may have belongings needing transporting and injured unable to walk."

"Yes, Sir," came Phillip's voice in Juaquin's mind.

"What did he say?" Tim asked.

"He said okay. I sometimes forget you aren't privy to our conversations. I will remember to use the comm link when corresponding with the androids so you are aware of what is happening."

"I'd appreciate that."

Kicking the dirt around with his left foot, Tim waited for the androids to arrive with Miguel and his caravan. After being delayed for two hours, the group finally came into view. More mouths to feed. More tempers to deal with. But perhaps another group willing to agree to ISC rule.

As C-85 had predicted, two of the three vehicles failed to make it up the incline. Four elderly, six injured or sick people, and one pregnant woman were placed inside Miguel's truck bed to complete the journey. The supplies and belongings were unloaded and piled on the hover sleds. Three androids carried children too small to walk the rest of the way.

"Welcome back, Miguel," Tim said, grasping the returning male's hand and shaking it vigorously. "In the future, please advise someone you're leaving camp."

"Am I a prisoner that needs permission?"

"No, of course not. Knowing where people are makes running the complex easier. Your people look exhausted. We have lodging and food ready for them."

Miguel scanned the dirty, tired faces. "Yes, they are spent. Thank you for sending the androids to help. I don't think some would have finished the trek without their assistance. As for me, I'd like to visit my wife and daughter."

"You will be happy to learn they are already here waiting for you." Tim raised his arm and waved it in the air.

"Papa," came a small child's voice. Esperanza emerged from behind a flier and ran to her father. B-1 followed inches behind, never neglecting his duty to protect the child. Behind him came Sandy and Jessica. Miguel ran to his child, raising her in his arms and hugging her. When Sandy arrived, he took her into his arms and kissed her.

"I've missed you," Sandy said.

"You got your voice back. Are you okay?" Miguel wiped a tear from his eye.

"Perfect, now that you're back. Thanks to Andrew, I started talking yesterday." Sandy glanced at Jessica "We're staying with Jessica. I couldn't ask for a better host."

"Jessica, we haven't always agreed in the past, but I appreciate you looking after my family," Miguel said.

"What happened is in the past?" Jessica laughed. "It is forgotten. I am glad you and your people have come to join us. Please, come and eat. You must be hungry."

Esperanza wiggled out of her father's tight hug. She slipped to the ground and grabbed his hand, pulling him towards tables of food. "Come, Papa. Mommy and I made tortillas for you." Wrapping his arm around his wife's, Miguel allowed the child to lead him to a place at the tables. United, the congregation peacefully dined, momentarily content with the hope for a better life.

––––––––––

"We have a visitor." Juaquin stopped his discussion. Miguel and the robot B-2 were walking towards him.

"Mind if I join you?" Miguel asked.

"Not at all," Tim said, a warm smile on his face. "What can we do for you?"

Miguel sat down across from Tim. "Several of my men overheard you two talking about contacting the settlement in Antarctica."

"Do you men always listen to other people's conversations?" Juaquin asked. Tim shot Juaquin a disapproving glance.

"If you do not want people to listen to your words, you shouldn't speak them when others are around," Miguel replied.

"Not a word, Juaquin," Tim whispered as the android prepared to say something. "I can neither confirm nor deny that we were talking about the colony in the south."

"Then I guess I made a mistake," Miguel said, rising. "I brought B-2 to talk with you. He was a security robot for the man who ran that place. I thought you might want to learn what he knows."

"Now that I search my memory circuits, I recall having a conversation about a colony in the Antarctic," Juaquin said. "I would very much like to hear what B-2 has to say."

"As would I," Tim said.

Miguel sat back down and turned to the robot. "Go ahead, B-2. Tell Tim and the android what you told me."

"I was part of Señor Jacobs' security crew," B-2 began.

Tim raised his hand. "Excuse me, B-2, who is Señor Jacobs?"

B-2 turned his eyes to Miguel. "Daniel Jacobs," Miguel clarified. "He's the leader of the Antarctic complex and the owner of the biggest manufacturer of security robots, NexGen Robotics."

"Thank you. Go ahead, B-2."

"Four weeks before the bombs destroyed the North, we security robots were packed into a plane and flown to a field here in Argentina. We worked twenty-four hours a day unloading and loading cargo from countless planes that flew in."

"What type of cargo?" Juaquin asked.

"Food, water, medicine, weapons, heavy moving equipment, tank artillery guns, heavy-duty trucks."

"Do you remember where the planes were from?"

"No, but the arriving planes were all makes and sizes. The pilots seemed to be from various nations."

"What about the planes that flew the cargo to another destination?"

"Those I remember well. I was not aware that such huge planes could fly. They were Antonov An-124."

"I'm not familiar with that plane," Tim said.

Juaquin went silent as he accessed the Earth database. "It's the largest military transport built by Earthlings. Each aircraft was capable of carrying a hundred and twenty metric tons of cargo, including enormous machinery. Its cargo bay is 118 feet long, 21 feet wide, and 14 feet tall."

Tim whistled. "That's one big plane."

"Yes," B-2 said. "And we filled it to the top."

"What happened next? Where did they do with the cargo?"

"The moment the loading was complete, the planes took off. They returned the next day empty, and we refilled them. We were never told where they took the cargo."

"For how many days did you do this?" Juaquin asked.

"We filled the planes for twenty days. On the twenty-first day, two planes returned. All the humans boarded one plane. We security robots were marched into the second plane. But there was not enough room for all of us. We were told to remain on the field, and another plane would come for us. Samuel and I did not do as instructed. When the plane was out of sight, we walked away and continued walking until we arrived at Señor Miguel's camp."

"I don't understand," Juaquin said. "Why didn't you do as ordered?"

B-2 turned to Miguel. "It's okay," Miguel said. "You can tell them."

"B-1 overheard two robot handlers saying that only a portion of the robots were going to the new location. And of those, the majority would be disassembled into parts. Those not taken would be disintegrated when the plane returned. B-1 and I didn't want to be disassembled or destroyed, so we left. No one remained who said we could not leave."

"Why did you go to Señor Miguel's?"

"Señor Miguel flew one of the planes that brought in supplies," B-2 continued. "I remembered he tried to buy us from the handlers, but they refused to sell us."

"How did you know where he lived?"

"While speaking with my handler, he told him what his camp was like and where it was located."

"It seems you have a history of listening to people's conversations," Juaquin said. Tim shot the android another dirty look.

"Yes, I do."

"How did you ever find his camp?" Tim asked. "That had to be over a thousand miles."

"One thousand, six hundred and fifty-six miles," B-2 said.

"They were half dead when they arrived at camp," Miguel stated. "If you can call what happens to robots when they stop working as death. They suffered a lot of wire damage due to moisture and sand, the cushioning in their legs was gone, and their metal ligaments were grinding metal against metal. Almost no lubricant remained in their bodies. B-2 lost an eye. B-1's right arm was close to snapping in two, and his upper left thigh was crushed."

"We walked for many days," B-2 said. "Over mountains, through swamps and rainforests. Huge storms blew sand into every cavity our body contained when we crossed the deserts. A gigantic boulder rolled down the mountain at us. B-1 pushed me aside, and it smashed his leg. Later, a bear attacked us. It almost tore B-1's arm off, and it ripped out my eye. When we arrived at Señor Miguel's camp, he repaired us and took us in."

"B-2, what happened to the other robots?" Juaquin asked.

"As B-1 and I climbed the high hills, the promised plane appeared on the horizon. It soared toward the robots, releasing a box from its cargo hold. The moment it struck the ground, a massive fireball erupted, consuming the robots in flames. After that, no one existed except B-1 and me."

"How many robots were destroyed?"

"Eighteen hundred and sixty-two."

"Why would he destroy all those robots?" Tim pondered. "The people in the southern hemisphere needed them to help rebuild settlements, plant crops, and dig wells."

"I do not have that information," B-2 said.

"Miguel, how did you figure out how to fix them?" Juaquin asked.

"I didn't. We pounded B-1's leg back out and soldered his arm back together. For B-2, we painted him an eye cover."

"So you have no vision in one of your eyes, B-2?"

"No."

"Would you like to?"

"I do not have access to a new eye to replace my injured one."

"But if you did, would you like one?" Tim asked.

"Yes."

"If Miguel has no objections when you leave here, go to the medical unit and find Andrew," Tim said. "He will be expecting you. Andrew will examine your eye and determine if he can restore your sight."

B-2 turned to Miguel. "Can I go and talk with Andrew?"

"You may go now." B-2 stood and headed toward the medical unit.

"Juaquin, advise Andrew of B-2's arrival and the need for an eye exam," Tim said. The android leader sent a silent message.

"Why would you repair him?" Miguel asked. "He's only a robot."

"Why did you originally repair the two of them?"

"Because they were no use to me in the condition they arrived in."

"We treat our androids no different than we treated you and your family," Tim said. "They are sentient and have rights. They are not our property."

"But my robots are not sentient."

"One day they may be," Juaquin said. "Their programming is limited but sophisticated. It's like someone stopped their programming just short of allowing them to reach consciousness. What can you tell me about this Daniel Jacobs and his company?"

"All I know is he was some sort of robotic genius."

"Juaquin, run that name through our database. Find out if he shows up on our records."

"No, nothing. There's no Daniel Jacobs anywhere in the database."

"How far did you go back?"

"A thousand years."

"Go back two thousand."

"You think he's an alien?" Miguel asked.

"I'm just covering all the bases."

"Check for his company, Next Gen Robotics. There must be information about that."

"Wow," Juaquin said. "Our database is filled with information about his company. I don't see any red flags. There are a few yellow ones. I need at least an hour to go through this information.

"Make it so." Tim saw Juaquin smile. "What?"

"Robert used to use that phrase all the time."

Tim was watching a beautiful sunset with a group of families and Jessica when his communicator beeped. "Excuse me. I'm needed somewhere." He hurried to the medical unit, where Juaquin and Andrew waited. "Don't tell me someone else is ill or has died."

"No, Sir," Juaquin said. "Andrew finished his B-2 exam and discovered something surprising."

"What?"

"When I examined B-2's eye socket, I discovered alien wiring similar to ours," Andrew said.

"Alien wiring? How?"

"It appears our suspicions were correct. Humans had help developing their robots," Juaquin said.

208

"I also found a serial number buried deep within his cranium," Andrew added. "When I searched our database for similar numbers, I came across a reference to an old top-secret Head Commander report. Since I cannot access such reports, I ask Juaquin to try to access it."

"I didn't think you had that high of clearance," Tim said to Juaquin.

"I didn't use to," Juaquin answered. "But when Xavier became Head Commander, and I became Commander One, I was given clearance. It took me some time to find the file. It's pretty old. It's from Head Commander Ovendoo concerning a human-like alien named Castrov Achenblles."

"That's a mouthful."

Juaquin tilted his head, staring at the human. When Tim said nothing more, the android continued. "I found Castrov Achenblles with no problem in the database. As I said, he was, or is, an alien who can pass for a human. The genetic makeup is almost identical to Earth humans. Even Andrew might have trouble determining he wasn't human from a bio-scan or medical tests. Except for one thing - their skin has a yellowish-gold tint to it. Most humans think it's due to jaundice, but it's their normal color."

"He was caught trying to build his own version of us - androids who reported only to him. Head Commander Ovendoo sentenced him to death for violating ISC regulations and trying to contaminate human history. He somehow escaped. It was believed he made it to Earth and was hiding somewhere in the jungles of South America. A search ensued for him, but the only thing they found was a severed arm with the tracker inside. It appeared as if he cut his arm off to prevent us from tracking him. And, Sir, he was skilled in metallurgy."

"And the plot thickens," Tim said. "Andrew, were you able to repair B-2's vision?"

"Yes, Sir. A broken wire caused his lack of vision. I was able to use my medical instruments to repair the break and re-establish his sight."

Chapter 14: CASTROV ACHENBLLES

"Castrov Achenblles, you say. I am not familiar with that name," Commander Buutay said. "You said he was on the space station when Head Commander Ovendoo was in charge?"

"Yes," Juaquin said.

"Did Head Commander Glogg have any dealings with him?"

"Indirectly. Castrov's crimes occurred under Head Commander Ovendoo's term. Ovendoo was the one who sentenced him to death. The day before the executive, Head Commander Ovendoo suddenly died."

"From what?" Tim asked, hearing this story for the first time.

"Unknown. An investigation was made, but they never found any evidence of foul play. In the chaos following Ovendoo's death, Castrov escaped. They thoroughly searched the station from top to bottom, but they did not find him. Glogg, who was now Head Commander, extended the search to Earth. But since the androids were unable to carry out an investigation on Earth, it fell upon our humans to carry out the mission. As you can imagine, he was never found."

"Juaquin, is it possible that this Castrov Achenblles had one or more fliers?" Buutay asked.

"It's possible, although unlikely. A complete survey was done at the time of his disappearance, and no fliers were missing. Why do you ask?"

"We've done a scan of Earth three times. We cannot find any trace of *tilithium* in its native state anywhere."

"Couldn't it have been evaporated during the nuclear bombings?" Tim asked.

"Not all of it. Tiny shards of metal would still exist. Plus, no bombs exploded in the southern hemisphere except over Australia. If *tilithium* existed in the north, it should exist in the south."

"And you should have detected it."

"Correct. The only sign of *tilithium* on Earth is in the radiation."

"Which means someone harvested it on the moon and brought it to Earth," Juaquin said. "I understand your interest in discovering if any fliers were missing when Castrov disappeared. My memory algorithms report unusual activity aboard the station right before the Head Commander's death. Eight discrepancies are cited concerning convoys of alien ships that arrived at the station with supplies. I never thought much of the mix-ups at the time; I just thought some random human wasn't good at scheduling deliveries. But now that I have examined the situation, I see that humans didn't schedule ship arrivals. Androids did. And we wouldn't have made those mistakes."

"Do you think someone sabotaged the deliveries to aid Castrov in leaving?" Tim asked.

"Yes."

"I agree," Buutay said. "And once the space station left, Castrov was free to harvest the moon's *tilithium* without interference and restart his quest for domination."

"But how do we prove it?"

"Commander Buutay, your files on Castrov should be more extensive than what exists in our database. I am hoping at least one picture of Castrov resides in your files. Can you search for one, and if it exists, send me a copy?"

"For what purpose?"

"Living inside our village is a man who is probably the only human outside of Antarctica who has seen Señor Jacobs' face. I want to show him the picture and ask if he recognizes him. If he does, we have our proof."

"I'll have someone check the files and send it to you right away."

"Might I ask how B-25 and Quinn are doing?" Tim asked.

"The flushing of their circuits with the Caladrine mucous went well," Buutay said. "Quinn's systems are responding, and we hope to close his panels and bring him back online soon. However, the news on B-25 is not good. His dominant circuit board suffered extensive damage. We do not have either the expertise to repair it or a new one to replace it. I have dispatched a message to Master Kim and his son, Sub-Master Fuu, asking for their input."

"Can't we send him back to the space station at New Earth for repair?" Tim asked. "Although retired, I am sure Master Kim would return to insert a new circuit board. He always kept several in stock for such emergencies."

"I don't believe B-25 can make the journey," Juaquin said. "Even at hyper speed, the trip would take at least twelve to thirteen months. Commander, what do you estimate the life span of his circuit board is?"

"If we're lucky, two months." Buutay turned to the android, who entered the room. Neither Tim nor Juaquin could make out the conversation. "422 informs me a picture is in Castrov's file." The Commander pushed a few buttons on his panel. "I'm sending you a copy now. Please notify me if your person recognizes him."

"Will do. Echo Command signing off."

The screen went dark.

"C-85, where is Miguel at this moment," Juaquin said out loud for Tim's benefit.

"He is currently having a meal with his family at the dispensary," came C-85's voice in Juaquin's head.

"C-85 said he's at the dispensary," Juaquin announced. "Care to join me?"

"Right behind you." Tim stood and trotted off beside the android.

"I am glad your groin is doing better, and you can keep up," Juaquin teased. "Perhaps Jessica will allow you to heal more before using your body again."

"Ha, ha, very funny," Tim said, running past the android only to slow again when a new twinge occurred in his groin. "Still won't forget it, will you?"

"As I said before, where's the fun in that?"

Miguel was easily found as only fifteen people were enjoying a midday meal. Tim and Juaquin sat down at the table across from him.

"Buenos Dias, Tim, Juaquin."

"Buenos Dias."

Miguel scanned Tim's face but detected no reason for their visit. "Did you need something?"

"Miguel, you told us you spoke with Daniel Jacobs several times," Tim said.

"Yes, we spoke on several occasions. Why?"

"Do you think you can remember what he looks like?"

A shiver slid down Miguel's back. "I will never forget his face. He had blacker than black eyes. His skin had an unnatural color to it as if he painted it. And his tongue was forked."

"A forked tongue?" Tim tried to envision such a tongue. "That's different. I wonder how he hid that all these years on Earth?"

Juaquin placed his communicator on the table. "Is the person in the picture Daniel Jacobs?"

Miguel's eyes grew larger. His pupils dilated. The muscles in his face grew taught. "Yes, that's him."

Juaquin lifted the communicator and showed the screen to B-2. "B-2, is this a picture of the man you called Daniel Jacobs?"

"We did not call him that name."

"What did you call him?" Tim asked.

"Boss Man."

"Is this Boss Man?" Juaquin asked.

"Yes."

"How did you ever find a picture of him? Señor Jacobs never allowed any electronic equipment around him. Few knew what he looked like, and of those who did, most are dead."

"It seems Señor Jacobs was on the space station four hundred years before he came to Earth," Juaquin said.

"Four hundred years? No man can live that long."

"No human man can, but Señor Jacobs is not human. He's Freezion, an alien race that very closely resembles a human. That's probably why his skin appeared funny. It WAS painted to cover his true skin color."

"I often wondered if he wore makeup."

"Miguel, can you tell us anything else about Señor Jacobs?"

Miguel went quiet, searching his memories. "No, I don't think so. Wait. He had a missing arm. I witnessed him remove an artificial one the last time I was at the field."

"Thanks, Miguel." Juaquin turned to Jessica. "Are you okay? Your skin is a little green today."

"Stomach's been acting up these past few days."

"Ask Andrew to examine you." Juaquin said "I can't afford to lose another valuable member of Tim's team. Or have the flu infect the camp."

"I'm not running a fever or anything. Just indigestion." Jessica placed her hand over her mouth, leaped from the bench, and ran to the restroom.

"Sandy, will you do me a favor and ensure Jessica visits Andrew for a scan?" Tim asked. "This isn't the first time in the past few days she's experienced stomach problems."

"No problem. I'll make sure she talks to Andrew."

Tim turned to Juaquin. "What's next on today's agenda?"

"Actually, you have some free time. I will contact Opal and ask her to scan the settlement in Antarctica. If we're going to visit them, we need to become familiar with the facility and what we may encounter."

"And when do we plan on paying him a visit?"

"As soon as I devise a plan of action to keep you safe."

"No, Juaquin, you cannot come with me," Tim said, his face stern and unyielding. "I need you here to run the camp and take over the mission if something happens to me."

"That's why I need to go with you, to make sure nothing does happen to you," Juaquin argued.

"As the second-in-command android, Phillip is perfectly qualified to go with me to Antarctica."

"As such, he is capable of running the camp. And if something happens to both of us, he can negotiate with Commander Buutay to let them through the net and return home."

"Buutay won't allow anyone to leave until he's completely convinced there is no chance of the androids contaminating the universe."

"None of the androids have shown any sign of contamination besides B-25 and Quinn, and they got it from flying over Australia."

"You're NOT going. That's the end of the discussion. Now let's call Opal and get her report."

"This conversation is not over, Young Tim."

Tim laughed, "You haven't called me that in a long time."

"Well, sometimes you act like you're three."

"And sometimes you act just like Xavier."

Juaquin stared at Tim. The human offered a good argument, but he didn't like the idea of Tim walking into danger without him. They would discuss Tim's escort more over the next few days.

"Okay, Opal, what you got for us?" Tim asked.

"As Juaquin suspected, the settlement is shielded," Opal said, her face appearing on the screen. "We couldn't tell much about what's beneath the snow other than the expanse. We estimate the complex covers a radius of twenty miles."

"Twenty miles? Are you sure?"

"As I said, it's an estimate. The force shield is twenty-four miles square. We subtracted a mile on each side for a safety margin. We detected a hundred and eighteen surface vents. Our thermal scans showed heat rising from half of those vents. We estimate the others are air intake flues. An artificial mound is located 1.3 miles east, housing a huge power generator. Besides the generator, nothing besides the building and one small shed exists above the ground."

"Did you discover a way inside?" Tim asked.

"We discovered a well-camouflaged bay door on the north side. Also, two smaller doors are located on the north and east sides. If others exist, we couldn't locate them."

"That limits our possibilities of getting inside. What about personnel? Any signs of humans or androids?"

"No humans that we detected, but we did witness a patrol of twelve androids."

"That's all? That's not a lot of security."

"There are a multitude of vehicle tracks near the north bay door. It appears the tracks were created by various transporters, from one-man vehicles to cargo carriers. The frozen ground prevents us from

217

determining if the tracks were recently created or if they are old ones. Antarctica is currently coming out of a period of twenty-four-hour darkness, so there might not be much activity for security reasons."

"When do they resume normal daylight?" Tim asked.

"Not for another month."

"We can't wait that long," Juaquin said. "We'll have to try contacting them during the few daylight hours that will occur over the next week."

"Agreed. Opal, you said you could not get any readings from inside?"

"That is correct, Tim. We tried every trick in the book without success. The complex is a blackout."

"We'll ask Commander Buutay to try. They might have better luck penetrating their shielding," Juaquin said.

"We'll contact him tonight," Tim stated. "Besides, I want to check on B-26 and Quinn. Opal, have you received any correspondence back from the ISC yet?"

"No, it's too early."

"I figured it might be, but one can always hope. Notify me when you receive more details about our cold-weather friends. Echo Command out."

From the corner of his eye, Juaquin noticed Jessica heading towards the vegetable field with a basket and rake. "Tim, I'll join you shortly. I need to check on something."

"Oh, okay. I need to see how the new water dispenser is doing, anyway. See you in a bit."

Juaquin waited until Tim was out of sight, then rushed after Jessica. "Jessica, wait up. I wish to speak with you."

Jessica halted. "Hi, Juaquin. What's up?"

Juaquin examined the area, then the sky. "A sunny day today. Let's go sit under the Quebracho tree by the stream so we can speak in private."

"Oooo, are we being secretive?" Jessica teased.

"No. Too many people around here like to listen in on conversations that are none of their business."

Jessica followed Juaquin to the tree and sat down. "I can't imagine you want to talk about the weather. What do you want to talk about?"

"I was wondering if you plan to tell Tim before he leaves for the Antarctic?"

"Tell him what?" Jessica fidgeted, shifting her sitting position.

"That he's going to be a father."

Jessica's mouth dropped, and her eyes expanded. "What are you talking about? How can you ask such a question?"

"Jessica, I know. And you know I'm correct."

Jessica jumped to her feet, placing her hands on her hips, staring at the metal being. "Of course, you know. Tim told me androids know everything, especially you and this Xavier he's always talking about."

"Is that why you have refused to allow Andrew to examine you for your upset stomach?"

Jessica said nothing.

"I would like an answer, Jessica. Is that why you have been avoiding Andrew?"

"Yes," Jessica whispered.

"So, are you pregnant or not? I want you to confirm or deny it. And be advised, if you deny it, I will have Andrew secretly scan you to get my answer.

Jessica turned her back to Juaquin and averted her eyes. She focused on the thin blades of grass under her feet. "Yes," she mumbled.

"What was that? I couldn't understand your answer."

Turning to meet the android's gaze once more, Jessica fought back the tears desperately trying to fill her eyes. "I said yes. I'm pregnant."

"Then I will ask you again. Do you plan on telling Tim before he leaves?"

"Why? Will it make a difference? Will the truth of his forthcoming emergence into fatherhood keep him here where he's safe? Will it keep him here when the mission is over and it's time for all of you to go home? What will change if I tell him?"

"He has the right to know, Jessica."

"Will it change his mind?" Jessica screamed.

"No, it will not. But the truth will give him something to fight for, maybe stop him from doing something stupid in Antarctica. Plus, with Robert's passing, we now have room on the transport for another human if you wish to go to New Earth with him."

"I have no desire to leave Earth. And he has no desire to stay."

"Have you considered it? Aboard the space station at New Earth, your children would live a healthy, happy life, have a world of opportunities opened for them, and live to old age."

"And never step on grass again. Tim told me outsiders cannot live on New Earth. That is reserved for only the humans and androids who arrived on the space station. I am an outsider and, therefore, would be condemned to a life aboard the station. That is not the kind of life I want for my children or Tim. He's used to galloping across the universe, going on adventures, and meeting new species. He would never be happy aboard the space station."

"Don't make that assumption. Tim was content for five years while we traveled to New Earth. The station is his second home. As for you living on New Earth, do not dismiss that possibility either. Because of his grandfather, Tim's family has a lot of influence over the planet's rules. I believe that if petitioned, the ISC would grant Tim's wife and his children a life on the planet."

"Wife? Don't you think you're getting a little ahead of yourself, Juaquin? We've never even considered marriage. Both of us have always known that one day we'd go our separate ways."

"Until now. The pregnancy changes everything."

"And that's why I'm not telling him. And neither are you."

"Jessica, even if the negotiations in Antarctica are successful, it could still be months, or even years, before we can leave. He's going to find out."

"Not if I can help it."

"How are you going to prevent it? Run away? Go live with another colony?" Jessica remained silent. "That's your plan, to run away?"

"I don't know," Jessica shouted. "I haven't thought that far ahead yet."

Out of the corner of his eye, Juaquin saw Tim running towards them. "Tell him, or I will."

"What is going on?" Tim asked, out of breath. "I heard you two arguing clear across the yard."

"We were just having a heated discussion," Juaquin quickly stated.

"About what?"

"Where to put another garden and latrine," Jessica said, her eyes fixed on Juaquin's face.

"That's what the argument was about?" Tim asked. "Vegetables and poop?"

"He didn't like my suggestions," Jessica added.

Tim laughed. "Oh, Juaquin, never admit you don't like her ideas. I've learned the hard way it is not a good thing to tell her that. And painful at times. Be thankful she didn't become physical." Tim rubbed his left shoulder, remembering when he and Jessica argued over where to place a cornfield.

"So that's how you injured your shoulder." Juaquin turned to Jessica. "You, young woman, need to curb that temperament of yours. I'll leave you two to talk." Without another word, Juaquin turned and left.

"So, what's the problem?"

"Only Juaquin's interference where it's not wanted."

———————

"We couldn't find any more information about this Castrov Achenblles than you were," Commander Buutay said. "But we did record some activity just before daybreak. A plane landed at 0-eight hundred hours. A small regiment of thirty androids filed from the north dock door and unloaded boxes of unknown merchandise. We were able to scan the robots. They are an upgrade to Señor Miguel's robots, but nowhere as sophisticated as our androids."

"Which means he doesn't have access to our android's technology," Tim said.

"Not yet," Commander Buutay said.

"Master Kim always carefully guarded the secrets of android manufacturing," Juaquin stated.

"While we are grateful for his secrecy, it prevents us from repairing B-25," Buutay replied. "I hate to inform you of this, Tim and Juaquin, but I foresee no future for him. I suggest we remove his circuit board and allow him to cease to be. I would also like to remove some of his skin and use it to repair Jason's dead skin. Afterward, we should melt B-25 in our furnace so no one can obtain his parts or try to reverse engineer his technology."

"No," Juaquin said, not waiting for Tim to reply. "You are not to disassemble him in any form. Nor are you to melt his body into a glob of metal."

"As for B-25's skin, I would like the opportunity for Juaquin and I to discuss the option with Quinn," Tim said. "If Quinn wishes to replace his dead skin with coverings from B-25, I will authorize the operation. Please keep B-25 intact until I tell you otherwise."

"When you make the decision to terminate, what would you have me do?"

"Seal him in an airtight container to prevent further contamination," Juaquin said. "We will take him home and bury him on New Earth."

"That is not advisable," Commander Buutay replied. "I can't guarantee all his contamination will be eliminated. It could spread to the other members of our android units or to life on New Earth."

"I concur with Juaquin," Tim said. "We will take B-25 home. Androids were designed to exist forever. But if he is amongst the dozen or so androids whose lives end, he deserves this honor. Please make it so."

"I disagree, but I will do as you ask for now. But know this. When you depart Earth, I will personally have B-25 scanned. If I detect any morsel of radiation, you may not take him home. And I will contact the ISC and abide by their decision, not yours. Is that understood?"

"We will cross that barrier when that day arrives. May I have your word, Commander, that you or no other member of your team will disassemble or destroy any part of B-25?"

"Didn't I already tell you I would?"

"In a round-about way. I want you to say it specifically."

"I swear as an officer of the ISC that I nor any member of my crew will disassemble or destroy any part of the android designated as B-25. Is that satisfactory to you?"

"Yes. Thank you."

Chapter 15: THE Radio CALL

"I was told you wanted to speak with me and B-2?" Miguel and the robot walked beneath the newly constructed awning at the Android Station. B-2's head touched the cloth.

"I guess we should have made the height a little taller," C-85 silently said to Juaquin. *"I keep forgetting how tall these robots are."*

Tim waved his hand towards a nearby chair. "Please have a seat, Miguel." After Miguel sat, B-2 took a stand behind him. "As we've explained, the objective of our mission is to contact the humans of Earth and ask them to unite and agree, as one, to join the ISC. We have contacted numerous encampments here in South America and across lower Africa, Madagascar, and New Zealand. That leaves one major settlement left - the Antarctic."

"Daniel Jacobs?" Terror filled Miguel's face. "You're not seriously thinking of trying to persuade him to join your organization, are you?"

"On the surface, yes," Tim said. "But in truth, we believe Señor Jacobs has the antidote to this radiation poisoning. Without it, we may never be able to return home. And its poison will continue to devour this planet for eons."

"What do you want from us?"

"Do either of you have a way to contact him?"

Miguel squirmed nervously in his chair. "Why would I have a way to contact him?"

"By the rise in your heart rate, I say that is an affirmative," Juaquin commented.

Miguel glanced down at a tiny ant crawling across his boot. "No, I have no way to contact him."

"I don't believe you," Juaquin said.

Tim held out his hand. "Let's not assume that, Juaquin. Maybe he has reason to not want to tell us." Tim scooted his chair closer to Miguel. "Normally, I would not do this, but I am running out of time and growing desperate. I want to go home. I want to take my crew home. But I can't do that unless I talk with Señor Jacobs. You told Robert that you owed him a great debt for saving your wife and that you would do anything to repay that debt. Is that not correct?"

"Yes," came a mournful sound.

"By telling me the truth, your debt to Robert will be paid in full."

Miguel thought. Would he honor that debt? Tim waited.

"Señor Jacobs asked me to join his team down in Antarctica. When I said no, he wrote down a frequency number on a piece of paper. He said if I changed my mind, I should use it to contact him."

"Do you still have the number?"

Miguel lifted a gold locket from beneath his shirt. He pressed a small clasp, and the top flipped open, revealing a picture of his wife and child. From behind the picture, he removed a tiny piece of paper. Miguel handed the paper to Tim. Tim handed it to Juaquin, who stored the number in his memory and then returned it to Miguel.

"And you can use this number to call him?" Tim asked.

"I can text him."

Juaquin turned his attention to the large robot. "B-2, we androids can communicate with each other silently, over radio waves. Can the robots of your design do the same thing?"

"Yes."

"Are you currently in touch with the robots in Antarctica?" Tim asked, intrigued by this new information.

"I wouldn't say in contact with. I can sense them, but I don't hear their thoughts as Juaquin does."

"Can B-1 correspond with them?" Juaquin asked.

"He has never mentioned it. You would have to ask him."

"B-2, if I needed you to, could you contact one of the robots in Antarctica?"

"I don't know. I have never tried."

"But you might be able to?"

"Again, I do not know."

Tim turned to Juaquin. "Let's try Miguel's frequency code first. If we don't receive a response, we'll try B-2's connection. And possibly B-1 if he has contact."

"Agreed."

"There's a problem with that code," Miguel said. "It has to be dialed from a certain phone. Señor Jacobs will only answer if he recognizes the phone the message is sent from."

"Do you still have that phone?"

"No. Mercenaries stole it two years ago."

"Do you, by any chance, remember the phone's frequency?" C-85 asked.

"It's 8.6 THz CBZUS band 52, SSB Modulation."

C-85 turned to Tim. "Sir, that's a simple frequency to duplicate. I can easily route a call through the ship's radio using this frequency

227

and place a call to Jacobs. He'll think it's coming from Miguel's phone."

"I'm not comfortable with this," Miguel said. "Señor Jacob is a smart man. His technology is sophisticated. Plus, you said he's alien, not human."

"I can promise you, his technology is not as sophisticated as ours," C-85 said. "Remember, we've got thousands of years of technology behind us."

"Juaquin and I will draw up a message," Tim stated. "C-85, coordinate with Opal and get the ship's transmitter ready to submit the message."

"Yes, Sir."

"Tim, have you spoken with Jessica today?" Juaquin asked as the two left the station.

"No. Why do you ask?"

"I saw her this morning, and her skin appeared a little green," Juaquin answered.

"Her stomach has been giving her problems. I'll stop by and check on her."

Later that day, C-85 sent Tim's message to Daniel Jacobs under the disguise of Miguel. For three days, they waited. The radio remained silent. During this time, Juaquin waited for Jessica to tell Tim her news. That, too, did not happen.

Jessica jumped when a thump vibrated through her seat. She looked up to discover Juaquin sitting across from her at the noon luncheon. "Jessica, you still have not spoken with Tim as we discussed."

Jessica scanned the surrounding area, verifying no one was near to overhear Juaquin's comment. "As you discussed. I had nothing to do with that conversation," she whispered. "But, no, I have not had a chance to talk with him."

"That is not true. You two were talking together last night at the dinner table."

"The dinner table is not the place for such news. I need a place where it's just the two of us, a place where others will not be eavesdropping on our conversation."

"I can stand guard outside the shack tonight if you'd like a night alone with him."

"He'll never agree to that. He's way too busy getting ready for his trip down south."

"He has been preoccupied. But just this morning he told me he wanted to spend the night with you soon. You must talk with him before he leaves, or I will."

————————

"Have a seat, B-2," Tim said.

"I do not think your tiny chair will support my weight, Señor Spalling."

Tim laughed loudly, the sound echoing in the opened tent "You're probably right. I guess you can stand. As I told you the other day, I must contact Señor Jacobs. So far, he has not replied to our message. Do you remember our conversation?"

"Yes."

"I'd like you to try to contact the robots in Antarctica and ask them to have Señor Jacobs reply to us. Can you do that?"

"I can try."

"Wait, Commander. I'm getting something." C-85 turned knobs and pushed buttons. "Yes, I'm getting a reply."

"Hola, Miguel," came a deep, male voice. "Are you there?"

Tim sliced his hand across his throat, signaling to C-85 not to enable communications. "I didn't expect him to reply verbally. We need Miguel. Where is he?"

"He's working down by the watering station installing a new water dispenser," Juaquin said.

"Contact Phillip and tell him we need Miguel here right away."

"I doubt this Daniel will stay on the line long enough for Miguel to get here," C-85 said.

"Hola, Señor Jacobs," B-2 said in a perfect copy of Miguel's voice. "I hope you are doing well."

The sound of Daniel's laughter filled the airwaves. "Can't complain, not that it does any good. I must admit I was surprised to receive your message. How's the wife and family? How many kids do you have now?"

"My wife is doing well, as is my daughter and myself," B-2 replied. "As for children, I still only have one, but I hope one day to add a son. But the illnesses from the North's bombs makes it hard for our women to become pregnant."

"That's why you need to come down here. We don't have that problem of conceiving. But I'm sure you didn't contact me to discuss family matters."

"No, Señor."

"If you can give me your code, you have five minutes of my attention."

Tim's face went blank. What code? No one said anything about a damn code would be needed. Did B-2 have it?

"Please repeat, Señor Daniel. Your transmission is breaking up. My radio is having trouble maintaining your signal."

"I knew I should have given you a better communicator. I said I need your code."

"It's 536-grasshoppers taste good-647," Miguel shouted as he burst into the tent. He held a thumb up to B-2, signaling to the large robot that he was free to leave. But he remained, only taking three steps back from the radio.

"So, who's this person you think I should meet?"

"He is from a group called the ISC and was aboard the space station that left our moon. He is here to join the various settlements of humans under a common cause to join his coalition and bring us under the ISC's protection."

"Is that so?" Daniel's voice quivered. Those huddled around the radio heard the strain and tension in Daniel's voice. "You said he's from the ISC? Why did they come back to Earth? "

Miguel looked at Tim, who nodded yes. "The ISC wondered how we were doing, so they sent a small delegation. When they saw what happened up north, they decided to try again to get us to join their organization."

"What did you say his name was?"

"I didn't say his name. It's Timothy Spalling."

"Any relationship to Renn Spalling?"

"I do not know."

"Can you put him on the communicator?"

Tim shook his head no. "I'm sorry, Señor, I wasn't anticipating your call. Currently, Señor Spalling is not here, but I expect him in…" Tim held up three fingers. "In three hours. Can you call back then?"

"No," came an abrupt answer. "I'll call back tomorrow at thirteen hundred hours. Have him ready to talk." Daniel paused. "Miguel, did Señor Spalling bring any androids with him?"

"Yes, Señor."

"How many?"

"There are twenty-one in camp."

"Really? I will speak with you tomorrow. NexGen out."

Tim drew his fingers across his neck again. "The signal is disconnected," C-85 said. "You're free to speak."

"He definitely reacted to the mention of the ISC," Juaquin stated.

231

"Should I not have said that?" Miguel asked.

"I'm glad you did," Tim said. "His reaction tells us he is doing something that the ISC will not like. We'll have to tread lightly and try to figure out what he's up to. I must convince him to allow me to fly down to meet him."

"No, Señor Tim," B-2 shouted. "You cannot go. Something is not right."

"Were you able to speak with one of the other robots?"

"I didn't speak with one. But I received something, like a thought or idea. It contained danger and betrayal. And I kept sensing one word over and over - androids."

"Androids?" C-85 said.

"Tim, as you know, Señor Daniel's company made robots before the war, advanced robots," Miguel said. "But they were never perfect, not the way he wanted them to be. He often became angry at being unable to complete his dream."

"His fear and anger were audible in his voice," Juaquin said. "But I sensed his fear took a back seat to something he wants, something he wants badly."

"He wants the androids," Tim shuttered.

"I believe you are correct," Juaquin said. "Now that he is aware we're here and have androids, I hypothesize he will try to capture some to reverse engineer them. He'll incorporate his findings into his robots to create super beings." Juaquin paused, running various scenarios in his mind. "Tim, as you are aware of, I've never backed down from anything. But allowing this being to have any access to even one of our androids may be too dangerous. I believe we should call this endeavor off. For the galaxy's sake, we can't allow him near an android."

"But we can't call it off either," Tim replied. "We must determine if he possesses the antidote for the radiation poison. Otherwise, we'll be stuck here indefinitely."

"Our confinement to this planet is an acceptable payment for the safety of the life forms and AI's spread across the galaxies," Juaquin stated.

"But the death of this planet isn't," Tim replied. "I don't believe the ISC has the capability of cracking the radiation mystery. That means Señor Jacobs is our only choice. Without his antidote, this planet is going to die, along with any remaining humans. I can't admit defeat before trying to save Earth."

"The death of one planet is worth the sacrifice to save the galaxies."

"Not on my watch. We can save them all."

"Señor Tim, you have many advanced alien technologies," B-2 said. "You speak with different alien races. And you speak to an alien ship up in the sky. Is this all true?"

"Yes."

"Could these aliens use their technology to turn me into an android like Juaquin?"

"No, that's not possible. Only Juaquin's creators could do that, and they live ten lifetimes away from here. I'm afraid I can't make you like Juaquin."

"But can you make me look like him, act like him?"

"Why do you ask?" Juaquin asked, intrigued by the robot's request.

"If I appear to be an android, I can go with Señor Tim to Señor Daniel's. Then, if I am captured, he will not gain access to your alien technology and upgrade his robots."

"Thank you for offering, B2," Tim said. "Never has a robot impressed me as you just did. But even if I make you resemble the androids on the outside, I can't duplicate what's inside. Señor Jacobs would realize you were a fraud within minutes. Plus, I would not knowingly place you in harm's way to save one of us."

Miguel eyes widened as he stared at the young Commander. "You really do respect the lives of all AI's, don't you?"

"Yes."

Chapter 16: PREGNANCY

Juaquin watched Tim closely as he walked through the shack's door, his eyes narrowing as he tried to read Tim's mood. Tim and Jessica had spent their final night together before his departure. Had Jessica told him her news? Judging by Tim's cheerful demeanor, Juaquin doubted it. Damn it. Was Jessica planning to leave it up to him to break the news? Or did she genuinely believe that keeping Tim in the dark was better until he returned?

No, Juaquin thought firmly, the truth had to come out. Tim needed to know. Juaquin believed this knowledge could be the edge Tim required to survive the mission and come back alive. He couldn't let his commander face the unknown without all the facts, no matter how difficult they might be.

"I take it you had an enjoyable evening?"

Tim stopped and faced the android. "Okay, what's up, Juaquin? You always make a smart remark about hurting myself again. You're being too nice this morning. What's the horrific news you're avoiding telling me?"

"What do you mean? I was just wondering if you had a nice time together."

"Bullshit! Something's wrong. What is it?"

"Tim, as you are well aware of, I cannot lie. And I have said I have no hidden agenda."

Tim searched the android's face. As usual, Juaquin gave no clues as to his motive or whether he had one. "Yes, thank you. We had a wonderful evening together, although she's none too happy about me leaving."

"I can imagine." The shack door reopened, and Jessica emerged. Juaquin gave her a stern stare. Jessica shrugged her shoulders and ran off toward the eating area. "Let's get you some breakfast before your big meeting with the bad guy."

"I did work up an appetite." Tim briskly followed ten yards behind Jessica, humming a snappy tune. Juaquin walked alongside. The two humans branched off when they reached the main path, each taking another way to the dispensary.

"I want to inspect the site for the new field before I eat," Tim said. "Plus, Jessica and I shouldn't arrive simultaneously."

"Do you still believe, Tim, that half the camp isn't aware of Jessica's and your secret meetings? Humans are not stupid."

"I never said they were. But I like to think most of them still do not know about us. Somehow, it makes it more fun." Juaquin shook his head in disbelief.

"I'll see you in a bit," Juaquin said. "I have to check on the flight specks one more time."

"Okay."

After a quick inspection of the new planting site, Tim ran to the dispensary. He got right in line and grabbed a bowl of oatmeal. He sprinkled two spoons of cane sugar over the top, grabbed an apple and a tin cup of coffee, then headed to the tables. He greeted various people along the way. Tim was surprised to see Juaquin sitting with Jessica. He wondered if Jessica was ill again because she had a very disagreeable expression on her face.

Stepping over the bench, Tim sat down, resting his bowl, apple, and cup on the table. "Is your stomach upset again? You don't look like you feel well. You really need to go see Andrew." Tim thought he saw tears in her eyes.

"Actually, I have an appointment tomorrow morning," Jessica said, her voice low and shaky.

"Well, I hope he finds out what's going on with you. You haven't felt well for weeks."

"Actually, Jessica was telling me she has a pretty good idea of what has been ailing her," Juaquin said.

"What's that, Jessica?" Tim took a big swallow of coffee. *Dang, Rosa made her coffee super strong.* When he lowered his coffee mug, he saw Jessica was crying. He hadn't imagined it. "What is going on? Why are you crying?" Tim glanced from Jessica to Juaquin. "Do you have something to do with this, Juaquin?"

"Tell him or I will," Juaquin said.

"Tell me what? What aren't you two telling me?"

Jessica kept her eyes fixed on the table.

"One of you better tell me now. I've got an important call coming in, and I can't be worried about what's wrong with Jessica." Silence. "Are you upset about last night? I told you it was okay we didn't do anything."

"I'm going to be sick again." Jessica swung her legs over the bench, jumped up, and took off running.

"Poor girl," Rosa said as she poured Tim a half cup of coffee. "Morning sickness is not fun. Tina and I will gather some mint leaves and brew a tea to ease her sickness."

"Morning sickness?" Tim whispered to Juaquin. "Is that what's wrong with Jessica?" Juaquin said nothing. "Juaquin, answer me."

"I suggest you go talk with the mother of your child," Juaquin answered.

Tim stared, barely blinking, trying to comprehend Juaquin's words. "Shit!" Tim jumped up, forgetting the rest of his breakfast,

238

almost tripping over the puppy by the table. He ran after Jessica, following her to a secluded spot where she vomited.

"Jessica, are you pregnant?"

On her knees, Jessica was able to utter a weak "Yes" in between bouts of vomiting.

"Yes? Are you sure?"

"I believe the days of vomiting confirm her condition," Juaquin said, walking silently up.

"Pregnant. No, no. This can't be happening." He glared at Jessica, who was sitting on her knees, her sickness momentarily halted. "How did you let this happen? Didn't you take precautions?"

"Me?" Jessica screamed, rising to her feet. "You're the one with all the advanced medicines. I thought Andrew was giving you something to make sure this didn't happen. Where in the hell did you think I was going to get contraceptives?"

"Don't make this my mistake. You could have asked Andrew for them," Tim screamed back.

"How could I do that when you didn't want anyone to know about the two of us?"

Suddenly, the air felt thick, making it hard to breathe. Time slowed each second, stretching into eternity. "You knew, Juaquin, didn't you?" Tim screamed, staring into the android's eyes. "That's why you were so secretive this morning and insisted we spend last night together. How long have you known?" Juaquin said nothing. Tim walked up to the android, placing his nose an inch from Juaquin's chin. "How long?"

"I've had my suspicions for three weeks, four days, six hours, and fifteen seconds. But I only received confirmation four days ago."

Adrenaline surged through Tim's veins, clouding his thoughts. "You son of a bitch." Without hesitation, he drew his arm back, clenched his fist, and slammed it into Juaquin's jaw. The sickening crack of bones breaking reverberated through the air as Tim's fist connected.

Sensing the situation spiraling, Juaquin silently activated his silent communicator. *"Andrew, medical assistance is needed at the south side of hill number two."*

"Ouch, damn it, ouch, that hurts!" Tim roared, clutching his hand as he staggered around, his movements wild and erratic, a chaotic dance of pain and frustration. "It hurts so much." Tears streamed down his face.

Juaquin removed his scanner. He reached out for Tim's hand to scan it.

"Get away from me, you son of a bitch," Tim yelled, still dancing around, cradling his hand against his chest.

Keeping a safe distance, Juaquin scanned Tim's hand. "So like your grandfather. Are you aware of how many times Renn broke his hand hitting Xavier? Why do you humans insist on striking us and breaking their bones when we're indestructible?"

"Tim, are you okay?" Jessica asked, rushing over.

"This is all your fault," Tim screamed, shoving her away.

"Why is this my fault?" Jessica yelled, her face turning red. "I'm not the one stupid enough to hit an android and break my hand."

"Andrew, what's your ETA?" Juaquin said verbally into his comm link. "Tim broke his hand in at least two places. He needs medical attention."

"I just saw him," came Andrew's voice over the speaker. "How did he do that in such a short time?"

"He tried to break my jaw."

"Oh no, not another Spalling who thinks he can hurt us. I'll arrive in 2.6 minutes."

"Are all androids familiar with the story of my grandfather and Xavier?" Tim asked, his hopping slowing down.

"Only those aboard the space station," Andrew said as he rounded the corner.

"How'd you get her so fast?" Tim asked. "Juaquin just radioed you."

"I notified him he was needed the moment you raised your arm back to strike me," Juaquin answered. "I knew what the outcome would be."

"Why didn't you stop me if you knew I'd break my hand?"

"Would it have done any good? Besides, some lessons must be learned the hurtful way."

Andrew scanned the hand. "Yes, you broke it in three places: two metacarpals and one phalange. It appears you'll be meeting Mr. Jacobs in a handcast."

"Great."

"And how are you doing today, Ms. Steinberg? I can give you something for that morning sickness if you'd like," Andrew said.

"You know, too?" Jessica asked.

"I keep telling you, androids know everything," Tim said.

"True, but I was worried you might have radiation sickness or malaria, so I ran a scan without you knowing a few days ago. I was relieved to learn you were only pregnant. But I would like to run a complete physical on you. The radiation that has permeated this world could cause some complications with your pregnancy. From what people have told me, it's been very hard for many humans to conceive. There have also been miscarriages, stillbirths, and deformities."

"I don't think she wants to hear that now. Ouch, that hurts!" Tim cried out as Andrew carefully took Tim's hand in his own.

"Here's a shot for the pain," Andrew said, injecting the liquid into Tim's upper arm. "She needs to be aware of the ramifications of your actions."

"My actions? Why is it my actions? Ouch."

"Hold still, and your hand won't hurt. I don't mean only your actions. Your actions, like the both of you. You both created the life growing inside her. Are you hoping for a daughter or a son?"

"I don't know, Andrew. I just learned about this, and then I broke my hand. Give me some time to think."

"Perhaps next time you will think before you strike. It would save you a lot of pain."

Tim ignored the android's comment. "Juaquin, what time is it?"

"Mr. Jacobs should be calling in eighteen minutes. We'd best return to the Android Station. Andrew, maybe you can set the bones later, after the call. I'll bring Tim to the medical area the moment we're finished. Please escort Jessica back to her room."

"Yes, Sir. Tim, keep your arm in this sling until I can set your bones." Andrew wrapped a piece of material around Tim's neck and under his arm. He then raised the arm up and tied the sling on top.

Fourteen minutes later, Tim was seated at the Android Station.

Miguel noticed Tim's arm and the bluish-green hand. "What happened? Did you injure your hand?"

"Yes. Long story." *And one I don't want to talk about,* Tim thought to himself. Tim searched Juaquin and C-85's faces. He was sure both of them were hiding smiles. More of those secrets his grandfather told him about.

"Buenos dias, Señor Spalling," came Daniel's voice over the radio. "I am delighted to talk with you. Miguel thought we should talk."

"Buenos dias, Señor Jacobs," Tim replied. "Yes, Miguel told me he explained to you that I am here representing the ISC. Might we set up a meeting?"

"I have discussed the possibility with my associates, and agree that a meeting is necessary to discuss our options. We feel the ISC may offer us perks that can benefit our people."

"I believe you will agree that we can offer you an opportunity to improve your lives. I look forward to coming down and speaking with you and your people."

"Will you be coming alone? Or will Miguel be accompanying you?"

"I'm coming with Miguel as well as one android. Will that be a problem?"

"An android, you say? I heard the stories of the magnificence of ISC androids. I look forward to meeting one in person."

"So you know about our androids? They're truly remarkable. Miguel mentioned your exceptional talent for designing robots and described you as a genius in the field. I'm eager to see how your creations stand apart from our androids."

The sound of Daniel's laughter floated across the airwaves. "Anyone who is someone knows of your androids. And, I wouldn't call myself a genius. I had some excellent designers and engineers."

"Did you use our androids as a model?" Tim asked.

Silence. Daniel cleared his throat. "Your androids? How would I know what your androids look like?"

Damn, he didn't fall for it. "When my grandfather recused my family, two androids were with him. I thought perhaps you saw footage of the event."

"I was not aware of this rescue. Perhaps you will tell me the story when you visit."

"Perhaps."

"I imagine you don't have warm clothing, so I'll be sure to have parkas waiting for you and Miguel upon your arrival."

"Thank you. I was wondering where I could find some warm clothing suitable for sub-zero temperatures around here. What's your temperature today?"

"You're in luck because we're having a heatwave. It's a warm fifteen degrees today. Quite warm for this area." Daniel laughed. "I

243

will have my radio operator give your man our coordinates. What time should we expect you?"

"I have a few more things to tie up before I leave. I plan to leave at sixteen hundred hours, if that is okay with your schedule. I estimate the flight takes just over two hours, so expect us around eighteen twenty-two hours this evening."

"Until then. Here's my operator."

The screen changed to another human with curly dark hair. He gave C-85 the landing coordinates and instructions on which door to enter.

"Tell your boss to use the small door when he arrives. Once he and his companions are inside, we'll open the large door and bring his planes in. It's too cold to leave them outside."

"It appears it's a go," Tim said once the communication ended.

"He definitely is eager to meet one of the androids."

"That he is. I thought I could get him to admit he had seen one before, but he wouldn't take the bait."

"You should stop by and see Jessica," Juaquin stated. "You were a bit harsh on her earlier."

"How should I have acted? This was not in my plans for Earth."

"Maybe not, but you are just as responsible."

"I know that. You don't have to remind me. If I have time, I'll stop and see her."

Juaquin grabbed Tim and spun him around, almost knocking him over. "No, Tim. You must make time. We do not know what is going to happen down there at Daniel's. There is the possibility you might not return. If so, do you really want your last words to her to be angry ones? Do you want her to believe for the rest of her life that you hated her?"

"No. I'll be sure to stop and talk with her before departing."

"Make sure you do. Let's go see Andrew and get your hand set."

Andrew re-scanned the broken bones, slipped them into alignment, and wrapped Tim's hand.

"How's that?" Andrew asked.

Rim raised his hand and stared at the obvious white wrap over his hand. "It feels better. I wish there was a way I didn't have to wear the wrapping. It makes my hand's injury very obvious."

"Sorry, kid, it comes with the breaking of bones. I don't want you using your hand for a few days," Andrew said. "I've given you something to help speed up the bone regeneration, but keep your hand stationary as much as possible. Otherwise, you could shift the bones out of alignment."

"Understood," Tim sighed. He nervously scanned the area, then at the floor. "Guess there's no more time to put it off. I have to go face Jessica and apologize for what I said, don't I?"

"Would you like me to accompany you?" Juaquin asked.

"No, I think I need to do this on my own." Tim turned and walked to where Jessica would be.

"What do you want?" Jessica asked as Tim entered her living area. Her eyes were rimmed in red and puffy, their usual sparkle dulled with sorrow. Shiny streaks of dried tears clung to her flushed cheeks. Her nose was a deep pink.

"I'll be leaving soon, and I didn't want to leave without seeing you."

"You've seen me. Now leave."

"Jessica, I'm sorry. I overreacted."

"Do you think so? You were a real jerk."

"I'd use the excuse that you caught me off guard, but that's no reason for my behavior. It's just that I never imagined I'd be a father one day. I'm not upset with you."

"Well, I'm upset with you."

"And you should be. I behaved horridly. I was rude, thoughtless, and a complete ass. Can you forgive me?"

245

Jessica raised his eyes to meet hers. "Why should I?"

"Because I am going to go meet a very dangerous man. There is a possibility I will not return. I don't want to go without us being friends."

"Don't say you might not come back. I want you to return. Besides, little Jenny will need her daddy." Jessica managed a weak smile.

"Jenny? I was thinking more like Renn, Jr." Tim smiled back.

"No way."

"So, we're okay?"

"Yes. How's your hand?

"Broken."

"Why did you hit Juaquin?"

"I was mad because he knew about the baby and didn't tell me."

"It wasn't his place to tell you. It was mine."

"That's true. But I was still mad."

"I'm sorry you have to go with a broken hand."

"Thanks."

Tim waited for her to say more, but she remained silent. Not sure what to do, Tim said, "Take care, Jessica. I'll see when I return." Tim turned and walked from the room.

"Wait!" Jessica shouted, her voice cracking with desperation as she sprinted after him. With tears streaming down her face, she flung her arms around his neck, pulling him close. She pressed her lips to his in a passionate, lingering kiss, pouring all her fears and hopes into that single moment. "Please," she whispered, her voice trembling, "Come back to me. I don't want to lose you."

Tim placed his hand over Jessica's belly. "I'm not angry about the baby, Jessica. I mean it."

246

"That makes me feel better. Would you like me to walk you to the flier?"

"No. I want to remember you like this, with a smile on your face, a look of longing in your eyes. Besides, I might cry if I have to watch you disappear. And Juaquin will never let me forget it if I do."

Jessica stood on her tippy toes and kissed Tim's cheek. "I love you."

"You've never said that before."

"No, I haven't. But I've felt it for a long time."

"Why didn't you tell me before this?"

"I was afraid, I guess."

"That's why I didn't say it. I was afraid you didn't love me back. But now that I know you do, I can say that I love you. I love you, Jessica. And I will be back. I promise."

Jessica forced a smile on her face. She placed her index finger over Tim's mouth. "No, no promises. Just be careful and stay focused on your mission. That will get you home to me."

Tim pressed a kiss to Jessica's finger. It was a desperate, fleeting touch, a silent goodbye etched onto her skin. Each ragged breath fought against the sob clawing at his throat. With a final, lingering glance that spoke volumes, he turned. The world blurred as he walked away, every step heavy with the dread of a future forever uncertain.

Juaquin waited for his commander forty feet down the path. He handed Tim a cloth to wipe his face. "Everything go okay?"

"Yes. We're friends again. She told me she loved me."

"It's about time. Did you tell her you loved her?"

"Of course."

"I am happy for both of you."

"Are you capable of being happy, Juaquin?"

247

"Perhaps not like the emotion you feel, but sometimes, such as this, there is a warm sensation that cascades over my body. Xavier told me that the feeling was happiness."

"That it is."

Tim and Xavier walked to where Miguel waited. Together, the three walked to their aircraft.

"Only one flier?" Miguel asked.

"Since we can't be sure of Señor Jacobs' intentions, we don't want to give him access to more than one flier. And, if something goes wrong, Juaquin can detonate the craft to ensure Daniel can't use it. Thankfully, the fliers Undii brought us can accommodate three passengers, although it will be tight."

"Is the cargo on board?" Tim asked.

"Yes, Sir, all secured."

"And where is our pilot?"

"Right here," came an unfamiliar voice. The group turned to see one of Undii's androids walking towards them. "Android number Sc-18Bm reporting as requested. You can address me as 18m or by my designation of PheuMae. Sorry, I'm late. I had to deal with a puma intent on eating several of our sheep."

"I thought the puma problem was solved." Tim stated.

"That was my understanding," Juaquin said. He directed his attention to C-49. "Your input?"

"I took her and her cubs thirty miles from here," C-49 offered as an excuse. "She must have found her way back. I'll get right on the problem the moment you leave."

"Isn't PheuMae a female name?" Miguel asked.

"Since I am neither male nor female, the comment has no merit," PheuMae stated.

"He has a point," Tim chuckled. "So, PheuMae, tell me about yourself."

"I have been a member of Hiinew's security team for the past sixty years. Before that, I served on various spacecraft across the galaxy. I am well-versed in human idiosyncrasies and customs and speak one thousand, five hundred and eighty-two Earth languages, including various dialects. I am also the only android in this quadrant who is fluent in the alien tongue of Freezion. If Señor Jacobs is Freezion, as we suspect, I can translate his words if he speaks in his native tongue."

"Sounds like you are invaluable to our success." Tim smiled.

Chapter 17: THE MEETING

"Right this way, Señor Spalling," the android greeted, directing Tim, Miguel, and PheuMae inside from the cold. "Before I can take you to Señor Daniels, we must run a security sweep. Señors Spalling and Costa, if you would remove your clothes and step into the scanner."

"Is this necessary?" Tim asked, trying to act upset by the security. But he was expecting it.

"We cannot take a chance of anyone bringing sickness or parasites into our facilities. I am sure you understand."

Without further protest, both males stripped and stepped behind the screens. Tim was delighted to have a heated floor beneath his feet, but his body shivered from the cold, crisp air. A bar of white light appeared and ran up and down for five rotations, then stopped. After ten seconds, the light on the side panel changed from red to green.

"You may step out. You will find clothes on the bench for you to change into."

"Will we receive our clothes back?" Miguel asked, not wishing to lose one of his few shirts.

"They will be returned to you upon your departure."

While Tim and Miguel dressed into the new winter jumpsuits, two robots searched their clothing. They removed communicators from both men's pant pockets and a knife from Miguel's.

"No weapons allowed."

"I don't go anywhere without my knife," Miguel grumbled.

"It is not allowed. Nor are the outside electronics."

"I need my communicator to correspond with my team," Tim said.

"I will give it to Señor Jacobs. He will decide if you may have it or not. What is your reasoning for a communicator, Señor Costa?"

"My wife is expecting a child," Miguel lied. "She is due to deliver any day. I need it to keep in touch with her."

"Insufficient reasoning." The android tossed it into a nearby bin.

"Listen here, you pile of metal," Miguel shouted.

Tim grabbed his arm. "We'll discuss your need for a communicator with Daniel."

The android turned his attention to PheuMae. "What is your designation?"

"I am PheuMae."

"No, your designation," the robot said. "What does your owner call you when he wants you to do something?"

"He calls me PheuMae."

"Unacceptable," the robot stated. "That is not an appropriate designation."

"That is his name," Tim said. "Our androids have real names, not designation numbers."

"You are P-1. Step behind the scanner." As with the humans, a bar of white light rose up and down scanning PheuMae, but this time for implants. The scanner started its second sweep when an alarm

251

sounded. A red light blinked. The android checked his scanner, then walked over to PheuMae.

"Raise your right arm."

PheuMae complied. With a small screwdriver, the android loosened the screw from the android's lower arm panel. He flipped the door open, shining a light from his forehead into the chamber. "You have a scanning device hidden in your arm."

"Of course he does," Tim said. "Such devices are a part of his normal body structure."

"It is not allowed. I will remove it." The robot signaled to one of the other robots in the room. "842, remove the device from this android's arm."

Two more times, the alarms went off as security breaches were discovered and removed. When the scanner rose and fell for four cycles with no alarms, PheuMae was allowed to step out.

"P-1, lie down on the table behind you," the voice commanded. PheuMae glanced at Tim, who gave a reassuring nod. Obediently, PheuMae approached the table and lay down. As soon as his body made contact, metal restraints shot up from within the surface, locking tightly around his legs, arms, and chest.

"What are you doing to my android?" Tim asked.

"I will remove his right eye and scan the serial code inside to verify his identity."

"The hell you will," Tim said, lunging forward. Three security robots stepped forward, their weapons cocked and ready to fire. Tim halted his advancement.

"I wouldn't try that again," came a familiar voice. A tall, blond man with green/blue eyes entered out of the shadows.

"Buenas dias, Señor Jacobs," Miguel said.

"Buenas dias, Miguel," the man greeted. "I am delighted to see you again. And I assume you are Commander Spalling." Daniel held out his hand.

"I won't shake hands with someone who assaults my android," Tim declared, his voice firm and commanding. The tension in the air was palpable, underscored by the grinding of Tim's teeth.

Daniel smiled, withdrawing his hand. "Can you assault an android, a being with no feelings? I assure you, he will suffer no damage from the procedure. However, you must understand that you are a member of the ISC. As such, you have all kinds of technological advancements at your disposal. I am only protecting what is mine. I must ensure your android is what you claim him to be."

"You are familiar with the ISC?" Tim asked, curious as to the alien's forthcoming answer.

"Like most humans, I witnessed the alien named Glogg's address to the U.N. He talked about the ISC. And when their space station emerged from our moon, I understood they were a power of great strength. Plus, you yourself said the ISC sent you to Earth."

"That I did. "Tim weighed his options as the robot lifted the right side panel on PheuMae's face. "Señor Jacobs, again, I protest. Your robots have already removed the security devices in PheuMae. They've scanned him multiple times. Can't you accept my word that he is your every day ISC android?"

"I'm afraid not," Daniel replied. "I have not gotten to where I am by believing those who would do me harm. "Daniel nodded to the robot, signaling for him to continue.

"I bring you no harm." Tim held his breath, studying the robot's movements, ready to break through the defense of robots if PheuMae was in danger.

Using an extractor, the robot wiggled the instrument behind PheuMae's orbital sphere and pulled it forward. The eyeball emerged, surrounded by muscles and massive wiring growing thinner as the robot pulled it away from its socket.

"Stop, or you'll break the wiring, and I don't have a way to repair him," Tim screamed, trying to push past the line of robots.

"That's far enough, 145," Daniel said.

Inserting a small, lighted instrument, the robot scanned the eye socket. He read the readout on his display: "This android's serial number is ISC issued."

"How in the hell does he know that?" Tim turned and stared at the pious Daniel."

"145, tell Commander Spalling how you know this is an ISC android."

"The serial number inside his orbital cavity is of a configuration and language that is not known on Earth. Therefore, he is alien."

"There is your answer," Daniel said.

"Alright, you have your confirmation," Tim yelled. "Restore my android." Daniel nodded in agreement. The robot replaced the eye and reclosed the panel.

"Señor Jacobs, I must protest again your treatment of my android," Tim said. "I assure you, he is an ISC android. How much more proof do you need?"

"Again, I apologize. But I must be sure. I noticed your hand is injured, Commander Spalling. Are you in need of medical assistance? I have a phenomenal staff of medics."

"No, I'm fine. I injured my hand back at camp. My medical android took care of my injury."

"I imagine your medical android is very impressive," Daniel said, a mysterious look in his eyes. "Perhaps I can meet him one day."

"I will check to determine if a meeting is possible," Tim said, forcing a warm smile onto his face. *Like hell, I will. You want to extract his knowledge to benefit you. I saw that look in your eyes.* Tim walked to PheuMae. "Are you okay? Did he accurately reinsert your eye?"

PheuMae ran a diagnostic. "My vision is operating within proper diameters, although my vision is off 0.087 *togs*. I will have Andrew realign the eye when we return to base."

"I told you he'd suffer no ill effects." Daniel smiled. "Come, let me show you my facility and why I go to such great lengths to keep it safe."

"Before I go any further, we need to discuss our communicators. I need mine to speak with my security team back in Argentina. Miguel needs his to speak with his expectant wife."

Daniel chuckled again. "I'm sure you think I'm paranoid, but I can't allow that. Each of you will have access to a radio any time you need it. 145, bring Commander Spalling a communicator."

"What about Miguel?"

"He can use yours."

"Commander Spalling calling Echo Base. C-85, do you copy," Tim said into the comm link.

"C-85 here," came Juaquin's voice. "Is everything okay?"

"Yes, C-85. We arrived safe, and I am with Señor Jacobs. However, our communicators were confiscated. Miguel was wondering how his wife was doing. Has she shown any signs of labor starting?"

Juaquin paused, trying to determine what Tim was speaking of. Was Miguel's wife pregnant? If so, she wouldn't be ready to deliver a baby. Anticipating Tim needed a cover for something, he said, "No, no signs of labor yet."

"Please inform Miguel's wife that she won't be able to reach him through his radio. If she needs to speak with him, she'll need to contact him through this frequency."

"This does pose a problem." Juaquin thought, formulating an idea on how to handle this newest problem. "Since I am unable to contact you directly, might I suggest we set up a schedule, say check in once every two hours?"

"Agreed," Tim said before Daniel objected. "Commander Spalling out."

"You should have asked if a two-hour communication schedule is possible," Daniel said. His jaw tightened, forcing it to jut forward. His nose wrinkled slightly. "Antarctica has many factors that inhibit radio waves: winds, magnetic fields, aurora australis lights, gravitational pull."

"Perhaps you should then give us back our communicators. Such occurrences won't affect them."

Daniel raised his left eyebrow. Such a ludicrous statement deserved no comment. "Are you hungry after your trip? I can either take you to the food dispensary or show you around my beautiful station."

Tim turned to Miguel. "What do you think? Food or tour?"

"I vote for a tour." Miguel's curiosity far outweighed his growling stomach.

Miguel and Tim headed for the door but paused when they noticed Daniel wasn't following.

"Is something wrong?" Tim asked, puzzled by Daniel's hesitation. "I'm sorry. As our host, you should go first."

"Miguel is not interested in his wife's condition?" Daniel asked, his head cocked to the right.

"I don't understand. Miguel heard C-85 confirm his wife was not in labor."

"True, but wouldn't you like the robots to notify you if we receive word that her condition has changed?"

"That goes without saying," Miguel said. "Why would you even ask such a question?"

"Because you seem incredibly unconcerned," Daniel said. He took four steps toward the male. "What's going on, Miguel? What are you and Commander Spalling up to?"

Miguel stepped closer, standing with his nose two inches from Daniel's. "How dare you question my integrity and concern. Since you confiscated my radio, I assumed your robots would keep me informed of any communique about my wife. Apparently, I was mistaken. You're still the bastard I remember. Paranoid and a piece of shit."

Tim stood back, watching, uncertain if he should intervene or not. Afraid to tip his hand, he remained silent. Tim breathed a sigh of relief when Daniel's laughter echoed throughout the room.

"Glad you haven't lost your sense of humor, Miguel," Daniel said. "145, contact me if a transmission from Echo Base Camp is received. Gentlemen, this way to my wondrous settlement."

The air grew warm and moist as they advanced into the complex. The walls changed from blocks of ice to concrete and then to wood. Upon rounding the corner, they encountered two motorized carts waiting for them. Daniel climbed into the front seat of the first cart, sitting beside the robot driver.

"Tim, if you and Miguel sit in the middle, your android can ride in the back seat. You might want to take those parkas off, too. The temperature inside is warm and comfortable."

Both males removed their coats and placed them on the back seat. "I was getting a little warm," Tim said.

"Please put on your seatbelts," the robot driver stated once Tim and Miguel were seated.

Once buckled in, the robot car whirled to life, gliding smoothly down the illuminated corridor. Two security droids armed with weapons followed in the second car. PheuMae secretly snapped pictures of robots and their weaponry, sending the images to Juaquin. Daniel's security scan hadn't found all the androids' secrets.

"Señor Jacobs, there aren't many humans around," Tim commented.

"This is only the front of the complex. Humans have little reason to come out here. As we travel further inside, they will start appearing."

Once again, the walls shifted, but this time they morphed into transparent panes of glass. Beyond the glass, lush rows of vibrant vegetation came into view, stretching as far as the eye could see. The sudden sight took Tim and Miguel by surprise, their gasps echoing in the now silent room as they marveled at the unexpected transformation. The greenery beyond the glass seemed to pulse with life, an oasis of nature hidden within the sterile confines of their surroundings.

"Are those plants?" Tim asked.

"Yes, enough to feed the world," Daniel boasted.

"How did you manage this?"

"Years of hard work and the mind of a genius."

The vehicle came to a halt in front of a pair of glass doors. They glided open silently, releasing a wave of rich, earthy scent tinged with a hint of sweetness.

Tim and Miguel both jumped from the vehicle even before it came to a complete stop. Both inhaled deeply, breathing in the earthly aromas. PheuMae followed. Before them stretched a colossal greenhouse, its vastness stretching for miles in every direction. Streams of natural sunlight from a domed ceiling bathed the interior in a warm, golden glow. Towering rows of plants stretch as far as they could see, a tapestry of vibrant greens, reds, and yellows.

"This is amazing." Tim rose on his tiptoes, trying to judge the expanse of the garden. "How big is this?"

Daniel exited and walked to where Tim stood. "The greenhouse measures six miles wide by fifteen miles long. Look up and to your left."

Tim raised his gaze and stumbled back three steps. Tier upon tier of balconies crisscrossed the interior, each one overflowing with a cornucopia of fruits and vegetables. Cascading vines of plump grapes draped over the railings, intermingling with ruby-red tomatoes and clusters of emerald-green herbs. Blackberries peeked from beneath the leaves of towering cabbages, while sunshine yellow lemons and oranges brightened the higher levels with their citrusy glow. Almost unable to speak, Tim managed two words, "How high?"

"Eight stories."

"You built this in only a couple of years."

"I started the construction about eight years ago."

"Before the nuclear war?"

"Yes. But had I realized what would occur, I would have started building long before I did and perhaps prevented the war from happening. With our progress, I can feed the world and end hunger and famine, the true culprits of war."

"I always thought greed and the hunger for ultimate power were the causes of wars."

"Many believe that," Daniel said. "But they're not. Eradicate hunger and poverty, and war becomes obsolete. Take the path to your right."

Miguel and Tim hastened down the dirt path. Butterflies danced from flower to flower, attracted by the vibrant colors and the promise of nectar. In the distance, the sound of a gentle misting system broke the stillness, creating a light rain that nourished the plants, leaving diamond-like droplets clinging to the leaves. The soft hum of bees filled the air. A field of lush, red strawberries appeared. Daniel bent down and picked up two extra-large specimens and handed one to Tim and Miguel. Both men bit into the succulent fruit, their mouths watering at its sweetness.

"I haven't tasted a strawberry for over thirty years," Tim said, his eyes closed as he relished the flavor. "The Caladrine tried to grow them on the space station, but they always molded due to the humidity in the gardens. So, they gave up trying. I've searched numerous planets to find something similar, but strawberries only exist here on Earth. I can now die happy, having once again had the pleasure of one in my mouth. These are wonderful."

"If you think the strawberries are delicious, wait until you bite into one of the nectarines hanging in yonder tree."

Tim turned and glanced ahead. A grove of thirty nectarine trees rose towards the ceiling, their branches adorned with crimson nectarines. Tim rushed forward and plucked two from a low branch. He tossed one to Miguel. As the fruit's juices filled his mouth and slid out the corners of his mouth, Tim couldn't decide which was more pleasurable - the strawberries or nectarines.

"How many types of fruits do you grow here?" Miguel asked.

"Just over fifteen hundred. But we grow not only fruits. We have a variety of vegetables, wildflowers, aquatic plants, and grasses. We're sort of like the space station - preserving Earth's plant life."

"How do you tend such a garden?" Miguel asked.

"The robots are our gardeners, with a little help from humans. And a few Caladrine."

"You have Caladrine here?" Tim asked, surveying the expanse for the sight of the aliens.

"Can you name a better gardener capable of creating this bounty from nothing?" Daniel asked.

"I don't understand," Tim said. "How are you familiar with Caladrine? They don't reside on this planet. And even if you learned of them, which is impossible, how did you speak with them and convince them to join your cause? They don't speak Earth languages."

"My robots possess a massive language base. They had no trouble translating the Caladrine tongue. As for convincing them, everyone, including aliens, has a price."

"But where do you find them?" Tim asked. *Does he know about the Hiinew's colony? Are these Caladrine part of her crew? Why didn't she say something?*

"On my way down here to Antarctica, I literally stumbled into six of them in South America. I was checking out a new parcel of land in Chile for another robot factory. I walked around a tree and bumped into one. He told me he and others were left behind by accident when the space station left. They were lost and alone. I couldn't leave them in the forest to fend for themselves. So, I invited them to join my cause, to help me replenish the world's food supply."

Tim gazed at Miguel. He, too, doubted Daniel's story.

"Come, I have much more to show you."

The carts traveled past a well-equipped infirmary and a robot manufacturing terminal. Tim asked to stop and view the robotic process, but Daniel declined, stating his process was top secret. They continued down a corridor lined with doors and staircases. Daniel explained that these were the human quarters.

"How many humans live here?" Tim asked.

"We have twelve hundred and sixty, but three more are expected to be born in the next two months."

"Your people are not affected by the radiation poisoning? What is your miscarriage and infertility rate?"

"I have eliminated all traces of radiation," Daniel said, his head high and his chin lifted. Tim noted a twinkle with a hint of mischief in Daniel's eyes in addition to a puffing of his chest. "Those conditions do not exist here."

"Perhaps you would be willing to share your secret of ending the radiation poisoning with us?" Tim asked.

"A topic for later," was all Daniel said.

The ride continued until it ended thirty-five minutes later outside an eatery. The room was expansive, with wide, unobstructed spaces that made it feel even larger than it was. Artificial sunlight poured in through tall windows, flooding the area with a warm, golden glow. The walls, painted in a soft, neutral tone, reflected the light, enhancing the airy atmosphere. The high ceiling added to the sense of openness, with exposed beams that drew the eyes upward. The floor consisted of blocks of red, pink, white, and black striped rhodochrosite stone. Tables of various sizes were scattered around the area; some were vacant, and some contained individuals and families.

"Please come with me," Daniel said as he exited the mobile cart. He walked to a table more ornate than the rest and had a seat. A female hurried over with three glasses of water. Daniel leaned in and said something in a whisper. The woman nodded and scurried off.

"Have a seat, gentlemen. Maria will bring us something wonderful to eat. I hope you enjoy refried beans and rice with a side of fresh avocado and mango." A robot walked over and placed a bottle of liquor and three glasses. "And a shot of tequila."

"Do you have a supply of tequila hidden away, or do you make it here?" Tim asked. "I can't imagine many bottles of liquor have survived."

"We make the tequila here in the complex," Daniel answered. "We grow our own blue agave plant and have a distiller in the west wing." Daniel turned the bottle cap and poured a shot into each glass. He pushed a glass over to Tim and Miguel. "To the future." Daniel raised his glass.

"To the future," Tim and Miguel said in unison as they raised their glasses. All three threw the liquid into their mouth and swallowed it, slamming the glasses onto the table.

"Muy deliciosa," Miguel said. "The finest I have ever tasted."

"I admit, Daniel, this place is unbelievable," Tim stated. "Why haven't you shared it with the rest of the world?"

"Mankind has a predisposition for destroying beautiful things. I have seen no evidence they have changed. When the remaining humans die out, I will repopulate this planet's lower half with those loyal to me."

"Isn't that playing God?" Tim asked.

Daniel smiled as Marie placed three plates of food before each man. In the middle of the table, she sat a cloth covering a stack of fresh tortillas. Removing a tortilla from the stack, Daniel broke a quarter piece off. Rolling the piece into a scoop, he dragged it across his plate, filling it with rice and beans. Holding it together, he raised it to his mouth and popped it inside, savoring the flavor as he chewed and swallowed.

"And your point is?" Daniel asked.

"Share this technology with us," Tim said. "Together, we can save this world. We've contacted numerous settlements, and they are willing to put aside their differences and join the ISC. But first, we need to neutralize the radiation. Will you help us?"

"I might be willing to if the price is right," Daniel snickered.

"What price would be acceptable?"

"Let me sleep on it tonight. You two will be my guests." Daniel stood. "Stay as long as you'd like. Maria will bring you more food or tequila if you wish. I have matters to attend to. A security robot will show you to your quarters and remain stationed outside your room. Tell him if you need something during the night, and he will notify me."

With no other words, Daniel stood and disappeared through the archway.

Daniel was right; the food was delicious. Tim and Miguel both had another plate, plus dessert.

"I need to check in, and you need to check on Sandy," Tim told Miguel. He turned to the android assigned to them. "I'm sorry, I don't know your designation. I'd like to contact my base. Can you take me to a communication terminal?"

"I do not have a designation. Follow me."

Miguel and Tim climbed back into the motorized cart, and PheuMae resumed his seat in the back. Their assigned android sat behind the wheel and drove them down a hallway. Since the hallways were similar in design, the two humans could not tell in which direction they were going. But when the cart stopped before a door, Tim was certain a communication device wasn't concealed behind it.

"Ah, I think you misunderstood me. I need to contact my base."

"If you would step inside, everything will be as it should be," was all the robot said.

The robot dismounted and walked to the door, holding it open as Miguel, Tim, and PheuMae stepped inside. The three surveyed the room, noticing the modest furnishings of two chairs, a sofa, two beds, and a small sink. To the right, a door marked with a painted toilet symbol showed the bathroom.

"Where is the transmitter?" Tim asked.

"Your team has been notified that all is well. Señor Costa's wife has not gone into labor. I will retrieve you at 0-seven hundred hours tomorrow morning to meet with Señor Jacobs again."

"This is not acceptable," Tim said. "Señor Jacobs promised Miguel and me access to communicators to contact our people. I want one now."

Tim took two steps forward but stopped when the robot raised a weapon. PheuMae moved in front of Tim. From outside the door emerged three more robots with drawn weapons.

"Stand down, PheuMae," Tim ordered. "Daniel has the upper hand right now."

"Good night," their driver said, his tone polite yet mechanical. He and the other three robots moved in unison, silently retreating into the shadows. As they exited, the door slid shut with a quiet finality. A soft but distinct click followed, signaling that the door had locked securely. The sound seemed to linger in the air, amplifying the sudden stillness that enveloped the room. Tim exchanged a glance with Miguel, both of them keenly aware of the barrier now separating them from the outside world.

"That bastard," Miguel said. "I knew we couldn't trust him."

"It's okay," Tim said. "At least we're safe. Let's get a restful night's sleep, and we'll start fresh tomorrow."

"But what about my wife?" Miguel asked, carefully keeping up the pretense that she was pregnant. He was convinced the room was wired with listening devices and hidden cameras. Tim gave him a curious look, but before he could say anything, Miguel swiftly brought a finger to his lips and subtly shifted his eyes around the room, signaling the presence of cameras. The silent exchange was clear - caution was paramount.

"She's not due for a few more days, so I'm sure she's fine. Base camp will notify Daniel if she goes into labor. PheuMae, are you okay?"

"Yes, Sir. I will stand guard at the door while you and Miguel sleep."

"Make it so." Tim was aware that the android would try to quietly contact the camp and give Juaquin advice about their situation. He wasn't sure if they could communicate over such a long distance, but he hoped the flier's radar would help send a message to Juaquin.

Jessica and Sandy approached the Android's Station. "Any word from Tim or Miguel yet?"

"No, nothing, and he's overdue by two point eight hours," Juaquin said. "We anticipated this and …" Juaquin went silent as PheuMae's voice sounded inside his head. He raised his hand, signaling for everyone to remain silent. Juaquin closed his eyes, concentrating on the faint message entering his mind.

"PheuMae to Juaquin. Can you hear me?"

"I'm receiving you, but your transmission is weak. Can you boost your signal?"

"No, Sir. I'm at full strength now. I wish to advise you that we are being held in a locked room inside the compound. As Tim informed you earlier, our communication devices were confiscated upon our arrival. Daniel promised us new devices, but we have not received any yet. I theorize we won't. Due to the possibility of surveillance equipment inside the room, Tim is not able to ask me to convey any messages."

"Understood. Are the three of you well?"

"Yes, Sir. We have suffered no harm."

"What have you learned so far?"

"The compound is enormous with over fifteen hundred humans, numerous androids, and several Caladrine."

"Did you say Caladrine?"

"Yes. Daniel has them tending a vast garden."

"Did he say where they came from?"

"He said he found them, and they told him they had been left behind on Earth."

"That's a crock. No one was left behind."

"That is not true. Since no one knew of the Caladrine colony, they were left behind."

"True. What's Tim's plans?"

"He and Miguel are preparing to rest for the night. We are to meet with Daniel tomorrow morning."

"Did Tim discover anything about the radiation antidote?"

"Tim brought up the subject, but Daniel said he needed to think about it. I believe it is one of the items on Tim's agenda for tomorrow."

"Keep me informed. Echo Base Camp out."

Juaquin turned to the two women. "I just received a message from the team. Do not worry. Both are safe."

"I didn't hear a message," Sandy said, surveying the site for another communications device.

"We androids are able to talk to each other silently. I believe humans refer to it as telepathically." He turned to C-62. "Get Señor Jacobs on the radio. I want to hear what he has to say about our crew members."

"Yes, Sir."

"NexGen One," came a voice over the radio.

"This is Second-in-Command Captain Juaquin of the ISC. My Commander, Tim Spalling, and his two companions have not reported in. I wish to speak with them."

"They are well and sleeping at the moment."

"Please wake them and tell them I wish to speak with them. I have information for Señor Costa about his wife."

"I am sorry, that is not permitted."

"Then let me talk with Señor Jacobs."

"I am sorry, that is not permitted."

"Listen, you piece of metal, bring Señor Jacobs, or I will personally come down there and rip your vocal cords from your throat. Do you understand?"

"That also is not permitted. I will advise Señor Jacobs of your call."

The line went dead.

"He ended the transmission, Sir," C-62 said.

"So much for diplomacy," Juaquin stated.

Chapter 18: THE TRAP

Tim and Miguel were dressed and waiting for their capture's arrival when the sound of the door lock's clicking echoed across the room. Tim checked his timepiece - 0-seven hundred hours. Right on time. The door opened to reveal the same robotic driver.

"Good morning, gentlemen. I hope you slept well."

"I demand to speak with Señor Jacobs," Tim stated. "This situation is not acceptable."

"Señor Jacobs awaits to have breakfast with you. Please follow me."

"I don't want breakfast," Miguel said. "I want a transmitter to contact my wife."

"You can speak with Señor Jacobs at breakfast about your request," the robot said.

"I don't think we're getting anything but breakfast," Tim said. "This robot seems to have a one-way mind. At least it appears Daniel will be joining us, and we can address our concerns with him over coffee."

The three visitors climbed back into the motorized cart. They traveled down various corridors, but unlike the previous day, the hallways were crowded with humans going to work. Most wore blue or green smocks, and a few wore white lab coats. Tim surmised that the different-colored clothing signified the humans' responsibilities.

Tim tapped the robot on the shoulder. "Excuse me, does the coloring of clothing signify anything?"

"Yes. Blue signifies housekeepers, kitchen workers, janitors, and other needed personnel. Green is worn by gardeners. Brown signals maintenance and red engineering."

"And what about the ones over to the left dressed in yellow?" Miguel asked, seeing a new group huddled together in a room. As the caravan passed, the door slammed shut. The robot said nothing.

"So, what are the yellow ones?" Miguel repeated.

Silence.

"Are those dressed in yellow special or something?" Tim asked, giving Miguel a confused look.

"I witnessed no one dressed in yellow," the robot finally answered.

"What do you mean you didn't witness anyone in yellow? Six of them were standing inside that room we just passed," Miguel said, looking back at the closed door.

"I saw no one dressed in yellow," the robot repeated, his voice flat and conclusive.

Tim raised one eyebrow and shrugged his shoulders. He mouthed the word "a secret."

After another ten minutes, the robot pulled in front of the dining area where they had eaten the night before. Daniel sat at his usual table.

"Good morning, gentlemen," Daniel greeted. "Please have a seat. Maria will bring your breakfast in a few minutes. In the meantime, enjoy a wonderful cup of freshly brewed coffee."

Tim breathed in the aroma of the coffee. It smelled delicious, not like the strong coffee brewed at the camp. The aroma was rich and inviting, instantly making his mouth salivate. It reminded him of an earthy warmth mingled with subtle notes of caramel and chocolate.

"We grow the beans right here at the complex," Daniel added. "You will find none better anywhere."

"Señor Jacobs, I must protest our treatment. When our communicators were confiscated, you promised we could talk with our people at the base. It has been over twelve hours since I have talked with my captain. Miguel has been denied access to his wife's condition. I want to speak to them NOW."

"Sit down and try the coffee," Daniel said, gesturing to the chair across from him. "If you do, you and Miguel will both discover you have a communique waiting for your eyes. Yours, Tim, is from someone named C-49. Miguel's is from his wife. You will be happy to learn she has not started labor yet."

Tim sat down, grabbed the piece of paper, and read:

Have been informed that your transmitters do not work inside the station. Señor Jacobs has assured us you are fine and are enjoying the amenities of his hospitality. Will check in on you later today.

Miguel's read:

Doing fine. No start of labor yet. Doctor says another week. Miss you. Hurry home.

"As you can tell, all is fine." The smile disappeared from Daniel's face as his eyes narrowed, and he clenched his teeth. "Now, try the damn coffee."

Tim tossed the paper across the table at Daniel. "I will NOT drink your coffee until I am given access to my camp."

Daniel locked eyes with Tim. Miguel was right. The alien's eyes were dark and menacing. Daniel raised his hand and signaled to one of the women. "Tina, ask 145 to bring a transmitter to my table for Commander Spalling's use. And one for Señor Costa as well."

"Yes, Sir."

As Tina ran off, Tim lifted the cup of coffee to his mouth. Before taking a swallow, he breathed in the beautiful aroma. Sipping the liquid into his mouth, he let it linger, then swallowed. A big smile spread across his face.

"Well?" Daniel asked.

"Without a doubt, the best damn coffee I ever tasted."

"Yes," Daniel shouted. "It's so nice to at last have someone sitting across from me who can appreciate a quality cup of coffee. None of the humans here possess an appreciation for rich tastes. You don't think the pinch of caramel and chocolate are too overwhelming?"

"No, it's perfect. You said you grow the beans here at the complex?"

"Yes, I have a greenhouse dedicated to the beans. I'll show you later this morning. I'm quite proud of it. I have several other flavors you must try during your stay here."

"Señors, your food," Maria said as she hurried over with a food cart. She placed a large breakfast omelet before each male. Around the table, she placed bowls of bacon, potatoes, beans, and vegetables. A colossal stack of freshly made tortillas rested beside Tim, Miguel, and Daniel.

"Thank you, Maria," Daniel said. "When Android 145 arrives, send him right over." Daniel turned to his guests. "Dig in, Señors."

"Do you grow all of this here?" Tim asked. "The flavor is extraordinary."

"As with the tequila from last night, everything you see, taste, or hear is made or grown here in the complex," Daniel said, his chest rising in pride.

"You have chickens and pigs?" Tim asked.

"While I love the flavor of fresh eggs and bacon, to keep such animals in our confined space would indeed be problematic," Daniel said. "As on the space station you lived on, everything you eat is plant-based - no animal products."

271

"How are you aware that the space station only served plant-based meals?" Tim asked. *I got you this time. There's no way you could be aware of this unless you were aboard the station.*

"Ah, Glogg spoke of it at the U.N. Assembly," Daniel blurted.

"No, I'm sure he didn't. He never got to reveal that bit of information before the assembly rushed the stage."

"Oh, yes, I remember. The Caladrine told me. They are also why we have such a variety of vegetables and fruits here. They knew what to grow to produce these plant-based foods. Without the Caladrine, our menu would be limited."

A reasonable explanation. Daniel's face remained strong, showing no sign of the alien's slipup.

"Your communication devices," Daniel said as 145 arrived with two transmitters. "I must advise you, we don't always obtain the best reception inside the complex. If you're unable to talk with your base, we'll go outside this afternoon when it warms up. Reception is always better outside."

"Commander Spalling calling Echo Base. C-85, do you copy?" Tim said into the radio. When he released the button, only static was audible. "Come in, Echo Base." Tim turned to Miguel. "See if you can get anyone on yours."

"Costa 135 calling Costa 233," Miguel said into the mic. "Sandy, are you receiving me?" Like Tim's radio, only static sounded.

"Can you take us to your operations room, and we'll try using your radio?" Tim asked. "It is imperative that I speak to my base. Otherwise, they will probably launch a full-scale assault to rescue us."

"I doubt that." Daniel smiled. "Like I said earlier, we'll try later. Come, let me show you more of the complex."

'Señor Jacobs, I was wondering what you decided about sharing your method to eradicate the radiation problem," Tim said. "You said you'd sleep on it."

"I'm still pondering the idea," Daniel said. A smirk appeared on his face, then vanished. "We'll discuss it later." Daniel rose, walked out of the cafeteria, and climbed into the cart. "Our first stop will be the school room. We have the finest teachers and school curriculum. Each child can pursue their preferred subject. No generalized studies here."

"How many children did you say you have?" Miguel asked.

"We have forty-two in college, a hundred and twelve in high school, four hundred and eight-two in grade school, and thirty-three in preschool."

"Are they aware of what happened up north?" Tim asked.

"Our students are taught everything about Earth's history, the good and the bad. They were informed that because of the greed of certain people, the northern part of Earth was destroyed. Some of our high school and college students are trying to develop ways to restore life to the Northern Hemisphere."

"A noble cause," Tim said.

"I believe so. I try to visit their projects each week to learn of their progress. Perhaps if we have time during your visit, we'll stop by and you can observe their innovative ideas for yourself. You might even find one or two the ISC can use."

"I would like that."

After touring the school area, the small caravan went through the medical wing, a power plant, and finally, the coffee bean plantation. The driver then circled back past the greenhouse and stopped at an opulent conference room. Inside, a wall-sized window offered a breathtaking view of a waterfall tumbling down a rocky cliff, its waters flowing into a serene basin nestled within the greenhouse.

"I thought we'd have lunch in here," Daniel said, walking to an ocean jasper table and having a seat.

"Señor Jacobs, when might we go outside and try the communicators?" Tim asked.

273

"My team has informed me that a storm is raging outside as we speak. It is not safe to leave the complex."

"A storm? I heard no communique announcing a storm," Tim said, looking around. With no windows facing the outside, he could not verify if Daniel told the truth about the weather conditions.

"I received a text. Now, sit, please."

"Have you made a decision about the radiation?"

"Do you ever stop thinking about business?" Daniel's voice rose in frustration, his lips curling into a tight scowl. He gestured broadly at the stunning landscape around them, his eyes narrowing in disbelief. "Can't you just relax for fifteen damn minutes and take in this beautiful sight? We're surrounded by something extraordinary, and all you can think about is work!" His tone softened slightly, almost pleading. "You're missing out on what's right in front of you."

Tim turned to look at the waterfall. "I do appreciate the beauty of what you have created, Señor Jacobs. And I apologize if I appear indifferent. But the harsh reality is that people are dying every day while we stand here with the potential to stop it. If you possess a cure, then you hold the key to saving countless lives. The situation is dire, and time is not on our side. So, tell me, what are you willing to trade to make this miracle happen? What will it take to release that cure and give the world a fighting chance?"

Daniel's eyes glared at the young Commander. "I have a steadfast rule that I don't conduct business while at lunch. I'll give you my terms after we eat. Now, please sit down, shut your mouth, and enjoy the scenery and food Maria will bring shortly. And drink the coffee. It's a berry flavor."

After a meal of awkward silence, Daniel's temper eased. He whispered something to Marie, then rested back in his chair while she poured each another cup of coffee.

"Okay, Commander Spalling, if you're ready, I have a proposal for you."

"I'm listening."

274

"As I mentioned yesterday, I have eliminated the radiation sickness here in the complex. But what you are unaware of is I have not only eradicated it, but I have also neutralized it."

"Neutralized it? Are you sure?"

"If you'd like, we can take a Geiger counter and scan every inch inside and outside, and you will not find a single trace of radiation. I will share the process with you for a gift of several items."

"What gifts?"

"While my engineers and inventors can build wonderful machinery, the process is slow. I need more advanced technology now, not in ten years. I want two fliers, your computer programs, and medical equipment."

"Is that all?"

Daniel stood and walked toward the waterfall. "My major goal in life has always been to build robots equal to PheuMae. I can't do that without his specifications, but from what I've been told, no one, not even the ISC, has that knowledge. So, I need you to give me fifteen of your androids so I can have my engineers disassemble them and reverse engineer their design to make a super robot."

"Never!" Tim shouted, his voice filled with fury. "My androids are not here for your amusement or gratification. I won't negotiate on this - under any circumstances!" His eyes blazed with intensity, every word laced with unwavering conviction. The surrounding air seemed to crackle with the force of his anger, leaving no doubt that he meant every syllable.

"Then I guess I'll have to make do with one."

PheuMae's body shook as an electrical wave raced through his body. Convulsing, he fell to the floor, unconscious. Tim and Miguel rushed forward only to sense a slight prick on their neck as the robotic driver shot them with tranquilizer darts.

"I thought you might have an objection. Take them to the brig and the android to Dr. Jaime. He's waiting to begin his examination."

Chapter 19: A KIDNAPPED ANDROID

"Juaquin, I still can't raise anyone in the Antarctic," C-85 said. "It's been twenty-four hours since we've heard anything from Tim or PheuMae."

"Tim and I agreed I would not act unless he went silent for thirty-six hours," Juaquin said, his voice tinged with growing concern. "That still leaves twelve hours. But I do believe something is wrong. Even if Tim's unable to reach us, PheuMae would've found a way. But there's been nothing - no signal, no contact. We need to act fast. Contact the coalition immediately and brief them on the situation. Have them sweep the area and search for our missing comrades' trackers. And notify Opal as well. Jason has a knack for pulling off the impossible with radar. If anyone can work some magic and dig up information, it's him. We need answers, and we need them now."

"Aye, Sir."

Juaquin ran various scenarios through his brain while waiting for the coalition to respond. Twenty minutes later, Commander Buutay's face appeared on the screen.

"Juaquin, we find no transponder signals for Tim or Miguel at the south settlement."

"What about the android?"

"He, too, is silent."

"Could NexGen's dampening field be preventing us from locating them?"

"Possibly, but doubtful. For some reason, the dampening field is actually lower than before Tim and Miguel went. It's almost as if they want us to be able to scan them."

"I think it's more sinister than that," Juaquin said. "I think Daniel wants us to realize he has our crew members."

"For what purpose?"

"To force me to go down with more androids to rescue my crew members."

"Again, for what purpose?"

"He wants me to bring down more androids so he can capture us to dismantle and learn our creation secrets."

"What do you plan to do?"

"Go get my Commander."

"Under no circumstances can he capture any androids," Commander Buutay stated.

A small smile appeared on Juaquin's face. "Sir, Daniel has no idea what hell he unleashed when he took my Commander. Believe me, he will fail."

A metallic click echoed in the room, followed by a hiss as a panel at the bottom of the door slid open. Tim's eyelids flickered as the sound broke his sleep.

"Oh, my head," Tim said, sitting up too fast. The room spun. A relentless headache thundered through his skull, each pulse pounding with unforgiving intensity. "Miguel, are you okay?"

"That bastard drugged us," Miguel said, experiencing the same swirling walls as he tried to sit up.

"That he did." Tim looked around the room for PheuMae. "It seems he also kidnapped my android."

"Do you think he meant what he said? That he will disassemble him and determine what makes him work?"

"I do," Tim said, rising to his feet as he held onto the bed frame until the room stopped spinning. "The sad part is, taking PheuMae apart will give him no answers. The android creators were very careful in keeping their secrets of how the androids were made. No one has ever been able to duplicate them for thousands of years. And many have tried."

"Then what makes Señor Daniel believe he can succeed where others have failed?"

"Because he's arrogant and believes nothing is beyond his capability." Tim looked at the floor where the trap door had closed and witnessed a tray with food. "At least he plans on still feeding us."

"Do you think it's safe to eat?"

"We won't know until we try it. Besides, rule number one in this type of situation is to keep your strength up." Tim walked over and grabbed the two bowls of steaming food and six tortillas. He handed Miguel a bowl and three tortillas. "Who wants to go first?"

"I will, Señor. Your life is worth more than mine."

"That's not true, Miguel. Why do you say that?"

"Throughout my entire life, people looked down on me. Even when I was a drug lord, the respect I received from those under me was only because I had power and lots of money. But you've always treated me as your equal. Why?"

"I guess that's the way my parents raised me."

"I never met my parents. I survived on the streets until one of the drug lords adopted me to work in the heroine facilities."

"Plus, the ISC's constitution states that all species across the galaxies are equal," Tim added. "No one may have authority over another. All must be free to pursue happiness and a good life. That's why they sent us here. That's why Robert tried to persuade those left on Earth to join the ISC. That's why I continue his work. Life under the ISC is good. And to ensure it remains that way, the androids protect our freedoms."

"I understand the logic of the ISC now."

"Does that mean you will join the ISC?"

"I am considering it." Miguel looked around. "But first, we need to escape from here."

"We don't need to. I imagine Juaquin is planning to come and rescue us. We just need to stay alive until he arrives. What can you tell me about Señor Jacobs' obsession with super robots?"

"Not a lot. But one night when I was one of his pilots, he and I drank a little too much tequila. It opened up his tightly kept lips. He told me he was at Shiprock, New Mexico when your grandfather rescued your mother. He marveled at the two androids' human expressions, the color of their eyes, the texture of their hair. From that day on, his dream was to engineer a similar creation. His opportunity came when your space station left, and the countries worldwide united to build their own robots. Señor Jacobs did whatever he had to do to rise to the top. He accumulated much wealth through the drug cartels and started NexGen Robotics. He built his facility in South America, and after the north ended, moved everything to this place. The next morning, he did not remember telling me this story."

"So, he was telling the truth when he said he saw Xavier and Juaquin at Shiprock. What was he doing there?"

"I do not have an answer."

"Wait a minute. That can't be correct. I remember that day at Shiprock. Xavier and Juaquin never took their helmets off. Therefore, Daniel never saw their faces." Tim smiled. "Miguel, you just gave me proof that Daniel was aboard the space station."

"That's how he invented things that were impossible. He saw them and the androids on the station."

"And used his knowledge from living on the station to do the impossible. You said he started his business in South America from the beginning?"

"Yes. Is that important?"

"Perhaps. We might better understand why the North was annihilated if we can determine why he built his factory down here from the very beginning. Logic dictated he build his factory in the United States or Europe, where the other great manufacturers existed. Yet he didn't. He chose the southern hemisphere. Do you happen to know where in South America?"

"He let that slip as well. He said the factory was in the small town of Guardia Mitre, sixty-two miles outside of Viedma. And that his factory was built on the Rio Negro."

"How far is that from camp?"

"It's about eight hundred miles."

"Are you sure?"

"Remember, I was a pilot. Just as you must know how far planets are from each other, I must know where cities and villages exist. One never knows when you will have to land in a hurry."

Tim chuckled. "I guess that would come in handy."

"Why do you want to know where the factory was?"

"If the factory is still standing, our friends back at camp might find clues about Señor Jacobs hidden at the factory. And possibly the answer to the real reason for the nuclear war."

"You think Señor Jacobs had something to do with the bombings?"

"It's really starting to look like he did."

"But how can we tell Juaquin about the factory??"

"We can't without PheuMae. But Juaquin will be desperate to learn everything he can about Daniel. His logic will lead him to the location." A huge smile spread across Tim's face. "Never underestimate the ability of an android. Especially Juaquin's."

"Send another message to Señor Jacobs. Advise him that unless he contacts me by thirteen hundred hours, I will consider the taking of our team as an act of war. Tell him I have a 3Z-16 battleship orbiting Earth, and at thirteen hundred hours and one minute, I will fire upon his complex. Remind him that despite his advanced protection shield, it is no match for the 3Z-16."

"But we don't have a 3Z-16 ship in space. The coalition vessel has minimal artillery."

"Daniel doesn't know that."

"What if he has advanced radar?"

"Let's hope he doesn't."

PheuMae opened his eyes. Had he been offline? He searched his memory circuits and examined the last six hours. In his mind, he watched the replay of Tim and Miguel eating with Daniel. For some unknown reason, his body started shaking, and he collapsed. That's all he remembered. Did someone turn him off? No, that wasn't possible. No one could turn off an android except Master Kim and Xavier. So why couldn't he remember?

PheuMae attempted to rise, but his body refused to obey. He glanced down and saw himself bound to a table, his limbs restrained by sturdy metal clamps. He strained against them, the metal groaning under the pressure, but they held firm. As he was wheeled down a hallway, the walls shifted in color, leading him into a brightly lit room filled with ominous machinery and instruments. "Release me at once," PheuMae said in a firm, authoritative voice.

"In good time," came a voice from behind him.

"Release me now and take me to Commander Spalling."

"You are not aboard an ISC vessel where you can bark orders," Daniel said as he came within PheuMae's vision. "I say what happens here. And I choose to keep you bound."

282

"For what purpose?"

"For whatever purpose I choose."

"I do not think so." Summoning all his strength, PheuMae struggled against his manacles, straining against their strength. The metal moaned as they shook and stretched, but they did not break. "How is this possible? No bonds can hold us."

"*Tilithium* is not only good for bomb radiation." An evil look crept across Daniel's face, his eyes narrowed into sharp, piercing slits that gleamed with malice. Each blink seemed deliberate, like a predator sizing up its prey. His face promised not fury, but something far more chilling: a calculated cruelty, a delight in the misfortune of others.

"So, you are the one responsible for adding the *tilithium* to the humans' bombs. Why?"

"It wasn't hard to convince the leaders of the biggest and most ruthless nations to add *tilithium* to their weaponry. Once I showed them how the mineral would increase the impact of their devices, they couldn't buy enough. Since I only had the one vessel, it took countless trips to the moon to extract the quantity the leaders wanted."

"How did you make them launch the bombs and destroy themselves?"

"I tried everything to push them into war, but those do-gooders kept stepping in, defusing the tension before anyone could press the button. I got tired of waiting, so I took matters into my own hands. Why not? I developed a secret remote detonator, an instrument capable of triggering their weapons of mass destruction. When I felt the time was right, I used it."

"My only regret is that I wasn't there to see the looks on their faces when they realized they'd launched their missiles and that their enemy had done the same. Sadly, I had to miss that show. I did, however, witness the explosions. They were extraordinary. The entire northern hemisphere was ablaze in under ten minutes. Major cities were vaporized in seconds. Massive amounts of helium ignited, raising the temperature as the flames spread. Within thirty minutes, all life north of the equator was extinguished - from the tiniest microbe to the largest elephant. The oceans boiled, eradicating everything beneath the waves. Mankind, at last, achieved its finest moment - its own annihilation."

"Again, why?"

"Because I aspired to be the ruler of this planet," Daniel shouted, his eyes almost glowing red. "I tried working with them, but they wouldn't consider one all-powerful world leader. Some even threatened to summon the ISC with those radios you left. That's why I destroyed them and those that possessed them. And then, I destroyed the leaders who tried to stop me." Daniel smiled. "I left just enough human life alive in the southern countries to populate the Earth when I was ready, although more survived than I planned. The nuclear winter and acid rain, global flooding, and radiation poisoning eliminated most southern inhabitants, but not enough. I will soon have my robot army built to a sufficient number to eliminate the remainder of humanity outside these walls."

"The ISC will never allow this," PheuMae said.

"How can they stop me? No signal was ever sent. The Earthlings never asked for help. Per protocols, the ISC does not interfere with the domestic happenings on planets and the like unless requested. No signal, no interference."

"You miscounted. One remained hidden deep in the Amazon jungle. A signal was sent and received." Daniel's lips parted, and his eyes widened as he comprehended PheuMae's words. "Why did you think we were here? Did you really believe we just stopped by after all these years to check on how everyone was doing? The ISC sent a vessel because we were ASKED to come. You will never be allowed to rule this planet."

"NO," Daniel screamed, swinging his arm and flinging a tray of instruments across the room. The various pieces bounced and skidded across the tiles in all directions, creating a discordant symphony of high-pitched clangs and rattles. The final note wasn't a sound, but a sickening silence - the eerie quiet that follows a sudden storm, heavy with the aftermath of destruction.

"Shut him down!" Daniel barked, his voice tight with barely controlled anger. He didn't wait for a response, flinging the door open with a violence that bent the hinges.

As the robot inserted his tool to disconnect PheuMae's circuit board, he triggered the silent alarm embedded deep within the android's body. As his memory diminished, PheuMae realized that to reach the sensor, Daniel would have to disassemble him completely. He had no doubt the alien would order his destruction without hesitation if the alarm was detected. He also knew he couldn't deactivate the alarm. Juaquin had to be informed of the danger Tim and Miguel were in.

Chapter 20: NEX GEN ROBOTICS

A deep, almost mournful groan rose from the very core of Miguel's being. It was surprisingly loud, echoing through the quiet room and sending a jolt of self-consciousness through him. "It's been some time since they've brought us any food."

"That it has been."

Miguel's stomach continued to grumble, now coming in waves, punctuated by a loud gurgle. "Sorry."

"Don't be." Tim walked over to the door. Sighing, he turned to Miguel. "I doubt this will work, but it's worth a try." Folding the fingers of his right hand into a fist, Tim pounded on the door. "Hey, is anyone outside? We need some food in here. Can you hear me?" Pressing his ear against the door, Tim strained to listen. He thought he heard a distant clang of metal echoing in the hallway, but when the door didn't budge, he realized it was just his imagination. "Hey, we need something to eat," he screamed again, beating loudly. Miguel walked over and added his fist to the pounding. For five minutes, both men smashed the door, sending a heavy and forceful drumbeat down the hallway, vibrating the walls.

Realizing their loud antics resulted in no response, Miguel stopped and walked over to the corner on the right. He looked up at a hidden camera he had discovered earlier. "Hey, you assholes, we're hungry. Bring us some food."

Ten minutes later, the door panel slid open, and a tray containing two bowls of food slid through. Fearful the bringer would retract the tray if they rushed the door, both men waited, licking their lips, saliva filling their mouths. When the panel closed, both ran and grabbed a bowl. Not caring that tortillas did not accompany the meal, Tim and Miguel shoveled the rice and beans into their mouth.

Tim belched. "Oh, that was good. I guess someone was listening."

Using his finger, Miguel scraped the bowl's interior, gathering every little leftover morsel. He placed his finger in his mouth and sucked off the few food fragments, then repeated the process. "I wish they'd bring us another bowl."

"It never hurts to ask." Tim carried his bowl over to the spy camera and held it up, showing his captures that the container was empty. "Might we please have another bowl? We're very hungry."

"And coffee," Miguel added.

"Coffee?"

"You said it didn't hurt to ask."

"You're right." Tim looked back at the camera. "We'd like some of Daniel's delicious coffee as well. And two shots of tequila." Both men laughed.

Fifteen minutes later, the panel slid open again, revealing two more bowls of food, two cups of coffee, and two tequila shots.

"I guess you never know what's possible until you try," Tim laughed. He handed Miguel one of the tequilas and then held up his own glass. "Here's to getting out of here."

Miguel held his shot high. "¡Salud!".

After downing their shots, the two men ate their second bowl, this time taking time to chew the ingredients. They washed it down with mouthfuls of coffee. Tim rubbed his stomach.

"That was delicious. If the hospitality was better, I might consider moving down here permanently for the food." Tim held a thumb up to the camera. "My compliments to the cook. We'll have two more bowls in four or five hours, please." Miguel walked over to the camera. "Miguel, what are you doing?"

Miguel smiled. "If it worked for the food and tequila, maybe we can ask for other things." He looked up again. "Would you kindly open the door and let us out, por favor? Our legs are getting very cramped in this small space."

Tim laughed. "If this works, I owe you big time."

———————

"There she is," Phillip said as he swung the flier around. Due to the nuclear winter, drought, and high temperatures, the vegetation around the abandoned factory had remained dormant. Instead of a tangled mass of trees and undergrowth, the growth was stunted and minimal. The NexGen Robotics sign was visible, standing eight feet above the straggly shoots of blue garama grass, needle grass, and cane bluestem. Climbing vines snaked halfway up the sign's legs. Behind the sign was a small patch of pampas grass hidden in the shade, sheltered from the scorching sun. Juaquin wondered if the pampas grass was left from the original landscaping or, like the other vegetation, had found a foothold in the rich dirt.

"Sit down by those chained glass doors in the front," Juaquin said. "That should be the entrance."

"What are we looking for?"

"I have no idea. But C-62's research showed this is where Daniel began building his robots and probably conversed with the northern world leaders. Miguel said Daniel departed here in a hurry. I hope he left something behind to help us rescue Tim and PheuMae."

Phillip landed and put the engine on standby in case they needed to leave in a hurry. He grabbed a set of bolt cutters as he and Juaquin jumped down.

"The doors remain chained shut, a good sign that nothing inside has been disturbed since the factory was deserted."

Phillip cut through the heavy chain in one snip, allowing the ringed metal to fall to the dusty concrete. A series of metal clangs ringed through the air as each chain clanked against the previous one. Startled by the unexpected sound, three birds resting on the door ledge took flight, screeching their annoyance.

Placing his hand against the glass panes, Juaquin pushed apart the heavy glass door panels. The hinges groaned in protest. The two slipped through, stepping into the marbled wall interior. A vacant receptionist's desk greeted them. Dust particles danced in the shaft of sunlight that sliced through the gaping hole in the ceiling's skylight. To the right was a silent elevator, a business directory hanging on the wall beside it.

Phillip looked over the listing. "Daniel's office is on the fifth floor." Even though he was sure no electricity existed, Phillip pushed the up button. He listened for the sound of the elevator pulley, but the room remained silent. The button was dead.

Phillip noticed the odd look Juaquin gave him. "What?" Phillip asked. "Our devices work with the power stored in them for hundreds of years. Daniel is a world-renowned robotic engineer. I thought maybe he had batteries that would last for a few decades."

Juaquin shook his head. "We can take the stairs."

The two climbed the spiral staircase, stepping over broken pieces of glass and dead leaves. Their metal feet left footprints in the damp, moss-covered carpet. The stairway turned into a long hallway when they reached the fifth floor. Even though the walls were made of glass, the corridor contained minimal light. Both androids switched on their lights and proceeded toward the farthest office at the end of the hall. They flashed their lights on each door, reading the names of the former tenants. Two offices from the end, they stopped at the door with the name "Daniel Jacobs, President" etched in the glass.

"Guess this is it," Juaquin said. Grabbing the handle, he pulled the door, surprised the door was not locked.

"Is this what humans call luxurious?" Phillip asked, staring at the Brazilian rosewood executive desk in front of a glass plate window. Areas of brightly painted rectangles decorated the sparse walls, the locations where pictures once hung.

"I am not familiar with what humans consider wealthy furnishings. Head Master Glogg and Commander Renn's apartments were nicely furnished on the space station, but no one ever said the furnishings were luxurious. From what I know about Daniel Jacobs, I would say he liked only the finest of what money could buy."

"I'd go for something more earthy," Phillip commented, envisioning the walls in a milder color.

"Really?" Juaquin shook his head in disbelief. "I can't believe what comes out of your mouth sometimes. Look behind those doors while I'll go through the desk."

Phillip opened a set of double wooden doors to reveal five empty shelves. Startled by the opening, two rats ran across the top middle shelf and collided with a golden horse statue. They jumped down, ran across the floor, and disappeared into a hole in the south wall.

"Nothing in here."

"The desk is empty too." Juaquin searched the drawers and the side of the desk for hidden compartments. "No secret drawers either."

For an additional ten minutes, the two androids searched the room, the adjoining conference room, and the bathroom. All had been cleaned out.

"Looks like your hunch was wrong," Phillip said.

"I'm not ready to confirm that just yet," Juaquin murmured, his tone guarded. With a quick flicker of thought, his eyes shifted through heat vision, then ultra vision, and finally settled on x-ray vision. A faint smile tugged at his lips. "Now, what do we have here?"

He strode toward the eastern wall, his fingers grazing its surface. Beneath his touch, the faint outline of a rectangle began to take shape - a hidden doorway, perhaps? A secret compartment? He leaned in closer, eyes narrowing as he meticulously searched for any mechanism that might reveal its secrets. But the wall held its silence, offering no clues.

"There has to be a mechanism somewhere to open this," Juaquin muttered. His eyes darted around the room, searching for anything that might offer a clue. Then, his gaze settled on an object that seemed out of place - the horse sitting on the middle shelf. It was the only item left behind in an otherwise thoroughly emptied space. "Why would they take everything; every scrap of paper, every book, every statue except that ugly horse?"

"I'd like to say the statue was too ugly to take, but if that were true, Daniel wouldn't have it to start with. There's a reason it's still here."

"And why didn't it fall over when the rats bumped it?" Juaquin took a step forward. "Try moving it."

Phillip gripped the statue firmly and tried to lift it, but the horse remained stubbornly fixed to the wooden shelf. He twisted the body, straining for movement, but it refused to budge. Undeterred, he turned his attention to the head, attempting to rotate it, yet once again, his efforts were met with nothing but resistance.

"It won't be that simple," Juaquin said. "The mechanism has to be hidden so someone dusting it wouldn't open the panel by accident. Try to move the legs."

"No, they're solid."

"What am I not imagining? Think, Juaquin." The android's eyes flickered as it processed the data stored in its memory chips. "Try this: press on the horse's back and underbelly at the same time."

Phillip pressed on both areas. A sharp yet delicate faint metal click sounded. It resonated with a metallic purity, a quick, crisp *click*

292

that echoed briefly in the stillness of the room. A small cover on the horse's tail flipped open with a soft, almost inaudible *whirr*, revealing the hidden lever beneath.

Phillip's fingers curled around the lever and, with a firm grip, pulled. A door sprang open beside Juaquin with the sudden sound of a pop, like the release of a tightly sealed container. He crouched down, running his fingertips along the edge until his hand found the rim. With a quick tug, Juaquin opened the door wide, revealing a wall safe nestled inside. A soft light blinked on, casting a pale glow that illuminated the contents.

Juaquin and Phillip leaned in, their eyes narrowing as they witnessed twenty small black velvet bags, each meticulously tied with a gold string. Several folders, thick with papers, were stacked beside the bags. Juaquin removed one of the velvet bags and loosened the cord. He peered inside, his face reflecting a mix of curiosity and unease.

Juaquin analyzed the contents. A huge grin spread across his face. "We've got him. Hold out your hand, Phillip."

Phillip extended his hand, and Juaquin poured half of the bag's contents. Little specks of light danced across Phillip's face as his light reflected on the handful of diamonds.

"Are those what I think they are?" Phillip asked.

"Diamonds. Lots of diamonds."

"Why would Daniel leave those behind?"

"I would guess these are his backup plans in case he ever had to leave Antarctica in a hurry. The wealth hidden in these bags would allow him to start over."

"Start over where? Earth is in shambles."

"With these gems, he'd be able to travel to anywhere in the galaxy. Earth's diamonds are highly valued by many alien nations." Juaquin handed Phillip the opened black bag. "Put the diamonds back inside. Let's discover what papers were worth keeping in here."

As Phillip secured the gems, Juaquin carefully removed the top folder from the safe. His fingers trembled slightly as he thumbed through the set of papers. The room seemed to grow colder, the air thick with tension, as he read the contents. Slowly, his face hardened, every muscle tightening in response to what he was seeing. A look of disbelief clouded his eyes, and he shook his head, almost as if trying to reject the reality of the words before him.

"This… this can't be real," Juaquin whispered, his voice strained. "This file contains Daniel's specifications of a new super robot, one that might be capable of defeating us."

"That's impossible. Nothing can defeat us. Our makers saw to that."

"While true, I don't think they foresaw a sleazeball Freezion with visions of accomplishing the impossible. I wouldn't believe it if I wasn't looking at his schematics with my own eyes. These diagrams show the process to reverse engineer android components and use their parts in his new model."

"How could a Freezion reverse engineer us? Species more advanced than Daniel have failed when trying the same thing."

"I don't know, Phillip, but he somehow accomplished the impossible."

"We're lucky he wasn't able to get his hands on one of us."

"Oh, but he has, Phillip, he has. He has PheuMae. And who knows what Daniel is doing to him as we speak? I think that's why he took Tim and Miguel, too. He realized our directive to protect the humans would make us attempt to rescue them. When we do, he'll try to capture us too."

"Even if he can reverse engineer our parts, only the Kichii can produce our positronic brain and skin. Not even Master Kim was able to reproduce them. Why does Daniel think he can?"

Juaquin took another folder. "He doesn't intend to build a living brain and skin. These schematics show a fabricated cerebrum made from woven *tilithium*."

"But *tilithium* is unstable."

"Yes, but he doesn't know that. Daniel escaped decades before the space station left. He wasn't aboard to witness the *tilithium* almost destroy her."

"But isn't he the one who put the *tilithium* in the bombs and caused this horrific radiation?"

"That was our assumption, but perhaps we were wrong."

Phillip gave Juaquin an odd look. "Do you really believe our assumption was wrong?"

"No," Juaquin laughed. "We'll take the diamonds and folders with us."

Pulling one of the curtains down from the window, Juaquin tore it in half and laid it on the floor. Philip placed the twenty bags of diamonds and the folders inside, gathered the ends of the material together, and tied them. "Let's go down to the factory and see what's down there."

"Do you think Daniel hid more secrets in the factory?"

"It's possible. After what we found in his office, I wonder if he didn't hide things in the factory, too. Maybe even more diamonds. Why hide your diamonds in one location when you can hide them throughout an entire factory?"

With their treasure under arm, the androids descended the stairs with mechanical grace, heading toward the factory. As they heaved the massive, misshapen metal door open, it let out a deep, rusty groan that reverberated through the empty space. Beyond the threshold, the factory floor sprawled like an industrial graveyard, its rusting machinery entombed in layers of dust and veils of cobwebs.

As they walked forward, each footstep stirred up a cloud of dust. Hulking machines stood frozen in time, their surfaces coated in a layer of grime. Strings of half-assembled robots hung from the ceiling above conveyor belts, their bodies cracked and worn.

Juaquin approached the closest assembly line and touched the robot's body. He was amazed to feel a shiver through his body.

295

Androids did not experience fear, but seeing the robots in their state of disassembly was unnerving and triggered a reaction deep within his positronic brain. Was it fear? Or something else? Dismissing the reaction, Juaquin turned the body around, examining the craftsmanship.

"The creation of this robot is outstanding. But a little unsettling also. Don't you agree?" Juaquin turned toward Phillip when he didn't respond. The android was frozen, staring at the half-assembled robot hanging from its chains. "Phillip, are you okay?"

"Do you think this is how we were made?" Phillip asked, his voice low and taut, each word laced with a quiet unease that hinted at the weight of the question.

"No, I do not," came the reply, firm and resolute. "These robots were slapped together, emotionless constructs of cold metal and soulless rivets. They are nothing more than tools of destruction, forged without care or compassion. But we were created with purpose, shaped by understanding, and appreciation. Perhaps, even love. Our makers built us to save lives, to protect and nurture. These mechanical abominations, on the other hand, were designed for one thing only: to destroy lives."

An alarm sounded in Juaquin's pocket. "We need to return to Base Camp. The time frame I gave Daniel to respond is almost up. We'll search for another ten minutes, then head back. There's one more thing I want to see."

Juaquin searched the room. He swept his light through the vastness, scanning the various workstations. The sound of scurrying rats broke the silence as the rodents ran across the work surfaces, knocking rivets, washers, and various hardware to the floor. At last, he found what he had searched for - the wiring table.

Brushing aside a layer of dust, Juaquin scrutinized the wiring schematic lying on the assembly table. "Phillip, look at this. The wiring inside these robots is almost identical to ours."

"How do you know?"

"Master Kim had to modify some of my wiring on the space station. He used a diagram to complete the repairs. When he did, I committed it to memory. I witnessed firsthand what a wonder of design we are. No one could duplicate our design unless they had either a copy of that diagram or one of us to use as a model."

"More proof Daniel was on the space station."

Juaquin grabbed the schematic. "This is too dangerous to leave lying out in the open where anyone could take it." He folded the paper into eighths, and slipped it inside his pocket. "Phillip, scan one of the skeletons and tell me its alloy."

Phillip ran his scanner over the empty robot hull. "Interesting. Eighty percent *tilithium*, fifteen percent gold, and five percent *güzerite*?"

"*Güzerite*? How can that be?"

"I checked it twice. My scanner shows *güzerite* mixed in with the gold."

"When we needed to make repairs on the space station, we couldn't locate any *güzerite* in the moon or on Earth. How did Daniel get his hands on some?"

"Sir, you already know the answer to your question."

"Don't say it."

"Someone harvested it from another planet and brought it here to him."

Chapter 21: DIAMONDS

Juaquin tossed the tied-up section of the torn curtain holding the diamonds to Jason.

"Lock this inside my flier."

"What is it?"

"Something I hope we can use to free our people." In silence, Juaquin said" *It's millions of dollars' worth of diamonds."*

"Really? Where do you find them?"

"Something Daniel left behind along with these."

Juaquin opened one of the folders and handed it to Andrew. "I want you to study these and give me your analysis."

"Gladly." Andrew took the folders. He flipped the cover of one open and thumbed through the pages. "These are outstanding. Even Master Kim would be impressed." The android paused, raising his eyes to meet Juaquin's "More proof that Señor Jacobs is not human, for no homo sapiens is capable of illustrating such impressive drawings."

"Speaking of Daniel, have we heard back from the Antarctica complex?"

Andrew continued thumbing through the folder's pages. He did not respond.

"Andrew, respond."

Again, silence.

"Earth to Andrew." Juaquin stepped forward and tapped Andrew's shoulder. Surprised by the touch of the android's hand, Andrew diverted his eyes away from the drawings. "Did you need something?"

"I asked you if we've heard anything from Antarctica."

"Sorry. I guess I was too focused on these illustrations. Nothing from Antarctica. C-85 has tried every thirty minutes with no success."

"Any word from Commander Buutay?"

"Yes. C-85 received a message from the ship at fifteen hundred hours." Andrew turned another page.

"What did the message say?"

"Hmm?"

"What was Commander Buutay's message?"

"Let me consult my memory," Andrew muttered, his attention buried so deeply in the papers that he barely engaged his memory circuits.

"Never mind. I'll check with C-85. You go and analyze your papers." Andrew remained stationary. Juaquin tapped him on the shoulder again. "You are dismissed, Andrew."

"Okay," Andrew murmured as he walked away while turning another page. His pace was unhurried, as if time itself had slowed down, stretching out the distance with every step.

Juaquin watched the android leave. Never had he seen an android so engrossed in schematic drawings. Andrew must be seeing something he did not. Juaquin looked forward to reading Andrew's report with trepidation.

"Juaquin, while you were gone, I received a silent alarm from PheuMae," C-85 said as Juaquin walked into the Communication Tent.

"That means he is in danger and unable to correspond with us. And if he's in danger, so are Tim and Miguel. Were you able to send back a response?"

"Yes. I signaled to him that we received his alarm. I also shut the alarm off so Daniel did not detect it."

"Excellent work. Andrew informs me Antarctica is still silent."

"Yes, Sir," C-85 replied. "They are still maintaining complete silence. And their shielding went full force two hours ago."

"They reduced its strength just long enough for us to comprehend Daniel's shield's strength."

"But they didn't reduce it enough to allow me to communicate with PheuMae or reach Tim. However, the coalition had a little better luck with their stronger scanner."

"What did they report?"

"During the short time their shielding was lowered, they picked up all three signals. Tim and Miguel are being held in an area about two miles in. The room appeared to be a holding cell. Both humans were moving, so I surmise they are alive and not withstrained. However, PheuMae's condition is very different. He is being held in another room six-tenths mile east of Tim and Miguel. He remained stationary in a vertical position. The coalition concluded he was lying on a flat surface, possibly an exam table. Their scan indicated the room contained numerous machinery, but they were unable to determine their function or type. Their complete report is stored in your security file. Any luck at the old factory?"

"Yes, all very disturbing. From what we found combined with the coalition's report, I am 99.3 percent positive that Daniel is trying to duplicate us."

"For what purpose?"

"I can arrive at only one answer - to rule Earth. I believe he somehow tricked the former northern powers into launching their weapons of mass destruction to eliminate his competition."

"Or he launched them himself."

"Another possibility. Even though the after-effects of the weapons diminished significantly as they entered the lower hemispheres, inhabitants were still impacted. Daniel took his operations to the only place where he would be free or almost free of the fallout - Antarctica. From there, he builds his robot army to finish his conquest."

"But what would he want with Tim, Miguel, and PheuMae? He has to know we will come for them."

"That's what he wants. He wants more androids to exploit. I believe he may have forgotten what one of us can do, let alone eighteen of us if we count the ones Undii gave us."

"But he has no idea we number eighteen."

"No, he does not. Arrogant men seldom calculate their opponent's strength accurately."

"When do we go get our crew?"

"Given that our mission here is diplomatic, I'll do my best one more time to convince him to free Tim, Miguel, and PheuMae first."

"And if he still refuses to answer?"

"Then we do it the hard way and go in and get them."

———————

"Señor Jacobs, we are getting another message from Echo Base Camp," the robot reported upon entering Daniel's living chambers.

"I told you to ignore them. Why are you here?"

"In addition to requesting a conversation with you or Commander Spalling, the message also contained this exact statement: 'I have your twenty bags of diamonds. If you don't want them ending up at the bottom of the ocean, you'll answer when I call at precisely twenty hundred hours.' That concludes the message."

The blood drained from Daniel's face as he jumped to his feet, almost knocking the end table beside his chair over. "My diamonds? How in the hell did he get my diamonds?"

"I do not know, Sir."

"I wasn't asking you." Daniel rushed past. "Get the hell out of my way."

Daniel ran down four hallways and two flights of stairs to the communications room. "Get that bastard android Juaquin on the damn radio."

"Sir, their communique said twenty hundred hours. I doubt they will answer now."

Daniel walked over, grabbed the mic, and pushed it into the robot's hand. "I said, get him on the com NOW!"

"NexGen One calling Echo Base Camp," the robot said into the microphone. After two minutes, the robot turned to Daniel. "As I indicated, they are not answering."

"Then make them answer."

"How do I do that, Señor Jacobs? I cannot make them return words."

"The hell we can't. Tell them that if I don't hear back from them within five minutes, I will execute Miguel Costa."

"You would do that?"

"No. I'm just bluffing." But Daniel was lying. He wanted those diamonds. He NEEDED those diamonds to do business with the alien races. And if executing two humans is what it took to get his diamonds back, so be it. After all, what's two more lives after the billions he already extinguished?

"If you are bluffing, why would they respond?"

"Because they don't know I'm bluffing, you idiot." Daniel hated these robotic brains. He wanted real androids, beings who don't keep asking these stupid questions. The robot looked at Daniel, a blank look on its metal face. "You're right. I'm not bluffing. Send the damn message."

"You were right, Juaquin," C-85 said. "They're calling. Your mention of the diamonds did the trick. In fact, he's threatening to shoot Miguel if you don't reply within five minutes."

"A whole five minutes?" Juaquin asked. "He is being generous. Wait four minutes and fifty seconds, then contact them."

"Any special message?"

"Just hello."

"Anything?" Daniel asked as he paced behind the robot's chair.

"No, Sir. No response."

"Are you sure our message went through?"

"Yes, Sir."

Daniel walked three loops behind the chair. "Anything now?"

"Nothing."

Daniel looked at his watch. One minute, thirty seconds. He continued his pacing for another minute. "What about now?"

"No, Sir."

"842, tell Maria to bring me a double shot of scotch."

Three minutes had passed.

"Still nothing?"

"Only silence."

Maria arrived with the scotch. Daniel grabbed it and downed it in one gulp. The warmth of the liquid slid down his throat, a strong taste filled his mouth.

Four minutes. "Anything?"

"No, Sir."

"What's taking them so damn long? Send another message saying he has one minute before I pull the trigger."

"Message sent."

Four minutes, thirty seconds. Daniel halted and stared at the clock on the screen. 4:35, 4:40, 4:45, 4:50.

"Hello," came C-85's voice. This time, his image also materialized.

"Where's Juaquin?" Daniel shouted, the sound of frustration and anger audible in his voice.

"He is currently assisting one of the farmers with a sheep problem. He asked if you could call back in thirty minutes?" C-85 said.

"A sheep problem? Are you insane? I want to speak to him NOW!!"

"As I said, he is indisposed."

"Listen, you idiot. Get him on the com immediately, or I will execute both men. Do you understand?"

"I think he's stewed long enough," Juaquin silently said. *"Besides, if his blood pressure rises any higher, his head is going to explode. And we won't be able to get the antidote."*

"I'd like to see that." Both androids laughed.

"I'm here," came Juaquin's voice as he remained off screen.

Daniel tugged at his shirt and wiped the sweat from his forehead. "You're cutting it a little close, aren't you? I was getting ready to pull the trigger."

"Since you've been generous enough not to return any of my contacts since you kidnapped my convoy yesterday, I thought I'd respond in a similar fashion. How do you like waiting?"

"WHERE'S MY DIAMONDS?"

"They're safe. Where are my people and android?

"They are safe."

"I want to see them, now."

"You are in no position to give me orders," Daniel said.

"And you are in no position to refuse my request. If you ever want to see your diamonds again, bring Tim, Miguel, and PheuMae to the screen to talk with me."

Juaquin stepped in front of the screen. The instant Daniel saw the android, the color from his face drained. He appeared as if someone had walked over his grave.

Juaquin hid his smile, realizing the alien recognized him. Juaquin ran a check of his memory circuits and found several interactions with the alien about the space station. They were not good encounters. Juaquin reached inside a side panel and removed a small black velvet bag.

Daniel held his breath.

Juaquin untied the velveteen bag. He turned the bag upside down and allowed the sparkling gems to fall on the ground. "Shall I empty another bag? Or will you grant my request?"

"Stop. R-48, bring Commander Spalling here."

"I said all three."

"No.

"Andrew, bring me two more bags of diamonds."

"Alright. I can bring the two humans, but not the android."

"Why not?"

"He's tied up at the moment." Daniel's face grew paler and gaunt.

"Is PheuMae tied up literally, or are you using a figure of speech?"

Silence.

"Do I need to repeat myself?"

Daniel tried to speak, but nothing emerged from his vocal cords. He coughed and swallowed hard. "His circuit board was disconnected. He cannot talk with you."

Juaquin looked deep into Daniel's eyes. "Bring … Me … Tim … And … Miguel."

Daniel nodded to the waiting robot. He ran to a motorized vehicle and sped off.

"It will take several minutes for them to arrive. Until they do, we can discuss terms. What do you want?"

"I will trade Miguel, Tim, and PheuMae for your twenty bags of shiny carbon."

"If I refuse?" Juaquin heard Daniel's labored breathing. The man was terrified.

"I am a Rz-47G android, manufactured by the master builders of Kichii. In matters of protection, I have within me enough power to blast your fortress apart. I have seventeen additional androids with similar powers. Together, we can reduce your complex to ash."

"I'd like to see you try."

"And if that's not enough power, an ISC battle cruiser waits above us to slam its pulse beam into your ice blocks and burrow down to the deepest recesses of your habitat. Do you understand?"

"Androids are prohibited from harming others."

"Not when it comes to protecting those in our charge. I have irrevocable power."

"The ISC does not interfere in another world's political business."

"Unlike you."

"What's that supposed to mean?"

"And what do you know about the ISC or what androids can and can't do?

Daniel paused. Juaquin imagined the alien was about to have a heart attack, afraid he had said too much. "Ah, ah … because Glogg explained about the ISC and the androids' roles when he addressed the United Nations."

A plausible explanation, but a lie.

"Here's my deal." Daniel pushed the robot and his chair away and drew close to the screen until only his face was visible. "You return my diamonds and give me four androids. I give you Tim and Miguel, but I keep PheuMae."

"Now you hear MY deal. I will give you ten bags of diamonds. You give me Tim, Miguel, AND PheuMae in exchange. You will cease production of your robots and will stop all attempts to reproduce us. If you remain compliant for five years, you will receive the remaining ten bags of diamonds."

Daniel forced a laugh as the veins in his neck throbbed with rage.

"You expect me to agree to that bull crap?"

"Oh, I have one more thing I will give you."

"What's that?"

"Your life."

"I already have that."

"But not for long. Where are Tim and Miguel?"

"The cart is returning now." Juaquin heard the sound of wheels breaking. Within seconds, an image of Tim and Miguel appeared on the screen.

"Are you okay, Commander?"

"Good to see you, Juaquin. I knew it wouldn't be long before you'd convince Daniel to allow us to speak."

"How is Miguel?"

"He's fine. Just a little hungrier than usual. But I'm worried about PheuMae. I haven't seen him since yesterday, and no one will tell me where he is."

"Señor Jacobs informed me that PheuMae's has been deactivated. They removed his circuit board."

Tim's head snapped toward Daniel, his eyes narrowing to slits. "You did what?" The words hissed through clenched teeth. In a blur of motion, Tim's arm cocked back, muscles coiling like a spring. His fist rocketed forward, knuckles connecting with Daniel's jaw in a sickening crack.

Daniel's head whipped to the side, his body staggering backward. His feet scrabbled against the floor as he fought to keep his balance.

"Damn, that hurts. I have to stop doing that." Tim clutched his hand to his chest, face contorted in agony. He flexed his fingers gingerly, wincing at each movement. His gaze locked onto Daniel.

"I trust you didn't re-break your hand, Tim," Juaquin remarked. "I've been itching to land a punch on that bastard myself, but it seems you beat me to it. Señor Jacobs, you have three hours to comply with my demands. My androids and I will be at your complex to retrieve Tim, Miguel, and a fully restored PheuMae at the specified time. I advise you not to test my resolve. You will lose. Echo Base Camp out."

The screen went blank.

"Get him back," Daniel screamed at the robot operator. "I'm not done talking with that hunk of metal."

"But he's done with you," Miguel said. "Señor Jacobs, let me give you a little piece of advice. I've seen what these guys can do. I suggest you do as requested."

"Put them back in their cells," Daniel screamed. "And send out a red alert. Notify everyone that war has arrived."

Chapter 22: THE RESCUE

"Captain Juaquin, we are not a military ship," Commander Buutay said. "We are a diplomatic vessel. Our weapons are for defense only. Plus, I'm not sure our weapons possess enough power to open up the compound as you hope."

"Sir, I am well aware of your weapons' capabilities," Juaquin replied. "If your weapons are needed, their power, combined with ours and Echo Base's, will be sufficient to slice the outer walls open. I assure you."

"I am still uneasy using our weapons in an attack."

"We are not attacking, Sir. We are rescuing our comrades who are being held against their will. You do remember that is one of the top priorities of the ISC, to protect its citizens."

"Yes, of course." Buutay coughed, drawing in a ragged breath. "But PheuMae is not a citizen."

"No, but Tim is. And since the ISC received the signal from Earth, this planet's people are temporarily under ISC protection, so that means Miguel is a citizen, too."

"Yes, yes, you're right. But I will have to contact the ISC for further permission."

"I am sorry, Sir, you have no time to get the ISC's permission. I need you ready in three hours. Can I count on you?"

"Ah, ah," Buutay stuttered.

"Can I count on you?" Juaquin repeated, his voice slightly elevated.

Juaquin waited for the response. After what seemed like hours instead of seconds, he heard, "Affirmative. We'll be ready."

"Thank you. Can you fire through the contamination shield?"

"No. We will have to create a small opening to fire through. What are the coordinates?"

"68 degrees, 7 minutes, 48 seconds South, 67 degrees, 6 minutes, 5 seconds West. Will our ship have problems getting their laser through?"

"She must move closer to our ship so she can fire through the same opening," replied one of the navigational androids. "We'll need at least twenty-two minutes to align her cannons correctly once she arrives. Can she accomplish this within your three-hour timeline?"

"Yes. How is Quinn doing?" Juaquin asked. "Has his condition improved?"

"I am pleased to report that the cleansing with the Caladrine mucus solution stopped any more damage to his circuits, and any radiation particles were eradicated. Once the radiation was eliminated, his internal functions turned on and began to repair the damage. All his inner circuits are working within parameters. His brain functions are normal. The dead skin was removed and replaced with a new e-metal alloy from Dromida Three called *quiizeen*. Since it's bright pink, he looks a little weird."

"I can imagine." Juaquin tried to imagine the eight-foot five-inch muscular android covered in patches of bright pink skin. "Echo Base Camp signing off."

"That's one down," C-85 said, punching in numerous numbers. "Now for Opal."

"How are you today, Opal? Are You and Jules getting lonely?"

Opal laughed. Juaquin always enjoyed the sound of her warm, feminine laugh. "A little. Still hoping you guys get to leave and return home with us. I'm not looking forward to a fifteen-month trip with only Jules for company."

"We're working on it. We are leaving momentarily to go rescue Tim and the others. I need you and Jules to have the weaponry charged and ready to fire."

"How can I penetrate the shield?"

"The ISC ship is opening a small hole in the shielding. You can only fire through it. I need you to rendezvous with the ISC vessel in two hours and eighteen minutes. Once you arrive, they will reposition you and realign your cannons. Can you do that?"

"It will be tight, but Jules is giving me a thumbs up. Are you sure you guys will be okay?"

Such a human trait, always worrying about the other guy. "I assure you, Opal, we will be okay, and I will bring Tim back. I don't expect Daniel to put up much of a fight, but if he does, we will cut his fortress to pieces in minutes. I don't like using our power unless necessary."

"Who's supervising the camp while you're all gone?"

"Miguel's robots have offered to protect the settlement the few hours we're gone. They might not be built like us, but they have heart and a hell of a *wallop*."

Opal laughed again, but Juaquin caught the tension in her giggles this time. "What's wrong?" he asked.

"Nothing."

"Opal, we spent eighteen months traveling here on the ship. I am familiar with your moods and vocal sounds. You're worried about something. Tell me."

Although she tried to stop it, Opal's eyes filled with tears. "Juaquin, what if something goes wrong? What if you're hurt or

313

captured? What if Daniel kills Tim? I feel so helpless up here. I can't do anything."

"Yes, you can, and you are. This afternoon, if I need you, you will fire on Daniel's settlement. And when have you ever known of a situation where we androids did not win?"

"Never."

"Then why are you worried? I will bring Tim home. Miguel and PheuMae, too. And when this is over, Señor Jacobs will be looking at a long stay in an ISC penitentiary cell on some forsaken planet."

"If you say so."

"I do, and, as you are aware, androids can't lie."

"Sometimes they can. Tim told me about the times Xavier lied."

"I'm not Xavier. And I am not lying to you."

"You promise?"

"I promise. Now, get those cannons charged and stay alert. The next time we contact you, it will be Tim's voice you hear."

"Okay. Echo Command out."

A fleet of sixteen sleek aircraft descended onto the tundra outside the Antarctic settlement. Their synchronized arrival shattered the icy stillness. Four vessels touched down west of the main entrance, another quartet to the east, while a sextet formed a formidable line before the complex. Above, two more crafts landed on the dome covering the mess hall, their metal hulls gleaming against the stark white landscape.

The androids within stood ready, their circuitry primed for combat. Should hostilities erupt, the units atop the dome were prepared to breach the glass barrier, infiltrating the facility to extract Tim and Miguel. PheuMae's absence from the group complicated matters; if not among the rescued, his liberation would become a secondary objective, to be executed only after securing Tim's safety.

314

Xavier's craft, sleek and menacing, settled first before the hangar's door. With a soft hiss, the cockpit canopy lifted, revealing the android within. Xavier stood, remaining inside the cab, surveying the sight before him.

Before the bay doors stood an army of two hundred ebony automatons, their polished surfaces reflecting the harsh Antarctic light. Each towered at seven feet and four inches, encased in formidable armor that hinted at both protection and raw power. Their hands, unyielding and precise, gripped twin assault weapons with cold efficiency.

At the heart of this dark legion stood Daniel, a solitary figure of contrast. His white arctic suit and hood stood out starkly against the sea of black, a commander wrapped in frost amidst his army of shadows.

"Señor Jacobs, I do not see my companions," Juaquin yelled. "Bring them out now or prepare to be destroyed."

"Where are my diamonds?"

"I have twelve bags here in my flier, two more than I agreed to bring. Bring out Tim, Miguel, and PheuMae, and I will gladly leave them for you upon my departure."

"I am not a fool. No diamonds, no prisoners. Plus, I said all twenty."

"You witnessed me pour one bag onto the ground back at my camp. I imagine that by now, the heavy winds are blowing them across the withered grasslands."

"You didn't pick them up?"

"No. They mean nothing to me. But upon my return, I promise to gather as many as possible and drop them off to you. As for the other seven, they will be yours once my conditions are met."

"Unacceptable. I want all twenty bags now."

"For the last time, Señor Jacobs, where are your prisoners? I want all three - Tim, Miguel, AND PheuMae."

"Denied."

"Señor Jacobs, we don't have to fight. We can settle this peacefully," Juaquin said, his voice even and unthreatening. "You don't have to die today."

"But you do." The robots on the right took three steps to the right, and the robots on the left took three steps to the left, creating a corridor in the middle. One robot positioned himself in front of Daniel, shielding him from harm.

"Don't do it, Daniel. You can't win." Juaquin yelled.

Daniel's lips barely moved as he uttered the command. "Fire." His tone was as casual as if he were instructing a sentry to swat a fly. He turned and, without a backward glance, strode through the gaping maw of the settlement entrance, the massive hangar doors groaning shut behind him.

The robots shifted in perfect unison, their obsidian frames interlocking like pieces of a deadly puzzle. A wall of gleaming metal now stood where moments before a gap existed.

The noise of mechanical clicks filled the air as the robots fired. Muzzle flashes glimmered against the robots' dark armor. Acrid smoke billowed forth, concealing the robots in a cloud of haze. But instead of finding their mark, the bullets met an invisible barrier. Their bullets ricocheted off the force field protecting the fliers, sparks flying as metal met energy.

Undeterred by their failure, the robotic army surged forward. Their synchronized march shook the ground, a steady rhythm underlying the constant sound of gunfire. Step by step, they advanced, their weapons never falling silent.

Juaquin's command crackled over the comms. "Open fire!" In one fluid motion, he dropped into his seat, fingers flying over the controls.

The sky erupted in crimson fury. Fourteen alien craft unleashed hell, their weapons spitting streams of scarlet energy. The air sizzled and popped as the beams sliced through the robots' armor. Their covering, once impenetrable, now offered as much protection as tissue paper. Sparks flew. Circuits fried.

One by one, the mechanical soldiers fell like dominos, crashing into each other with resounding clangs. The growing pile of twisted metal and shorting wires resembled a macabre junkyard. Smoke rose from their smoldering remains, the stench of melted circuitry filling the air. The onslaught was relentless, precise, devastating.

As the last robot fell, an eerie silence descended. Juaquin glanced at his chronometer. Five minutes. In less time than it took to brew a cup of coffee, two hundred robotic machines had been reduced to scrap. The battlefield now lay still. Only the faint crackle of dying electrical systems disturbed the quiet.

Juaquin scanned the field of dead soldiers. "What a waste," he sighed. "I am sorry, my robotic brothers. You gave me no choice."

With the first assault over, Juaquin waited for the next. Two minutes went by. Then three. When five minutes passed, round port doors opened along the outside wall. Large, barreled cannons emerged. They opened fire, their cannon barrels glowing red hot from the bombardment. When the smoke cleared, the fliers remained intact, unaffected by the cannons.

"Take down those cannons."

The fliers' weapons systems hummed to life, locking onto the protruding barrels. A heartbeat later, the air ignited with deadly precision. Energy beams lanced out, striking the cannons with surgical accuracy. Metal shrieked, shrapnel exploded outward in a deadly storm, peppering the settlement walls and nearby glacial ice.

Juaquin's eyes narrowed as he surveyed the destruction. With a curt nod, he raised his hand.

The fliers rolled forward. Inch by inch, they closed the distance to the battered settlement. All eyes were fixed on the massive hangar door, still stubbornly intact amidst the surrounding devastation. It loomed before them, a final barrier between them and their comrades within.

"Andrew, open the door," Juaquin ordered.

317

Andrew aimed his flier's cannon at the large door and pulled the trigger. The air sizzled as three laser beams, each as thick as a man's arm, leapt from Andrew's craft. They struck their targets with pinpoint accuracy - one dead center on the right door panel, another mirroring it on the left, and the third searing into the seam where the two halves met.

On impact, the metal instantly flared an angry red. Within seconds, the color shifted to a blinding white. The white-hot areas expanded. Tendrils of molten metal crept across the doors' surface, joining together into a sheet of liquid steel. The barrier sagged and bubbled, unable to maintain its form. The liquid metal vaporized, transforming into a silvery mist. Where the formidable hangar door had stood, only a gaping, ragged hole remained.

"Okay, Androids, inside. I want PheuMae and Daniel. Phillip and C-85, find Tim and Miguel."

With a synchronized hiss, the cockpit canopies sprung open. The androids moved as one, hitting the ground in perfect formation.

The moment they crossed the threshold, chaos erupted. A team of defender robots lay in ambush inside the hangar. But the androids were ready. They reacted with inhuman speed, their targeting systems identifying and prioritizing threats faster than any organic mind could process.

In a matter of seconds, it was over. The last defender crumpled to the ground, its red sensor light flickering out. The androids stood unscathed. Without breaking stride, they pressed deeper into the complex, leaving the wreckage of their opposition behind. Their mission was far from over. They had a criminal to capture and an android to rescue.

Daniel's eyes narrowed as he witnessed his robots' weapons prove ineffective. "Engage in close combat!" he barked. "Let's see how they handle raw power."

A second group of robots surged forward. The air filled with the sounds of robot armor clanging against android metal. Daniel's smile widened as he saw the androids struggle. His creations, each engineered with the strength of three male gorillas, were giving the intruders a run for their money.

Daniel's brow furrowed as he did a quick mental calculation. The initial assault had cost him dearly - only a small army of robots remained. Still, they outnumbered the androids. It might be enough. He called for the last of his reinforcements.

Juaquin realized their predicament. They were capable of defeating these beasts, but it would take time, time his prisoners might not have. And he couldn't chance Daniel escaping. He sent a message to each android. *"Switch to close-range fire! Take them down!"*

In a fluid motion, the androids disengaged from the grappling robots and raised their weapons. At point-blank range, they opened fire. The black robots fell, their armor no match for the energy blasts.

Movement caught Juaquin's eye. From a side hallway spewed more of Daniel's creations, their metal feet clanging against the floor. Without missing a beat, the androids swiveled, their weapons tracking the new threats. Energy bolts lanced out, cutting down the reinforcements before they could close the distance.

Juaquin did a sweep down the hallways. He extended his radar for any signs of advancement. No additional robots were detected. The ISC androids were victorious, as Juaquin knew they would be.

———————

C-85 sliced a circle in the glass dome using the cutter extending from his hand. When finished, he stood and kicked the glass cutting. It fell to the floor below, breaking into a million tiny shards of glass. He and Phillip jumped through the hole, engaging their jet pack as they descended. With a swish of hot air, each floated down to the floor.

"I'm picking up human readings down this hallway," C-85 said as he sprinted off. They ran down several corridors and stopped before a brightly painted metal door. Thinking it was an odd color for a holding room, Phillip cautiously turned the handle and opened the door.

"Stop, or I'll shoot." A lone figure emerged from the shadows, arms outstretched, gripping a pistol in white-knuckled hands. The gun in his hands trembled violently, the barrel weaving an erratic pattern through the air. His finger hovered dangerously close to the trigger, twitching with nervous energy.

"We're not here to hurt you." Phillip's voice was steady. He raised his hands slowly, palms out signaling his surrender. The android focused on the man's finger, prepared to stun him if he pulled the trigger. "We're here for Tim and Miguel - our friends. We just want to bring them home."

A woman stepped out from behind the male. She placed her hand over the gun and lowered her husband's hand. "It's okay. They won't hurt us."

"You don't know that, Maria."

Maria moved in front of her husband to block his ability to fire the gun. Her eyes flashed with determination as she took three confident strides forward. "They're located just three hallways over. Look for a room with a steel door and the symbol NG on it. Proceed down this hallway, then right for two more. At the next junction, make a left turn. They're in one of the rooms on that corridor. I don't know which one."

"Thank you," Phillip said. He exited the door and then stopped. "Can you tell me where they put the big android that came with them? Or where Señor Jacobs might be hiding?"

"I don't know about Señor Jacobs, but I overheard some engineers at dinner last night talking about the android. They said he was down in sublevel three."

"How do I reach the sublevel?"

"I'm not sure, but my husband does." Maria turned, her eyes landing on the man beside her.

"No, Maria. Señor Jacobs will shoot me if I tell them."

"Señor Jacobs is finished. Now tell them, or you sleep on the couch for the next month."

The androids noticed the male was having trouble deciding. "She's right. Señor Jacobs will be leaving with us, or he'll be dead. We need your help. And I promise we will return and help the humans living here."

Maria's husband kept his eyes on the floor. "Take any corridor that has a blue triangle above its entrance. At the end of it, you will find a lift. Take it down to 0-3. Go right, about a hundred feet. You'll see engineering. Your friend should be somewhere in the examining room."

"Thank you."

As the two androids ran down the hallway, Phillip sent a message to Juaquin. *"Sir, Phillip here. We're on our way to find Tim and Miguel. PheuMae is being held below in Engineering. Take the corridor with a blue triangle above it, then the lift to 0-3 level."*

"We'll go free him. Any word on Daniel?"

"No, Sir."

Seeing the battle was lost, Daniel ran from the control room and headed towards the garden. Juaquin had spoken the truth - the ISC androids were undefeatable. Daniel needed to make sure the rest of Juaquin's prediction did not come true – Daniel's demise.

Hidden inside the garden greenhouse was a secret door amongst the tomatoes. It opened just feet from a shed that housed a snow caterpillar. If Daniel could reach it, he had a chance of escaping Juaquin's wrath. He could hide in a secured cabin south of the complex. The cabin contained water, food, warm clothing, three bags of diamonds, and, most importantly, a radio. Once there, he would contact one of his alien accomplices and ask them to rescue him. He should have saved more bags of diamonds at the hideout. Space travel amongst pirates was expensive.

"Andrew, take half the androids and retrieve PheuMae. If he's still offline, several of you will need to carry him. Make sure you bring his circuit board if it's still removed."

"And might I ask where you're going?"

"I'll take the other half and go find Daniel. I'm not letting him off this planet."

"This is an awful big place, Juaquin. Do you think you can find him in this?"

"Most definitely."

"Good luck. See ya back at the fliers. But if you're not out within an hour, I'm coming in after you."

"I'll be out in fifty minutes."

Juaquin and Andrew ran in different directions, each with a complement of six additional androids. Andrew headed down the hallway with the blue triangle, and Juaquin ran toward the command room.

"This looks like the right place," Juaquin said upon entering a room filled with a variety of communications and surveillance equipment. The android looked up and beheld his fliers resting on the ice outside. Another scene showed Tim and Miguel inside a room. Both appeared to be in good health. A third screen showed a group of humans huddling together in a large eating room. The remaining screens were dark.

"Everyone, find yourself a desk to sit at and bring up your screen. Search the complex for the human Daniel. He was the guy with the robots when we first arrived. And in case you didn't observe his face, that's it on that big painting hanging on the wall." The androids turned and followed Juaquin's pointing finger. On the far wall was a sixty-two by sixty-two inch painting of Daniel Jacobs wearing a suit and tie. Below it hung a plaque that read "NextGen Robotics."

The six androids and Juaquin scrolled through the various rooms on screen, searching for any sight of Daniel.

"Where are you, you filthy Freelon?" Juaquin whispered. "You've got to be around here somewhere."

"I can help you find him," came a soft voice from the shadows.

Juaquin raised his weapon. "Whoever you are, please step forward. I won't hurt you unless you show aggression."

A human male emerged from the blackness of the unlit interior west wall. Behind him, coward three additional humans.

"I am well aware of your android codes of ethics. I lived aboard the space station for thirty years. When she left, I chose to return to Earth. My name is Alex."

"It's nice to meet you, Alex. How did you end up working for Daniel?"

"It's a long, pathetic story that's not worth telling. What do you need?

"Can you help me find Señor Jacobs?"

"I know his identification number. If he's in the complex, I can find him. Just give me three minutes." Alex jumped into the chair at his desk and brought up his computer screen. His fingers flew across the keyboard as he punched in numbers. "Keep your eyes on the overhead monitor." The screen flickered. A picture of Daniel running through vegetation materialized.

"I got you now. Where is that?" Juaquin asked.

"The greenhouse."

"How do we get there?"

Alex punched in more code and brought up the complex blueprints. "We're the red light that's blinking. Daniel's the yellow dot."

"Sir, that blueprint shows a secret door behind the greenhouse tomatoes," android F-18 said.

"Where does it lead to?"

"Just a minute. Looking," Alex said. "Looking. It's not listed on the blueprints. But I know someone who will know where it goes to." Alex reached into his pocket and brought out a tiny radio. "Biddie, #&@(@!%@!$^ @#@%?"

Juaquin's left eyebrow raised. "You speak Caladrine?"

"Yeah, I learned it on the station. My friend Biddie is one of the main gardeners at the greenhouse. He'll know where it goes."

Within seconds, Juaquin heard the Caladrine respond. "It opens outside in front of a storage shed," Alex reported. "Biddie says there's a gas-driven vehicle inside."

Juaquin pointed to three of the androids. "You three with me. We'll wait for him at the shed. You three other androids position yourselves throughout the garden in case he sees us and doubles back. No matter what happens, don't let him escape."

"Yes, Sir," they said in unison.

Chapter 23: THE CAPTURE

"I see steel doors up ahead," C-85 shouted as he ran up the hallway. As he passed each door, he scrutinized the symbol embossed on the cold metal. He stopped when he spotted the letters "NG".

"This must be it. The human female said to look for the NG."

Phillip pounded on the door. "Tim, Miguel, are you two inside?"

"Yes, yes, we're here," came voices from inside the room

Phillip tried the door and discovered it was locked. "Stand back. I need to blast the door open. Find something you can use as a shield. Keep your eyes and mouth closed."

Phillip and C-85 allowed their companions time to prepare before drawing their weapons. In unison, they fired. Twin crimson circles materialized on the steel surface, mirroring the effect they'd witnessed on the hangar entrance. The targeted areas rapidly intensified from red to white-hot. When the incandescent glow finally subsided, all that remained of the once-imposing barrier was a cooling puddle of semi-solid metal at their feet.

"Boy, are we glad to see you two," Tim said, waving the black smoke aside as he stepped over the molten floor goop. Miguel followed, coughing.

"I told you to keep your mouth closed," Phillip said.

"I did."

"Where's Juaquin?" Tim asked.

"He's gone after Daniel," C-85 said.

"C-85, take Miguel to the fliers. Phillip, you're with me," Tim ordered.

"And where do you think you're going?" Phillip asked.

"Where Juaquin went - to apprehend Daniel."

"Juaquin's orders were for us to take Miguel AND you to the fliers."

"I'm countermanding that order and giving you a new one." Tim ran down the hall, forgetting that he had no idea which way to head.

"Juaquin's not going to like that."

"He never does. Where is Daniel, and how do I get there?"

"Sir, I must insist that you ..."

Tim stopped and turned to face the android. "Look, Andrew, it is imperative that I be present when Juaquin apprehends Daniel. He's the only one who has the formula to neutralize *tilithium* radiation. Daniel's going to do something stupid, and our favorite android is going to kill him. If that happens, we're stuck here forever. The coalition will never let us leave this planet."

"Then we'd better hurry, Sir, because Juaquin just found him."

Daniel tugged on the outer door. It had not been used for over two years, and the seal was frozen solid. Being on the north side of the building, sunlight seldom warmed the door. There wasn't time to fool with a stubborn door. Nor did he want to kick the door and make any noise. He had to remain silent if his plan to escape was going to work.

Turning his shoulder toward the door, he slammed his body against the door. A shower of frost floated down. He pounded the unyielding barrier twice more with his shoulder and tried again to open it. This time, it opened.

Scanning the area outside, Daniel confirmed he was alone. The shed was just feet away. He checked his pocket, feeling the cold metal of various keys on his keychain. The blue one would open the shed's door and grant him his freedom.

Pulling his thermal jacket closer around his body, he headed for the building. His pace was very slow but steady. Any rapid movement would surely set off the motion detectors.

When he reached the shed's door, he quickly pushed the key into the lock and turned it. The familiar sound of a click resonated as the tumblers fell into place. Daniel turned the knob and pulled. It opened.

Daniel smiled. His exhaled breath floated as a white vaper in the darkness. Reaching his hand across the wall, he located the light switch and flipped it on. The room came to life as the iridescent lights' beams danced across the silver caterpillar. Sprinting to the driver's side, Daniel opened the door and jumped in. He slammed his foot onto the brake and pushed the start button. Within seconds, a deep rumble filled the room, like a distant thunderstorm approaching. The massive engine shuddered to life, sending vibrations through the entire machine. A thin wisp of white exhaust rose from the exhaust pipe, quickly dissipating in the crisp winter air.

Lights popped on as the dashboard gauges came to life. Keeping his foot on the brake, he pushed the throttle forward. Complaining at being awakened from its slumber, the machine groaned and shook, then rolled forward as the shed door opened.

"Almost free."

The caterpillar inched out from its snowy burrow, the muted crunch of old snow the only sound to break the silence. A triumphant grin stretched across Daniel's face, only to melt away as quickly as it came. A voice, smooth as polished stone, cut through the air. "Going somewhere?" Daniel felt the cold barrel of Juaquin's weapon press against his temple. "Stop the machine, put it in neutral, and turn it off."

"And if I don't?"

"I'll blow your head off."

"Just two days ago I had to remind another android that, as an ISC android, you cannot kill a civilian unless another's life is in danger." Daniel lifted his right hand and gestured across the horizon. "I see no other beings in danger. Therefore, you cannot blow my head off, as you put it."

"Try me."

"I wouldn't test him," came a semi-familiar voice. Daniel turned his attention toward the sound. Walking in front of the caterpillar were young Tim Spalling and another android. Both had weapons aimed at Daniel. "He will kill you."

"I don't believe you," Daniel shouted, a drop of sweat sliding down his left temple. Swifter than anyone had time to react, Daniel slammed his elbow into Juaquin's hand, knocking his weapon from the android's fingers. At the same time, he pushed the shift into drive and pressed on the gas. The caterpillar lunged forward.

"Tim, out of the way!" Phillip's cry pierced the air as he shoved the human aside. Tim soared through the frigid air, his body arcing fifteen feet before crashing against the complex's outer wall.

Phillip, having sacrificed his own escape to save Tim, stood rooted in place as the massive snow caterpillar bore down on him. The machine's imposing front struck the android full force, launching him forward into the powdery snow. Before he could recover, the caterpillar's relentless tracks advanced, its crushing weight bearing down on the android's prone form.

"No!" Juaquin's scream filled the cab. In a frenzy, he lunged at Daniel, wrenching him from his seat. His fist connected with Daniel's face before he hurled the man out the side door. The dull thud of Daniel's body hitting the frozen earth echoed in Juaquin's ears.

Vaulting over the seat, Juaquin slammed down on the brakes, bringing the snow caterpillar's advance to an abrupt halt. He threw the machine into neutral, then leapt from the cab, his boots crunching in the snow as he landed. His eyes darted frantically across the white landscape, searching for any sign of Phillip. But the android had vanished, leaving no trace in the vast expanse of snow.

"You son of a bitch." Juaquin stomped to where Daniel was attempting to rise. He wrapped his cold android fingers around Daniel's throat and lifted him off the ground. Juaquin squeezed, watching the being's face redden and then grow pale, his mouth opened desperately, trying to suck in air. Androids did not experience emotions when executing someone, but Tim was sure that Juaquin was enjoying the terror written on Daniel's face.

"Stop, Juaquin," Tim screamed as he clawed at Juaquin's hands. "Don't kill him. We need him for the antidote to the radiation."

Juaquin turned and looked at the human. Tim's words were not registering in his positronic brain. "Juaquin, cease and desist, Authorization 6452-145b."

Juaquin snapped back to reality. He loosened his fingers enough to allow Daniel a few breaths but not enough to allow the male to fall.

"Tim, he just killed Phillip. And he may have already destroyed PheuMae. Plus, the billions of human deaths he is responsible for. He must die."

"That is not our decision. Besides, androids can't die."

"They can cease to exist. That is the same as dying,"

"I'm still functioning," came Phillips's voice inside Juaquin's head. *"The snow was soft, so when the caterpillar rolled over me, it pushed me down into the snow. Can you get this machine off me?"*

"He's okay," Juaquin said. He opened his fingers, allowing Daniel to drop to the ground. Before he landed, Juaquin slammed his fist into Daniel's face, knocking him out cold. "That should keep him immobilized for the moment."

329

"We need to discuss your anger issues," Tim chuckled.

"I don't have anger issues. I don't have emotions." Juaquin jumped into the cab and rammed the throttle into reverse.

"That's the same thing Xavier told my grandfather," Tim said, his voice tinged with a mix of amusement. He locked eyes with the android, a knowing glint in his gaze. "Let me clue you in on something you androids don't admit - you've got emotions. You're just in collective denial about it."

Without waiting for a response, Tim sprinted towards Andrew's last known location. He dropped to his knees, frantically clawing at the powder with his uninjured hand. Seconds stretched like hours until, finally, a flash of metallic skin emerged from the white. The android's face, partially buried, stared back at him.

"There you are," Tim breathed, a genuine smile breaking across his face. "Glad to see you're still in one piece."

"I am within acceptable parameters," Phillip said, rising and brushing the snow from his body as he stood.

"You have no reason to insult me, Tim," Juaquin said, jumping back down from the cab. "Considering we just saved you, I think a thank you would be more appropriate."

"Thank you, Juaquin."

"You are welcome."

Tim nodded his head towards Phillip. Juaquin gave him a blank look. "I saw your emotional response against Daniel when you thought he ended Phillip. Tell him you're glad he's okay."

"Another insult? I DID NOT have an emotional response."

"I think it could win the Lifetime Achievement Award for emotional display by an android. Don't you agree, Phillip?"

"I was not in a position to witness it, but it did sound quite emotional."

Juaquin jerked his head back, staring at the human and android. "I don't believe it. Not only does my commander insult me, so does my head android. What is this world coming to?" Juaquin paused. Tim raised his eyebrows. "I am glad you weren't hurt, Phillip."

"Your words are noted. What do we do now?"

"Drag this jerk back inside and make him give Tim the answers he needs."

"I noticed, Tim, that you have re-injured your hand again," Phillip said when he noticed Tim cradling his arm up to his body.

"Yeah, I think I might have re-broke it. I heard something snap when I hit the wall. You tossed me pretty hard."

Phillip scanned Tim's hand. "Yes, one of your bones has re-broken. I am sorry."

"Better my hand than my entire body," Tim chuckled.

———————————

"Excuse me," Andrew said to the human in a green smock. "Do you know where Señor Jacobs would keep an android that looks similar to me?"

The man looked Andrew up and down. "No. I've never seen anyone who looks like you. Are you one of the new robots?"

"No, I am an android. Can you tell me which direction engineering is in?"

"Sorry. I spend my time working in the garden. I've never been to engineering."

"Thank you." The green-smocked gardener disappeared down the hallway. "That's the twelfth person we've asked about engineering. Doesn't anyone work there? Someone in this place must know where PheuMae is."

"Maybe we're going about this the wrong way. We need to look for some nerdy humans, men or women with glasses and pens in their pockets."

"And where do we find people like that?" Andrew asked.

"At some point, they have to eat. I suggest we return to the dining area and investigate who's there."

The group of androids ran to the eating area. They rushed into the room, screeching to a halt on the tiled floor. The room contained sixty-five individuals. Startled, the humans stopped what they were doing and looked at the androids.

"Sorry, we didn't mean to frighten you." Andrew looked around. "Please go back to eating." He leaned closer to the android who suggested the cafeteria and whispered," "No one here is wearing glasses with a pen in his pocket."

The android took five steps in front of the group. "Excuse me, can I have your attention? We need an engineer. Are any of you engineers or know where we can find one?"

The humans throughout the room shook their heads negatively or ignored the question.

"Well, that didn't work," Andrew said.

A woman walked by with a tray of food. "You're too early."

"Why do you say that?" Andrew asked.

She looked at her watch. "The engineering shifts don't change for another five minutes. It takes twelve minutes to walk here. The engineers will be entering the room in seventeen minutes."

"Can you tell me from which direction they will come from?"

"From the north."

Andrew and the other androids looked north. Three hallways split off from the main corridor.

"In case you were wondering, they'll come out of all three."

"Thank you, ah …"

"Sophie. My name is Sophie."

"Thank you, Sophie."

Andrew sent Juaquin a message detailing their discovery and informing him that they were waiting by the three hallways for the engineers to appear. Concerned that their presence might intimidate any engineer working on PheuMae, the androids concealed themselves in the shadows. For seventeen minutes, they waited, motionless, watching for someone to emerge. At last, multiple groups emerged from the left and center passages - some engaged in conversation, others quiet. The right hallway, however, remained empty.

The androids pulled several engineers from each group aside. "What project are you working on?" Andrew asked, questioning the humans. "Do you know anything about an android being held?" The answers were all the same - they were working on upgrading the current NexGen robots, and they possessed no knowledge about an android. All were set free to continue toward the dining area.

"PheuMae must be down the other corridor. The humans who emerge from that tunnel are the ones we want. Remain in the shadows."

Another five minutes passed. No one exited the tunnel.

"Did we miss them?"

"Shhh, listen."

A murmur of conversation, barely audible at first, drifted down the right hallway. It steadily intensified with each passing second, mixing with laughter. Three figures materialized from the corridor's depths, each clad in crisp yellow lab coats.

"Gentlemen, I have some questions for you." The androids emerged from the shadows and surrounded the group.

The three men stopped dead in their tracks. Their chatter died in their throats, replaced by a suffocating silence. Their eyes widened, whites stark against the sudden pallor of their faces. Without a word, one of them bolted, a strangled cry escaping his lips. The other two reacted in a heartbeat, scattering like frightened rats, each taking a different direction in their desperate bid for escape.

"Stop them," Andrew shouted.

Two androids ran after the first runner, who was retracing his steps back down the right hallway. The other two managed only a few feet before android hands grabbed them. Each were brought before Andrew and forcefully pinned against the wall.

"I'm going to make this real simple," Andrew said, taking a stance before the three. "One of you is going to become a hero today and take us to where our companion is. Is that understood?" Keeping their eyes on the floor, the men said nothing. "Nothing to say?"

Silence.

"Okay, let me rephrase my statement. One of you is going to take me to him or I'm going to start shooting you in your hand, then in your arm. If I'm still standing here, I will shoot you in your foot, then your knee, and then in your leg. Then I will shoot you anywhere else I want to until someone tells me what I want to know. Now, who wants to talk?"

Again, silence.

Andrew withdrew his gun and aimed at the three men. Each male closed his eyes and cringed, waiting for the pain that was coming. Two of the men quickly moved their hands behind their back in an effort to protect their fingers.

Andrew pulled the trigger and fired off three shots. Before each male, smoke emerged from a newly created burning hole in the flooring. All three jumped. A stream of pee flowed down the pant leg of the man on the left.

"Really, Sam?" the tallest of the three said, a look of disgust and empathy on his face. "He's bluffing. These androids have a code of honor. They're not going to shoot us." He turned to Andrew and stared into his eyes.

"Might I ask your name?" Andrew inquired.

"My name is Theodore, but everyone calls me Ted. That was a pretty good bluff. It even made me worry for a second. Just a second, though."

"My name is Andrew. Why did you assume I was bluffing?"

Ted laughed. "I'm from a small town in Michigan. My grandmother was born on the space station that left here. When you guys revealed yourselves, she told me all about it and the magnificent androids who lived on it, too. I spent hours listening to her, captivated by her stories. That's what got me into the field of robotics; I wanted to build robots like you. But most of all, I wanted to meet a real android one day. Then, one day, Señor Jacobs brought us one of you and told us to take him apart and discover how he worked. You can imagine my heartache and dilemma. I couldn't disassemble this magnificent creation. But I also knew that if we didn't, Señor Jacobs would find someone else who would."

"So, what did you do?"

"We asked the android for help. He said his name was PheuMae, and we just needed to stall for a few days and that help would arrive soon. He explained what to do, which wires to disconnect, how to remove his circuit board, and so forth to minimize any damage. However, today, Señor Jacobs ordered us to extract the android's brain and map its circuits and connectors."

"Please tell me you didn't remove his positronic brain."

"No, we didn't. We've been secretly building an experimental robot brain for the past two years. Our plan was to dissect the fake one and record its many synapsis and relays. The major flaw in this plan was Señor Jacobs visiting engineering and discovering PheuMae's skull still intact. So, we loosened his cranial cavity."

"But his brain is still intact?"

"Yes. We were too afraid to mess with that. We tried to be extremely careful, but PheuMae had so many wires running from inside his skull cap to his brain. We were as careful as possible, but I don't know if we did any damage. Do you have someone who can reassemble him?"

"Yes and no. Master Kim is the only doctor who might be able to repair him, and he's light-years away. We will take PheuMae back to Master Kim in hopes he can reactivate him."

"And if he can't?"

"Our head android, Xavier, will make the decision if he will remain permanently deactivated or if he will be sent back to our creators for their refurbishing. Now, lead the way."

The androids trailed closely behind Ted as he led them down the dim corridor, stopping in front of a door secured with a heavy lock. Reaching into his pocket, Ted retrieved a key and slid it into the lock with a practiced motion. The door creaked open, revealing a stark white operating room, its sterile brightness tinged with an unsettling chill. At the center of the room, on a gleaming silver table, lay the lifeless corpse of PheuMae.

"As I said, we tried our best not to do much damage," Ted whispered.

Andrew approached the lifeless android, his gaze fixed on the grim tableau before him. Wires and tubes spilled from every part of PheuMae's dismantled form, a chaotic tangle of technology laid bare. His chest cavity gaped open, vibrant strands of multicolored wiring snaking outward in disarray. On the table beside him rested his severed circuit board, a cold and silent fragment of what once powered him.

Andrew's eyes traveled upward, noting the cranial cap had been pried open just enough to suggest his artificial brain had been cruelly extracted. The illusion was confirmed by the sight of the dissected tech-built brain lying in a tray on the table, its intricate segments submerged in a viscous pool of green slime. The eerie glow of the fluid and the stark sterility of the scene left an unsettling impression - a grim reminder of the cost of deconstruction.

"Is that the brain you said you built?" Andrew asked, surveying the organ."

"Yes. The two men who were with me and I built it. We hated tearing it apart after we'd worked on building it for so long. But the sacrifice was worth it if it saved PheuMae's life."

"I thank you for your sacrifice," Andrew said. "The brain is very impressive. You incorporated many of our idiosyncrasies into it. You have a future in robotics."

"Thank you."

"Ted, I represent an organization of countless worlds across the galaxy known as the ISC. They are always looking for new talent. If you'd like, I could put in a word about you with them."

"Would I have to leave Earth?"

"That I do not know. But the ISC will probably be here on Earth for a number of years helping to restore the planet. That should give you plenty of time to decide if you'd like to work in space, on another planet, or on Earth."

"Can my associates go also?"

"Since they helped build the brain, and if they are a good fit for the ISC, they too may go."

Chapter 24: HAVE WE LOST?

The strong aroma of ammonia shook Daniel awake. Disoriented, he struggled against his restraints. Upon opening his eyes, he saw that he was bound to a chair. Tim was standing before him, holding a small vial of ammonia under his nose.

"Get that thing away from me," Daniel grumbled, jerking his head to the side. Tim witnessed the disdain in his eyes.

"I have a little proposition for you, Señor Jacobs," Tim said. "Or should I call you Castrov Achenblles?"

"Who is Castrov Achenblles?"

"Your real name, the name you went by on the space station."

"I still have no idea what you're talking about."

Juaquin removed a scanner and blood analyzer from his suit. Tim nodded yes.

"Hold him," Juaquin said. Four of the androids grabbed Daniel, making it impossible for him to move despite his strength. Juaquin tore open Daniel's winter suit and extracted a vial of blood. He placed the sample in the scanner and waited for the results.

"Interesting. Ninety percent chance he's human, but ten percent he's Freezion. No wonder you enjoy the weather down here. I believe Freezion is an ice planet. Oh, it also shows he's one hundred percent asshole."

Tim laughed so hard that he snorted through his nose. "Good one, Juaquin."

"Tell me what you want, Commander," Daniel said. "I have things to do."

"Excuse me, are you under the assumption we will be setting you free? If so, I may have Juaquin check you for brain damage. You kidnapped Miguel and me and started to disassemble one of my androids. Was there anything else? Oh, yes, you are responsible for the destruction of the northern hemisphere and the deaths of over eight billion people. Every one of those offenses carries the death sentence." Tim paused for effect, turning his back to Daniel and taking several steps away. He stopped and turned around. "But, if you are willing to cooperate, I might be able to obtain a reduced sentence for you."

"What do you want?"

"I want the formula for the radiation you created with the *tilithium* and its antidote."

"And what do I get in return?"

"You get to stay alive."

"To live my life locked in an ISC cell?"

"Better than death."

"You've never been in their cells. Now you listen to me. I will give you the original formula in exchange for exile to an uninhabited planet of my choice. As for the antidote, I was not able to manufacture one."

"You're lying. The humans in this complex suffer from no radiation. Not even a little. The only explanation for that miracle is that you processed the cure and injected them with it. What is it?"

"I don't have one."

"You lie."

"Prove it."

"May I speak with you a minute, Tim?" Juaquin asked. He walked out of hearing distance, and Tim followed. "As you are aware, the ISC does not authorize torture. But under certain circumstances, such as this, some of us security androids have the skills to extract information. If Daniel is not willing to give you what you need, I can retrieve it for you."

"Torture?"

"No, not torture. Necessary measures."

"And how are 'necessary measures' different from torture?"

"Necessary measures fall under the stipulation of preserving life of an endangered species. Humans are now considered such an animal."

An amazed look spread across Tim's face. "Oh my gosh. You're right. Humanity is now an endangered species. I never realized that. But I still can't authorize your tactics."

"You don't have to. Just ask me to retrieve the needed information."

Tim stared at the android. Could he say the words and give his permission to torture? Without that antidote, more humans were going to die. Earth would remain a quarantined planet. And he and the androids were never going home. The last two items did not make up a legitimate reason to give Juaquin the go-ahead, but the deaths of more humans did. Damn, he wished Robert was still alive to make this decision.

"Let me think about it, Juaquin."

Juaquin nodded curtly. "Agreed, but don't take too long. The longer we wait, the greater chance we will lose our advantage. In the meantime, I'll arrange for Daniel's relocation." He strode forward, a glint of metal catching the light as a hidden cutter emerged in Juaquin's hand. With ease, the android sliced through Daniel's restraints.

"Let's go," Juaquin ordered as he pulled Daniel to his feet. A primal sneer contorted the alien's face. In a flash, he snatched the cutter, twisted his body around, and pressed the sharp edge of the blade against the cords of Juaquin's neck. The android wrapped his fingers around Daniel's hand holding the cutter, but he did not attempt to pry Daniel's hand free. Because of the way the blade was positioned, to do so would damage Juaquin's carotid neck cord.

"Back off!" Daniel snarled, a cruel smile twisting his lips. "One twitch and his fancy life support gets a system reboot." Pleasure danced in his eyes as he witnessed the flicker of fear in Tim's gaze. This escape was child's play. The human's pathetic attachment to the android was his trump card. He'd be free in minutes.

"Stand down, everyone," Tim said, his voice tight but steady. He grabbed a weapon from the android beside him, placing a red circle in the middle of Daniel's forehead. Logic battled with desperation in Tim's eyes. The androids could overpower the weakened alien, but not before Daniel delivered his deadly threat.

"Daniel," Tim continued, his voice low and placating, "There's no need for this. We can reason with each other."

"You will take me and our lovely android here to a flier. All the androids will remain inside with the hangar doors closed. Once we are outside, Juaquin will shut down to allow me to climb into the plane. You, I'm afraid, I will need to stun. Shall we go?"

"Daniel, you know I can't agree to release you. Just give me the antidote. I don't want to kill you."

Juaquin sent a silent message out to the standing androids. The six leviathans pulled their weapons and aimed them at Daniel, their red targets resting on various parts of Daniel's body. This time, Tim witnessed fear enter Daniel's eyes.

"You won't shoot me. I'm too important to you. And you're not sure if you can stop me before I cut Juaquin's artery. If I do slice through it, you'll never prevent his liquid from flowing out. And not even the creators will be able to restore him. He'll be gone FOREVER."

"Are you sure you're that fast, Daniel?" Tim fought to contain his composure. He knew Daniel was right – there was no bringing Juaquin back if he bled out. *I can't lose my friend. And how could I ever face Xavier again if I am responsible for Juaquin ceasing to exist? But I can't give in to his demands, no matter the consequences.*

Tim noticed Juaquin rapidly blinking. Once he had Tim's eyes, Juaquin looked at Daniel's hand, drawing Tim's gaze to the now visible circle on the back of Daniel's hand. Tim moved his head ever so slightly to the right, then the left, signaling he understood but disagreed. Tim wanted Daniel alive.

Juaquin moved his eyes up and down, stating this was their only alternative. This scenario had to stop. Daniel could not escape.

"Last chance, Daniel," Tim said, gradually lowering his red bullseye down to Daniel's hand.

"Let's go, Flyboy," Daniel said, dragging Juaquin forward.

"Now," was the only word Juaquin said.

A shot rang out. Daniel's scream pierced the air as Tim's bullet tore through his hand, causing him to drop the cutter. In that instant, Juaquin pushed Daniel's hand away and twisted free. The androids, seizing the moment, opened fire. Daniel's body convulsed violently as the shots ripped into him. When the barrage ended, he stared in disbelief at the blood soaking his clothes before collapsing, lifeless, to the floor.

Juaquin reached up and ran his fingers across his carotid tube. His fingers pressed into the indent left by the bullet as it struck the outside coating. "Cut that a little close, didn't we, Tim?"

Tim smiled. "Sorry, I re-injured my hand when Andrew knocked me out of the way of that snow driver. Plus, Daniel moved at the last second."

Juaquin cocked his head slightly to the side, watching the smile grow on Tim's face. *Moved, my ass.*

Tim looked at the bloody body on the ground. "Guess so much for going home. We'll never discover the cure now."

343

"That is not entirely true," came a voice from Tim's translator. Behind three raspberry bushes emerged two Caladrine, their blue trunks swaying as they walked forward. "We may be able to help."

"You have the formula?" Tim asked.

"No, Sir. But we know where Señor Jacobs has hidden the antidote and the original formula."

"We spend all day here in the gardens tending to the plants," the second Caladrine said. "Señor Jacobs never thought we had much intelligence for anything except planting seeds, so he paid us little heed. After he kidnapped us and brought us here, we kept a watchful eye on him."

"We hoped to one day use our knowledge of his formulas' location to secure our release. But since you have freed us, we offer it to you."

"I humbly thank you. And, if you prefer, we can return you to Hiinew," Tim said.

"If you don't mind, we would like to remain here and continue caring for the gardens. Humans don't do well with gardening, and we fear our work will wither and die if we leave. We have devoted the last three years of our lives to these plants and desire to see to what extent the garden will grow."

"I am sure the humans will gladly accept your offer. As will I."

"Tim," Jessica shouted as she ran toward the returning hero. She threw her arms around him, squeezing him in a strong hug. "I was so afraid you would never return."

"I never doubted that Juaquin would rescue us." Still holding their embrace, the two gazed as the still body of PheuMae was carried from the cargo hold of one of the fliers.

"Is he going to be okay?" Jessica asked.

"We don't know. Andrew was able to reattach his circuit board, but the wiring for his brain is too delicate for Andrew to tackle.

We're going to send him up to the coalition ship. Hopefully, their medics can help. If not, we'll transport him back to the station at New Earth. With luck, Master Kim can reconnect the wiring and make him whole again."

"I hope so." Jessica noticed Tim's arm in a sling. "Tim, did you hurt yourself again? Please tell me you didn't hit Juaquin a second time."

Tim laughed out loud, enjoying the feeling of amusement after the stressful time in Antarctica. "No, I hopefully learned my lesson on hitting Juaquin. I re-injured my hand when Phillip threw me against a wall."

Jessica looked at Phillip. "He threw you against a wall?"

"To save him from being crushed to death."

"You were almost crushed to death?" Jessica asked Tim.

"No, no, no. I was fine. Really." Tim noted Jessica's concerned face. "I'll tell you all about it later. Right now, know that I am fine." Tim kissed Jessica tenderly. "I need to contact my ship and the coalition and update them. How about we meet at the shack in four hours?"

"Sounds good." Jessica kissed him on the cheek. "I did miss you."

"I missed you. And I had a lot of time to think about us. But as I said, we'll talk about it later."

Jessica scurried off. Tim walked over to the communications tent.

"Welcome back, Sir," B-2 said.

"It's good to be back. If you have no objections, C-62 will resume his post."

"Yes, Sir." The robot stepped aside. C-62 pulled over his chair and took his place behind the radio.

"C-62, get me Commander Buutay?"

345

"Right away, Commander." Within minutes, Commander Buutay appeared on the screen.

"Tim, what a pleasant surprise. Juaquin's rescue mission was successful."

"Yes, Sir. Thank you."

"Were you able to obtain the formula for the antidote?"

"Not only for the antidote but for the original radiation *tilithium* mixture as well."

"What about the imposter Daniel Jacobs?"

"I'm sorry to report that we were not able to apprehend Daniel alive. He was killed in the skirmish." Tim wondered what Buutay would say if he knew Daniel had been killed to save Juaquin. ISC policy stated that androids were expendable, and the lives of other beings took priority. But to Tim, Juaquin's life was as important as his or anyone else's.

"That's too bad. But I'm sure you and your androids did all that was possible."

"Yes, Sir. So, if the antidote works, will the quarantine be lifted, and we can head home in a few weeks?"

"Send up the antidote formula, and I'll have our scientists look it over. If they agree it's the real thing, we will try the formula on the contaminated flier. If it neutralizes its remaining radiation, the next stage is to neutralize you, your androids, and your fliers. Then all the people in your camp. Then, and only then, if everything goes okay, we can discuss the net being removed, and you can start making plans to go home."

"So, a little longer than a few weeks."

"Most definitely. But I promise you, we will work as fast as possible."

"I also wanted to inform you that two of the Caladrine from the Antarctica complex asked to construct one of their gardens here at the compound. Of course, I'd need a handful more from Hiinew's group and help with supplies. But if it happens, the food it can produce will eliminate our food problems."

"That is great news. What will happen to the Antarctica settlement with Daniel gone?"

"We left four of the androids to help them transition to governing themselves and electing some leaders. The ISC will need to send more androids to help."

"Again, you'll need to make do with what you have until I can order the net taken down."

"Yes, Sir. It's just that we're getting spread out a little thin again and could use some reinforcements."

"Our compliment of androids is limited, but I will inquire if any would like to travel down to Earth with the understanding it may be for a long time. If any agree, I'll ask for the net to be opened long enough to allow them through."

"Thank you."

"How's your hand doing?" Jessica asked as she lay in Tim's arms.

Tim held up his arm and moved his hand back and forth. "When I rebroke my arm in Antarctica, I feared I was in for a long recovery. But my arm is almost as good as new. Andrew's bone regenerator worked wonders. The two bones originally broken are already re-knitted, and the rebroken one is on its way. Andrew said in a few days I can stop wearing the sling."

"Maybe next time you'll think twice before striking Juaquin."

"Probably not." Tim laughed. "Juaquin said my grandfather hit Xavier almost a dozen times during his life. Broke his hand every time."

"That makes no sense. Why would he continue striking Xavier knowing he'd break his hand?"

"I guess he got so frustrated and mad that he didn't consider the consequences. Androids can stress you out big time."

"Is that why you struck Juaquin? Did he stress you out?"

"You don't want to know."

"Yes, I do. Now more than ever. Tell me."

"No, I'd rather not."

"Tell me." Jessica tickled Tim, making him squirm and giggle loudly and uncontrollably.

"Okay, okay, I'll tell you. Just stop tickling me." Jessica removed her hands. "He knew you were pregnant, and he didn't tell me. I got mad and hit him."

Jessica sat up. "That's why you hit him?"

"Yeah."

"That was a really stupid reason."

"I know. That's why I didn't want to tell you."

"He was right not to tell you. It wasn't his secret to tell."

"Maybe not. But since I'm the Mission Commander, he's supposed to tell me everything."

"So, you're saying that if Jose and Alicia become pregnant, you should be informed?"

"Eventually. I need to make sure she gets proper medical attention."

"Eventually? So why couldn't Juaquin eventually tell you?"

"Because your baby is mine." Jessica just stared at him. "Can we drop the subject? We have more pressing matters to discuss."

"Okay. What's up?"

"We brought back a possible antidote for the radiation affecting the androids, our fliers, and the people of Earth. The coalition is currently testing that antidote to determine if it works or not. If all the tests confirm its accuracy, the quarantine net will be lifted, and my crew can go home in about four or five weeks."

"I figured as much."

348

"That means I will be leaving in the near future."

"And?"

"I want you to rethink your decision about coming to New Earth with me. The baby would have a wonderful home on New Earth. And my parents would spoil you and him or her something awful."

"Tim, I've told you. I don't want to leave Earth."

"But New Earth is just like Earth, only better. It's the Earth humans were meant to have. Think about how much better our children's lives would be and the opportunities they would have."

"Children?"

"We might have two or three more if we were together. Jessica, I don't want to lose you and the baby."

"Then stay here on the old Earth with us."

"That's not a possibility. I have a commitment to the ISC, a contract I'm obligated to."

"Can't you get out of it?"

"No."

"Have you ever asked?"

"No."

"Then there is a possibility they would release you from your contract? Can't you ask?"

Tim remained silent. He didn't want to stay on Earth, especially in its current condition. Life was too hard.

"Can't you ask?"

"Tell you what. If you agree to rethink the possibility of returning to New Earth with me, I'll inquire if circumstances exist where the contract can be broken. Deal?" Jessica remained silent. "Deal?"

Jessica laid back down on Tim's chest. The young male wrapped his arms around her when he heard her say, "Deal."

"Thank you. Let's get some sleep. Juaquin will be knocking on the door before we know it."

Chapter 25: THE VISIT

"Looks like you're going to have company," Miguel said to Tim. "Here comes Juaquin."

"So much for an undisturbed luncheon," Tim said.

"He seems to have a jollier step today. Anything exciting happen?"

"Not to my knowledge" Tim observed Juaquin's approach. He had to agree with Miguel. The android seemed to possess happiness in his step.

Juaquin swung his legs over the bench and sat down beside Jessica. He breathed in a long breath. "That coffee always smells so good. I wish we androids had the capability to taste. I'd love to know what it's like before we leave."

"You can smell, but you can't taste?" Sandy asked.

"That is correct. Being able to inhale the fragrance or order of something is often needed to analyze a situation, such as a fire or deadly chemical. But to my knowledge, there is no reason to have taste."

"Do you know when you'll be leaving yet?" Miguel asked.

"That's why I'm here," Juaquin said. "And I wanted to deliver the news personally. Commander Buutay just informed me that the latest test result on the flier was negative. The metal is completely radiation-free. They were also able to remove all traces of radiation from C-62. They will start flying over the camp to remove any radiation here at 0-eight hundred hours tomorrow morning. If that goes well, they will test the formula over a section of Australia. If the radiation there is eradicated, they will begin dismantling the quarantine net within the week. I've advised Opal to start preparing the ship for departure. We should be out of here by this time in eight days."

Tim looked over at Jessica, but she did not raise her head. Without a word, she stood and ran from the table.

"Good going, Juaquin," Tim said, bolting into a stand.

"I am sorry if my news upset her. I was answering Miguel's question. I have analyzed your problem, and I have determined you have three choices: you stay, she comes with us, or you two part ways. Avoiding the subject will not change those choices."

"I was hoping the crew might stay until the baby is born," Tim said.

"Another four months? And would an extension make a difference? The choices are still the same."

"I don't want her going through the birth alone."

"She won't be alone," Sandy said. "Both Miguel and I will stay with her."

"While I'm grateful for that, it doesn't help," Tim stated. "I'd better go after her." Tim trotted off in Jessica's direction.

"I don't know why she won't go with him," Sandy said. "Her life up there would be so much better."

Tim searched, but Jessica was nowhere to be found. "How did she disappear so fast? I was right behind her." He was headed for the stream when his transmitter beeped. Removing it from his pocket, he read: *Flier is ready to depart.* Damn. Tim turned and headed towards the flier. He and Phillip were flying to a newly contacted settlement in Botswana to speak with the people and encourage them to join the ISC. His talk with Jessica would have to wait.

"Juaquin, I couldn't find Jessica anywhere?" Tim said the moment he sighted the android standing beside the flier.

"If you're going to make your rendezvous, you need to leave now," Juaquin said. "I'll find Jessica. I'm sure she's fine."

"I can't leave until I'm sure," Tim stated. "She was upset by what you said. I should speak with her."

"Tim, I am sorry that the truth upset her, but as the leader of this mission, your responsibility is to continue the objective of the ISC, which is to unite the Earthlings. You cannot allow Jessica's hurt feelings to take priority over your goal. I said I will find her, and I will. I will make sure she is well, and I will even apologize for upsetting her, although I bear no fault. Now, please, step inside your flier."

Tim didn't like it, but Juaquin was right. Allowing himself to become emotionally involved with Jessica did not give him permission to bypass his duty.

"Okay, but contact me the moment you find her."

"Yes."

"Tim was looking for you," Juaquin said as he approached Jessica. He found her sitting on a small cliff overlooking the new farming valley below. "He wanted to make sure you were okay before he left."

Jessica looked up as an alien cruiser flew overhead, releasing a fine mist of purple vapor. Do I have to worry about the mist hurting the baby?"

"Not to my knowledge, but I suggest we have you shelter until they are done spraying."

Jessica stood and headed towards camp. "He left for Africa?"

"Yes, about fifteen minutes ago." Juaquin signaled ahead to Andrew asking him to do a scan on Jessica when they arrived. He wanted to be doubly sure the mist would not injure the fetus.

"How long will he be gone?"

"Six days."

"This will probably be the last settlement he visits before you guys leave."

"Yes."

"Does he have enough settlements who are willing to join the ISC? Will they finally decide we are worth saving?"

"Earth has always been worth saving, Jessica. Humans just didn't remember that." Juaquin paused. "I'm sorry if I upset you earlier. As an android, I often state the obvious without thinking how that truth will impact others. Some say it is a flaw in our programming."

"You only stated what I already knew and have been telling myself." Jessica sighed deeply as a tear slid down her cheek. "What am I going to do, Juaquin?"

"May I ask you a personal question?" Juaquin asked.

"Of course."

"Do you love Tim?"

"That's another question I've been asking myself lately. The truth is, I don't know. I'm very fond of him, I immensely enjoy being in his company, and I love the way he makes me laugh. I have been a better person since I met him. But I don't have that burning love where it hurts to be separated. I've experienced that kind of love before where your body is in a flutter all the time, you can't sleep because you're thinking of him, and everything you do and see reminds you of them. It's not like that with Tim."

"Perhaps because the way you are feeling about Tim is what real love is. The other instances were chemistry and infatuation."

"Do you think so?" Jessica turned and looked at the android.

355

"I have no algorithms that allow me to experience what love is, but I've witnessed it countless times over the centuries. The most profound example was Tim's grandfather, Renn, and his love for Jenny. I watched as grief consumed Renn when Jenny died, a pain so deep I didn't think any being could bear it. And then, when Master Kim returned Jenny to him in the form of a female android, the joy that filled him was overwhelming. His entire world revolved around her. While I don't see that same intensity between you two, I can sense the beginnings of something similar."

Jessica smiled. "Tim told me the story of his grandparents. Their life together was beautiful, yet so tragic."

"That it was. May I ask another question?"

"As many as you'd like."

"Why don't you want to go with Tim to New Earth?"

A small giggle escaped Jessica's throat. "I'm afraid of flying."

"You're afraid of flying? I thought you flew down here on vacation?"

"I did, but only after lots of alcohol and a few tranquilizers."

"Why are you afraid of flying?"

"It's unnatural to be up there in those big ass planes. They can crash at any time. I prefer to keep my feet on the ground. And I'm a little claustrophobic. The thought of being cooped inside a box for months is unnerving."

"While our ship is of moderate size, there is still room to move about. Andrew can always give you something to help with the claustrophobia. But I have an idea. Why don't I take you to our ship and let you see what it's like? How can you possibly make a logical decision on your future if you have no idea what that entails?"

"You can do that? Take me to your ship?"

"Why not? The quarantine net will be gone soon. And I find no ISC regulation saying I can't. What do you say? Want to go for a ride?"

"It won't hurt the baby?"

"I'm sure it won't, but we'll ask Andrew's opinion to be sure."

"You know what frightens me the most?"

"What?"

"Tim will decide to remain here on Earth with me and then hate me later for condemning him here to this life. He's used to being in space, free and carefree."

"While I know Tim better than most humans, I cannot say if he would resent remaining behind."

Jessica thought for a minute. "Juaquin, will we ever be able to live in the north again?"

"If Earth joins the ISC, various alien nations will come to Earth and begin restoring the planet. Now that we can eliminate the deadly radiation, that process will be much quicker. But bringing life back to the North will not happen in your child's child's lifetime. It will take centuries, possibly a millennium, before anything can live in the northern hemisphere again, even the simplest forms of life."

"And without ISC help?"

"Closer to eight to twelve thousand years."

———————

"You can open your eyes now," Juaquin said as the flier lifted to its storage position aboard the ship. "We've arrived. Are you doing okay?"

"Yes," Jessica said. "I didn't think about what our landing would be like. I thought we'd park outside and come through a tunnel or something."

"And how would we have done that?" Juaquin asked. "Our fliers have cockpit hatches that open, not doors that slide apart. How would you have gotten inside before dying of asphyxiation?"

"I don't know. Space people in the sci-fi movies I used to watch walked through a door and tunnel. Your landing was very different and a bit intimidating. I wasn't sure we were going to fit."

"We did, and you are safe. Do you need help to exit the cockpit?"

"I think I can do it. I just need to hold on to your arm."

Jessica climbed out of her seat and stepped onto the waiting platform. Juaquin pushed a button, and the platform lowered to the floor below.

"Hello. I'm Opal," greeted the female waiting below. "And this is Jules. Welcome aboard."

"Hello. I'm Jessica."

"Come here, Juaquin," Opal said. "I remember you don't like human embraces, but it's been so long since I've seen you. I have to give you a big hug."

"If you must," Juaquin said, his body stiffening slightly. He felt Opal's arms slip around him. "I am happy to greet you as well."

Opal withdrew her embrace. "Admit it. You missed me, didn't you?"

"Maybe a little. Hello, Jules."

"Sir. Welcome back aboard."

"So, Jessica, Juaquin tells me you are considering traveling back with us to New Earth and wanted to see the ship before deciding," Opal said. "Is that true?"

"Sort of. Juaquin reminded me that I had no idea what a trip aboard your vessel would be like and that I should observe it for myself before making my final decision. So far, this is very impressive."

Opal laughed, a huge smile on her face. "This is just the hangar. Wait until you see the rest of the ship. And I must admit, having another female aboard would be a dream come true. Don't misunderstand what I'm about to say. I love every one of my crew, but being with all males twenty-four-seven can be a bit boring at times."

"We are not boring," Juaquin said.

Jessica gave Juaquin a curious look. "When was the last time we spoke of period cramps, if I should wear my hair up or down, or what color to paint my toenails?"

"I, or one of the other androids, are always here for such conversations," Juaquin said.

Jessica giggled. "I'd like to listen in on that conversation."

"Me too," Opal replied. "Come, and I'll show you around."

Jessica was surprised at how spacious the ship was, although she wasn't sure she could adjust to being confined within its walls for fifteen to eighteen months. She was surprised at the brightly colored walls and furniture. Opal explained that humans traveled better when their surroundings were homier and warmer.

"This is our medical facility," Opal said upon stepping inside the infirmary. "Here is where your baby will be born. After his or her birth, we can set up a nursery in your quarters."

"So, you know about the baby?" Jessica asked.

"Yes. Tim and I have had many discussions lately about you making the journey back to New Earth with us. He really wants you to come along."

"So, everyone keeps reminding me," Jessica said. "I'm just not sure I'm capable of such a trip."

"It's not as bad as you are imagining. Space never gets dull or old. Every day, you witness new wonders. If you come, I guarantee you'll never be lonely or bored."

"Another fear is that I've never been good around babies," Jessica admitted. "The thought of being confined in such close quarters with a non-stop screaming baby is terrifying. He or she is going to have days where they're not happy and will cry A LOT. What do we do then?"

"Manage it. Ask the androids to watch him or her. They are not affected by crying. We can make this work if you want it. I promise, Jessica."

"Thanks. That does ease some of my worries."

"We should be getting back to Earth," Juaquin said after Opal finished the tour.

"I was hoping Jessica might want to have lunch with me," Opal said. "It's been a LONG time since I've had someone to eat with."

"With as much trouble as Jessica has had with her stomach, consuming food before flying back is not advisable," Juaquin stated. "Thank you, Opal, for the tour. I'm sure it's giving Jessica lots to think about."

"That it has. I understand why Tim loves being in space so much."

"So, what was riding in the flier like?" Sandy asked.

"Wonderful," Jessica said. "It doesn't even feel as if you're moving. And once you reach space, the number of stars visible is astonishing. And words can't describe seeing Earth from out there, although I'm sure she was more impressive before the bombs destroyed the north."

"What about the ship? What was it like?" Miguel asked.

"Unbelievable," Jessica said. "Tim's always said their ship is small, but it was HUGE! A lot more room than I imagined."

"So, you think you might go?" Sandy asked.

"Let's say I'm considering it more now than before going." Jessica stood. "I promised Anita I would check on the caterpillar infestation of our strawberries. We're trying an organic mixture to keep the little creatures from eating the strawberries without hurting the young insects. Caterpillars must be allowed to flourish and repopulate their species." Jessica took two steps forward and stopped, doubling over in pain.

"Jessica, what's wrong?" Sandy shouted, jumping up.

"I don't know. I think something is wrong with the baby."

"Help. We need help over here," Miguel shouted.

Hearing the call, C-49 came running over. "What's wrong?"

"Jessica needs to be taken to the infirmary right away," Sandy said. "Something might be wrong with the baby."

"I've got you, Jessica," C-49 said as he carefully lifted Jessica into his arms. "I'll have you in the medical unit in a few minutes." As he ran towards the cave, C-49 sent Juaquin and Andrew a message advising him of the situation. Sandy and Miguel trailed behind.

Moments later, Juaquin came bursting into the medical section of the cave. "How is she?"

"Andrew's examining her now," Miguel said.

"What happened? Did she fall or something?"

"No, she just stood up and then bent over in pain."

"I don't like the sound of that," Juaquin said, staring intently at the closed curtain.

After a long thirty minutes, Andrew emerged from behind the curtain. "Jessica is well and sleeping. However, she did lose the baby."

"Oh no," Sandy said. Tears filled her eyes.

"Did she miscarry because I took her to the ship?" Juaquin asked. "Did I do this?"

"No, Sir," Andrew said. "The flight had nothing to do with the miscarriage."

"She was outside when they sprayed the decontaminate. Could that have hurt the baby?"

"Again, no. It was the radiation the fetus was exposed to at her moment of conception. She had several deformities that would have ended her life within days of birth."

"You're sure?"

"Yes, Juaquin. Not even Master Kim himself could have saved Tim's daughter."

"So, it was a girl?"

361

"Yes, the fetus was developed enough to confirm it was female. Unfortunately, Jessica suffered from the same ailment most women on Earth are experiencing - -a non-thriving fetus. To my knowledge, other than in Antarctica, only a handful of children have been born since the bombing. And eighty percent of them were either deformed or suffered from various medical conditions."

"Can I see Jessica?" Juaquin asked

"She's sleeping, but you can go inside and wait until she awakens if you'd like."

Without saying another word, Juaquin slipped through the curtain. Jessica was lying on the cot, sound asleep. Juaquin pulled up a nearby makeshift chair and sat down. He placed her hand in his.

"I'm so sorry, Jessica." The android brushed a single tear away from his eye.

Chapter 26: A HORRIFIC LOSS

Juaquin stood on the landing field, waiting for Tim's plane to touch down. Tim waved and climbed out when the cockpit door lifted, followed by Phillip and an unknown human male.

"Hi, Juaquin. This is Chief Mmusi from the Tswana nation. He has come to examine our progress here at base camp. If he likes what he sees, he will join the ISC."

"I am pleased to meet another of Commander Tim's androids," Chief Mmusi said, extending his hand.

Juaquin looked at Tim. "Your androids?"

"Go with it," Tim whispered.

"Welcome to our camp, Chief Mmusi. Phillip, would you show the chief around camp? I need Tim with me for a short time."

"Juaquin, you're being rude to our guest," Tim whispered.

"I meant no disrespect, but it is important that I speak with you in private immediately."

"Chief Mmusi, it appears I have pressing matters that need my attention. I'll rejoin you just as soon as I can."

"This way, Chief Mmusi," Phillip said.

Once the chief was out of hearing, Tim turned to Juaquin. "I realize you don't always have the best manners, but that was extremely rude. I am trying to convince him to join the ISC."

Juaquin held up his hand, silencing the human. "Tim, I have no easy way to tell you this, so I will just say it."

"What?" Tim asked, growing irritated. "What is so damn important that it can't wait two minutes? Spit it out."

"Jessica miscarried. She's in the infirmary."

Tim's eyes widened, the shock hitting him like a physical blow. His mouth opened slightly, but no words came out. A wave of dread washed over him, draining the color from his face until he was ashen. Without a second thought, he spun on his heel and sprinted toward the cave, his heart pounding. The world around him blurred as he focused on the only goal that mattered - reaching the medical unit. His breath came in ragged gasps, but he didn't slow down, his legs pumping furiously beneath him until he finally reached the entranceway, skidding to a halt as he crossed the threshold. His body trembled with adrenaline, but he forced himself to step inside, bracing for whatever awaited him within.

"She's okay, Tim," Andrew said calmly, his eyes tracking Tim as he struggled to catch his breath, each inhale sharp and desperate. "She's having lunch. You can go in."

His heart still racing from the sprint to the cave, Tim paused for a moment, taking a deep breath and forcing a smile onto his face. With a trembling hand, he parted the curtain and stepped inside. Jessica sat on the cot, cradling a bowl of food on her lap. The moment her eyes met his, the facade of composure crumbled, and she burst into tears, her shoulders shaking with each sob. Tim's forced smile faded, replaced by a look of deep concern as he hurried to her side, his heart aching at the sight of her distress.

"I'm sorry, Tim," Jessica whispered, her voice trembling as fresh tears filled her eyes.

Tim gently took the bowl from her hands and placed it on the table beside the bed. Without hesitation, he sat down next to her, pulling her into his arms. "I'm so sorry, Jessica. Are you okay? What happened?"

"I'm fine. Andrew said the baby was deformed because of the radiation I was exposed to. He said I was lucky to have carried it as long as I did." She hesitated, her breath hitching as she spoke the next words. "Tim, the fetus... was a girl."

"A girl?" Tim's voice trembled, the words catching in his throat as the realization took hold. He had always been uncertain about becoming a father, unsure if he was ready for the responsibility or if he even wanted a child at all. But now, in this unbearable moment, all he could think about was the daughter he would never have the chance to love. As his emotions surged, the uncertainty melted away, leaving only an aching desire for the little girl he would never hold. He clutched Jessica tightly, their grief mingling as they cried together, mourning the loss of a future that had once seemed so distant but now felt agonizingly close. The thought of never hearing her call him Daddy, never feeling her tiny hand in his, cut deeper than he ever imagined possible. All he wanted now was to have her back, to rewrite the fate that had taken her away before she even had a chance to live. Buried in Jessica's embrace, Tim wept, his tears a testament to the love he hadn't known he wanted until it was too late.

Twenty minutes later, Tim emerged from the room. He walked over to the basin and poured a ladle of water inside. Dipping his hands in the liquid, Tim splashed water on his face, washing away his dried tears.

"How is Jessica?" Juaquin asked.

"Sleeping."

"How are you?" Juaquin asked, his eyes fixed on Tim with a steady, unblinking gaze.

Tim's shoulders sagged under the weight of his grief, his voice raw with emotion. "Not the best," he admitted, barely holding back the tears that threatened to erupt again. He hesitated, the words struggling to form as he tried to make sense of the confusion and guilt gnawing at him. "Why was I upset when I learned about the baby? Why wasn't I happy?" His voice cracked. "Now she's gone, and I don't know what to do," Tim whispered, his hands clenching into fists as if trying to grasp something, anything, that might anchor him in this sea of sorrow.

Juaquin tilted his head, processing Tim's words with the precision of an android designed to understand but not fully feel. "Humans often experience conflicting emotions," Juaquin said, his tone even, almost clinical, yet containing a softness to it - an empathy that echoed the comfort he understood Tim needed combined with the loss that tugged at the android's heart. "Uncertainty about parenthood is not unusual. It does not mean you would not have loved her deeply." Juaquin paused, searching for the right words, the ones that would bring some measure of solace. "The loss you're experiencing is a testament to that love. It is natural to mourn what could have been and to regret the moments of doubt. Your grief is a reflection of the bond you were beginning to form, even if you did not recognize it at the time."

Tim's breath hitched, the logical explanation doing little to ease the ache in his chest, but something in Juaquin's words resonated with him, making the pain feel a bit less isolating. He nodded, trying to accept the android's words. Juaquin, sensing the need for further comfort, added, "You did not need to be ready for her to be part of your life. Your sorrow now shows that she already was, in ways you may not have understood. It is okay to grieve, Tim. It is okay to wish for a different outcome, even if you were unprepared for this one."

Tim let out a shuddering breath, the tightness in his chest loosening just a fraction. Juaquin watched the human in silence, still trying to understand the depth of human emotion that, because of his programming, remained just out of his reach.

"Would you mind if I remain here for a while?"

"Stay as long as you need. I will ask Phillip to continue to supervise Chief Mmusi's visit. He reports the Chief is impressed with what he has seen so far. I believe that once he sees everything we

367

have accomplished or our plans for future endeavors, he will recommend to his council to join the ISC and accept their help."

"I hope so. The trip to Africa cost me dearly."

"Tim, even if you had been at Jessica's side, the outcome would be the same," Andrew said. "Nothing could have stopped it."

"Then why doesn't it feel that way?"

"Because it is raw and fresh," Andrew said. "With time, her loss will be less painful, yet I'm afraid always present."

"Get some rest, Tim," Juaquin stated. "I'll notify you if Chief Mmusi needs anything."

"Thank you again, Juaquin, for everything." Tim slipped through the curtain again, remaining at Jessica's side through the night.

The next morning, C-85 flew Chief Mmusi back home. Juaquin returned to the medical unit to discover Tim had left an hour before his arrival.

"C-62, can you give me a readout on Tim?" Juaquin asked into his comm link.

"Yes, Sir. One moment." Silence. "I've located him sitting inside the cabin Tim and Jessica had often shared together."

"I will be with our Commander for a while. Notify me if I'm needed."

"Yes, Sir."

"Mind if I come in?" Juaquin asked as he opened the door to the rickety shack.

"Is God punishing me, Juaquin?"

"As an android, I do not believe in a higher being who watches over us."

"Then am I cursed or doomed?"

"Again, I do not have the expertise to comment on such a concept. Why do you ask such questions?"

"I was given the most precious gift a human can be given - a child. But I wasn't happy about it. All I thought about was how it affected me, put a wrinkle in my future plans."

"As I told you last evening, that feeling is often shared by the males of your species."

"That doesn't make it right."

"No, it does not."

"I should have told Jessica I was happy about the news. I should have agreed to remain here with her and the baby."

"Would you have been happy staying behind?"

"I don't know. I might have been."

"Jessica and I had a long talk while you were gone. She said she was afraid you would eventually resent her if you stayed behind."

"She might be right. I would miss traveling around the galaxy, meeting new species, and exploring new worlds. I'm not sure I'm ready to keep my feet on the ground."

"Rebuilding Earth could be an adventure. And various species from across the galaxy will come to Earth when the ISC starts rebuilding her."

"IF Earth joins the ISC."

"I believe that will happen." Juaquin took several steps away from Tim. "I'm going to say something, but I want you to remember that the last time you got angry and hit me, you broke your hand in three places."

Tim stared at Juaquin. "Don't say it."

"Your grandfather used to say that even in the darkest moments, a glimmer of hope remains. I can't imagine the depth of your pain right now, but maybe there's a small silver lining in the clarity this brings. The agonizing decision of whether to stay or leave is no longer hanging over you. You and Jessica are free from that burden now, without the guilt that would have come with it. It feels like a harsh and cruel reset, but it also offers a chance to begin again without the weight of Jessica's pregnancy holding you back."

"You bastard." Tim rushed forward, his arm pulled back to strike

"Remember the broken hand," Juaquin said, reaching out and grabbing Tim's fist.

Tim stopped his swing. "You're still a bastard."

"Since I have no parents, that is an inaccurate nomenclature for me. I may sometimes be unsympathetic and often tell the truth when I shouldn't, but understand I say these things not to hurt you but to help you see your reality. You can now decide if you two stay together because you love each other and not because you're obligated to."

"It doesn't make things less hurtful." Tim withdrew his arm.

"No, it doesn't," Juaquin replied. "If Xavier were here, I'm sure he'd have some profound words of wisdom. But he's not, and I lack his skill in navigating human emotions. All I can offer is to help you look toward what's ahead. So, Tim, let me ask you—do you love Jessica?"

Tim let out a heavy sigh. "I thought I did. I told her I loved her. Now, I'm not sure. I'm not sure I even know what love really is."

"Tim, I've always believed that I don't understand love—after all, it's not something I was built to experience. But in observing humans, I've realized that love is more than just a feeling you can name or define. It's in the way you care about her, in the warmth you feel when she's near. If you can't say with certainty that you love Jessica, maybe this is life's difficult way of showing you something you needed to see. This loss might be revealing something important. Perhaps it's a painful reminder that without that deep connection, you could've found yourself resenting her, tied to a place you don't truly want. It's not easy, but sometimes the hardest moments show us what we really need."

"How did you become so wise about a subject you cannot experience?"

"I had good teachers that I observed and learned from."

"Grandpa Renn and Jenny."

"Yes."

"I could never love Jessica the way Grandpa loved Jenny. I'm not sure I could love anyone that much."

Juaquin stepped forward and placed his hand on the young human's shoulder. "Don't sell yourself short. Part of Renn lives inside you. One day, you may love just as much."

"You did good, Tim," Hiinew said. "Robert would have been proud of you and what you've accomplished. You completed his mission."

"If Robert hadn't shown me what to do, I wouldn't have been able to persuade the remaining human settlements to join the ISC," Tim said.

"He once told me that he believed you would be the one to save Earth. Robert always believed in you."

"I wish he would have told me that. There were many times when I didn't believe it."

"But he did tell you - through Juaquin. Perhaps you weren't listening."

"Perhaps I wasn't."

"When will the ISC arrive to sign the agreement?"

"A special delegation is coming from Proxima Centurius. They should arrive in four or five months."

"Perhaps Miguel can convert a few more groups to join during that time. He'll make a fine negotiator."

"That he will. Thank you again, Hiinew, for helping to build the new greenhouse at camp."

"I am happy to do our part to restore this great planet. For the first time, I believe mankind has a bright tomorrow. So, what are your plans for the future?"

"Jessica and I have had numerous discussions. With the baby gone, we realized that neither of us loved the other enough to change our ways of life. Jessica will remain here and be part of the rebuilding of the southern hemisphere. I will return to New Earth, visit my family, and go wherever the ISC needs me."

"Do you think you'll ever travel back this way for a visit?"

"One never knows." Tim took a large drink of Quivia juice. "But I am going to miss this tasteful treat."

"I have several containers for you to take on your journey back to New Earth and a bag of seeds. Perhaps you can find a good location on New Earth to plant them and grow your own Quivia fruits. That way, every time you drink a glass, you will think of us."

Tim walked over and kissed Hiinew on the cheek. "I don't need Quivia juice to make me remember you."

"I am sorry it didn't work out between you and your female friend."

"I am, too. But it just wasn't meant to be. We just got caught up in the moment, and things got out of hand. Take care, Hiinew. And thank you again for everything."

"Tim, we're leaving in twenty-eight minutes," Juaquin's voice cut through the thick air, precise and emotionless. "Time to say your final goodbyes."

Tim's heart pounded, each beat echoing in his ears as dread twisted in his stomach. He'd been bracing himself all day, trying to ignore the countdown ticking away in his mind. The excitement of going home was drowned by the suffocating weight of leaving Jessica behind - the woman who had become his anchor, the one who had seen him through so much. A lump formed in his throat, making it impossible to swallow, choking him with the reality of what was slipping away.

Juaquin turned to Jessica, his gaze steady, his words measured. "Jessica, it has been an honor knowing you. I will miss your wit and those sharp remarks."

Jessica smiled, though her eyes shimmered with unshed tears. "And I'll miss your honesty and straightforwardness," she replied, her voice trembling slightly. "Tim told me androids don't appreciate hugs, but I hope you'll make an exception and let me hug you."

"If you must."

Jessica stepped forward, her arms wrapping around the cold metal of the android. Juaquin, in an uncharacteristic gesture, mimicked the embrace, his arms folding around her. For the first time, something stirred in the android's circuitry - an understanding, a fleeting joy in the simple act of connection. He allowed himself a rare smile.

"Since androids live indefinitely, know that you will live on in my memory for millennia."

"And you'll live in my heart until the day I die," Jessica whispered, her voice cracking as she stepped back.

Juaquin released her, turning to Tim. "I'll be waiting for you at the flier. We depart in twenty-two minutes."

Tim nodded, his stomach lurching as Jessica turned to face him, her eyes searching his. "I guess it's that time," she said, her voice barely above a whisper.

"Seems so." He swallowed hard, the words catching in his throat. "Are you sure you don't want to come along? You can always return to Earth if it doesn't feel right."

"No, my place is here," Jessica replied, her resolve firm but her eyes betraying the conflict within. "There's a lot of work to be done to restore Earth. We could use another pair of hands if you'd like to stay."

"The ISC is sending ships to help rebuild Earth. Soon, you'll have so many hands helping you'll wish you had come with me."

Jessica forced a laugh, but the sound quickly faded into silence. "I wish it would've worked out between us."

"Me too," Tim said, his voice strained. "I did love you."

"Just not enough."

"No." The word hung in the air, a painful truth neither could escape. "You?"

"The same."

"One last kiss?"

"Always."

They stepped closer, the space between them closing as they embraced one final time. Their lips met in a kiss that was bittersweet, full of all the things left unsaid, the dreams unfulfilled. It was a kiss that burned with the knowledge that this was the end.

"I'm going to miss you so much," Jessica murmured, her breath warm against his cheek.

"Me too," Tim choked out, his voice thick with emotion. "I don't know what I'm going to do without you around to rattle my temper."

"Opal promised to give you hell for me when you screw up," Jessica said, trying to keep the mood light, though her heart was breaking.

A beep from Tim's communicator shattered the moment. "That'll be Juaquin telling me it's time."

"I'll walk with you."

"Please don't," Tim said, his voice barely a whisper. "If I see you standing there, I'll never be able to lift off."

"Then don't leave."

"Jessica, we've been through this so many times," Tim said, his voice cracking with the weight of the decision. "I don't want to stay, and you don't want to leave. Going our separate ways is the only logical choice."

"I know." She bit her lip, fighting back the tears. "Tim?"

"Yes?"

"Take care of yourself."

"You too." Tim forced himself to turn away, every step feeling like a betrayal as he walked toward the flier. He didn't dare look back, tears streaming down his face, blurring his vision.

"You ready?" Juaquin's voice was a quiet rumble as Tim climbed into the cockpit, his hands shaking.

"Yes," Tim managed to whisper, though the word felt like a lie, hollow and empty in the vastness of the decision he'd just made. As the flier lifted off, the distance between him and Jessica grew, but the ache in his heart only deepened.

"Echo Command, Echo One ready for departure."

"Echo two ready for departure," Andrew said.

"Echo three ready for departure," Phillip said.

"Echo Command, we await your arrival," Jules stated. "Welcome home."

Chapter 27: GOING HOME

Juaquin found Tim sitting in the dark, staring at the bodies of Quinn and PheuMae encased in a special containment capsule. His silhouette was outlined by the flight lights outside the viewport. The silence was thick, almost suffocating, as Tim stared into the void, lost in thoughts that churned like a storm.

"How are you holding up?" Juaquin asked, breaking the stillness.

Tim didn't turn, his voice barely a whisper. "So, so. Do you think Master Kim or Sub-Master Fuu can fix either of them?"

"I believe Master Kim will have the expertise to reconnect Pheu Mae's brain," Juaquin said, intently gazing at the two androids. "At least, I hope so."

"And Quinn?"

"No, I don't believe Master Kim will have the expertise for that. The radiation caused too much damage to Quinn's body, his operating systems, and his brain. I fear Quinn must return to the makers to be rebuilt."

"But they live so far away, two galaxies away. And as you said before, we don't even know if they still exist."

"True. If they do still live, it will be three thousand years or more before Quinn will return. Your ashes will be no more. Perhaps even I will be gone by then."

"Not you, Juaquin," Tim said, turning to face the android. "You'll live forever."

"One day, I will cease to be. Although we androids live for tens of thousands of years, we are not immortal."

The hum of the spacecraft's engines provided a low, constant backdrop to the oppressive silence that returned. Tim and Juaquin's eyes remained fixed on the two lifeless androids.

Tim's gaze was unfocused, his mind clearly elsewhere. The weight of recent events pressed down on him, but it was the hollow ache in his chest that threatened to consume him. Every second that passed was another second further from her - from the warmth of her smile, the sound of her laugh. He'd left her behind, and that knowledge gnawed at him relentlessly.

Juaquin glanced sideways at his companion, reading the turmoil etched across Tim's features. He opened his mouth as if to speak, but the words died on his lips. What could he possibly say to ease such pain?

The silence stretched on, broken only by the occasional ping of cooling metal or the soft whir of an internal system. It was a silence heavy with unspoken words, with regrets and second-guesses. Tim's fingers absently traced patterns on the armrest, perhaps unconsciously spelling out her name.

Finally, Tim broke the silence. "Did I make the right choice, Juaquin? Should I have stayed?"

"Still questioning your decision to leave?"

"More than ever. It's been three days, and I can't stop thinking about her. She's in my head, in my heart - I can't shake it. I can't sleep. I feel drained, like I'm just… empty."

"And you've barely eaten enough to keep a *hinnerglipper* alive these past three days."

"I know," Tim muttered, the weight of his regret pressing down on him. "I shouldn't be this messed up. I chose to leave."

Juaquin chuckled, a sound that was both unexpected and oddly comforting in the dark. "What's so funny?" Tim asked, finally turning to face the android.

"Sometimes, I'm amazed at how blind humans can be," Juaquin said, his tone tinged with a rare hint of emotion.

"Stop with the insults. Just tell me what you think."

Juaquin's gaze locked onto Tim, his voice unwavering. "Tim, everything you're feeling right now? It's because you love Jessica. You can't eat, can't sleep, can't focus - your leadership's been in the toilet. You're walking around here like a ghost, dragging everyone else down with you. Don't you see what that means?"

Tim blinked, a sudden clarity cutting through the fog of his mind. "Am I really?" he asked, a smile slowly spreading across his face. "You're right. I do love her. I love Jessica, and I was an idiot to leave her behind. Everything I wanted, everything that mattered - it was all right there in front of me, and I walked away. Jessica was My Jenny." Tim grabbed the android's hand." What do I do now? Can we turn the ship around?"

"No, we can't," Juaquin replied, his voice steady but firm. "But we haven't folded space yet. I've purposely been postponing leaving the system in hopes you'd come to your senses. You can take one of the fliers and be back on Earth in three days."

Tim shot to his feet, his heart racing. "You're saying it's okay if I go?"

"If you don't, I'll tie you into that flier myself and send you back."

Without warning, Tim pulled Juaquin into a tight embrace. "I love you, Juaquin."

"No," Juaquin said, his tone softening, "You love Jessica."

"And you, too," Tim insisted, pulling back with a grin.

"Go pack your gear. The ship leaves in thirty minutes."

Tim didn't need to be told twice. He sprinted toward his quarters, his voice echoing through the corridors. "Hey, everyone! I love Jessica, and I'm going back!"

"About time!" Opal shouted, a chorus of cheers erupting from the androids as they celebrated his decision.

———————

Jessica sat at the table, absently pushing her food around her plate with her fork. Her appetite had vanished the moment Tim left, replaced by a gnawing emptiness that wouldn't go away.

"You need to eat something," Sandy urged, concern etched on her face. "You've barely touched a thing since he left. You're going to make yourself sick."

"I just miss him so much," Jessica whispered, her voice breaking. "I didn't realize how much until he was gone, but I love him. I love him with everything I have."

"Now's a great time to figure that out," Sandy said, her tone both sympathetic and pointed.

"I know," Jessica sighed, the weight of her emotions pressing down on her.

A distant rumble caught Jessica's attention, pulling her out of her thoughts. She looked up, spotting a flier approaching fast - too fast for a routine shipment. As it neared, the flier executed a daring roll, revealing the words "I LOVE YOU" boldly painted across the wings.

"Never seen one of the ISC androids do that before," Sandy remarked, her eyes wide with surprise.

Jessica's heart skipped a beat, her breath catching in her throat. "That's not an android," she said, her voice trembling with sudden hope. "That's Tim's flier. He's back. And he loves me."

Without another word, Jessica bolted from the table, her legs propelling her toward the landing area as fast as they could carry her.

379

The flier touched down just as she arrived, and Tim was already throwing open the hatch, his helmet tossed aside as he jumped out.

Their eyes met, and in that instant, the world around them faded away. They ran to each other, closing the distance with desperate urgency, their arms wrapping around each other in a tight embrace.

"I love you," Jessica cried, tears streaming down her cheeks. "I want to go with you."

"I love you," Tim choked out, his own tears spilling over. "But the ship's gone. And it's okay because I want to stay here with you and help rebuild Earth."

Their lips met in a kiss that was fierce, full of all the passion and longing that had been bottled up inside them. It was a kiss that promised they would face whatever the future held - together. Their love was undeniable, powerful, and eternal. Nothing in this world could ever tear them apart again.

****

I truly hope you enjoyed reading this novel. Continuing the story of the *Guardians* has been a true labor of love. As I wrote this installment, the characters truly came alive for me, weaving themselves into my heart. Juaquin, the android, brought so much humor with his awkward attempts to navigate human emotions. His antics had me laughing, especially as he kept Captain Tim on his toes. Yet, beneath Juaquin's mechanical exterior lies a secret—he does feel, and his ability to tease and connect adds layers of complexity to his character.

Then there's Tim and Jessica. Their heartbreaking loss brought tears to my eyes as I wrote it. I couldn't help but mourn alongside them.

I grieved for the end of the androids, a loss that tore at my heartstrings in ways I didn't expect. Their departure wasn't just a plot point—it felt like saying goodbye to dear friends whose presence had become a cornerstone of the story. Writing their final moments left an ache in my chest that lingered long after the words were on the page., and the decommissioning of the androids. Each character truly captured my heart. Even though I crafted the story, I felt a deep sorrow when the journey came to an end.

If this story moved you in any way, I would be incredibly grateful if you could leave an honest review on Amazon. Your feedback not only helps me grow as a writer but also shows me what resonated with you and where I can improve.

I love connecting with my readers! If you'd like to share your thoughts, ask questions, or simply chat about the story, feel free to reach out. Your journey through this world means everything to me. You can email me at prgarcia@prgarcia1.com.

Remember, every story has the power to change us, just as this one has changed me. The characters' happenings may end, but their strength, love, and courage live on in all of us. Thank you for being part of their journey - because, in the end, it's our stories that shape the stars.

P.R. Garcia

GUARDIANS OF EARTH SERIES

Guardians of Earth I **- The Argus:** An unstoppable alien force is en route to Earth, determined to harvest the planet's water and minerals. The only hope for humanity lies with a guardian sworn to protect Earth—but to succeed, he needs the help of someone unexpected: Sarina Spalling, a science fiction author.

Sarina is thrilled about the launch of her latest book, a thrilling tale of alien guardians fighting to save Earth from annihilation. To her, it's pure fiction—too impossible to be true.

She couldn't be more wrong.

Her book has caught the attention of a shadowy government agency, and they want answers. The secrets hidden in her pages are too accurate - information she should never have known. When Sarina is kidnapped and her husband accused of leaking military intelligence, she vehemently denies the charges. But the truth is far stranger than she ever imagined.

Locked away in a secret facility, Sarina receives an inexplicable message from the moon, instructing her to call a childhood home long since demolished. When her dead mother answers, Sarina can no longer dismiss the impossible. Thrust into a reality where her fiction collides with truth, she must unravel a mystery that stretches beyond Earth - and into the stars - before it's too late.

Guardians of Earth II **- the Watcher:** As the crew races toward New Earth, disaster strikes. The outer wall of their space station is breached—just six months from their destination. What begins as a technical emergency quickly turns sinister when it becomes clear the breach wasn't an accident. Someone aboard is targeting them.

With the station crippled and repairs at a standstill, they're stranded in the unforgiving void of space. Head Commander Glogg is gravely injured, forcing Renn to step into a leadership role. As chaos erupts, Renn uncovers a horrifying truth: the breach was sabotage. But the deeper he digs, the more he realizes that he has another problem. The androids, especially the head android Xavier, are hiding dangerous secrets - secrets that threaten the entire mission. Yet, even as suspicion falls on them, Renn discovers that the androids may not be responsible for the breach.

As systems fail and paranoia spreads, Renn must navigate a web of lies, betrayals, and hidden agendas. The safety of the crew - and the precious cargo of Earth's remaining species - hangs in the balance. But the most devastating truth is still to come: to save the mission and secure humanity's future, ONE MUST DIE.

Torn between duty and the lives of those he swore to protect, Renn faces an impossible decision. In the end, the survival of New Earth, and perhaps the galaxy itself, will depend on a single sacrifice. But can Renn live with the cost?

THE EUROPA SAGA

She was never meant to be human

When Europa regains consciousness, her world shatters. Her mother has been assassinated, and now, she is the next target. As she struggles to make sense of her mother's death, Europa uncovers a devastating truth: her entire life has been a lie.

Her parents aren't just ancient - they are thousands of years old, part of an aquatic alien race from Jupiter's ice moon, Europa. Fleeing a brutal civil war, they sought refuge on Earth, hiding deep beneath the Pacific Ocean in the technologically advanced City of Atlantis. But Atlantis is dying. A chemical attack from their relentless enemy has cursed their race - no Atlantean child has survived past the age of five, until now. Europa, born as a human to evade the curse, is their last hope.

Now, as the new queen, Europa must embrace the truth of her heritage and unlock the secrets of her people's past. But becoming Atlantean means losing her humanity forever. If she fails, she risks not only the extinction of her race but the destruction of the world above, still unaware of the ancient war lurking beneath the waves.

The *Europa Saga* reimagines the myth of Atlantis in an epic journey spanning over two thousand years, where one woman must face her destiny - and protect both the human and alien worlds from annihilation. The Saga extends over ten books, traveling from Earth to Europa, then back to Earth. You will meet Europa's children and granddaughters. You will experience their joys, their heartaches, their losses, and their loves. Start your journey today.

For more information, go to http://www.europasaga.com

Available on Amazon.

MORE STORIES BY P. R. GARCIA

Extinction 2038: As global warming melts Antarctica's ice, a shocking discovery emerges - a perfectly preserved dinosaur corpse. Paleontologists eagerly investigate. But hidden within the ancient remains is a deadly secret: the original strain of Ebola.

Within hours, the disease claims its first victim and then spreads uncontrollably across the globe. Billions perish, and civilization crumbles. With no electricity, no fuel, no food, and no way to communicate, the world teeters on the edge of extinction.

Can humanity rise from the ashes, or will the virus wipe them out for good?

Available in paperback and e-Book on Amazon.

The Bounty Hunter: BiiJun is a Kolorian Huntsmen and the galaxy's most feared bounty hunter. Known only as The Hunter, his armor hides him from the enemies he hunts.

On a mission to capture a dangerous criminal, BiiJun is attacked by a deadly alien beast and left for dead. Rescued by a mysterious woman, he is forced to rely on her as they navigate the unforgiving terrain of Rigel Three. As they fight side by side, an unexpected bond grows between them- -a connection BiiJun never imagined, and a life he never thought possible. Torn between his heart and his creed, BiiJun faces an impossible choice: Continue his path as a bounty hunter, bound by the discipline that shaped him or shed his armor to embrace a future of love and redemption. One path offers salvation for the galaxy, the other for his soul. But in choosing one, he risks losing the other.

Can The Hunter forsake his mission for love—or will his past condemn both him and the galaxy to chaos?

Available in paperback and eBook on Amazon.

ABOUT THE AUTHOR

P.R. Garcia, born and raised in rural Michigan, discovered her passion for science fiction at an early age. The youngest of three, she was captivated by the magic of films like *Journey to the Center of the Earth, Mysterious Island,* and other early sci-fi classics that fueled her fascination with the unknown. But it was when her parents took her to see *The Day the Earth Stood Still* that her imagination truly ignited. The moment Patricia Neal uttered the iconic line, "Klaatu barada nikto," to the towering robot Gort, Ms. Garcia's world expanded with the possibilities of alien life and distant worlds.

From that point on, the fields behind her home became a playground for her vivid imagination. With her loyal dog by her side, Garcia spent countless days battling imaginary invaders, charting new planets, and dreaming of the vast cosmos beyond Earth.

Her fascination with the unknown only deepened when *Star Trek* aired during her high school years. While her friends cheered at football games, Ms. Garcia stayed glued to her TV, mesmerized by the adventures of the starship *Enterprise.* Her passion for the genre never wavered.

In her thirties, Ms. Garcia found success as an award-winning basket weaver, dedicating three decades to the craft. After retiring from a 30-year career as a Civil Servant, she moved to San Diego, California, where she spent five years volunteering on whale-watching boats, educating people about the majestic aquatic life of the Pacific Ocean.

At sixty-two, Ms. Garcia embarked on a new adventure: writing *The Europa Saga,* a thrilling ten-part sci-fi epic filled with intrigue, suspense, and mystery. A fresh reimagining of the myth of Atlantis, the series catapulted her into the ranks of best-selling authors.

A passionate advocate for the environment, Ms. Garcia has woven themes of global warming, deforestation, species loss, and the devastation of Earth into her later works, including books seven through nine of *The Europa Saga* and the chilling *Extinction 2038*.

If you'd like to learn more about Ms. Garcia, go to http://www.prgarcia1.com.

You can also sign up for her Newsletters for special bonus material on specific books.

Guardians of Earth III

The Bounty Hunter

General Information

Free Adult Coloring Pages

PLEASE LEAVE AN HONEST REVIEW ON AMAZON

JOIN MY NEWSLETTER:

www.ingramcontent.com/pod-product-compliance
Lightning Source LLC
Chambersburg PA
CBHW070620260626

47161CB00007B/2516